FEAR

LAURA RYE

BAILEY R. HANSEN

LAURA RYE BOOKS

FEAR

LAURA RYE

LAUREN HANSEN

FEAR

Thank you for buying this A MONSTER BY ANY OTHER NAME paperback.

For bonus Freak Camp stories and early access to the rest of the series, sign up for the monthly Freak Camp newsletter at **freakcamp.com**

Book 3 FREEDOM will be released Fall 2023!

FEAR

A MONSTER BY ANY OTHER NAME

BOOK TWO

ABOUT FEAR

Jake's finally rescued Tobias from Freak Camp. It's a dream come true, even though it cost him more than he could have imagined. He's sure the hardest part is over.

But Tobias has never known anything but the stark existence of Freak Camp. He doesn't believe he's a human being, let alone that he has the right to walk down a city street at Jake's side.

Tobias forced himself to survive six months of brutal training all in preparation to be a monster worthy of Jake. He thought he was ready for anything Jake wanted him to do – except to pretend he's a real human.

All their dreams of a life together crash against the reality that Jake doesn't know Tobias as well as he thought, or why Tobias is so afraid of him, and how impossible it seems for Jake to help him.

Jake would never take Tobias back to Freak Camp, but maybe Tobias doesn't belong with him after all.

FEAR is the second book in the A Monster By Any Other Name series. Readers may skip book 1 and start with this book if they prefer not to read the horrors of Freak Camp in detail. Please take note that FEAR includes references to past sexual and physical abuse, torture, and neglect of children. This series is the slowest of burns, but each book comes with a happy for now / happily ever after.

FEAR

A MONSTER BY ANY OTHER NAME

BOOK TWO

by

Laura Rye and Bailey R. Hansen

Published by Laura Rye.
www.freakcamp.com

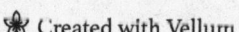 Created with Vellum

CONTENT NOTES

A MONSTER BY ANY OTHER NAME is a series about trauma recovery. The previous book (FREAK CAMP) is the part of the story when the trauma takes place.

The sequel you are about to read (FEAR) does <u>not</u> contain any of the graphic scenes of abuse or violence that are present in the first book. However, there are references to those past scenes of sexual and physical abuse that happen to Tobias as a minor.

This is a hurt/comfort story to the max: for every ounce of hurt, there will be a pound of comfort down the line. It is a very slow burn, but each book guarantees a happily ever after.

PREVIOUSLY IN A MONSTER BY ANY OTHER NAME

Another Wednesday found Tobias kneeling against the wall of the Director's office. He was still numb, hollow, stiff from the night that almost killed him, but he could feel that wearing off, and that terrified him more than anything else. The Director could have him beaten—he had done that last week because Tobias had hesitated too long before responding to one of the senator's commands during another visit—but nothing could hurt more than the return to feeling.

Still, some of his survival skills were returning, and he supposed he should be grateful like the Director had taught him to be grateful for all the hours of work he had painstakingly put into Tobias, an unidentified monster with no known supernatural abilities, to make him useful. He had never said that the aim was to make Tobias useful for Jake, the young hunter who for some reason cared about Tobias and had promised to get him out, but Tobias wanted to believe that was the case. Even though one of his very first lessons in Freak Camp, the one the witch Becca had taught him when he was still very small, was that freaks were not allowed to want things.

Six months into the Director's training, Tobias didn't need

to look at more of the Director than his hands, and he was no longer consciously aware of watching them. Each long finger was buried deep into his brain, locked into his spine where all the nerve impulses radiated out, and any twitch of his finger, any snap of his wrist could make Tobias act without conscious thought. *Come here, pick it up, stop, sit, kneel, crawl,* and Tobias would find himself moving.

Tobias would have felt relief at that if he felt anything at all. Responses so ingrained as to be instinct were responses that wouldn't earn him a beating, responses that would keep him alive without requiring him to feel, think, or process.

Victor stood stiffly next to the door. True to the Director's word, Crusher had never joined their sessions again, and other guards learned quickly what the Director liked, what he wanted, what his little nods and gestures meant. Today, the Director sat at his desk scrawling his elaborate signature over a pile of pale red forms. He used a dark fountain pen that gave his *J*'s a particular swooping look and bled through the sheets onto the plain white paper he kept beneath them.

Tobias recognized the color of the papers. He had been assigned sometimes to sort piles of paperwork for the Agency for Supernatural Control, and execution permission requests were always that shade. He had been grateful, at the time, not to come across numbers for himself or Kayla (the shapeshifter girl younger than him, who was definitely not his friend, even if they looked out for each other; monsters did not have friends). Now he wondered dully who was going to die in the next few days and if they had been in Special Research for very long already, or if part of what the forms authorized was their induction there.

The Director let Tobias kneel for a while, the scratch of his pen the only sound in the office, and then he glanced up and made a tiny scooping, jerky motion with his left hand. *Stand and come here.*

Tobias stood and walked forward. He stopped when the Director's hand told him to stop.

The small table that usually held the Director's interrogation tools stood in the middle of the room; a black handgun rested on top of the pristine white sheet. Tobias didn't look at it, didn't let his hands stray.

The Director signed the last sheet with a flourish and dotted an *I* with enough force to punch a hole in the paper. Tobias flinched—he had scrubbed the Director's desk once, trying to get those little black dots out of the hardwood—but otherwise gave no reaction.

"Good," the Director said. "That's done." He turned the full force of his brown eyes on Tobias, and Tobias felt a throb of terror beneath the hollow and numbness. The Director's eyes flickered to the gun and then back to Tobias's face. "Pick it up."

Eyes locked on the clawed feet of the Director's desk, Tobias picked up the gun. In all his sixteen years, he had never touched one before. His hands were shaking slightly. He willed them to stop.

"Take the safety off, put it to your head, and pull the trigger."

It was an awkward angle, and Tobias couldn't manage it as smoothly as he should have. The fumbling gave him time, too much fucking time, and thoughts tumbled like hail pounding on the aluminum roofs of the barracks, like broken bodies thrown out of a black van.

Was this really it, the moment of death, the moment of release? Should he angle the blast so that brain matter flew more toward the less expensive—and easier to clean—area around the conference table, or move it to be sure that Victor wouldn't catch any of the gore? What would Kayla do when she learned? Would it hurt? Would he still be numb in hell? Oh God, would the Director really make it this easy? Would Jake know that he was dead? Would he care? Had he asked that Tobias be put down because he couldn't come get him after all?

Did the Director wait until he signed my execution form to give the order? was Tobias's last thought before he pulled the trigger.

The empty click of the chamber was loud in the room, and the hammer vibrated through his skull. He clenched his eyes shut—they had been open, fixed on the Director's desk, locked onto the Director's hands—and fought to keep any other reaction off his face, any sound coming from his mouth.

Of course the Director would never make it that easy. He would have done it in the yard or in his interrogation room, not in his office. Tobias had been a stupid freak even to guess, to wonder, to hope.

He should have known better from the start than to wish the gun was or wasn't loaded. That was the lesson.

He forced his eyes open again, homing in on the Director's hand. He kept the cold barrel of the gun pressed against his temple and hoped his expression gave away nothing, even though the Director knew it all.

"Clean it. Put it back. Get out," the Director said.

Tobias quickly and silently used the plain white sheet to rub down the gun—get the filthy monster fingerprints off the shiny black—placed it back in the middle of the table, turned, and left. He didn't change his pace as he walked out of Administration, across the yard, and into the showers. He made his movements there as methodical, impersonal, and obedient as they had been cleaning the gun.

In the library, Tobias hunched over the massive spell book, occasionally checking that the notes in his notebook were still legible. He took a moment to close his eyes and massage his right hand, ignoring how the healing flesh screamed at him. He was off computers for the week since he had failed to report a possible demon sighting. The Director didn't want him back on the electronics until his hands healed enough to be decently fast on the keyboard, but he could still do research work for hunters.

In some deep place of him he would not acknowledge, he liked the library with its smells of musty paper and bindings. Sometimes he could almost hear Becca's voice in his ear, though he hadn't heard it since he was seven years old, as she'd taught him to read and do his numbers in this room.

The other reason he liked the library was that he was often alone. Not that that would keep him safe, but the camera in the corner wouldn't catch him closing his eyes, rubbing his hands, or taking the time to think of nothing at all. As long as he got the work done, no one caught him not working.

When the door opened, he didn't flinch.

"Freak, you're going!" Lonny stood at the door and smacked his billy club against his thigh. "The Director says put everything away, you're not coming back."

Tobias's jaw clenched. That could mean anything from *He doesn't need what you were researching* to *You're not ever coming back to the library*. Or worse.

But he didn't let it show on his face. He closed his books and replaced them on the shelves, mentally filing away the page numbers and notes in case the Director asked. He closed his notebook and set it on the shelf with the rest of the research documents.

The first inkling Tobias got that his luck had run out was when Lonny took a heavy lead line from his belt and snapped one end onto his collar.

Tobias froze, too shocked and horrified to not let it show.

The guard grinned at him. "I told you, freak, you're *going*," and he jerked the line down hard, sending Tobias crashing to the floor.

He caught himself on his knees, but what was the point of keeping himself together when his luck was gone? Eleven years of surviving, eleven years of clawing onto nebulous hopes, and here was the ultimate outcome.

You're going.

There was only one place Tobias could possibly be going. *Special Research.* It was where witches went for their executions, where monsters went when they couldn't behave. It was the place freaks went so that hunters could study them until the freaks left in the salted smoke of the incinerators.

Stumbling after the guard down the stairs, Tobias couldn't stop shaking. What did it matter? What the fuck did it matter anymore? He could feel everything in him shutting down, trying to brace for . . . the end. He'd wished for death so often in the last six months, but since the Director had had him put the gun to his own head, he'd understood that was something too good for him to be granted easily.

Instead of taking the door out into the yard, Lonny turned toward Reception. When Tobias tripped again, sheer terror making him unsteady, the guard pulled him up by the collar. Tobias welcomed the more normal form of pain. He had been here before. He had walked this way to interrogations and those brief, lightning-flash moments with Jake.

Lonny stopped outside the resource room, ducked in, and emerged with a short stack of clothes that he shoved into Tobias's arms. Then he towed Tobias deeper into the dark corridors. Other hallways in Reception were for the important visitors, the ones through which senators and civilians walked; scratched, fluorescent-flickering halls like this were for freaks and guards. *Paperwork*, Tobias thought. *Monster comes in, monster goes out, you have to have the right forms with the right numbers.*

At the last door in the hallway, a heavy metal one with sigils keeping demons and other malevolent spirits from crossing the threshold, the guard turned to Tobias and dropped the lead line. "Clothes off."

Tobias couldn't tell what he wanted, fast obedience or a show—Lonny could go either way, depending on the day and his mood—so he compromised by going fast but facing him.

When he was naked and shivering under the fluorescents, old gray clothes neatly folded in one pile, the guard pointed his club at the set Tobias had carried. "Put those on."

Silently, Tobias crouched for the new clothes. The boxers and jeans—like a hunter wore, like a *fucking hunter* wore, just the thought made his hands shake—were like his usual pants, until he got to the buttons and zippers. He'd opened enough flies that he knew the theory, but doing it to himself was different, his hands stumbling. The shirt's buttons took a long time to open and then meticulously hook together again, but the guard gave no indication that he would start hitting Tobias with the club he tapped against his thigh.

When Tobias was dressed, head down, hands still, Lonny turned to the door with a grunt and punched a string of numbers into the key box. He waited a few minutes, muttered something into the intercom, and then the red light above the huge iron door turned green. Tobias only half listened. He could probably remember both the password and the number sequence if he had to—lately anything he saw went straight to long-term memory, a Director-induced survival skill—but at the moment he couldn't care less about what Lonny was doing.

Becca had told him never to fear death, to look forward to it as something that would bring him to an infinitely better place where none of the guards would be able to touch him, but Tobias had stopped believing that sometime while Crusher had used the hot irons according to the Director's cool direction. It was too much to hope for, and he had learned well her other lesson: it was better not to believe in anything that sounded good. Death sounded too nice. He didn't expect that transition into peace and darkness. Much more likely was the hell of Special Research sliding seamlessly into the hell after life. He doubted there could be much difference.

But when Lonny grabbed the lead line again and jerked Tobias through the open door, everything he had expected shattered into a vast and uncertain lightness.

Standing in the bare white room beyond the door, face in profile, hands in his jean pockets, was *Jake*.

And Tobias could not imagine death, or hell, or true pain, if Jake were there.

~

When the guard came in with Tobias trailing him on the leash, Jake almost reeled in shock.

It hadn't occurred to him that he had never seen Toby in anything but the gray shirt and pants provided by the facility. In jeans and one of Jake's button-up shirts, Toby appeared like a person Jake had never seen before, one with the look of a long-term survivor who didn't have the resources to survive much longer. Jake's shirt on him was baggy, several sizes too big for Toby's skin-and-bones frame.

"Here you go, Hawthorne," the guard called as he shoved the door closed. He carried Tobias's leash like it was just another weapon, like the club hanging from his belt. "Dressed up and pretty like you wanted. Madison get that paperwork to you yet?"

"Not yet," Jake said.

"Can't leave until you get that." The guard grinned. "Always better to inspect the merchandise before you sign the contract. 'Specially secondhand goods." He slapped Tobias on the shoulder, and Tobias winced and swayed.

Jake swallowed hard, his hands clenched. He wanted to get a look at Toby, a good look. Toby was rail-thin and pale, like he hadn't gotten as much sun as he used to, and there was something else about him, something brittle that Jake hadn't seen the last time he saw him, six fucking months ago. Jake wanted to put his finger on the difference, but first he needed this asshole to go away. Otherwise he would never get Toby to look at him, wouldn't be able to see if Toby could forgive him for taking so goddamned long, for not even explaining why.

"Can you leave us?" Jake asked. "Maybe check on where the forms are?"

Lonny's grin faded, but only slightly. "Yeah. Sure. Hey!" He extended the leash. "You want this, or should I check it on the wall?"

Jake felt his jaw jump, and the guard must have seen some of the rage on his face, because he backed up to the door, ran the leash through the hook on the wall, and left through another set of doors to the Reception desk behind the bulletproof glass. Tobias's head followed the lead, his body leaning back toward the door, but he didn't move his feet, didn't move in any way that wasn't necessary.

Jake waited until the door shut behind the guard before he moved forward. Toby cringed away from his hands, a slight movement that Jake might not have noticed if he weren't looking, but he couldn't balk or hesitate now. He caught Toby's face between his palms and pushed him back with the same movement, moving him closer to the wall so that the leash wasn't twisting his head around.

"Toby, you okay?" *You okay?* Seriously, that was the best he could do when he had just *left him*? But Jake had nothing better.

Toby stared at him, some kind of shock in his face, and then he almost smiled. It was a slight flicker in his mouth, in his eyes, gone in an instant, but even that softening notched Jake's tension down. But then his eyes fell to Jake's shoulders. "Jake."

Jake figured that was about the best he was going to get.

"Let's get this fucking rope off you." He reached under Toby's chin for where the line connected to the collar.

Toby took a deep, shaky breath, but tipped his head up, eyes closed, while Jake fumbled with the clips. When he got the head of the leash off Toby's collar, Jake threw the fucking thing as hard as he could against the wall.

When Toby jumped, Jake laid a hand on his shoulder and smiled at him. "You never have to wear one of those again, Toby. I promise."

Toby nodded and then smoothly stepped away from him, out from under his hand, when the door opened to let in Lonny, Madison, and an older man with his hair fading to gray at his temples and a small smile not quite reaching his eyes.

Tobias didn't know the woman—well-fed, dressed in a business jacket and skirt, carrying a pile of papers—but with the Director *and Jake* in the same room, he had a hard time breathing.

It had been easy to forget, if just for a second, what he was and what he could expect when Jake was touching him, sliding his hand beneath Tobias's chin, resting his hand on his shoulder—not to restrain him but, as far as Tobias could tell, for the contact alone. He had been able to forget the next logical step after a hand on his shoulder—the fist in his gut, the order to go to his knees—and he let the small voice in his head say Jake's name over and over again, the shock, the *joy* so overwhelming that it squeezed his lungs.

Oh my God, you're seeing Jake again. Even one more time was more than he'd had any hope left for.

But now: impossible, unthinkable, to forget anything with the Director in the room.

Jake looked at the other real humans, tension in the line of his neck, but not the stark panic that Tobias felt. Jake looked ready for a fight, a fight he knew he would win. It was the same brash confidence Tobias had seen from the day they'd met, so many years ago now, the first time that Jake had smiled at him and made him feel almost like a real person.

The woman eyed Tobias warily, but the Director strode forward. It was everything Tobias could do not to run, not to call attention to himself. He had pulled away from Jake—the Director hurt everything he loved, Tobias couldn't risk Jake being too close to him—but it was hard not to drop to the floor or to fumble the leash back around his neck to prove that he hadn't meant to pretend to be something he wasn't.

To Tobias's relief, the Director ignored him completely. To his tight-throated horror, the Director reached out a hand to Jake, smiling, and Jake took it, still tense even without realizing who it was he was touching, not realizing how close he was to pain, death, and a calm voice directing the whip.

"Jake Hawthorne," the Director said, shaking Jake's hand and never dropping the smile. "It's a pleasure to meet you at last. I've heard good things about you. You're cousin Sally's son, of course." When Jake stiffened, the Director's face fell into the clear lines of sympathy, mouth down, eyes sad. "I'm sorry, that was callous of me. Jonah Dixon, Director of the FREACS facility and the ASC. May I call you Jake?"

Jake nodded. "Sure, Mr. Dixon."

The Director laughed, and Tobias shuddered. "Please, call me Jonah. Though most around here just call me Director. It seems I gave up first names when I stepped into Uncle Elijah's shoes." The Director's smile invited Jake into the joke, shared with him the pressures of responsibility. "Some days I wish I could just get back out there where the worst I had to worry about was a mated pair of wendigos and no backup. Now I have to deal with politicians and law enforcement."

The more the Director talked in that bright, conversational

tone he reserved for reals he wanted something from, the more Tobias had to fight the urge to flinch or whimper, but the words seemed to loosen something in Jake, easing a line of tension in his shoulders.

"Cops," Jake snorted.

Tobias wanted to scream at Jake to run, not to believe a single word said in that cold, smooth voice, but he was afraid of breaking the illusion the Director was creating. He didn't give a damn what happened to him, but what if Jake did something that made the Director see him as a threat? Jake was strong and had fought monsters tougher than Tobias would ever be, but there was no way that he could defeat the Director. Tobias lowered his head and focused on giving no sign that he knew the false cheer and charm was a lie.

"Indeed." The Director changed tones smoothly, into one that Tobias recognized as looking for one right answer. Any other answer ended in pain. "You can imagine I don't have much time anymore for hands-on work, but when I heard you were requesting a permanent removal of one of our inmates, I showed a special interest. Did you know this is the first one we've approved in over two years?"

"I do now," Jake said. "But everyone hears rumors they get out all the time for bait permits."

"Not at all. Well, I assure you there should be no problems with your new charge from our end, but if there are, know that we can always take him back or give you support. At any time, if the monster proves to be unmanageable, we will take him back. Just because you are signing for permanent responsibility for his actions doesn't mean that we aren't here for you, Jake."

Tobias didn't dare look up to see Jake's reaction, and his voice betrayed nothing. He could have been anything from angry at the suggestion to honestly grateful. "I appreciate the thought, Jonah."

"Good." The Director sounded less than pleased, but he

waved the woman forward. "Then I'll leave the rest of the details to Madison, who is so much better at keeping the forms together than I am. Without her and the rest of the staff, this organization would combust faster than a salted ghost. If you have any more questions, don't hesitate to contact me through anyone here or at headquarters. Good luck."

With that the Director squeezed Jake's hand for one last friendly shake, and then turned to leave.

Only then did Tobias realize that Jake wasn't just there for a visit. Jake was taking him away.

It was true. The Director had talked to Jake, the Director was walking away, and Tobias still stood near Jake, not leashed, not dragged back through the doors to Special Research. The Director hadn't said a thing make it clear to Jake just how much of a waste of time Tobias was, how much of a disobedient, useless dog.

Jake was signing papers. It was real, all real, not a fantasy or hallucination. Jake was taking Tobias away.

Tobias closed his eyes, breathless and so afraid he would show everything he felt, everything he had never expected to feel. Only distantly did he notice the Director pulling Lonny over, whispering a few words before he left. Only vaguely did he see the frightened glances the woman kept shooting him as she handed Jake page after page to sign. Every time she took the signed document and placed it back in the folder, Tobias felt lighter and lighter. He was dizzy imagining days upon days with Jake, every day a good day: only one person who could hurt him (Jake never had, but he could and Tobias wouldn't care), only one person he had to please, and being willing and happy to give that person any fucking thing he wanted.

Tobias kept from passing out only by taking a deep breath and reminding himself that this wouldn't be forever. He was, after all, worthless—he knew that, it had been made abundantly clear—with few assets or abilities that would hold the interest of a man like Jake. But even a year, a month, a week, *any* moment spent with Jake would be a time he could hold on to for the rest of his miserable, short life. It was even easy to believe in death, in peace and contentment, when heaven had come for him.

Jake and the secretary moved to one of the tables to finish the paperwork, but Tobias stayed where he was, watching Jake from under his hair, overwhelmed that Jake's promise was coming true. What would Kayla say if she could see him now? He hoped she'd find out, that she would know he hadn't just gone to Special Research.

He didn't notice Lonny coming up next to him until he grabbed Tobias's collar and pulled Tobias's ear to his mouth.

"Don't fool yourself that Hawthorne's gonna make you a pampered pet," he whispered. "He's a hunter, and he'll treat you exactly like you deserve—pimping you out to his dogs. And when you stop being a good little bitch, you'll end up right back here."

Tobias didn't flinch. He knew that Lonny was just trying to rattle him, and it wasn't going to work. He knew this wasn't forever, he knew he wasn't good enough for Jake to keep, but he wasn't going to be thrown off by a threat that wasn't true. Unless something big had changed in the last six months, he knew that Jake didn't even own dogs.

Finally, the last paper was signed, and the woman put on the last seal and gave Jake a tense, hopeful smile. "That's it, Mr —Jake."

"We free to go now?" Jake asked, glancing at Tobias.

She nodded, marking something down on the edge of one form.

Jake smiled at her. "Good. Come on, Tobias."

Tobias hurried to Jake's side, and they kept a steady pace through the last hall.

Leaving Freak Camp and taking those first steps outside the

facility were so unreal that Tobias had trouble putting one foot in front of the other. When the last door swung shut behind them, Tobias had to fight to keep his eyes on the loose gravel under his feet. The sky seemed bluer, the dry desert air fresher, though he knew it was the same air, the same sky, that he had known his entire life.

He would have known the Eldorado anywhere from Jake's loving descriptions and photos, but the sleek black car looked bigger, more dangerous and alive, when the real thing gleamed before him in the sunlight.

He saw Jake's smile out of the corner of his eye: he liked Tobias's reaction. That meant Tobias was safe showing that he was happy. Just the idea of being *safe* to be happy felt so fucking good. "I'm really glad you get to see her at last," Jake whispered.

When they stopped next to the Eldorado, Tobias closed his eyes and took a deep breath. Being able to show happiness was one thing, but this feeling, this rush . . . he was still close to passing out, and Jake hadn't done a fucking thing to him but smile.

Jake was leaning against the Eldorado, arms crossed, grinning at him, when he opened his eyes again. "Well, Toby. I did it. I got you out. Sorry it took so long."

"It's okay," Tobias managed to say past the lump in his throat, the lightness in his body. "You came back." He couldn't believe that he was here, outside Freak Camp, standing beside Jake's car, staring at Jake without fear because the guards were back behind the razor wire and he was all Jake's now.

Jake couldn't seem to stop smiling either. Then his eyes flickered down, and he frowned and pushed himself up from the car. "Hey, we should hit the road, but before we put this shithole in our rearview mirror, there's something we gotta take care of."

He opened the trunk and withdrew a pair of heavy-duty wire cutters as long as his forearm. Tobias's brain immediately shut down as he braced for pain. Not a new reaction or one he could help—it was the same automatic response he had when he saw the electric prod or the Director handling a whip.

He was about to lose . . . a finger? Maybe. Probably not his nose, Jake wouldn't want him to look any more of a freak. He briefly considered his genitals—he'd been told often enough he didn't need them to be useful, in every way, to a hunter—but everything he knew about Jake told him he wouldn't cut something off Tobias just because it wasn't useful to him, just to cause pain. He wasn't like the guards.

Probably just an ear, then. Even assuming that Jake cut into the ear canal and damaged something internal instead of just taking off the outer skin, Tobias would still be able to hear orders fine with just one. Even better, this might mean Jake wanted him for more than just a couple of weeks' hard ride, wanted to mark Tobias as his. And *that* was more than okay. If he was Jake's, Jake was much more likely to salt and burn him somewhere when he got tired of him than to let an old possession get passed around back in FREACS.

Tobias could deal with losing any body parts right now if it meant that Jake was claiming him. And even if he was too hopeful, if Jake had no problem dumping him back at Freak Camp after he'd had his use of him, at least it would be a reminder that he had once been Jake's.

Tobias's whole thought process took just a couple of seconds. By the time Jake stepped up to him, Tobias's heart rate was back down, and he watched Jake and the wire cutters almost hopefully, trying not to let his daydreams fly away with him.

"Tilt your head up," Jake said. "I want to get a good angle so I don't hurt you."

The last sentence didn't make any sense, and it almost shattered the edge of Tobias's happy calm, but he obediently closed his eyes and lifted his head, hoping Jake hadn't noticed how the blood beat harder in his jugular.

The slide of the wire cutters' cold metal against his throat and the sharp *snap* next to his ear made him clench his jaw. The lack of pain nearly made him panic because *oh God, what happened that I can't even feel it?*

Then something hit the ground. Something that sounded too heavy to be an ear.

Tobias opened his eyes, and Jake was smiling at him, the smile that always made Tobias's heart race in a way that had nothing to do with pain or fear. Jake tossed the wire cutters back into the trunk and reached toward Tobias, making him flinch slightly, and rested a hand against his neck. His bare neck.

Tobias looked down, Jake's hand warm and gentle against the naked skin of his neck, and saw the collar in the dirt by his feet. Slowly, hardly believing that he wouldn't touch blood and bone, he reached for his neck on the side opposite of where Jake's hand rested, brushing his own fingers over the exposed skin.

He looked up, so filled with emotions he couldn't even name—was this shock, terror, wonder?—that he stared straight into Jake's eyes, incapable of hiding himself, of not looking and looking his fill. He couldn't read Jake's face, but what Jake saw in Tobias's expression made his eyes flicker with something that Tobias couldn't put a name to, that made him nervous without being afraid.

Then Jake enfolded Tobias in his arms, pulling him to his chest in a grip that was warm and secure but strangely not confining. Tobias felt warmth unlike anything he'd ever known spreading through his body, leaving him weak-kneed. He let his eyes close. Jake was so close that when he took a breath, Tobias felt his own chest lift. It was a sensation—like electricity buzzing through his body, but without pain—that made him understand a feeling he'd never known before.

It felt like safety.

Jake held him, anchoring them together, and Tobias could think of nothing else that there would be in heaven.

It ended. Of course it ended, and it left Tobias shaky but smiling, not afraid to open his eyes. Jake smiled back.

"Come on, Toby," he said, sliding around him and opening the passenger door of the Eldorado. "Let's blow this joint."

Tobias got in, clumsy in the unfamiliar space. He couldn't keep a grin off his face, and he didn't care. While Jake walked around to the driver's side, Tobias ran both hands down the leather seats, savoring the smell of Jake's car, the feel of Jake's life beneath his hands, the knowledge that Jake had come back for him, had taken him away from hell. He had kept his promise.

No matter how long it would last, no matter what happened to him after this moment, Tobias didn't think anyone could take that joy, that peace, away from him.

A MONSTER BY ANY OTHER NAME

BOOK TWO: FEAR

1

Tobias's first car ride was the most exhilarating experience of his life.

The highway sped away under their tires, the landscape outside flying by too fast for him to take in. There was so much flashing past, all the real world he had dreamed about but never imagined he would get a chance to see—but Jake was telling him they'd have time, Toby, *and this is nothing, wait until you see the Rockies or the Mississippi or until we get to the Atlantic.* It sounded like Jake wanted to keep him around for a while, which was another rush of euphoria, enough to make him feel dizzy and light enough to float away. Over and over, Tobias had to remind himself that all this hung on whether he screwed it up. He could make this last, he was sure; he was good at being obedient and meeting expectations.

It was almost impossible to think of how precarious it all was, though, with Jake grinning at him and talking nonstop of where they were going, what they were going to see, the diner in Utah where they would eat that night ("They have the best onion rings this side of the U.S., Toby, wait until you get a bite"). Tobias could almost believe this was forever, that he could be here next to Jake, driving farther and farther from those sigil-engraved iron walls, forever. That he wouldn't ever have to go back or go anywhere away from Jake.

Eventually, Jake's voice ran hoarse, and he turned on the tape deck. He glanced at Tobias, still grinning wide. "I guess we'll finally find out if you like AC/DC."

Tobias had no idea what that was, but he knew that absolutely nothing Jake could do—and he meant nothing—could bother him right now. He grinned at Jake, his face feeling stretched wide enough to crack. Maybe it would; he'd never smiled so much before.

"Absolutely," he said, sure that was the right answer.

Jake seemed pleased with it, turning the volume up a notch.

AC/DC was an all-encompassing *noise* that Tobias couldn't have begun to describe, but it was as big and bold and free as Jake himself, and Tobias loved it.

Then Jake reached over and found Tobias's hand, palms curling together, and Tobias forgot how to breathe.

He had to close his eyes to narrow his senses down: the constant thrum of the car engine, steady and reassuring already; the joyful cacophony of Jake's music surrounding him; and most of all, Jake's warm hand, sure in his. Jake was here, really and truly here. He'd fulfilled his impossible promise, coming to claim Tobias and bring him out of Freak Camp, into the light of the real world that Tobias had never been supposed to see. And he wasn't even afraid to hold Tobias's hand like there wasn't a chance in the world that Tobias could contaminate him by that touch.

It would've been terrifying if Tobias could've felt anything other than giddy. Giddy and safe, so safe, like he'd never been in his entire life. The guards were already miles and miles behind them, farther away every minute. Their voices and hands, their knives and whips, could never reach him, as long as Jake willed it.

It couldn't get better than this.

THE SUN WAS JUST STARTING to set—the clear view of the horizon before them was so breathtaking, Tobias could hardly look away—as they pulled into Tooele, Utah. When they stopped at a gas station, Tobias shook his head when Jake asked if he needed to use the restroom inside or wanted to stretch his legs. He already felt safer inside the Eldorado than he had anywhere in his life, and he never wanted to get out, unless he was going to be close to Jake. Besides, he could see other reals nearby, standing outside their vehicles as they filled their tanks, and just looking at them from inside Jake's car made him nervous. He didn't want to get any closer.

Jake had given him hunter's clothes—he could still hardly believe it when he glanced down and rubbed the denim fabric —but it wouldn't be enough to disguise what he was, even if he didn't have any distinguishing marks apart from the scarring around his neck, hidden beneath the collar of the soft flannel shirt. Even if he could keep that covered, he knew there was no way that he could pass himself off as a real. The thought of what might happen if someone mistook him for a real and then realized what he actually was . . . Tobias shuddered. He had no idea yet what Jake had in store for him, if he would be kept most of the time in the Eldorado or in a room in Jake's house (that did sound wonderful), but he hoped Jake didn't expect him to have much contact with reals. Better—*safer*—for everyone that way.

When Jake opened the driver's door to slide back in, relief flooded Tobias, and he couldn't help leaning toward Jake. This was already far longer than any visit they'd had before, and to think it would continue—*every day* seeing Jake—Tobias didn't know how he could cope with that much happiness. His heart might beat itself out of his chest, his fingers and entire body alive and ecstatic to be out, away, and *safe* with Jake.

Jake grinned back at him, pleased. "So, the guy inside said Rosie's Diner is right ahead, like I thought. We just gotta keep following Vine."

Tobias nodded, unsure why Jake was telling him, but he filed it away in case Jake checked later to see if Tobias had listened.

The parking lot for Rosie's Diner was nearly full, and Jake had some trouble squeezing the Eldorado into a spot between two cars larger than his. "Damn minivans," he muttered, shutting off the engine. "C'mon, Tobias, let's see if we can get a booth."

Tobias froze. He had glimpsed the crowded tables inside, reals wearing uniforms and carrying trays, and wondered how this was going to work. He had thought maybe Jake would go inside to get food and later give him a share, but now it sounded like Jake wanted him to go *inside* with all those reals. He couldn't have understood right. The Director would never ...

Jake, however, was already outside the car and looking at him expectantly, and Tobias fumbled for the door handle, just realizing he hadn't obeyed.

"Sorry," he gasped as soon as he joined Jake by the curb, but Jake just shrugged and smiled before turning to swing open the diner's door. He paused there, waiting for Tobias to go through, and Tobias took a shaky breath before stepping over the threshold.

He stopped just inside the entryway, overwhelmed by the sounds and smells and *so many reals*, all talking and eating and moving around, and none of them had seen him yet. Not yet. They were bound to notice soon, though. Then they would know there was a monster in their restaurant and they would look at him and Jake would have to—

He jumped when a hand brushed his elbow, but it was only Jake, and the sight of him so close eased Tobias's pounding heartbeat. Jake looked a little concerned, like Tobias wasn't doing something right, but not as if he was angry about it. "You feeling okay? You looked like you were about to pass out for a second."

Tobias nodded, taking a step closer to Jake's side before he could stop himself, but Jake didn't seem to mind being seen with a monster. He left his hand on Tobias's elbow as he glanced around. "Pretty sure this is a seat-yourself type place. I think I see one over there." He led Tobias to a booth near the back of the crowded room and slid into the far seat facing the door. He nodded toward the seat across the table from him. "C'mon, have a seat."

Tobias had no idea what the consequences would be for this—the audacity of a monster to sit at a table as though he was a real, despite being given the command to do so—but he didn't hesitate this time. He lowered his body into the unfamiliar frame, the strange fabric of the cushion sinking a little under him. He folded his arms on the edge of the table, the cold sweat on the back of his neck prickling against the collar of his new shirt.

Jake watched him, brow creased. "Sure you're feeling okay?" Tobias jerked his head in a quick nod, eyes down. "I mean, I know this is your first time you've been to a diner, but the onion rings, man, they're four-star." Jake reached across the table to lay a finger on the back of Tobias's hand, and Tobias couldn't keep from a full-body jump like the touch had been a rod of hot, blessed iron. Shit, he was already fucking up. Jake thought Tobias could do this without anyone noticing he was a freak, and Tobias couldn't, he didn't know how. This had never been one of the Director's lessons (he would be so angry). Tobias had never imagined he could be allowed to be around so many reals, much less to have the audacity to imitate them.

Before he could try anything, to apologize for failing or beg before Jake got angry with him, a woman stopped at their table. "Welcome to Rosie's, guys, what can I get you to drink?"

"I'll take a Coke," Jake said.

"What about for you, hon?"

She was talking to him. The real was talking to him, thinking he was a real too, and the second he opened his mouth—

Terrified, Tobias squeezed his eyes shut and shook his head, bowing it to the table.

"Two Cokes," he heard Jake say.

The woman walked away, and Tobias still couldn't move, every joint in his body and thought in his head locked up tight. He couldn't do this, and he knew he was disappointing Jake, already couldn't meet his expectations, and Jake was about to realize how worthless he was—

"Hey, Tobias," Jake said softly, and Tobias hunched down tighter. Jake's fingertips brushed the back of Tobias's hand again, and Tobias barely managed to minimize the flinch this time. "Hey, it's okay. I know this is all really new, but . . . do you want to come sit by me?"

Shocked, Tobias dared to peek up through his hair. Jake didn't look remotely angry, just that same strange worry and concern on his face. He tilted his head toward the unoccupied cushion next to him.

Tobias chose to believe in the offer, to believe it was okay to accept. He nodded.

Jake let go of his hand to slide out of the seat, standing up, and Tobias scrambled out and around, pushing himself in as far as he could go. Jake settled in next to him and, after a second's hesitation, laid his arm over Tobias's shoulders. Instantly, Tobias relaxed, the tension rolling down and out. The weight of Jake's arm was immensely comforting, and with Jake as a barrier between him and the reals, he felt reassured. He breathed out, slouching down.

"You're okay," Jake said quietly, then slid a large laminated sheet over in front of him. "Anything look good?"

It was hard to make any sense out of the text. He recognized ingredients, food—but he couldn't begin to think about any of it as actual choices, as food that would appear in front of him, just like for any real. Impossible—and besides, his stomach was still roiling as it had from the moment he'd stepped out of the car. He hadn't eaten since breakfast (a few spoonfuls of something that was supposed to be porridge, though it left a strong bitter aftertaste), but he didn't feel remotely hungry, wasn't sure how he'd be able to swallow anything even if somehow he did manage to choke out the words to order it like a real.

Finally, Tobias shrugged, bending his head to speak into Jake's shoulder. "Whatever you want."

Jake's fingers tapped a nervous rhythm against Tobias's arm, then slowed to rub more deliberately. Tobias breathed out, closing his eyes.

"I'm thinking a basic cheeseburger," Jake said, in a good attempt at his usual easy nonchalance. "Plus fries and onion rings. The onion rings are the real attraction, they don't make them like this anywhere else. Trust me, I've looked."

As Jake talked, Tobias relaxed a little more. This was more familiar now: even when he didn't really know what Jake was talking about, the confidence and sound of Jake's voice alone was enough to lull him almost into believing he was safe, that no one could hurt him. The idea that he was *out of Freak Camp* was still too enormous, too overwhelming to feel true, but as alien and terrifying as the real world was, he could believe now that Jake would take care of him. Jake got him out; he wasn't going to let Tobias walk into something that would get him thrown straight back in. Jake knew Tobias better than that, trusted him to be better than that. Tobias felt a little ashamed, like his fear was an insult. If Jake thought he could eat with reals, sit beside him like an actual person and order real food, then he could.

All the same, when their drinks and food arrived, he couldn't bring his head up to look at the waitress. Jake pressed his shoulder against Tobias's once more before letting go to move one plate in front of Tobias and pile the baskets between them.

The cheeseburger was similar to the ones Jake had brought him before, only so much larger and more vivid and *real*. Tobias recognized the fries from the greasy paper bags with the M logo that Jake had brought him before, which left the fried circles as the "onion rings" Jake had mentioned.

Jake grinned at him, nudging him with his elbow, and picked up his own cheeseburger. "C'mon, Tobias, eat up."

Tobias obediently reached for his burger like Jake had, brought it to his lips, and took a bite.

The flavors and textures exploded in his mouth, slid down his tongue, and he had to stop chewing and put the burger down just to marvel at the moment. Bread and meat and cheese, but nothing like any bread and meat he had had in camp. This tasted good, completely good, and not a bit like insects or rot or dirt. He didn't even have words for the flavors, the sensations on his tongue, except he knew that this food was a hundred percent *real*. Perhaps everything Jake had brought him before had lost some of its realness as it passed through the walls of Freak Camp.

Jake was halfway through his burger already but paused before another bite to check on him. "Your burger okay?"

Tobias hurriedly snatched the burger back up and took another bite, working hard to ignore how fucking fantastic it tasted in the need to show Jake that he was appreciating the food Jake had given him, hoping that Jake wouldn't take it away.

Then he had to swallow, and almost choked, but it worked

out okay. "No, Jake. It's good. It's fine. It's . . ." Tobias struggled for the words that would show Jake how much he truly appreciated the food, how grateful he was that he had lived long enough to experience this. *Heavenly, so fucking good, cosmic.* "It's delicious," he said at last, and he must have said it with more intensity than he intended, because Jake laughed. Tobias felt an instant of nerves, but the fear of losing the rest of the meal faded away when he saw the smile on Jake's face.

"I'm glad you like it, Toby." Jake's bright grin was almost as wonderful as the taste of burger on Tobias's tongue and even more satisfying than how the food eased some of the hunger he hadn't known he was feeling beyond the roiling of his stomach. "Come on, keep going."

Tobias ate, and Jake ate, and it was, again, the best moment of Tobias's life. He did his best not to make excessive noises of sheer joy and wonder when he crunched into the onion rings, and he watched Jake eat. He marveled at Jake's lack of hurry or watchfulness. Sure, Jake ate quickly, but who wouldn't with food this good? At camp, no matter how bad the meal had been, the monsters had scarfed it down so other monsters couldn't take it away, and so the guards wouldn't start to think that the monsters were overfed and needed smaller rations. But none of that fear was in Jake as he savored his food, and just like always in Jake's presence, Tobias couldn't hold on to it for himself either. None of the reals were looking in their direction; the waitress barely glanced at them. It was just him and Jake, eating, Jake's arm brushing his every time he lifted french fries to his lips.

At the end of the meal, there was pie. Jake ordered a slice for each of them, apple and cherry with a scoop of vanilla ice cream on each.

As he gave the waitress the order, Jake slid his hand over Tobias's on the table. Tobias stared at it, then dropped his head, unable to stop the smile on his face or the way his heart rate picked up when Jake touched him. He hoped the real waitress hadn't noticed, but he also didn't really care. All that mattered was what Jake wanted. Jake could do anything he wanted to Tobias. And Jake had *touched* him again, hand to hand, every time so gentle.

The slices of pie came to them in neat wedges, each on its own plate, covered in ice cream and whipped cream. Tobias felt a little nervous when Jake picked up his fork to cut off a bite— he recognized the utensil from his studies and from serving the Director, but he'd never handled one personally before. To his relief, he managed to copy and master Jake's movement. A lot had depended on him learning basic physical maneuvers quickly in the last year—gestures to neutralize a witch's hex bag, knife moves, the basic choreography necessary for the consecration of defiled ground—so he had no problem bringing the brightly colored red pie to his mouth.

It was again an explosion of mind-blowing flavors in Tobias's mouth, nothing he could begin to process. He had to stop for a moment, fork in hand, and Jake laughed again and nudged their shoulders together. He still wasn't upset.

"Better than when it comes from my pocket, huh?" Jake asked, and Tobias almost shook his head, but Jake's tone was light and he was still smiling. "I'm just glad that I finally get to feed you the real stuff. It's been a long six months, Toby."

A long six months. It seemed at once impossible, absurd, that it had been only six months since the last time Jake had visited Tobias at FREACS, when they had played cards in a quiet room that usually contained screams. But it also seemed infinitely longer, that the last time Jake had visited Tobias was as ancient and dream-insubstantial as the memory of Becca's single-handed hug. Six months, but they had been worth it. This was heaven. He had been in hell, and somehow Jake had broken in and taken him to heaven. He never would have deserved this without having first endured that hell, without finishing the Director's training. It was all worth it now to be with Jake.

BACK IN THE CAR, Jake turned the key in the ignition, though not before reaching over to squeeze Tobias's hand. He held on longer than he had in the restaurant. "I'm so happy, Tobias," he said, warm gaze on him. "I'm so happy you're here. Look, I got us a place in Boulder, but that's a bit of a drive. What do you say we just check into a hotel here, get a good night's sleep, and then head out in the morning?" He smirked. "Not that I couldn't drive it. I've made longer drives with less sleep and shrapnel in my shoulder to boot, but it'd be nice to get into Boulder when you can actually see things, since it's your first time seeing . . . anything, you know? What do you think?"

"That sounds wonderful, Jake," Tobias said. *You are wonderful.*

Jake pressed his hand lightly, not at all to hurt. "Cool."

There was less to see in the small town in the dark, but Tobias could lean back against the leather seat and listen to the purr of Jake's car. This day had been so good. Jake was so good, as Tobias had always known he would be. But Tobias knew what a *hotel* meant from the things the guards said to each other about what they liked to do there. Hearing that word in Jake's voice made something clench in his stomach, reminded him that Jake hadn't taken him out of FREACS for the hell of it, or because Tobias was a real or something. Jake had been damn good to him, and now that they were away from camp, with its cameras that Jake had never liked, and now that they'd eaten, Jake would expect him to start paying him back.

Back in Freak Camp, Tobias wouldn't have worried quite as much. He was obedient. He was good with his mouth. He knew what was expected. But nothing since Jake had taken him from

Freak Camp's walls was familiar, and anything unfamiliar was dangerous. Jake had been *so good* to him today. Tobias couldn't remember the last time he had been this well-fed or gone without any kind of pain or threat of pain for so long. Despite everything the Director had painstakingly taught him, he wasn't sure he had enough skills or understanding of what Jake wanted to pay for that wonderfulness.

His stomach wasn't so full he didn't feel a knot of nerves forming. He knew what was coming, though he also *didn't* know. For years he had been saving himself for Jake, but his total lack of experience with this one crucial act made him more apprehensive than any prospect of pain or degradation could. Jake was so kind to him—getting him out, feeding him the best food, reals' food—that Tobias didn't care if Jake turned out to be as vicious as Crusher in bed. That was hard to imagine, anyway, but even if that were the case, Tobias wouldn't mind. He'd undergo anything for Jake and thank him for it. He'd be glad to thank him, not like when the Director made him express gratitude for a beating that made him a tiny bit less of a useless monster-whore. However Jake chose to treat him was more than Tobias deserved, just because it would be Jake's hands.

While the prospect of intense pain and blood didn't faze him (it really didn't, not if it meant that he was Jake's at last), he was worried about how he would handle it since it was his first time. God, what if he did something that disgusted Jake or made him uncomfortable, something *monstrous*? Tobias would rather Jake drove nails through his hand to hold him down than for one second regret getting him out.

He still couldn't believe this was actually about to happen, tonight, what he'd been holding on to for all those years. All those threats and close calls with Crusher and others—the possibility of getting fucked by them had been the one thing he had been truly afraid of, far more than his own death. If

Crusher hadn't been interrupted those times when he'd pinned Tobias down in the shower and breaking room, all Tobias would have been able to hope for would have been not to survive the experience. There would have been no point, no hope remaining that Jake would ever come back for him. Tobias had never let himself linger long on that nightmare, but now that he was here beside Jake—finally *safe* for the first time in his life, with nothing to stop Jake from being his first that same night—he couldn't help shuddering at how very close it had been.

Jake glanced at him, hand still gentle over his. "You okay?"

Tobias smiled, unable to hold back his giddy relief. "Yeah. I'm—I'm so glad, Jake."

Jake's warm gaze had him closing his eyes, overcome with bliss. *Everything*, he thought. *Everything was worth this, right now.*

The high lasted until they pulled in front of a building with a sign reading Holiday Inn, and Jake paused as he turned off the car. "I'm gonna run in and get a room. You okay waiting here?"

Tobias nodded automatically and watched Jake stride past the glass doors.

Alone, his uncertainty grew, along with the gnawing suspicion that he would end up badly disappointing Jake if he didn't find out, right now, what was expected of him. He knew it wouldn't be exactly the same as what the guards did and liked. For instance, Tobias was pretty positive Jake wouldn't want to hear him scream or cry, so he had resolved not to make a sound, no matter how bad it got.

But he couldn't decide whether Jake would mind if, afterward, he got up to clean off the blood. Sometimes the guards and hunters wanted to leave it to show what they'd done. He was almost sure Jake wouldn't mind (it didn't pay to be sure of anything, ever; Tobias couldn't trust his judgment), but he should ask to be certain. But what if that made Jake angry? Maybe he was just supposed to know one way or the other. God, Tobias had never been so afraid of making the wrong move. The consequences of failing, disappointing, *losing* Jake were more dire than any punishment he'd ever faced.

His building apprehension was cut short when Jake opened the driver's door, dropping back onto the seat. "Okay, we're all set. Room 112, it's on the other side, she said. Two singles, hope that's okay." He slid a quick glance over to Tobias.

Tobias had no idea what that meant, but he nodded quickly before Jake could interpret his silence as reluctance.

As Jake drove them around the parking lot, Tobias reviewed his resolutions. *No sounds. No hesitation. Don't blank out, no matter what, you have to stay aware to respond to whatever cues he gives you. If he wants you to move, move and move quickly. Best not to get up afterward until he tells you to.*

But his certainty wavered again. What if Jake expected . . . what if Tobias disgusted him by doing the wrong thing? Surely it would be better just to ask now. Jake couldn't get angrier with Tobias now for asking than he would be when Tobias actually fucked up in the middle of everything because he didn't ask. Jake had to forgive him for being stupid, especially since surely this counted as the early stage of training—

"I think this is as close as we're going to get. Everybody always wants to park by the pool, you know."

Tobias jumped, but Jake was already out of the car, heading toward the trunk. Tobias scrambled after him, breath caught in his throat. The opportunity had passed. He could only hope now that he could wing it to Jake's satisfaction.

Jake pulled out two duffel bags from the black hole of the Eldorado's trunk, and Tobias reached to take them, but Jake slung them over his own shoulder before slamming the trunk shut. "Nah, I got it."

Tobias yanked his hand back, face burning. *See, those are the kind of stupid assumptions that make you so worthless, that are going to get you thrown back into Freak Camp before you know it, that are going to make Jake hate you.* He should have known better than to think Jake would want a freak handling his personal things.

Jake was already fiddling with a key at a door, one of an identical series along the wall, only marked with sequential numbers. Tobias swallowed hard before hurrying to Jake's side. That had been a mistake, but he was lucky that Jake didn't seem angry about it. Tobias was still okay.

But when the door swung open and he saw two beds set apart, he couldn't smother a brief flash of disappointment. He had been hoping he'd get to lie next to Jake afterward, but it seemed Jake wanted to keep his bed clean. Which made sense, really, he shouldn't have been surprised.

Jake swung his bags onto the nearer bed, and one of them landed with a clunk and clatter. Tobias's body locked up, his mouth gone dry. Jake's *tools* were in there. Tools he had brought in to have on hand with Tobias.

Jake spared him a half-glance over his shoulder. "C'mon in, you're gonna let the bedbugs out."

The order unlocked his paralysis. Tobias hastily stepped inside, shutting the door behind him, and forced his attention away from the closed bag on the bed.

Then he realized that for the first time in eleven years, he didn't know what to do in the presence of a real or where to go. With the Director, he'd be on his knees in a corner, head down, waiting for the first instruction—but Tobias's brain balked at putting Jake and the Director together, refused to finish the thought or let it send him to his knees. Not yet, not now.

Where did Jake want him?

"Here, Tobias." Jake was holding something out to him, and Tobias moved forward to take it. It was a bright yellow toothbrush, still sealed in its packaging. He stared at it uncomprehendingly.

"I, um—" Jake scratched the back of his neck, a gesture incongruous with the easy confidence that Tobias had always seen. "I picked you up a few things, since I figured you wouldn't be bringing much with you out of . . . uh, anyway, it's just to tide you over until we get home and you can pick out stuff for yourself." He offered a clear plastic bag. When Tobias looked down at it, he could see a dark green comb, an oval container of some kind of plastic, and a tube of toothpaste.

Jake grinned nervously. "What, not your favorite color?" Then the smile faded a little. "They had toothbrushes in Freak Camp, right?"

God, Jake looked almost worried, not like this was a test but like it actually mattered to him that Tobias knew what they were. Tobias nodded, a little frantically, knowing that whatever else he did, he couldn't let that worry stay on Jake's face. Jake had nothing to worry about. Jake couldn't be anything less than perfect, and not just because he was a real and a hunter, but because . . . he was Jake.

"Yes. Of course. We had to brush our teeth every day." The toothbrushes were one of the few things that had been specific to each monster, their ID numbers printed on each handle. He took the bag perhaps too quickly from Jake's hand. "Thank you, these are wonderful, this is perfect. Thank you, Jake."

Jake looked more relieved than Tobias thought the information warranted, but maybe not. Maybe monster hygiene was very important to reals everywhere. "That's cool, then. I mean, I'm not as good with brushing as I should be, but . . . yeah." Jake took a deep breath and nodded toward the bathroom. "You can go ahead and use the bathroom first."

Tobias hesitated, not sure if that was an order or just a statement, but when Jake only looked at him, he hurried into the small room and closed the door softly. He didn't close it all the way—guards had broken bones when monsters seemed to be hiding from them—but he thought that Jake would tell him to open the door or would just come in if he wanted to.

In the bathroom, Tobias washed his hands and thoroughly brushed his teeth, never looking in the mirror. The guards had told him he was pretty (*Pretty Freak*, Crusher hissed right into his ear, real enough to make him convulse hard). But no, Jake had him now, and if Tobias was good enough, he might never hear anyone call him that again—or at least no one but Jake, and that wouldn't be so bad, Tobias was nearly sure.

Whatever they had called him, mirrors had only ever shown him a bony, ugly monster, nothing at all like the well-fed hunters. He'd been told often enough that his ass was his only advantage that he didn't bother looking at his face or wondering whether Jake thought he was pretty the way the guards did.

At least until he'd rinsed his mouth. Then he tipped his face up and stared himself in the eye, like he would have looked at any other monster.

He wished he knew if there were something he could do to that face in the mirror, the face he almost didn't recognize as his own, to make this night better for Jake. He wished there was something he could do to make his heart slow down. Jake might be able to hear it all the way in the other room.

He hesitated, looking around and wondering if there was something else he was supposed to do. White towels hung from a nearby rod, but he didn't even think about touching them. After Tobias had been used, Jake would tell him what to use, what to do, because he was so kind. Tobias trusted him.

When he stepped out of the bathroom, he saw a small stack of clothes—T-shirt, boxers—on the end of the bed closer to him. Jake was fiddling with a pair of mismatched socks, but he set them aside and stood up. "All done?"

Tobias nodded, moving out of the doorway to set his back

to the wall, eyes on his shoes. Before going in, Jake stopped beside him for a moment but went inside without saying anything. Tobias listened to the water running, not moving a muscle. It was easier this way, just to wait. Then he realized he was retreating, the same way he did during the Director's sessions or any interrogation, and he tried to stop, to stay here. Jake had gotten him out, and Tobias wanted to give him everything, because he deserved all Tobias had. It wasn't much to offer a man like Jake, but he wasn't going to cheat him of anything.

The door opening took him by surprise, and he jumped before he could stop himself.

"Hey," Jake said. Jake was looking at him, Tobias could tell, but he couldn't bring himself to risk meeting Jake's eyes. "Sure you're okay?" Tobias nodded quickly, hands twisting in the sides of his shirt. "I put those clothes on your bed for you to change into, dunno if you saw . . ." His hand slipped over Tobias's, warm and reassuring, and Tobias forced himself to be still.

Jake rubbed his thumb over Tobias's knuckles and stepped closer. His other hand lightly touched the side of Tobias's head, sliding through the curls of his hair. Nothing like how the Director had petted him, but Tobias shuddered anyway.

"Hey, you're okay." Jake's hand settled on Tobias's shoulder, and he leaned in until his forehead rested against Tobias's temple, and Tobias felt a wave of dizziness. "You're with me now. They'll never touch you again, I swear it." His hand tightened real-solid on Tobias's freak-skinny shoulder. It was almost like the warm, beautiful embrace Jake had enclosed him in outside the walls of Freak Camp. Almost.

It would've been so easy for Tobias to lean into that touch and forget everything else. He couldn't let himself do that, though. He couldn't forget how much—*everything*—depended on this night, and he needed to keep his head. He would show

Jake he was ready, that he wouldn't dawdle or resist for a moment.

He drew in a shaky breath and dropped his hands to the small space between them, fumbling to work the button open on his jeans. He could have opened Jake's fly and had Jake down his throat in about two seconds, but instead it took him almost six to get the button open; the material was stiff, tricky, and he wasn't used to opening a fly on himself.

Jake pulled back. "Tobias, what are you—"

But Tobias finally managed to pop the button free, and he didn't need to get the zipper down to drop the jeans, with his boxers, to the floor.

Jake jerked away, his hands flinching off of Tobias's shoulders. "Whoa, hey." A nervous chuckle rose in his voice, the only gauge Tobias had for his reaction, since Tobias still couldn't force himself to look up.

He swallowed hard, trying to keep his breathing under control, even though he had already screwed up. He should have gone to his knees first. That was obvious now, since that was what he actually had experience in. Stupid, stupid monster. But maybe he could still make this work if he was very good. If he did everything right, there was still a chance . . . *Please, God, let there be a chance . . .*

He reached for Jake's belt buckle but had hardly touched it when Jake grabbed his hands, hard. Tobias flinched, drawing a shuddering breath. He wished his hands weren't starting to shake.

"Tobias." Jake's voice sounded odd, his breathing uneven too, but not in the way Tobias was familiar with, that meant they were ready to push him down. Tobias risked the briefest of glances at Jake's face. Jake was looking at Tobias's groin, but not with the lust or amusement Tobias usually saw on guards' faces. If anything, Jake looked slightly sick. "Tobias, wait. Just— just hold on a second."

He didn't move, and Jake didn't let go of his wrists. After a moment, Jake said, still in that strange, tight voice, "This isn't—we're not going to do this."

The ground teetered, threatening to fall away under him. He couldn't draw breath in a way he'd only experienced with bonds and weights on his chest. He didn't know what he'd done, what he'd failed to do, why Jake suddenly didn't want to take him, when Tobias had *waited*. He'd kept himself for Jake no matter the cost (he would have paid any cost, and he had), and Jake had gone to such lengths to get him out, to claim Tobias. How could he have destroyed everything, all of Jake's interest in him, so fast and with so little effort?

He struggled to speak, to get his tongue working again. "No, please—I'm ready, Jake, I swear I am, I can do anything you want—"

"That's not what I want!" Jake let go at last, pushing Tobias's hands away and stepping back as though he couldn't stand to be close to him for another second. Tobias flinched, pressing back against the wall with his chin lowered to his chest.

For several moments, there was no sound but Jake's strange breathing. When he spoke, it sounded like he was struggling to keep his voice steady. "Just . . . pull your pants up. Please."

It took Tobias a horrifically long amount of time, almost five seconds, before he could obey, tugging the jeans and boxers back up over his hips. It was harder this time to get the button closed.

When Tobias finally looked up, Jake had turned away, hand pressed to his forehead. Another minute passed before he spoke. "Look, it's—been a really long day for both of us. You must be wiped. Let's just go to—let's just get some rest, okay?"

Tobias didn't move, even as Jake went over to the bed with the bags and pulled out a set of clothes with quick, tense movements. Jake finally glanced over at him, mouth twisted. "If you want, you can change in the bathroom. Or sleep in that, whatever—whatever makes you happy. I'm going to bed." He dumped the duffels on the other side of the bed, snapped off the lamp between the beds as he pulled the covers down, and got in with his back to Tobias.

Tobias took a deep breath, struggling to get control of himself and to *think*. Jake had put out the clothes, so he must have wanted Tobias to change, but he also definitely didn't want Tobias to undress anywhere near him. Tobias took the clothes on the bed to the bathroom and changed there without turning on the light, folded the clothes he'd been wearing, and carried them back out. He stopped just inside the darkened room, but Jake hadn't moved, and it only seemed logical that the other bed was for him. He had been whipped for assuming less, but he figured that at this point, it wouldn't matter. Jake didn't want him. He'd be back in Freak Camp by the next night.

IN THE MORNING, Jake took him to the hotel lobby, which had an array of food set out along a long table. Thankfully the room was empty of reals, apart from a gray-haired couple eating at a table by the window. They didn't look up from their plates as Jake and Tobias came in.

Jake motioned for Tobias to get a plate, and Tobias picked up a plastic-wrapped round of soft bread (a muffin, he remembered it was called—Jake had brought him one once before, wrapped just like this from his pocket) while Jake loaded his plate with a little of everything.

Jake glanced back at Tobias but didn't meet his eyes, looking only at his plate. "That all you want?"

Tobias nodded. He wasn't hungry, but Jake had seemed to expect him to pick something up.

He dawdled uncertainly at the end of the bar. Jake sat down

at a small table, then sighed and nudged the opposite chair with his foot. "C'mon, Tobias."

So Jake still wanted to share a table with him. Tobias hadn't been going to assume anything, not after last night. He sat down carefully, gingerly tearing the plastic open and breaking the muffin into smaller pieces. It would be his second and last meal out of Freak Camp, and even though he had no appetite, he was going to try to savor it. A few more reals were coming in now, lining up casually at the bar and chattering as they got their own plates of food, but Tobias couldn't bring himself to care. There was nothing they could do to him now, anyway.

He could feel Jake watching him. Perhaps he was trying to figure out how he could have picked such a stupid monster, or how Tobias had tricked him. Tobias's gut clenched harder, and he wondered, even as he brought another piece of soft bread to his lips, if he was going to be able to keep it down. He'd probably be able to make it outside before he vomited, assuming no one tried to stop him—

Then Jake pushed over one of his two plastic cups, filled with a bright orange liquid. Tobias stilled.

"Here," Jake said. "It's orange juice."

Tobias picked up the cup slowly, sipped, and almost choked in surprise at the taste. Sour, but *good*. Very good. Without thinking, he looked up to meet Jake's eyes, unsure of how much he was supposed to have.

Jake's lips flickered in a smile. "Finish it. I can get some more."

Tobias drank the orange juice and ate his muffin, pacing it so he finished his at the same time as Jake with his large plate of food. Jake dusted his hands off and wiped his mouth with a napkin, eyes lingering on Tobias's empty plate with its few crumbs scattered across. "Did you like it?"

Tobias nodded quickly. The muffin had been delicious and very filling, but he hadn't gotten nearly as much enjoyment out of it as he had with the cheeseburger and onion rings from last night.

"Well, let's hit the road. Daylight's burning, and we got a long way to go." Jake stood up. Tobias followed quickly, swallowing hard, the good food he just ate turning hard in his stomach.

The drive that morning was nothing like the one yesterday. Jake didn't talk, only turned on his tape deck. Tobias couldn't stop himself from replaying the night before, wondering what he should've done differently. Even though they were fucking useless, hopeless thoughts—he'd already fucked up far too much for a second chance with Jake, and that was all that mattered.

Lost in his despair, he hadn't been paying attention to anything passing outside, but a sign caught his eye, the information registering automatically: 15 miles to Salt Lake City, 450 to Cheyenne. Salt Lake City was the capital of Utah, Cheyenne was the capital of Wyoming. Both were east of Nevada, and the road sign wouldn't be giving them those distances unless they were headed toward those cities . . .

. . . away from Freak Camp.

Tobias felt his brain freeze in shock. That couldn't be right. Freak Camp was the only place Jake could legally dump a monster (though a shallow grave and kerosene would work as well; no one but Jake would have to know). And he had fucked up, and Jake hadn't even bothered to punish him, to teach him to be better, which meant that Jake couldn't possibly want him. But if they weren't going back to Freak Camp, if they were going *away*, that meant he still had a chance. A chance to persuade Jake he was worth keeping around. Maybe Jake didn't realize how well-trained Tobias was, how he could do anything. Maybe if Tobias acted right now, if he was brave enough to push a little bit, he could make Jake understand that as stupid, fucked-up, and worthless as Tobias was, he could learn, he could be anything that Jake wanted him to be, or nothing at all.

"Jake," he said, softly.

Jake glanced over at once, the crease deepening between his eyebrows. He almost looked apprehensive. "Yeah, Tobias?"

Tobias wet his lips. "You can—you can do whatever you want with me, you know."

Jake looked wary. "What do you mean?"

So Jake wanted to hear it explicitly—that was okay, Tobias knew how to do that. A lot of guards had liked to hear Tobias talk as he jerked them off. He ran his tongue over his lips again, keeping his voice soft, even if he couldn't keep his words from tumbling out like blood gushing out of a wound.

He tried to tell Jake what he could do with him, but he must not have used the right words, because he saw nothing on Jake's face indicating arousal, interest, anything Tobias could understand.

"You could hurt me," he said more urgently, "anyway you like, I won't mind. You could cut me, whip me, choke me—"

Jake jerked the wheel to the side, and there was an awful crunching noise as they left the pavement and hit loose rock that threw up a wave of dust around them. The Eldorado came to a hard stop, throwing Tobias back against the seat behind him.

"Stop," Jake said, voice shaking with anger. "Stop right now."

Tobias froze, lips still parted.

Jake couldn't even look at him, but what Tobias could see of his face was dark with a rage Tobias had only ever seen on him once before. That terrible day when Jake had shaken him and then *left* him. "What kind of monster—why the hell do you think I'd *want* that?"

In the stillness after the damning words—*Just a fucking monster, too stupid to know what Jake would ever want*—every meager shred of hope Tobias had managed to rekindle from ashes for a life with Jake fell through his fingers, as insubstantial as smoke. That was it. His last chance, gone. Jake had stopped the car, had made it clear Tobias couldn't do anything that would make him worth keeping. Any second now he'd order Tobias to get out, or pull out a silver-loaded shotgun from the clanking duffel in the backseat, or turn the car around back to the camp.

Tobias had fucked it all up, like the guards, the Director, Kayla, *everyone* had told him he would, because he was so useless he couldn't hold Jake's interest for twenty-four hours. The one good thing he'd ever been offered in his life, the thing for which he'd waited and fought for years, and he'd lost it.

He almost didn't recognize the sensation of his throat closing up. It had been so many years since he'd cried—without hours of pain first and a guard sneering above him—that he couldn't believe it was happening now, in front of Jake, nor could he stop it. Jake was the only thing in his life he had dared to hope for, and from the day he'd allowed himself to believe Jake would keep his word and take him away, he'd reminded himself it wouldn't be forever—just a few weeks, maybe. But he'd never thought he'd fuck it up *this* fast.

And he still didn't know what had gone wrong.

Sobs worked their way out of him, shaking his shoulders, but he never made a sound—that lesson was intact from interrogations and punishment innumerable. He kept his head tucked to his chest, pressing himself into the space between the door and seat.

"Tobias," Jake breathed, something like anguish in his tone that Tobias couldn't comprehend. Jake didn't touch him, though. Tobias didn't expect him to.

A moment later, Jake eased the car back on the road. Tobias waited for the inevitable U-turn, but a mile on, Jake only said, "We'll be home soon."

2

They stopped every few hours to refuel, use the bathroom, and get drinks. Tobias hated getting out of the car, never sure if Jake was looking for an ASC checkpoint to dump him, but that had yet to happen. Usually, he just followed Jake to the bathroom—dirtier but less crowded than the Freak Camp facilities, and without any visible cameras —and then stood behind him while Jake paid for his Coke or candy bar.

"Get what you want," Jake had told Tobias—without looking at him—the first time they stopped, but Tobias hadn't had the foggiest idea what that meant. Besides, he hadn't been hungry. Just that one meal with Jake at the diner and the muffin in the morning was more than he usually ate in two or three days, and his stomach knew better than to start demanding more food at this point. Really, the only thing he wanted was to know how badly he had fucked up with Jake. In the past, if he'd failed to satisfy anyone to this extent—whether that was a hunter, the Director, a guard, or some real stranger—he would have bruises to show for it, or more likely be chained to the floor and beaten or whipped or branded. And that only if the Director wasn't feeling creative.

Usually, the Director was creative. But Jake . . . Jake did nothing, and Tobias was almost blanking out just to keep control of his instinctive terror. Because this *mattered*, like following the Director's instructions mattered, and he couldn't escape the fear that because Jake wasn't telling him to do *anything*, Tobias was just fucking up more and more.

He had assumed when Jake got him out that he would have a grace period, that Jake would tell him what to do, train him, and accept that there would be mistakes in the first few days because Tobias was so damned stupid.

Now, he suspected that he wasn't going to get instructions or a grace period. Jake was just going to do what he always did and expect Tobias to know and do what was required. But Tobias didn't have one clue what that might be, except it certainly wasn't anything he had tried so far. Jake hadn't turned the Eldorado around yet, and Tobias desperately wanted to take that as a sign that he still had a chance, but he couldn't quite believe that. More likely, Jake wanted to make sure that he was a screw-up before he took Tobias back. And for once in his life, Tobias didn't think keeping his mouth shut and his head down would be enough to keep him safe.

Jake gave him a funny look after the second stop, and Tobias had to fight the urge to run. Or to drop to his knees and beg. But he didn't do either, because there was a real watching —a man working behind the counter—and, given Jake's reaction to his begging earlier, that would be the worst thing to do.

When they left the store, a small bell above the door chiming cheerily, Tobias was tempted—briefly, wildly—to try begging anyway, just to see if he could get some kind of reaction from Jake. Even knowing what would finally earn him a boot to the balls would be a welcome relief to the sensation that he was falling and that Special Research was below.

He forced the thought away and settled himself in his corner of the passenger seat. There, at least, he could watch the endless fields flying past and let his dread and panic fade into the back of his mind where he didn't have to feel it.

At the third stop, Jake bought two Cokes, a bag of M&Ms, and an Almond Joy candy bar. Before they stepped back outside into the sunlight, he turned and, before Tobias quite realized what was happening, shoved all four items at Tobias. Tobias felt unnervingly clumsy as his hands closed around the two bottles of soda and plastic wrappers.

"Think you got all that, Toby?" Jake said, smiling tightly.

Tobias swallowed. He would carry some of it with his mouth if he had to. Jake was letting him *do* something. "S-sure, Jake. I've got it."

Jake nodded. "Good."

Tobias followed him out of the gas station convenience store and barely twitched when Jake held the Eldorado's passenger door open for him. He probably didn't want to risk Tobias dropping his soda.

When they were settled in the Eldorado, Jake grabbed one of the bottles of Coke and the M&Ms, leaving Tobias unsure what he should do with the last soda and the candy bar. He stared at them worriedly. If he just held onto them, the soda would get warm and the candy bar would melt. But he wasn't sure where he could put them so that Jake would be able to reach them easily when he wanted them.

"Those are for you," Jake said, ripping open the M&Ms and tossing seven or eight into his mouth before setting the big bag on the seat between them. He slid the keys into the Eldorado's ignition. "Well, the soda is. I claim half the candy bar. If you'll help me out with the M&Ms." He glanced over, and he still looked a little strained, but Tobias felt a big part of himself ease up just seeing Jake smile again. Maybe, somehow, impossible as it seemed, Tobias hadn't fucked everything up beyond repair.

And then he realized that Jake had *given him food*, just like he had when they were kids, and Tobias had to look down for a second.

When they were younger, Jake coming to camp had always meant that there would be a candy bar or squashed bag of chips or some other esoteric real-person food that to Tobias tasted like a piece of heaven. It almost hurt to remember the times when being with Jake had been the best thing in the world, a time when, because he was with Jake, he didn't have to be afraid of anything, because Jake would take care of him and never demanded anything in return.

Jake had always taken care of him. Of all the reals in Tobias's life, Jake was the one he had never needed to be afraid of.

Maybe he should try not to be afraid now. That went against a lifetime of being a monster and six months of the Director's training, but by those standards, he should've been dead already.

Tobias's hands shook a little when he twisted the cap off the soda, as he had seen Jake do, but he took a long drink of it even though Jake hadn't told him to. And then he promptly choked when it fizzed down his throat.

Jake looked at him, eyes wide and alarmed. "Tobias, are you—"

Tobias coughed a couple more times, and then fumbled the cap back on. He liked the flavor. He just hadn't expected the *fizz*.

"'Sokay," he choked out. "Bubbles." He could feel them crawling up his nose. How fucking weird. Not painful, just *weird*.

Jake stared at him for a second before beginning to laugh. It was a little choked, filled with more relief than humor, but it made Tobias smile, really smile, for the first time since they'd left the restaurant the night before. Tobias's smile seemed to make Jake relax, seemed to suck half the tension from his shoulders, the tension that Tobias had instinctively believed meant trouble and pain for him.

"Damn, Toby," Jake said, wiping his eyes. "Guess you never tried the Coke last night, huh?"

Tobias shook his head. He'd forgotten about the drink Jake had ordered for him, overwhelmed by all the food. Very daring, he took another sip. It was better this time when he expected the bubbles. Still weird, but at least he wasn't choking.

The rest of the drive to Boulder was . . . better. Even good. Tobias still wasn't sure what to do when they stopped, couldn't quite figure out what he was supposed to do with his hands, his eyes, his feet, but he managed to answer when Jake asked him a question ("Ever had beef jerky, Tobias?" "No, Jake." "Well, we better try it. Enough salt to keep the both of us well preserved") and use the reals' bathrooms. But it felt almost like it had years ago, when Jake sat beside him against the concrete wall, his shoulder warm against Tobias's, and for a little while it had felt like even the glares of the guards were far away, something that couldn't hurt him, at least so long as Jake was there.

By the time they started seeing signs for Boulder, Tobias could almost believe that he wasn't going back to Freak Camp. Not today. Not now.

Maybe tonight. Tobias's stomach twisted every time he thought about another night, about the possibility of walking with Jake into another room with another pair of beds. He still didn't know how he had messed up the last time, and there could only be a limited number of times that Jake would forgive him. Inexplicably, Jake *had* forgiven him for last night, so he had to believe that there was still a chance, that maybe tonight Jake would tell him what to do, how he had fucked up. The Director . . .

Tobias forced his mind away from the Director's cool, implacable voice, away from *tonight*, and focused on the here and now. He didn't know what was going to happen, and speculation had never helped—*Stupid dog, you really thought you could guess what I required this evening?*—and he had a whole world of unprecedented experiences, vistas, and sensations to experience now.

He watched the rugged mountains covered in thick, dark trees slide past the Eldorado's window in an always-changing green, tan, and brown blur beneath the brilliantly blue sky. He felt the way the Eldorado shifted gears, slowing down as Jake eased up for curves and speeding up to pass what Jake muttered under his breath were "blue-haired road hogs."

But more than anything else, Tobias watched Jake from under his bangs. The sunlight lit up the curves of his face, gilded the edges of his short dark hair, and brought out the light gray of his eyes. Jake's hands on the steering wheel fascinated him with their ease and grace. Even the thin scars over his knuckles and the backs of his hands, lines that Tobias had somehow never noticed before, proved his resilience. Nothing could touch Jake and survive, Tobias was sure of that. Whatever had left those scars was nothing but ashes and scattered molecules and the tales Jake had brought to him.

He looked both like and unlike how Tobias had always seen him in the camp. Infinitely more *real*. This was how Jake should be: free and strong in the car he loved, racing along the endless highways outside of Freak Camp. All these roads belonged to him. He was more beautiful than ever, in a way that stopped Tobias's breath, made him wonder if he was hallucinating near death in the way he'd heard about. How could this be real? What had he ever done to earn this?

Tobias soaked in the moment as Jake hummed softly along with the low-playing cassette, glancing now and then in Tobias's direction or munching one-handed on whatever snacks they'd gotten at the last stop.

He had seen sunlight and Jake's features before, but now, when the unending pavement and the sky and mountains made his eyes water and his head spin, he could watch Jake out of the corner of his eye. That sight grounded him, made him feel safe, awestruck, and light-headed. The sun outside of Freak Camp gave off a different light entirely, and Jake outside of Freak Camp . . .

Tobias took another deep breath and pushed any other thoughts far away, where they couldn't hurt what he had here and now.

When they finally reached Boulder, the sun was casting a sunset behind the mountains, and Tobias was distracted from the new colors playing against the tan of Jake's neck by the houses, the shops, all the *buildings*.

He could guess at the purpose of most of them from all his reading and researching, but he had never seen a home for reals before. He'd never been close enough to possibly step out of the car and touch a door or peer into a window. All the safe places meant for reals and to keep monsters out—monsters like him, and this was exactly why he'd been put into Freak Camp in the first place, so there wouldn't be a chance of him contaminating reals who were just living their lives.

Tobias didn't realize that he'd clenched his hand around the armrest in the door, fingers digging into the vinyl, until they started to go numb. He hastily let go, afraid to leave a mark on Jake's car.

Too many things, places, details, possibilities, a panicked voice in the back of his head hissed. *How the fuck can you manage all of that? Understand and account for all of that? When Jake isn't telling you what to do and you have to figure it all out yourself? There's no way . . .*

He told the little voice to shut up and let himself blank out a little. Just a little. Not so much that he wouldn't be able to respond the second Jake told him to do anything, the second Jake demanded anything of him—*please God, want me, use me* —but enough that the buildings and the streets and the *reals*

teeming in them went away for a little bit. The world narrowed
down to the rumble of the car and Jake's solid, warm presence
next to him. That was a good world, more than enough for
Tobias. So much better than a cocoon of ratty blankets or the
memory of Becca's arms that wouldn't really keep him warm or
safe from the guards.

He was so calm, so focused on *Jake* and *the Eldorado* that
when they stopped, he almost had to pull himself out of a
trance.

"Hey, Toby, wake up, we're here." Jake's hand was on his
arm, touching gently, not even shaking him awake the way
Kayla had when he'd needed to be *up fast* and an injury was
keeping him from reacting quite as fast as he needed to.

Tobias knew that he would always have to leave the safe
places in his head where the fear went away, but all things
considered, having Jake touch him on the arm and call his
name wasn't so bad of a way to wake up to reality.

THEY HAD PARKED in a small lot next to a two-story building.
There were only a few cars nearby and no reals in sight. Tobias
got out of the car cautiously, keeping his head down as he
trailed after Jake toward the trunk. This time, Jake held out one
of his duffels, the lighter one—Tobias could tell, even in the
twilight—as though he wasn't sure if Tobias would take it and
didn't want to force the issue.

Tobias took it without hesitation, sliding it onto his
shoulder with all the care Jake's belongings deserved, and
managed a quick smile. This was already different from last
night. *Different* in Freak Camp had always meant terrifying, but
last night had been awful in a way he'd never imagined. Tobias
would take almost any kind of different over that.

He was sure it could get worse (it could always get worse),

but if this turned out to be exactly like last night, he might not be able to keep from falling apart in front of Jake. Feeling the fuck-up coming and having no ability to stop it, when the stakes were *Jake*, would be the true nightmare.

Now, at least, he could hold onto the moment, the feel of the duffel bag strap over his shoulder, the way Jake's shoulders moved beneath his shirt as Tobias followed him up the stairs.

On the landing lit by a single overhead light, Jake fumbled with the keys—awkward in a way he'd never been with the Eldorado's keys—before pushing the door open. He took a step back, waiting for Tobias to go first.

Tobias set his jaw and walked in, sliding the bag to his back so that if there were traps before them, they'd be less likely to damage Jake's belongings. He tried to look everywhere without appearing to look at anything, and he kept his hands spread at his sides, ready to move instantly between Jake and anything— monster, ghost, human, booby trap—that might fly out at him.

When nothing happened and Jake came in behind him to shut and lock the door, it was a little anticlimactic.

Jake gave him one of the funny looks that was becoming stomach-churningly familiar before he switched on the light. "Well, here it is, Toby. Home sweet home. I know it, uh, needs a lot of work, but I hope you like it."

Tobias blinked in the sudden light. Freak Camp had either had nothing but light or nothing but dark, and the guards had always controlled which one the monsters got at any particular moment. It was strange to see Jake so easily flip a switch and imagine that he, Tobias, might be able to do the same thing. If Jake would let him, at least. If Tobias got up the courage to ask.

He followed Jake out of the narrow entryway into a large room, its walls painted a more gentle shade of the stark white rooms Tobias was used to. In the opposite wall was a closed wooden door; the left wall had two windows without any bars, only covered in thin plastic shutters. On the right, a half wall separated another room, and next to that a passage led somewhere else.

The room before them had a small wooden table with two padded chairs near the half wall, a sofa next to the closed door, and a television across from the sofa, with a short bookshelf against the left wall. The carpets were a worn white-gray, and the only other notable thing was a single poster, bearing the legend METALLICA across the bottom, tacked up on the left wall.

"So, uh, grand tour." Jake clapped his hands. Tobias started, then cringed. Jake paused before continuing. Maybe he'd just been collecting his thoughts, or maybe he was waiting for Tobias to apologize, and Tobias *couldn't tell.* "This is the living room, and right around the corner is the kitchen." He walked over to the open doorway that led into a small kitchen, then looked back at Tobias expectantly. Tobias felt his heart rate pick up again—*already too slow, fuck, not anticipating at all*—and stepped quickly to Jake's side. Jake glanced at the bag Tobias still clutched to his shoulder. "Just throw that down anywhere, man."

Tobias didn't think he meant that literally—Jake's *possessions* were in that bag—so he lowered it carefully to the carpet. He must have still done it wrong because Jake looked slightly unsettled in a way Tobias had never imagined Jake could be. Tobias had just begun to brace himself for the consequences when Jake started talking again, ignoring Tobias's lapse without giving any correction *again.*

"So, yeah, kitchen—kinda cramped, I know, but it's got a working dishwasher, stove, and fridge, which is more than a lot of places got, I can tell you that. This way—" Jake turned down the hall, and Tobias moved after him, step by step. "Bathroom here, laundry room right after—and that's pretty sweet, I gotta say, not having to worry about the weirdos in laundromats taking off with your boxers—this is my bedroom." Jake reached toward the partially open door at the end of the hall and rapped on it with his knuckles. "Back this way—"

He pushed past Tobias toward the living room, suddenly enough that Tobias jumped to get his back against a wall. Then he remembered that he didn't fucking deserve to dodge Jake (though maybe it had been a good idea to get out of his way), took another shaky breath, and followed Jake back to the living room, where Jake was standing next to the previously closed door, now open.

"This is your room, Tobias."

Tobias stopped at the doorway beside Jake. Up until now, he'd understood well enough—at least, he could have repeated everything Jake said if asked, and he hoped memorizing the name for each room would be enough for now, that he could later figure out the purpose and rules of each—but now he couldn't suppress the cold terror of complete incomprehension. This was clearly important to Jake, and Tobias didn't have a clue what Jake meant. *His room?* Would he stay there when Jake didn't want to see him? Was he going to be fucked there (*when when when*)? Was he in charge of keeping it clean? *Please don't do this to me, please just tell me, Jake.*

And this was clearly not the reaction Jake had been expecting. Tobias's idiocy was fucking everything up *again*. Jake was watching him, and though Tobias couldn't bring himself to look Jake in the face, he could still feel his—he didn't know what to call it, but he knew it wasn't good, that Jake wasn't happy with him. The terror slid into his throat, became unbearable, and Tobias was just about to crumple to his knees and *beg* Jake to be patient with his stupidity, please give him the mercy he didn't deserve, just a little and Tobias would swear he'll pay him back tenfold—when Jake spoke. Words alone could have made Tobias okay, but the note of desperation in Jake's voice actually made him *listen,* helped him break out of his rote response.

"We could switch if you want the other one with the big bathroom—I grabbed it just because, but it won't be a big deal to switch. Whatever you want, Tobias. I know this one doesn't look great yet, but I figured we could go out and you could pick out what you want to put in it, instead of whatever shit I got, 'cause I don't know—yeah, so, it's just, up to you, man."

Head tucked down, Tobias listened. He still didn't understand, but Jake sounded—not angry at all. It was almost like he was *worried*, and that didn't ease Tobias's fears, but it broke the terror into manageable pieces, small enough that he could speak, look, smile, and pretend that he understood what was happening and it was okay with him. That seemed to be what Jake needed right now, and anything Jake needed Tobias was there to provide.

"This is fine, Jake." He sneaked a peek into the room, at the huge, neatly made bed and wooden set of drawers that was almost like the filing cabinets in the Freak Camp library. It couldn't possibly be *for* him, not for a monster to use the way a real would, but whatever Jake was worried about, he shouldn't be. "This is great," Tobias said, more firmly.

When Jake let out a sigh, Tobias glanced at him and saw unmistakable relief on Jake's face. "Well . . . awesome. That's awesome. And we'll go out and get more stuff sometime so you can make it however you like." Jake ran a hand through his hair and blew out his breath again. "It's . . . good to have you here, Tobias. I'm really glad."

Before Tobias could soak in the joy of those words and how much Jake clearly meant them, Jake moved forward, almost like he was going to pull him close again, and Tobias had to fight down twin surges of excitement and terror. Last night had started this way too.

Maybe he did something wrong this time too, even though he didn't move at all; maybe he looked less than ready, because Jake caught himself and backed up against the doorframe.

"How 'bout I make dinner? I mean, I'm not that great. Got better since me and Dad . . . yeah, well, let's just say that credit card scams aren't as fun when you know the Dixons are looking over your shoulder."

Tobias nodded and smiled with very little idea of what Jake was talking about. But that was okay, because he was following Jake to the half wall beyond, which led into the narrow kitchen. Tobias saw metal doors and wooden cupboards but couldn't really get a good look before Jake motioned to the table through the open partition.

"Why don't you take a seat while I forage? I'm not sure where I put the pizza pan, and this kitchen's not really big enough for both of us not to run into each other."

It was almost a physical relief to be told what to do. Tobias hadn't been active that day, just riding in the car and soaking in Jake's presence, but he was bone-deep tired, like he'd been cold too long with not enough food. But Jake's car had been warm, and Jake had given him plenty of food, so probably it was the constant struggle to be something more than a crawling, whimpering monster for Jake, and the inescapable knowledge that he was failing.

So Tobias sat, his heart rate slowing slightly. He was used to tables. Tables featured in interrogation rooms, the least painful Director sessions, and those precious meetings with Jake. He felt safe and grounded.

And then Jake tossed two plastic plates over the counter, the too-loud sound of them clattering on the table filling the mostly empty apartment, and Tobias was no longer safe, no longer calm. A monster might eat huddled at a table with other monsters, might use a plate with them, but he did not belong or deserve to sit with real people.

Last night in the restaurant and this morning in the hotel, he had sat to eat where Jake had told him to, because it had been important to demonstrate to all the other reals how obedient Jake's monster was. But now, there was no one else to observe. No one except Jake, who knew exactly what Tobias was and how wrong it was for Tobias to pretend they could eat together.

If Jake had been the Director, Tobias would have known what to do. He would've left the table, maybe thrown himself down before the guard could come and move him. But Jake had told him—asked, did that mean the same thing?—to sit, so Tobias sat and fought to keep his breathing steady, fought not to shake, desperately reminding himself that Jake would tell him what to do. Jake would not bring him back to Freak Camp just because he stayed at a table too long. He was almost sure of that, though he knew it was never safe to assume anything with his malfunctioning freak-brain.

But the longer Jake didn't look at him and just kept moving in the kitchen—was he really unconcerned? Was this some kind of test?—the less Tobias could hold himself still in the chair, mimicking calm.

Then suddenly Jake was there, crouching by him. "Hey, what's wrong?"

Having Jake close to him again felt good. He didn't seem angry that Tobias hadn't moved yet, but it was so wrong that Jake was lower when Tobias knew that *he* should be kneeling by the table, not Jake. He slid to the edge of his chair, instinct driving him that far before Jake's hands fell on Tobias's knees, the contact a sudden shock that stilled him. If he moved forward any farther, he would be throwing himself into Jake's arms, which he wouldn't—shouldn't—do.

Tobias swallowed. "I don't know." *I don't know what you want or what I should do. I don't know how long you'll keep me or what will send me back. And you won't tell me.* "Please just tell me, and I'll . . ."

Jake touched his face, thumb brushing his cheek, fingertips grazing his hair. Tobias fell quiet at the familiar touch—only

two days he'd felt it, and it was already familiar and as necessary as air. Tobias could go without that touch like he could go
without food, but it *hurt* to be without it. Jake touched him like
it was a miracle that Tobias was there. Like Tobias was something special, something *real*. "Tell you what?"

What I should do so you'll touch me forever, fuck me, keep me.
"What I should do. I'm sorry, Jake, so sorry."

Jake smiled, but it was tight, not quite genuine, and Tobias
felt his nerves spike, tightening his spine, clenching his stomach. It was last night all over again, and he was going to fuck it
up, and Jake was going to—

"You're fine, Tobias." Only Jake crouching there in front of
him, his fingers against the too-hot skin of Tobias's face, kept
Tobias in his chair, kept a lid on the panic. "I don't really need
that much help with pizza. I mean, I haven't tried making it
here, you know, though I bought one a couple months ago when
I signed the lease for the apartment. I used to cook them all the
time whenever we had an apartment and Dad was . . . yeah,
well, I'm going to try to do better, you know? *Cooking* and stuff.
Tobias. Talk to me. Anything you want, anything, just say it, and
I'll do my best. I mean, I know that's not always that great,
but . . ." Jake snapped his mouth shut and took a deep, slow
breath. "Just tell me, okay? What do you need?"

Tobias couldn't process the question, couldn't think of
anything to say in response. He stared down while Jake's hand
slid from his cheek to the back of his neck, and the *ohsogood*
sensation of Jake's hand on his bare skin warred with the
inherent *wrong* that Jake (his master? a real? a hunter? perfect
and so much better than he deserved) was reaching *up* to him, a
monster, a freak and a worthless—

"You're on the floor," Tobias choked out, when the disso-
nance and his own emotions threatened to break him down
faster than even the Director's soft voice. He wanted to blame the

fact that he was stupid, that he hadn't slept hardly at all, but the truth was that this mattered so much that he could barely think about what he had *right now* without being terrified of losing it. Life always got worse for monsters. It had to. But right now, he was with Jake, gently touched by Jake, and there was only one way that his life could get worse, and that was if this contact, this connection, stopped. And it would the second Jake realized he was kneeling beneath a *freak*. He couldn't ask Jake to stand, he couldn't beg to be lower—*I didn't give you permission to beg yet, freak*—but Jake had told him to say what he needed, and maybe, just maybe Jake would be merciful enough to understand.

Jake laughed. It looked like it hurt. "Yeah," he said. "You wanna come down or should I get up?"

Thank you God, Tobias thought, as he slid off his chair and to the floor where he belonged, where Jake was.

WHEN TOBIAS just *dropped* from his chair—like he was desperate to get off of it, like he'd been shot—Jake couldn't help but flinch back. He expected . . . fuck, he didn't know what he'd expected. Maybe for Tobias to laugh at him and tell him to sit in a chair, to stop swooning like a tragic lover, or maybe to drop down next to him like he had when they were kids, nervous, but not like *this*.

When Tobias hit the floor, he didn't try to move closer to Jake. He just knelt, shoulders hunched until his head was well below Jake's, even when Jake sat back on his heels. Monsters had begged Jake for their lives, and he'd watched broken civilians weep over their loved ones' bodies, but he had never in his twenty years seen someone assume such an abject, groveling, demeaning position.

Tobias assumed it like it was the most natural thing possi-

ble, like it was a *relief* to be kneeling on the floor with his spine
bent.

A little voice in Jake's head was panicking, hissing, *What the
fuck? What the fuck!* over and over again, like repeating it would
give him some kind of answer, would bring back the Tobias he
had known when they were kids. Fuck, he'd take the Tobias he
had left in Freak Camp six months ago, who had been tense
and half-starved but who had smiled so much more easily, who
hadn't flinched at *everything* Jake did.

The worst thing, really, was that this was still Tobias. Same
smile, same face. Same expression in his eyes when he looked
at Jake, like Jake was the best thing in his world. But at the same
time, he was a broken stranger, someone who expected . . .
horrible things. Jake couldn't even—wouldn't even try to
imagine—

What the fuck did they do to you, Tobias? he thought, angry
enough to break something and also sick with the knowledge
that this was all his fault, that everything that had happened to
Tobias was his fucking fault as much as if he'd been the one
beating the joy out of him.

And then Tobias looked up at him from his twisted, groveling position and smiled that same tender, vulnerable, oh-so-
breakable smile that cracked Jake's heart when he was just
handing Tobias a bag of chips. Right now, with Tobias basically
cowering beneath his (fuck, *their*) kitchen table, it made the bile
rise in Jake's throat.

Moving slowly, he pulled Tobias up and close to his body,
wrapping his arms around him. Not because he necessarily
wanted to hug Tobias or just pull him close—though he
wanted all that, but he didn't know if Tobias did, and how the
fuck would Jake be able to tell if he wanted it or just wouldn't
say no to anything?—but because if he didn't touch Tobias
right now, if he didn't stop seeing that smile combined with the
way his body said he had absolutely no hope that Jake wouldn't

hit him, then Jake was going to punch something (the floor, the table, the chair, *never* Tobias) or throw up over the floor.

Tobias didn't come to his arms like girls or guys usually did. Or even, fuck, Dad, though the last time they'd hugged—

Yeah, Tobias's body was tense, like he was shocked that Jake was holding him, like he couldn't understand. And fuck, for all Jake knew, he didn't have the least clue and just thought that Jake was—

Jake cut off thoughts of anything but the slight weight of Tobias in his arms, the smell of his hair as Jake buried his face by Tobias's shoulder, feeling the knobs of vertebrae under one hand and the meatier flesh of his thigh under the other. Felt Tobias's breath against his ear and the even rise and fall of his breathing—even as he registered how each deep breath, coupled with the wire-tight tension in Tobias's body, indicated more panic than any sound he could make.

"Shhhh, it's okay," Jake murmured. "You're okay."

Tobias just sat there, stiff in his arms, and it was horrible. Jake rubbed Tobias's back, feeling every rib—*remember these, Jake Hawthorne, all your fucking fault*—hoping to ease some of the tension, to find a way out of the hug without pushing Tobias away. That was something he would never, could never, do. "I'm going to do my best, Tobias. I promise. I promise."

After a couple minutes of being held, Tobias relaxed. It was almost worse, because Jake could tell—he was close enough to hear Tobias's heartbeat in his throat, feel every muscle in his back—that Tobias wasn't *relaxing*, exactly, so much as he had finally forced himself to go limp and accepting in Jake's arms. Jake could hear the blood beating harder through his veins.

Accepting was not relaxing. It was not the same as willing. And Jake had damn well better remember that.

"Hey, Toby," he said, trying to keep cheer and ease in his voice for Tobias's sake. "You hungry?"

Tobias's head twitched, which Jake decided to interpret as a yes because, fuck it, he didn't know how to ask and actually get an answer.

"Me too," he said. "Here's the plan for tonight, low stress. I'm gonna—we're going to cook up the frozen pizzas. I've got pepperoni and sausage, so you'll get to figure out which one you like better." *Please tell me what I should do*, Tobias had said, and Jake hated that; he wanted Tobias to do what *Tobias* wanted, but he had no idea how to say that, no idea what to do to prove to Tobias what it even meant. Jake swallowed. "And then we're both going to sit at the table. I don't want you to . . . we're equals, Tobias. I mean, I'm a little older." Jake grinned a little, but the statement didn't even qualify as a joke and his expression died right away. "Anything I do, you can do, okay? I mean, you don't *have* to, I don't want to . . . to force you to do stuff you don't want to do, but we're together. I'm at a table, you can be at the table. And the same goes for me, too—if you're on the floor, I'm gonna come right down there with you. You got that, Toby?"

"Y-yes, Jake," Tobias whispered.

And that fucking hurt too.

"Up we go," Jake said, aware even as he said it that it wasn't something a guy like him would usually say to any sixteen-year-old. It sounded more like something that parents said when their toddler skinned a knee. Sounded like something that Mom might have said . . .

He withdrew from the hug, but only enough to stand and pull Tobias up with him. Tobias didn't struggle, just looked confused and a little lost.

They were nearly eye to eye, almost the same height. The same. Jake had to remember that because it didn't look like Tobias was going to be able to believe that on his own for a while. Jake felt lost himself, not at all qualified for anything that was happening.

But he was the best Tobias had right now, and he would damn well make it work.

It was weird and a little disturbing, making a frozen pizza with Tobias following him around like a desperate puppy or a lost five-year-old. The kitchen wasn't exactly big. As Jake had suspected, they were touching almost constantly while searching for the tray and taking out the pizza. He almost whacked Tobias in the face opening the freezer door, and he definitely bumped into him when he ripped open the package on the pepperoni pizza a little too enthusiastically, but . . . it worked. Tobias ducked the door and only looked nervous for a second before actually grinning—just a flash—at Jake's "Fuck, sorry, damn door." Then when Jake stumbled into him, Tobias leaned forward, supporting him, and Jake had to make an effort to focus and not to get lost in how goddamn surreal and wonderful it was to have Tobias *right there*, alive, a soft heat against his shoulders, those eyes locking on him every time he opened his mouth.

Jake gave up on finding the pizza tray—he'd bought it because it had seemed like a good idea at the time, and Chad, the guy at the store, had been really persuasive, not to mention the damn sexy smile he'd flashed at Jake. Anyway, the directions on the cardboard said they could just put it in the oven, so Jake did. Then they waited, the second sausage pizza thawing on the stove. It felt awkward to Jake just to stand in front of an oven waiting for the food to be done, like it was a jack-in-the-box about to give them a prize, but he didn't want to suggest that Tobias sit down or go sit down himself.

It was only a little burnt around the edges when Jake slid the pizza out (thank God Chad had mentioned oven mitts). "Sit down, Tobias. I don't want to dump cheese on you."

Tobias jumped back and took his original chair, and Jake plopped the pizza down between them.

Jake let himself sit and close his eyes for a second. Cooking was exhausting, and being so aware of Tobias every second was exhausting, and he was going to pretend they were letting the pizza cool and not that something was really, really messed up and he didn't know what he was doing.

Of course, stillness didn't last long. Jake's stomach growled, so he opened his eyes, smiled at Tobias, who was *watching* him —as though the apartment could be firebombed and Tobias wouldn't move unless he saw Jake reacting first—and reached for a slice. He almost burned his fingers off.

"Dammit," he said, shaking his hand. Tobias jumped when he swore, his eyes widening, but relaxed and almost smiled when Jake grinned ruefully at him. "That pizza is *hot*," Jake said. "Be careful, okay?"

Tobias nodded and watched while Jake used a hastily retrieved fork to scoop a piece of the soggy, cheesy pepperoni pizza onto his plate.

Jake got a sick, niggling feeling in his stomach when Tobias didn't reach for his fork or make any move toward the pizza, but he ignored it. Instead, he used his own fork to put the most pepperoni-laden slice of pizza on Tobias's plate. He couldn't decide if the way Tobias's smile widened—like Jake had just done the most wonderful thing in the world—made him feel all warm and fuzzy inside or just increased the queasiness.

Jake decided that this was another thing he couldn't think about right now, and he started to eat.

Halfway through his first slice, he acknowledged to himself that Tobias hadn't taken a bite. When he picked up his second, he did his best to smile. "You can eat it, you know. It's not too hot anymore."

Tobias started slowly, cautiously, eating about half of his slice in the time it took Jake to swallow his second. When Jake helped himself to a third, he put a second on Tobias's plate. He wasn't sure what this was, if Tobias didn't think that Jake wanted him to eat or if he was just being careful. Jake knew that if you didn't eat for a while—he'd gotten lost in the woods once —if you ate food too fast, it would just come right back up. And Tobias certainly hadn't been eating like a king in Freak Camp.

Maybe, a little voice inside Jake murmured, *maybe he didn't eat anything at all, and you just let it keep happening.*

Tobias ate a little faster with the second piece on his plate, so Jake made sure that every time he got himself a slice, he put another on Tobias's plate. Sure, he was still a slice ahead, but that was better than watching while Tobias ate one slice and Jake finished off the entire pizza—which he suspected would be the other possibility.

After the last slice had disappeared, Jake decided he wasn't going to ask if Tobias was still hungry. Jake was still hungry, and Jake had gotten one more piece.

He stood, then paused to look at Tobias. "Want to hang out in the kitchen while I make the next pizza?" He thought that it would be pushing it a little to say that Tobias could help him *make* it when all Jake had to do was rip the plastic off and put it in the oven, but he wanted it to be clear that he didn't mind if Tobias followed him. That he seriously *did* want Tobias close, he just didn't want to accidentally push him into the oven.

Tobias bounced up right away, as Jake had known he would.

Making the second pizza was easier because Jake had the hang of it and Tobias stayed farther away, leaning against the cupboard. It hurt, the way he kind of leaned away from Jake, but Jake figured Tobias also didn't want to be accidentally pushed into the oven.

When the timer went off, Jake took out the pizza—slightly more burnt than the last one, probably preheating or some occult curse or something, what the hell did he know about any of this?—and Tobias hurried back to the table.

This time, Jake put two pieces of pizza on Tobias's plate right away just to ease the gnawing feeling that he was cheating him. It wasn't like Jake would starve to death because he was missing one piece of pizza or something, and Tobias . . . yeah, maybe Tobias could.

Tobias looked at the pizza, looked at Jake, and then ate, finally losing an edge of tension that had been in his shoulders through the first pizza. So subtle that Jake hadn't noticed before, but now that it was gone . . . hell.

"You can help yourself to pizza too," Jake said. "That's cool, Tobias."

Tobias stopped smiling, stopped eating, just looked him in the eye for a second. Then he looked back down to his plate and picked up the slice. "Okay, Jake."

From then on, Tobias ate, not fast, not slow, just at about the same pace as Jake. He never reached for his own piece of pizza, but Jake put slices on his plate anyway.

When the second pizza was gone, Jake leaned back, as satisfied with the food as he wasn't with how everything else had had gone tonight. Still, he had to admit, it had gone better than the previous night.

Even just thinking that made him wince. Not much from last night could have gone worse. But tonight . . . tonight was better. Jake would take *better* when he could get it.

TOBIAS WAS CAUTIOUSLY willing to believe that this night was going well. He couldn't wrap his head around a lot of what Jake had said—*I'm gonna come right down there with you, Toby*—and didn't dare try, afraid he'd lose it the instant he understood, but what he was able to grasp could be boiled down into one major fact and three minor:

He was with Jake.

He was warm. He was fed. Jake hadn't so much as slapped him; Jake was still with him, and Tobias had hope that it was going to stay that way. Maybe for a while. Maybe longer.

When Jake took his last bite of pizza and Tobias quickly swallowed his own, they both just sat for a second, staring at the empty plates and *digesting*—food still so damn good that Tobias couldn't believe that Jake had given it to him, so many pieces of pizza that his stomach was *full*, full for two days straight—absorbing the silence of the apartment and the distant sounds of the neighborhood (cars, motorcycles, voices, music) slowly filtering through the walls.

Finally, Jake shook off his reverie and picked up their plates. Tobias nervously grabbed the glasses and the cardboard tray that had been under the pizza and followed Jake to the kitchen.

He wasn't sure that Jake would want him to help or touch or follow, but Tobias felt safer in some presumption, now. No, he wouldn't dare initiate contact with Jake without express permission—he was so fucking lucky that Jake wasn't the Director, or even a guard, or he doubted he'd still have hands right now—but Jake hadn't beaten the shit out of him when Tobias caught him in the kitchen, hadn't said anything when Tobias brought a spare oven mitt to the table to set the pizza on top of (so it wouldn't hurt Jake's table). Tobias was cautiously testing what would make Jake angry, what would earn him a whipping, a blow, a sharp word, *anything*.

So far, disturbingly, nothing had. But Tobias had faith that Jake wasn't just saving up all his transgressions for a new kind of Wednesday session. Jake really would tell him when he was being too much of a freak.

The smile Tobias got when he came into the kitchen with the cardboard made him feel almost dizzy with relief.

"Glasses go in the sink, and you can fold up the cardboard, shove it in the trash," Jake said, nodding at the bin where he had put the plastic wrap.

Tobias carefully folded the cardboard and tucked it into the garbage while Jake dumped their plates in the sink with the glasses. He felt a twinge throwing away something that still had crumbs and cheese residue—three days ago he would have begged for permission to eat those scraps, maybe the cardboard too—but it was minor compared to the complete satisfaction of being full and with Jake and *happy*. Not the same kind of happy he'd felt yesterday before everything had gone to hell, but happy nonetheless.

Even thinking about *yesterday* stripped away a lot of the good feelings from the pizza and Jake's smile. But before that memory could sink in, Tobias turned and Jake was there, smiling at him. His expression was not quite happy, not quite satisfied, but still familiar, because it was the same way Jake had always smiled at him.

Jake raised one hand to Tobias's face, hesitated, and then rested his fingers lightly on Tobias's cheek. Tobias closed his eyes and leaned into the touch. The part of him terrified of making the same mistake of last night—and he *still* didn't know exactly what it had been—was temporarily overwhelmed by the part of him saying *JakeJakeJake* like it was a chant to keep all the bad things away for just a few minutes longer. A few days, *please*.

Jake's hand caressed his cheek, and it was better than anything he had ever dared hope for. Tobias took a shaky breath—it felt so *good*—and then forced his eyes open, his face up to Jake's, because Jake liked him to look him in the eye and Tobias would. He *would*.

Jake's expression was tender, and sad, but there was a bit of happy in it too. Tobias was glad that Jake didn't look miserable, that even when Tobias fucked up, it couldn't make Jake sad for long.

"Hey, Tobias." Jake spoke like he had trouble forming the words right, like some of the worries plaguing Tobias were eating their way into him too. "I'm . . . I think we've had a really long day. I bet we could both use some shut-eye before we figure out what else we need around here."

Tobias tensed. That sounded like last night. Last night when he had fucked everything up.

"If you want me . . ." he started, hating the way his breath faltered, afraid it would make Jake think that he wasn't willing and ready. It was just that he was terrified that he would do the wrong thing *again* and break this beautiful, brittle chance Jake had offered. "I don't have to. We could . . . *anything,* Jake. If you want . . ."

"No," Jake said quickly, but he didn't take his hand away. He brushed his fingers through Tobias's hair, then rested both his hands on Tobias's shoulders. Gently, so gently, no pressure at all to make Tobias think he ought to go to his knees. "Let's just get some sleep, all right?"

He guided Tobias out of the kitchen and nudged him in the direction of "his" bedroom.

Tobias went, even though the last thing he wanted was to be parted from Jake. But Jake had told him he should go to the bedroom and sleep, so he went, even though it hurt when he couldn't see Jake anymore. He left the door open, so that if Jake reconsidered, he wouldn't think even for a second that Tobias wasn't willing.

The bed was softer than any bunk he'd ever slept on, any chair he'd ever touched, or even the breaking room couch. It definitely wasn't meant for a freak, and yet Jake had pointed him toward it. It would be ungrateful of him to sleep on the floor, but Tobias didn't think he could sleep in that bed. For the first time in his life, he was in a room without cameras (at least, he couldn't see any, and Jake never wanted their meetings recorded, so why would he put them in his own home?) or without a guard just outside the door. He couldn't quite believe that there weren't any other monsters nearby to jump him in the dark, nor could he process the unfamiliar shapes, scents, noises, and the all-pervasive fear that Jake wasn't going to fuck him, wasn't going to keep him, that this was all just a wonderful illusion that would crumble the second he closed his eyes for too long.

Tobias didn't think he would sleep. He couldn't shake the feeling that the instant he lay down, there would be a guard to beat him awake because he was hallucinating during a sleep deprivation test, or maybe Jake would decide after all to claim what was his, and Tobias had to be *ready*.

But the second Tobias pulled his legs up on the mattress, letting himself curl into a protective ball, the world went dark, his breathing evened out, and he slept. His stomach was full, Jake was moving quietly in the other room, and Freak Camp was miles and miles away.

3

The next morning, Jake was up well before Tobias and had no idea what he should be doing. Sure, he could sleep twelve hours or so as well as the next guy, but they'd gone to bed pretty damn early the night before, and . . .

Jake had to admit that part of what had gotten him out of bed was that he *couldn't* hear anything. What if Tobias was gone, hurt, or—shit, had somehow never been there at all? More than once in the months when Jake had been getting the apartment ready (buying all the shit that normal people apparently needed took more time and effort than he had ever expected), he'd sprawled over his big bed and thought about Tobias, hoping that tomorrow would be the day. He lay there hating the Dixons, struggling with how surreal it felt that busting Tobias out of Freak Camp was finally happening but not happening at the same time; Tobias's life with Jake—and Jake's promise—was in the hands of Washington paper-pushers, for fuck's sake.

Now, Tobias was with him, and Jake felt just as useless against the forces fucking with Tobias's head.

He got up at the crack of dawn because he couldn't sleep anymore and stood at Tobias's door like a complete creeper for about ten minutes before he could assure himself that Tobias was breathing behind the wood—finding Tobias's toiletries bag in his duffel last night had made it real too—then set about finding something to occupy his time.

Tobias finally appeared around ten, after Jake had washed last night's dishes, cleaned his guns, dusted—if this kept up, he was going to become a goddamn housewife—and finally settled in front of the TV with a big mug of instant coffee. Jake craned his neck around when he heard the door squeak open —he kept meaning to oil it or pound on it or something, though his instincts still insisted that doors *should* squeak and give him advance warning when baddies started coming through.

Tobias blinked, and his knuckles were white where they clenched the edge of the door. "D-did I sleep t-too long?"

"Nope," Jake said, taking a swig of coffee. "You needed it, so no problem. You hungry?"

Tobias hesitated, and Jake interpreted that as yes. He set his mug down, lowered the volume on the TV, and went into the kitchen. "I got Cheerios and Lucky Charms—I figure cereal is always good, yeah?—but we're going to start with the Lucky Charms because I need sugar."

Jake took out bowls, glasses, and spoons and was cheered when Tobias divided them between their two spots on the table without being told, asked, or nudged. He overlooked how Tobias glanced at him every time he touched a new object, like he expected . . . fuck, Jake didn't want to know. He just put out the milk, orange juice, and cereally goodness and kept smiling at Tobias as he sat down.

Jake didn't wait for Tobias to reach for the cereal. He didn't think he would, and Jake *hated* that, but if it were a choice between spoon-feeding him or Tobias not eating, there was no question what Jake would do.

He filled both bowls with Lucky Charms and milk, then hesitated over the orange juice. He glanced at Tobias, whose eyes were wide and delighted, like they were every time Jake put food on his plate. "You okay with OJ?"

It was a fucking simple question, but Tobias froze like Jake had asked him if he wanted fried scorpion for dinner. He nodded stiffly at the bowls. "W-w-whatever you want, Jake."

That wasn't really an answer, but Jake shouldn't have been surprised. And he wasn't, really. Which sucked.

Jake poured milk into both bowls and resolved that the second Tobias started feeling more comfortable, relaxing a little bit in this apartment that was *theirs* and not just Jake's, Jake would start asking him what he wanted and actually push to get an answer. He would not just take over Tobias's life because that was easy and seemed to make Tobias stop twitching. Tobias deserved better than that. Jake would *ask*.

But Jake figured for now they were both entitled to take the easy way out a few times.

Jake sat, nodded at Tobias's spoon, and dug in.

He watched out of the corner of his eye as Tobias cautiously picked up his spoon, visibly braced himself to take a bite, and then fell back against his chair, eyes flickering closed in something like bliss when he crunched into his first super-sweet marshmallow.

Jake grinned to himself and let Tobias chew before looking up. "Like it?" Not that he didn't know the answer, but he wanted to hear it. Partly because he wanted Tobias to be comfortable enough to tell him these things, and partly because when Tobias was filled with this much joy, Jake wanted to hold onto it as long as he could.

Tobias looked up, eyes sober, intent, and for one stomach-dropping moment Jake thought that he wasn't going to say it, that Jake had read him wrong, or maybe Lucky Charms was such a wonderful experience that Tobias wouldn't want to share it with Jake. "These are really good, Jake. I . . . thank you. I l-like them a lot." Tobias looked down and filled his spoon with vaguely pink milk. "This is milk? It's really good. I'm sorry I . . . I'm sorry. Thank you."

Jake decided not to think right now about what that response meant. He grinned at Tobias. "That's good. Awesome. Want some more?"

Tobias made another one of those vague motions that Jake decided meant yes, and he refilled both their bowls.

They ate for a while longer, and then Jake cleared his throat. "So, I've been thinking." He paused to take another bite and chew, ignoring how Tobias twitched, tensed, and then visibly forced himself to relax. His spoon came to a rest at the edge of his bowl. "This is all really new for you and stuff, I get that. So, here's what's going to happen. If I'm going too fast for you, or something happens and you have questions, you ask them, and I'll do my best to figure it out with you, okay?"

Tobias relaxed a little bit more, and Jake felt heartened. So he got to the next part, the part that had been plaguing him all night and that he really didn't want to bring up, though he knew he had to. Not just because of how nervous and . . . *pliant* Tobias was, but because of how disastrously their first night had gone and the kinds of expectations Tobias seemed to have. They were . . .

Well, they were sickening, that was what they were. Jake didn't want to think about it for even a second longer. But he had to say this.

"I know . . . this is a big change for you, so I'll say this once, a hundred times, as many times as you need it. I'm *not* going to get rid of you, and getting you out of FREACS wasn't about you doing anything for me or . . . to me, or . . . sex. I want you with me, Tobias, until you want to walk away, and there's nothing you can do that's going to make me toss you out, or take you back, or *anything*. Does that make sense?"

Tobias had let go of his spoon at the beginning of the speech, then watched Jake's face intently, staring so hard that Jake felt a little uncomfortable, like Tobias could stare straight through him to all the dirty corners of his mind. At the end, Tobias hesitated, took a sharp breath, and then shook his head, hard. He lowered his eyes and his hands twisted together at the edge of the table, hard enough to whiten the skin.

Jake reached over for one of his hands. He thought that he might have to wrestle it out of Tobias's death grip, but it loosened easily at his touch. Once again, Tobias looked like Jake had done something miraculous.

"Hey, look at me," Jake said, and Tobias did. Fuck, with that *look* again. "I'm *not* getting rid of you, I swear to God. And I'm not making any demands either. I'm not even looking for anything to get PG, okay? We're gonna keep it strictly G."

Tobias licked his lips, and his hand tightened around Jake's. "P-P-PG. What does that . . . does that m-mean?"

Jake stared at him. "PG, like, movie ratings. You know?"

Tobias didn't know. That was written all over his face.

Jake leaned over the table, one hand still wrapped in Tobias's. He rested an elbow on the table and his head in that hand and breathed for a moment. Tobias's hand in his was a warm, solid comfort, and Jake was grateful for it. If this kept up, he was going to need as much G-rated comfort that he could get. "Okay, well. We've got a lot to cover, but I'll watch out for you. Don't worry."

Tobias offered another small, heartbreaking smile, and together he and Jake cleared the table. Jake gave Tobias his toiletries bag and pointed him to the bathroom through Jake's room so he could shower. When Tobias came out, hair wet, wearing a new set of Jake's old clothes, Jake glanced up from taking inventory of his first aid kit and smiled, and Tobias smiled back cautiously before settling on the couch.

Eventually, Jake noticed that Tobias kept glancing at the bookshelf, then away, over and over again. It made Jake smile, his best smile yet that morning, remembering the little kid who loved to tell him about his reading and researching.

"You can read those," Jake offered. "I got most of them for you, anyway."

Tobias stared at him, wonder bright in his eyes. He moved off the couch, cautiously approaching the sparsely filled bookshelf—Jake had been planning to get some more books for him, but he hadn't been sure what Tobias would like, and bookstores weren't his usual hangouts. Finally, he withdrew a book: one of the thickest and most boring-looking. He glanced at Jake, but Jake smiled encouragingly and continued searching the kit for any other bloody gauze that had somehow ended up back in there.

Tobias moved back to the couch and settled in almost like he was really comfortable with his book in his lap, turning pages like each was made of gold. Jake hummed an Ozzy tune to himself, relieved to see Tobias happy and definitely doing something he liked.

Around noon—Jake didn't bother asking Tobias, he was getting a little hungry—he pulled the last two pizzas out of the freezer, then realized that there was nothing left in the fridge besides breakfast stuff, a half-empty six-pack of beer, and a pack of cream cheese.

Yeah, this wasn't going to cut it. This was only Tobias's third day out of Freak Camp. Jake had to take better care of him than feeding him frozen pizzas every day. Sandwiches and hamburgers at least, he could do that. "Hey, Tobias!" He slid the first pizza onto the pizza tray (damn thing had been in his *closet*, no fucking idea how it had ended up there).

"Y-yes, Jake?"

Jake held his breath for five seconds before letting it out. It would get better. Tobias would not always sound like that. It was just going to take time, a little progress each day. "How about we head to the grocery store? We can pick up some stuff for dinner tonight. See what looks good." Yeah, that was a good idea. Tobias would be able to look around, pick out what he wanted to try. This would help him get a sense of options. A change of scenery couldn't hurt, either. Jake was already feeling the walls start to close in.

They ate and cleaned up the food quickly. Tobias stayed quiet, head down, on the way out of the apartment, but Jake tried not to read too much into it. He was already obsessing over every move Tobias made, and adding fuel to that fire would lead nowhere good.

He slid in a tape for the short drive to the market. Boulder was a real artsy-hippie kind of place, and everyone he'd talked to had raved about the farmers' markets, but Jake felt more comfortable in a standard, run-of-the-mill grocery store. Safeway it was.

～

As SOON AS Jake suggested leaving the apartment, Tobias felt cords tightening around his chest, but he said nothing. If Jake wanted to go somewhere, that was what they would do. Surely just stepping outside, going somewhere else, couldn't be as bad as things he had done in camp. But at least those had been familiar. Still, Jake had given no indication they'd be splitting up and he didn't seem to think this would be any trouble for Tobias, so Tobias had to trust him.

All the same, he blocked out most of the drive, refusing to focus on anything going by. That was dangerous if Jake asked him later about something they passed, or if he had to remember their route, but until Jake made it clear that was what he expected, Tobias couldn't focus on the buildings—*each one filled with reals*—flying by.

They pulled into the parking lot for one of the largest buildings, and Tobias could only blink at it. It was as big as—bigger? — than the Warehouse in Freak Camp, but with bright signs and multiple entrances.

"C'mon, Tobias." Jake was watching him, and Tobias jumped for the door handle, hoping Jake wouldn't notice his hands shaking. This was the first test. God, he couldn't disappoint Jake, couldn't let him think Tobias couldn't handle what Jake thought was nothing.

The Eldorado was surrounded by hundreds of other cars—all empty. Which probably meant the reals who owned them were inside the massive building. Where they were also heading.

He broke it down to one simple task: *follow Jake*. If he stayed two steps behind, as they walked across the pavement and through the doors that slid open automatically before them, no one would question what he was doing. Even if he couldn't help jumping a little when the doors moved.

He blocked out everything: the hard gust of cool air as they crossed the threshold, the tall shelves ahead, the squeaking and clattering carts and bustling people. They mattered as little as a guard standing on the periphery of a Director session. He focused on Jake like he was the Director, who was just waiting for a moment when Tobias was distracted to give him vital orders. Though Jake hadn't used any hand signals yet, at least none that Tobias had noticed—and wasn't that a nightmare thought, that he might have missed them and Jake was just waiting to get back to the apartment before punishing him—so he focused on the bottom of Jake's jacket and kept two steps between them.

He almost panicked again when he realized that Jake had been talking to him and Tobias hadn't noticed.

"... Tobias? Hey, Tobias, you with me?"

Tobias lifted his eyes to meet Jake's, and the stark concern there took him aback, made him lose focus. He took a deep breath, then another. This could not be as bad as it felt.

"You sure you're feeling all right?" Jake stepped closer. He started to raise his hand, and Tobias flinched hard before he could stop himself. Jake stopped and slowly withdrew his hand.

Ashamed and furious at his body's lack of control, Tobias nodded quickly. "Y-yeah. I'm fine. This is fine. What—what did you say earlier? I'm sorry I didn't..."

"'S fine. I just wanted to know if you wanted to try Pop-Tarts or these funny granola fruit things." He held out two different boxes, cocking his head and grinning hopefully.

Tobias looked at them blankly. He couldn't remember ever seeing or tasting either before. Had Jake given them to him before when they were kids? What did he want Tobias to say?

"I," he began at last—he had to answer, even inadequate as it was, even as he was appalled to hear his voice quaver. "I don't know, Jake..."

"Okay," Jake said at once. "Okay, okay, Tobias, it's fine." He turned and placed both items on the shelf.

Only then did Tobias really look at the display and see dozens of similar packages in a line. And others on the rows above and below, stretching down endlessly around him on both sides.

Then his stupid brain put together what should have been obvious all along just from what Jake had said before they left the apartment: this was a store of food for reals. The gas station stores they'd visited during the drive away from Freak Camp had already been too much for him to grasp or think about (that reals could go in and have anything they wanted, at any time), but looking at *hundreds* of boxes of food, just sitting there, without anyone fighting for them—

He wasn't even hungry. Jake was amazing—constantly

giving him food, so many times a day, and insisting he eat, that Tobias hadn't felt cramps for days. It wasn't that he wanted any of the packages around him or that he couldn't stop thinking about anything but how it might taste if he snatched one and tore it open. He didn't know why the sight of so much food, sitting neatly as though no one had ever fought for it—never killed, clawed out someone's eyes, or dropped to their knees for it—made him feel like Crusher had him by the throat and was fumbling at his belt buckle. Or like the Director was looking at him in that thoughtful, calculating way that meant he was about to test a new way to teach Tobias not to be so stupid.

So much food. *Right there.*

He wasn't aware that his lungs had stopped pulling in air, that the world was spinning with black spots crawling over his vision until Jake grabbed his shoulders and Tobias heard him saying, "Shit, shit, *shit*. Breathe, Toby, breathe—" and then Jake was pushing, propelling him out of the aisle and farther, until Tobias's shoes stumbled on pavement and the summer sunlight warmed his face while the roughness of a brick wall anchored him from behind.

When Jake's hands on his shoulders guided him down, Tobias had a wild, sickening thought that it was the guard Victor again, that he had hallucinated the food, Boulder, *Jake*— but Jake's words came through before he lost it, before he could try to fight off the guards because the contrast between that dream and the reality that he deserved hurt too damn much for any kind of sense and the rules he'd known all his life.

"Easy, easy." Without pushing or forcing, Jake brought Tobias's head down to his knees; there, with Jake's hand warm on his shoulder, Tobias felt contained enough to remember how to breathe. Inhale followed exhale until he could regain some semblance of control, even as his reaction scared him almost as much as it had drained him. He'd never felt anything like that in camp, ever.

It was easier to come back to himself surrounded by tangible physical sensations: sunshine, a light breeze, the rough wall behind him, concrete beneath him, and Jake's hand steady on his shoulder. Tobias put everything else out of his mind and focused on being alive, not in pain, and *with Jake*. Though when he finally risked a glance at Jake's face, Tobias had to fight down another surge of panic. He had never imagined Jake looking like that—*scared*. And Tobias had done that.

"Okay," Jake said at last. He did not sound okay. Tobias could see it was not okay. "You—you're all right now, Tobias. Feeling better."

Tobias nodded fervently, though he had to shut his eyes again and felt inches from vomiting. He wouldn't do that, he had more self-control than to vomit over Jake's shoes—that would certainly be the end at once, if it wasn't already here.

With a shudder, he jerked his thoughts away from the possibility that this was the end. He couldn't think about that right now, not when his control was so threadbare.

"Okay," Jake said again, and rubbed his shoulder in a quick motion. "I'm . . . going to get you a water, okay?" He stood, starting to move away, and Tobias's eyes snapped open as he lunged forward, seizing Jake's jacket. A part of himself was appalled—*You can't act like that, filthy monster, can't grab Jake in public, should barely look at him*—but he couldn't stop himself.

Jake knelt back down immediately, grabbing and squeezing Tobias's hand in one of his and resting his other warm palm on the back of Tobias's neck. "Hey, hey. It's all right, I'm not—I'm not going anywhere, Toby."

Tobias shook his head and squeezed his eyes shut. He was being so pathetic in front of Jake, doing all the wrong things . . .

"Listen to me," Jake said, in a low, soothing voice. "We're right outside the grocery store, okay? There's no one around—no one even watching us. I'm not going to let anyone touch you or come near you, Toby. It's just us, and we're okay. There's a vending machine six feet away, right there, you can see it. I'm going to walk over, stick some quarters in, and get you a water. Nothing's going to happen to you when I get up. You'll be able to see me the whole time."

At last, Tobias nodded, and with a supreme effort of will, he made himself let go of Jake's jacket, tucking both hands between his knees and pressing tight. Jake stayed for a moment, rubbing Tobias's neck and shoulders until his breath evened out again. Only then, slowly, did Jake get up. Tobias didn't move a muscle, keeping his hands between his knees and his eyes level with Jake's calves.

Jake walked to the vending machine—Tobias could see him the whole time, just as he'd promised—and came back with a water for Tobias and a soda can for himself. He sat down beside Tobias, their shoulders touching. With difficulty, Tobias released his hands to take the bottle and unscrew the top. The water was cold and very good, and Tobias focused only on how good Jake was to him instead of the easily retrievable supply of clean water inside the black box.

When the bottle was half empty, Jake—who had been rolling his soda can between his hands—exhaled. "All right. So, game plan—I take you back home, then swing back around to pick up the basics, and we'll stay in tonight. I'll . . . make hamburgers, and then we'll . . ." Jake rubbed his forehead.

Watching him, Tobias felt a different, more familiar knot of anxiety twisting up his insides. It was so wrong for Jake to look like this, so worn down and uncertain. Was being around a monster really taking its toll on him that fast, even on someone as strong as Jake, after only three days?

Tobias swallowed, pushing past the trepidation and whispers that told him all he should ever say was *yes, Jake,* and said instead, "You . . . you don't have to take me back now if you need to buy things here. I'll—I'll be okay now." *I'll be good, I promise.*

Jake peered at him through the fingers of his hand, worry visible on his face even though his eyes were shadowed. "You sure? You don't have to go back in. You could wait in the Eldorado if you wanted."

"No." Not that he didn't like being in Jake's car—it was the best place he could be, other than the apartment with Jake—but he didn't want to sit alone in that vast parking lot where anyone could look at him and see a monster where he shouldn't be. Besides, he was sure the shock (he had never, ever dreamed so much food existed, let alone in one place) had made him fall apart like that. Now, he could push it down the same way he controlled his reactions to what he saw, did, or felt in a Wednesday session. Only the first time was he ever so vulnerable. "No," he said, clearly. "I want to go back."

Jake watched him with sharp skepticism, like he wasn't sure he could trust Tobias. But of course he couldn't trust any monster. Tobias was glad he knew that. "You positive? I wouldn't mind taking you home."

Tobias shook his head. He was determined to prove to Jake he could learn, adjust, do whatever Jake wanted. He didn't go through months of training to be this weak. "No, I'm ready now." He twisted the cap back on the bottle and stood, Jake rising quickly with him and slipping a hand behind his back.

"Hey, hey, take it easy, there's no fire."

It was so overwhelmingly good for Jake to offer him that, even now, that Tobias bit his lip and dropped his head until he had control again. "I'm ready," he said softly.

Jake didn't protest again but turned them to walk slowly back inside the store. Despite being braced for it, Tobias felt a wave of dizziness when they passed through the doors and under the cold fan; once again his hand moved without permission, catching hold of the hem of Jake's jacket. That was all, but he knew better than to think Jake wouldn't notice, that Jake wouldn't shake a freak off, though maybe in a way that wouldn't draw attention from other reals.

To his shock, Jake didn't hit him or order him to let go— Tobias could have then, but somehow, he couldn't get his fingers to relax of their own accord. But Jake gently disentangled Tobias's fingers, and then folded his hand around Tobias's —not crushingly hard, just *there*, here where anyone could see. His hand was warm, firm, so everything *Jake* that Tobias had ever known.

That wonder was more than enough distraction from the aisles and aisles of food in the vast store that would surely swallow him if he looked up or if Jake stepped away. Tobias didn't raise his eyes; it was all he could manage to keep his feet moving behind Jake's, stopping when Jake stopped. He was okay now, though. He was more certain of that than he had been since Jake first drove away with him from Freak Camp.

Jake didn't talk to him again in the store, but he also didn't let go of Tobias's hand until they reached the checkout line. Tobias knew that the hour of grace was over even before Jake squeezed his hand and let go to start piling items onto the conveyor belt. Tobias was still okay, though, quiet and calm. Maybe also stunned. Why would Jake do that for him in public, with other reals around? But he had, and that reassured Tobias: if Jake would do that, even after Tobias had fallen apart on him and been so utterly *useless* and unreliable, then maybe he didn't have to fear being taken back to Freak Camp tonight.

ONCE THEY HAD everything loaded into the Eldorado's backseat and Jake had shoved the cart off into an open parking space, Tobias slipped into the passenger seat and curled against the door, locking his eyes into the inside of his right hand as he pressed it to his forehead, as though the sight of anything outside the window was fucking unbearable.

Jake tried to focus on driving. The novelty of concentrating on making scrupulously safe turns, maintaining the speed limit, and using his turn signals was nearly enough to distract him from the way Tobias huddled against the window, one white-knuckled fist clenched in his lap. His posture indicated pain—Jake had curled up that way once or twice when a hunt had gone sideways and both he and Dad were banged up bloody—or an instinct to shield himself from the next attack.

Damn, Jake was so stupid, he'd get a call any day now to pick up his Idiot of the Year Award for being a complete waste of headspace. But he hadn't known. He could figure out a haunted object with a handful of pointed questions or know from a casual glance which babe at the bar was a sure bet, but he hadn't seen this coming, even though the warning signs had been all over the place. Practically a train whistle telling him to get the fuck off the tracks. But he hadn't seen any of it, and now Tobias looked like he had internal bleeding, wouldn't look at him, would barely move, and it was all Jake's fault.

It was never supposed to be like this, with Tobias afraid to look him in the eye, afraid to speak, reduced to grabbing at Jake's jacket like it was a life vest that couldn't hold their combined weight. Jake would do anything to make Tobias feel safe, but maybe he didn't have enough to give.

But he was it. The only line of defense between Tobias and the world. And even though that was going to be a hell of a lot more work than he had thought—*What, Hawthorne, you thought it would be fucking easy? That* Tobias *would be easy?*—he wasn't going to give up, not one single fucking inch.

When they pulled into their parking spot in front of their apartment, Jake turned off the car and leaned his head back, staring up at the headliner like the car itself could give him strength. Like that could make him enough for Tobias when he didn't know that anything could make Jake enough for anybody. When he looked over, Tobias's gaze was nervous, broken, wide-eyed, hopeful, like Jake wasn't the greatest fuck-up in the world, and just . . . Jake.

"Hey," Jake said. "Let's get the groceries inside."

Tobias obeyed, like he always did. Jake just had to say a word, and Tobias would be moving, halfway there, no hesitation unless what Jake had asked him to do was so far out of his range of experience that he couldn't even conceive of the order applying to him. Like when he told Tobias to take an extra helping for himself.

Jake wanted Tobias to feel comfortable close to him, wanted him to know that Jake wouldn't push him away. But when they got inside the apartment—Tobias following Jake silently, setting his share of the bags on the counter of their too-small kitchen and then just standing there, hands, eyes, and posture empty of any purpose or emotion—Jake couldn't watch Tobias anymore, see him *waiting* for Jake to tell him what else to do. Because he would, Jake was realizing. Tobias would stand and wait and wait until hunger and thirst overcame him or Jake told him to move.

There was no way that one Jake Hawthorne, hunter and good-as-orphan, should have that much control over another person's life.

"Tobias, you look wiped," Jake said, which was true. "Why don't you go relax, lie down for a while? I can handle putting these away."

Tobias blinked once, as though he hadn't heard or didn't understand, then slowly took a step back, never raising his eyes. "O-okay, Jake."

Jake waited until Tobias disappeared into his room—he didn't wait for the click, Tobias always left his door slightly ajar; maybe he felt claustrophobic or worried about being locked in—before exhaling, dropping his elbows to the counter and pushing his hands through his hair. He held that position for a full minute before moving to unpack the groceries.

Tobias slept for the next four hours. Jake kept himself busy with things other than glancing at his watch: checking the wards he'd put down in front of the doors and windows, turning on the TV—volume on low—and watching a couple '80s films. For a while he kept himself from peering through the crack into Tobias's room to make sure he was okay—he could *not* start hovering, or he might lose his mind completely —but after the third hour, he muted the TV and leaned against the wall next to the door, just to see if he could hear Tobias breathing. He could—barely audible, but enough. And it wasn't that crazy for Tobias to be so tired after the day he'd had (*the one Jake had put him through*).

It was almost seven p.m. when Jake decided to see if Tobias wanted any dinner. He pushed open the door but hesitated a long moment before moving to sit on the bed, where Tobias slept half-curled on his side, hands pressed between his thighs.

"Hey, Toby." Jake dropped his hand lightly to Tobias's back and tried to focus on something other than how easily he could trace Tobias's shoulder blades and spine through his T-shirt. His warmth, maybe, and the slow steadiness of his breathing, deep in sleep.

It took a few minutes of touching him and saying his name before he began to come out of it, moving sluggishly. "Jake?" he whispered, the uncertainty so palpable that Jake had to swallow.

"Yeah, it's just me. You're here in Boulder, in our . . . our apartment."

Tobias curled a little tighter, closer to Jake's leg, yet still without touching him.

Jake moved his fingers through Tobias's hair, feeling a disquiet he couldn't explain. "You hungry? I was going to let you keep sleeping, but I didn't know if you wanted to have dinner before it's time for breakfast."

"Did I sleep too long?"

"No, no. It's cool. You were wiped, like, run-over-by-the-Titanic wiped, you needed it. Wanna get up for a bite?" He knew he was pushing, but it was important as hell to him that Tobias not miss any meals. He wanted to show Tobias that he was in a different world now. Really, Jake suspected he wouldn't feel completely at ease until Tobias's face lost some of the sharp angles of taut skin over bone, until he seemed less like he could be folded away in a duffel or broken by a glancing blow. "I know I mentioned burgers earlier but, well. I've got a lasagna in the oven, should be done soon."

Tobias shifted slightly, and Jake stilled his hand before moving it away. Maybe he should stop petting Tobias, give him a little breathing space. "Okay," Tobias said at last, and he sat up so groggily that Jake reached for his shoulders to steady him.

"You feeling okay, dude?"

Tobias nodded, head falling forward to his chest, then rubbed the back of his hand across his eyes.

"All right," Jake said, and he got up before he couldn't keep his hands to himself for another second. Tobias had been through enough today without getting manhandled into another embrace he wouldn't know how to deal with. "I'll see if I can get garlic toast going without setting anything on fire."

Tobias didn't look much more awake when he emerged from his room, but he sat at the table with Jake and ate his share of the lasagna. They were silent, and it wasn't a great silence, but it didn't seem like Tobias was going to collapse again or anything, at least. After they put the food away and the dishes in the sink, Jake thought briefly of suggesting a game of cards or that they watch a little TV or talk or something, but Tobias looked exhausted, and he himself felt . . . just bled out.

No activity he could think of would actually help either of them feel otherwise right now.

"I'm beat, man," he said at last. "You chill going to sleep again?"

"Yeah, Jake." Tobias got up quietly, went back to his room, and for all intents and purposes crashed, even though he had already slept for at least four hours that day. Jake went to his big master bedroom alone.

❧

THE NEXT MORNING, they had Cheerios. Jake kept meaning to try out his frying pan now that he had eggs and cheese and butter—he knew he could handle mixing up scrambled eggs, maybe throw it on some toast to get Tobias more carbs—but he'd taken one look at Tobias's hunched shoulders, the way he twisted his hands, and any energy he had for turning on the stove and cooking something drained out of him. He got out two bowls, the cereal box, and milk.

Tobias stayed huddled at the breakfast table, leaning toward the wall, head bowed over his bowl. At least he didn't look for a signal now before picking up his spoon. That was already better.

But it was still hard to feel good about anything when the grocery store debacle remained vivid. He didn't know how Tobias felt about it or how he could rebuild the thin threads of trust between them—trust he had never earned—or how he could keep his word and protect Tobias when Jake didn't know half of what Tobias needed to be protected from. Jake couldn't even summon the energy this morning to try a conversation, not when he could see all too easily how that would go down: Tobias flinching, dropping his spoon, trying and failing to keep his eyes on Jake's. No matter what Jake said, Tobias probably wouldn't understand, he would only get upset and anxious, and Jake wouldn't know where to begin explaining.

So yeah, small talk didn't sound that appealing.

He had to, though. Yesterday had changed his plans, but there were still things they couldn't put off. Like how Jake didn't have many more clothes to loan Tobias. Sure, they had a new supply of detergent and their own washer (plus a dryer that didn't look like it might light his jeans on fire), but that wasn't going to fly. Tobias needed his own clothes.

Solving that problem was, of course, not so easy.

Jake waited until their bowls were nearly empty before he made himself speak. "So—"

Sure enough, Tobias started and glanced up for a second before looking back down to his bowl, shoulders visibly tauter.

Jake pressed on anyway. "We need to get you shirts and stuff, things that are yours instead of my secondhand crap. I was thinking . . . I mean, you seem to be fitting all right in my things." That stretched the truth more than a little. Jake's clothes hung off of Tobias; it was a wonder he could keep the jeans up. "I could go out on a run and get some more in about the same size. That way you don't have to worry about . . . going out, the hassle."

This was not how Jake wanted to do it. He didn't want to pick out Tobias's clothes for him. He wanted Tobias to choose his own clothes for the first time in his life, to have options and *use* them. But after yesterday, he wasn't about to push Tobias into something he wasn't ready for.

Tobias twisted in his seat before visibly forcing his head up, and the pain and fear in his expression struck Jake cold and soured the milk in his stomach. Tobias struggled to speak—it was clearly even harder than usual, but Tobias seemed determined to get the words out. "N-n-no, I—I want to go. I want to t-try again. I can d-do better, Jake, if you'll let me t-try."

"Tobias." Jake reached across the table and laid his fingers over Tobias's hand, and Tobias stilled at once, dropping his eyes even as some of the tension left his shoulders. Jake didn't understand how Tobias could react that way to Jake's touches when the rest of the time, he seemed to expect Jake to swing at him. "You do not *have* to go. I'm not going to be disappointed in you or . . . anything. I want you to take all of this slow, easy . . ."

Tobias shook his head, eyes shut. "I can," he said, in no more than a whisper. "I can do this."

As soft as they were, Tobias's words held a confidence and determination that Jake had never heard in him before. They sent a thrill through him, followed by a surge of amazement and hope. He tightened his hand around Tobias's. "Okay. Good. We can do this, Tobias. We'll get through it."

Tobias opened his eyes and met Jake's, and he smiled—a little tremulously and not very big, but a smile all the same.

It was hard to shake the feeling they were crossing a salt line when they'd stepped out the front door. Well, they were—Jake had packed lines of salt under the carpet when he moved in—but the *feeling* of moving into danger made his hand drift toward the knife at his hip and sharpened every sense. Tobias kept close to Jake, eyes lowered, but he seemed calm, braced, and nowhere near the panic of the other day, so Jake wasn't going to complain. The short walk was uneventful and the drive quiet, with Tobias looking out the window—that was something, at least—and Jake shooting him glances when he could take his eyes off the road.

Jake had scouted out the town more than once in the months he had waited and agonized about Tobias's fucking paperwork, and he'd found some big department stores. He'd planned to bring Tobias there and give him the biggest selection of decent, brand-new clothes he could, whatever Tobias wanted.

Today, Jake knew better.

He drove them just a few blocks to a small thrift shop

attached to an auto garage. He couldn't guarantee Tobias would be okay in it, but at least the type of place was familiar territory for Jake, and he'd be better able to react when—if—something went wrong.

After shutting off the engine, he hesitated, watching Tobias. "You okay?"

Tobias nodded. His eyes seemed distant, but he looked calm.

All the same, when Jake held the door open for them to enter the store, he couldn't stop himself from grabbing Tobias's hand. He hadn't planned the move, but it seemed to be the right one, because Tobias gripped back tightly, even as he kept his eyes studiously on the carpet.

The shopping was pretty straightforward. Clothes didn't seem to have the same effect on Tobias that packaged food did, or maybe he was just prepared this time for the aisles, passing people—whatever had set him off before. At any rate, Jake knew now what to do. Picking out a handful of jeans, plus a pair of sweatpants, was the easiest. He just had to throw a couple belts into the basket to make sure the jeans wouldn't fall off Tobias's hips. He wasn't sure about asking Tobias if he wanted to hold the basket—he didn't mind holding it *and* Tobias's hand, but he needed another hand free to browse— but Tobias took it without hesitation, folding his hand carefully around the handles.

The selection of men's shirts didn't leave many hard choices either. Jake wasn't exactly the height of fashion, but what he usually wore—solid-colored tees and long-sleeved overshirts with subdued prints—blended in nearly everywhere, which was pretty much what Tobias needed about now. Jake picked up some jackets—he'd already caught Tobias hugging himself like he was too damned cold, probably lacking the reserves to produce enough body heat on his own—a couple sealed packages of boxers, another of socks, and there, mission accomplished. Under fifteen minutes.

The whole time Tobias never raised his eyes, never showed any interest in what Jake was throwing in the basket, but he wasn't crumpling up in a wreck and forgetting how to breathe either, and that was a major improvement. Jake only let go of his hand to pay.

After they were safely back in the Eldorado, he released a big breath and glanced at Tobias. That had felt riskier than scouting a Chupacabra nest without backup. "Well, we may never get hired to shop for those chicks on *Clueless*, but I think we pulled that off pretty good." He held up one of the shirts, grinning, but it was hard to hold onto the joke when he felt like he'd won a very small battle in a very large war. The last bit, the bit he had to say, came out more seriously than he meant it to because he did mean every word. "You did good, Tobias. That was really good."

Tobias's mouth curved up into a small smile, though he still didn't raise his head.

I'll work on that later, Jake thought to himself, but his hand didn't see the need to wait. He touched Tobias's chin to turn that delicate, so-breakable smile up so he could see it, so he could let it soak into him like rain, opening the flowers, softening the earth.

I want to end everything that ever wiped away these smiles, Jake thought fleetingly. Without thinking, he brought Tobias's hand to his lips, pressing them to the back of his hand.

Tobias's mouth parted in astonishment, but there was no fear—only an indescribable look that maybe, just maybe, Jake dared to call joy. Then Jake gave in the rest of the way, leaning into the plastic bags of clothes piled between them, and pulled Tobias to him.

To his relief, Tobias didn't freeze but relaxed into him. His cheek settled against Jake's chest, and his hands cautiously rose

—not to wrap around Jake's back in return, but to take hold of Jake's jacket. Not in a death grip but something easier, more comfortable and trusting, and it was the best thing Jake could have asked for after the previous day of hell.

There would be more curveballs to come, but in this moment, they could just relish being *together* and safe. For the first time in what felt like years but had barely been days, Jake felt content.

4

Jake's exhilaration lasted during their journey home, when Tobias tried on his new clothes—some things were baggier than others, but at least Tobias had his *own* stuff now—and for dinner time to roll around.

Once more, Jake found himself looking morosely into the refrigerator. They had plenty of food (damn grocery trip was worth something, at least), but somehow there wasn't much he felt confident cooking.

He eyed the hamburgers warily. He had made Hamburger Helper a few times and not burned anything—actually, he loved Hamburger Helper, it was the closest thing to childhood comfort food that didn't come out of plastic wrap or get cooked over a fire—and he'd felt optimistic about the little preformed patties when he'd seen them in the store. But now, resting expectantly on the white wire shelf, they looked very raw and pink and uncooked. Given the way most of the week had gone, Jake would probably give them both salmonella. Or burn the apartment down.

Definitely won't get the deposit back then. Jake closed the refrigerator grimly.

"Hey, Tobias, what do you think about going out tonight?" After the grocery store meltdown, Jake had seriously considered locking them in and eating nothing but delivery Chinese food for the rest of their natural lives—and depending on the quality of the Chinese food, that could be long or short, you never knew—but Tobias had done so much better at the thrift shop. Even though there had been a couple creepers lurking in the corners, and one asshole had looked at Tobias in a way Jake did not like at all. He'd resisted the urge to pull his knife on the bastard, instead meeting his eyes and pointedly placing his hand on his knife's hilt.

The guy had scrammed, Tobias hadn't noticed, they had made a clean escape, and life was good again, except for the whole Jake-afraid-of-cooking thing. Their first night at a diner had gone okay.

Tobias looked up, like a rabbit hearing a sound in the woods. "O-out? If . . . you want." His hands found and tightened around each other. "I c-could . . . whatever you want, Jake."

Tobias looked nervous but determined, the same look he had had before the thrift shop, with just a little more confidence this time. It seemed like they were both getting better at all of this, and while part of Jake thought *it's about damn time*, the rest of him was just grateful.

"Yeah, we can go, take a ride around Boulder, see what places might have good grub. It'll be fun." Jake grinned. If it was a little forced, he hoped Tobias didn't notice.

It wasn't like going out didn't have precedent. They'd eaten at the diner that first night and Tobias had been . . . well, he hadn't exactly been chatting up the waitress, but he had done really well (compared to everything since), and they had sat together, and the look on Tobias's face when he bit into his cheeseburger for the first time . . .

That decided it for Jake. Tobias deserved food that would put that look on his face, experiences that wouldn't leave him lost and broken, and Jake wasn't sure that he could produce that from the kitchen.

"Let's go. Put on your coat—it might be chilly out there." Jake strode to the hall closet, got out the lighter of Tobias's two new coats and his own, and then they stepped out into the evening air. It wasn't really that cold, but Jake didn't want to see Tobias shiver. Or let himself use the excuse of sharing body heat to get more into Toby's space than he probably wanted. Not that he was likely to tell Jake off, so. No.

They both relaxed when they were settled into the car. For Jake—now as always—the Eldorado was home, all the more so with Tobias in the seat beside him, and the car seemed to have a de-stressing effect on Tobias. He actually gave Jake a real smile when the engine started up, and then leaned back into the seat, eyes closing, breathing deeply.

This will be good, Jake thought as he reversed out of the parking lot. Things were definitely getting better.

He decided not to go to an actual bar. For one thing, all that alcohol would be more tempting than was wise when he had to watch out for the dumbasses and predators. Not so much for himself—he could handle himself in any kind of fight a civvie wanted to bring—but there was Tobias to think of now.

For another thing, Tobias didn't look legal. Even if his age and his unhealthy bony frame didn't set off alarms, it would attract the wrong sorts of people. The sorts of people that Jake would rather stab than let anywhere near Tobias.

Jake, of course, had had a fake ID since he was sixteen. It was pretty good, thanks to a pal of Roger's, but for the first couple of years, some bartenders wouldn't buy it. He hadn't had trouble in a while, though. Twenty might as well be twenty-one.

They ended up at a Mexican restaurant about ten minutes away from their apartment. Jake didn't really want to go that far, and Three Amigos looked okay, though he never had much faith in any Mexican joint above the New Mexico border. Most of them wouldn't know how to make decent mole sauce if it was their only way to appease a culebrón who'd gotten a taste for Latin food.

Despite his intentions leaving the apartment, Jake slung his arm over Tobias's shoulders as they walked toward the door, and he was rewarded by the way Tobias pressed back into his side. The early summer evening was still awash in warm sunlight, but it was cooling down quickly. Jake was glad he'd gotten Tobias to wear his jacket.

The restaurant was what Jake had hoped for: not too noisy or busy on a Thursday night, but enough chatter that he and Tobias wouldn't be easily overheard. Tobias seemed okay walking inside, though he studied his shoes as they waited to be seated.

The red and green bunting across the ceiling looked cheap but cheerful, and one wall had a decent mural of a pastoral landscape with señoritas flaring their white skirts mid-dance. The mariachi band playing over the speakers was one that Jake half-recognized from his last time in Ciudad Juarez. That had been a couple of years ago – the last trip he'd taken with his dad south of the border, he suddenly remembered. He and Leon had gone on the track of a Chupacabra that turned out to be an ornery goat. Then they'd found a cheap place outside the city and decided to stay for a week, drinking and playing poker with the locals.

For as long as Jake could remember, Leon's pervasive obsession had kept them on the road with endless hunts, rotating hotels and shitty monthly rentals that looked the same no matter where they went. But for a minute, the Hawthornes' lives had been quiet, easy.

Jake couldn't have imagined then that in less than eighteen months, he and Leon would have the fight to end all fights. That that night would be the last time he and Leon ever spoke.

"I would rather see you dead than welcoming a fucking monster into your life."

Jake forcibly shoved the memory back. He was with Tobias now—Tobias who was alive, safe, and not being fucking tortured anymore—and that was all that mattered. He'd make the same trade every single day if he had to. Leon could go to hell for all Jake cared. Maybe he was there already.

When they got to their booth, Jake let Tobias get in first so he could slide in after him, providing a buffer from the world. See, Jake could learn.

A curly-haired white kid with a University of Boulder T-shirt under his brightly patterned apron appeared, notepad in hand. "Hey, welcome to Three Amigos. I'm Steve. Anything to drink?"

Jake bumped Tobias's shoulder with his own. Tobias looked up, nervous, his hand clenching Jake's under the table. Jake smiled at him to show he was proud that Tobias was looking up, but he didn't try to make him choose anything. Jake would ask him someday what he wanted to eat (maybe the same day Jake had the courage to actually cook something), but for tonight it was enough that Tobias was there with him, holding his hand.

"I'll have a Corona, and a Coke for him," Jake said. "And we'll have two beef enchilada plates." He could've ordered in Spanish, but he doubted Steve had taken more than a couple of years of high-school Spanish.

Steve made a couple of scratches on his notepad. "Gotcha. Anything else?" He glanced at Tobias and then back to Jake, clearly dismissing him, which made Jake simultaneously relieved—Tobias didn't need more stress right now—and pissed.

"Yeah, bring us some queso and guac."

As Steve walked away, Jake nudged Tobias's shoulder again. "Just wait, something here is gonna blow your mind. Maybe the queso, if it's any good. Hopefully they don't put any dry-ass beef in the enchiladas. But if they at least get enough sauce and cheese on them, that'll be a decent start for your first taste of Mexican. Someday I'll take you to this family restaurant in Las Cruces that makes fajitas so far outta this world they'd make 'em on the moon."

Toby smiled back at him, even if it was a little shaky.

Steve returned with the queso and guacamole. At the first bite of warm melted cheese, Tobias's eyes went wide with incredulous delight that made Jake grin like a loon. He didn't even mind that the guacamole was bland as hell.

As they emptied the basket of tortilla chips, Jake looked for Steve to get a refill. Out of habit, he assessed the bar for threats. He'd scanned the room as he'd walked in, but as his focus was getting Tobias safely to a booth and settled and *protected*, he hadn't really taken a good look around.

He realized immediately what he'd been missing.

The brunette at the bar perched on her stool like she knew she was the damn sexiest thing in the room and everyone else better know it too. She had a slim waist and long legs and wore her little black spaghetti-strap dress like its sole purpose was to highlight everything it wasn't covering.

Jake let out a soft whistle. When Tobias looked up, Jake nodded in her direction. "You see her?"

Tobias glanced once at the woman and immediately dropped his eyes. "W-what?"

"The hot chick in the minidress. Sitting alone, like some crazy bastard left her." She had two drinks near her on the bar and the utterly pissed expression he was familiar with from picking up more than one guy's dissatisfied girlfriend. "I mean, that is either one damn impressive push-up or supernaturally levitated, and either way I would definitely—"

Then Jake realized how Tobias had stilled next to him. If he thought that the shivering earlier had been bad, this was worse, and he didn't know how long Tobias had been frozen. Maybe he should work harder to fucking notice what was going on right next to him and catch on when he was doing things Tobias didn't like.

That was when he realized that from the second they'd stepped out of Freak Camp's gates, he'd maybe been way more handsy than he should have with anyone who'd grown up inside a prison. Even if he hadn't meant anything by it—fuck, that had to be why Tobias had had such fucked-up expectations from that very first night. Jake had been crossing lines left and right and never paying attention to clues like this that said Tobias really didn't want Jake touching him.

Jake felt more than a little sick. "Shit, Tobias. I shouldn't have—" He broke off and drummed his fingers on the table, too aware of how Tobias's hand in his had gone slack, dead. Skin crawling, he pulled his hand free, then took a breath and tried to backtrack to where he'd first screwed up, but the wrong question came out. "I just meant—I dunno if you've ever thought about a girl like that, or if you'd ever want to —"

"No." Tobias didn't raise his head, didn't move in any way, but the word had a forcefulness—and deeper than that, a horror, like Tobias was completely appalled Jake even asked— that Jake hadn't heard from Tobias before. "No," he said again, and there was no hesitation in it.

WHEN FIRST JAKE pointed out the woman, Tobias thought he wanted to show him something about reals that he should be aware of, or maybe a lesson. Then he worried there was some kind of threat. But as Jake kept talking, two possibilities swelled in his mind, and both had bile rising in his throat, horror and panic mingling into a potent, toxic combination.

First, this could be a test. A nasty, dirty, unpassable test.

Because Jake seemed to be asking if he wanted to have sexual contact with—to *rape*—that woman. The question could mean that Jake really did think he was the kind of depraved monster that would want to do *that* to a human being. But Tobias didn't. The very idea made him sick, shaky, devastated that Jake would ask because that had to mean Tobias had given some sign or had done something so wrong that Jake would think he *wanted* to hurt people. The Director had almost never asked a question without knowing how he would respond to it.

That was one possibility. But Jake's rough grin a moment ago indicated worse worse *worse*. It suggested that *Jake* wanted to do that.

This was nothing like Tobias's expectation of Jake fucking him. That wasn't about enjoying the act—though Tobias hoped Jake would enjoy it enough to keep him. It was about being Jake's, serving Jake, and giving Jake everything he had, including his blood and pain if that was what he wanted. And besides, Tobias was a monster. This woman was a *real*.

But maybe she wasn't. Maybe Jake had been speaking literally when he made that supernatural comment. And that meant any second now, Jake would get up and . . .

Tobias knew what hunters did to monsters. He had been forced to watch. He had been the one at the interrogation table, though never nailed down, never fucked. But in none of Jake's stories had he made even one comment indicating that he did anything but kill freaks as efficiently as possible.

Tobias didn't understand how he could have so horribly misunderstood Jake's interests.

Or—far worse—how a mere four days in contact with a freak could warp him so badly.

Jake was still talking, though Tobias could barely focus enough to process his words. "I know I grabbed you out of there kinda fast and then maybe—I swear I wasn't trying to make any moves. I've always been cool swinging both ways, but you might prefer chicks or not like guys or something . . . Whatever you want is cool with me. Not now, I get that, but whenever you do—"

Was Jake suggesting that *Tobias* might want that woman? Or that he'd want Tobias to join in?

Tobias had thought he was done watching. He had thought —and still clung to the hope—that it would only be him, that he wouldn't ever have to listen to someone else scream again.

"You can tell me, Tobias, just lay it on me and I'll understand—"

"I don't want to hurt her!"

The words tore out of Tobias with more force than he had intended—more force than he wanted to use against Jake, ever —but he couldn't just keep quiet, couldn't say nothing. Even if that was wrong. Even if, because he had said that, because he had spoken out against something Jake wanted to do, Jake would do all of it to him, would hurt him the way Crusher hurt the freaks he fucked, or how the Director hurt monsters that didn't obey or understand their place.

Tobias had never thought Jake was like them. He had never believed that Jake was even capable of doing what other hunters and guards had done to monsters at Freak Camp. But time after time, the Director had shown him that he was just a stupid freak that didn't understand *anything*, and he was fucking stupid if he thought he could even imagine what a real wanted.

Jake was staring at him, and Tobias couldn't stop himself from hunching lower, from digging his fingernails into his arms through the new shirt that Jake had bought for him. He didn't know what would be worse: if Jake hit him now in front of all those reals and announced what Tobias was and why Jake was justified in kicking him to the floor, or if Jake dragged Tobias out to the car. If he waited until they were back in the apartment to take out the whip, the knife, the Director's other tools

Tobias hadn't seen Jake carry but certainly all hunters kept just in case they had to use them.

And now Tobias had given Jake a reason.

"Tobias," Jake said. "I . . . I didn't think you did."

That was it, then. Tobias was wrong and too fucking stupid to know what Jake had meant. In only a few words, Jake had made it clear just how twisted Tobias was, how much of a nasty, perverse freak he was that he had thought those things in the first place. Tobias tightened the grip on his arms, using the pain to ground himself, to hold back the sobbing, the begging, the panic that clogged his throat and threatened to choke him.

"I'm sorry," Tobias forced out, through the nausea, the panic, the terror, the hard truth that in this new world, he had no idea what was going on, and that was going to cost him everything. He didn't understand, he never understood, and one day Jake would teach him that. Jake would be forced to teach him that the way monsters were always taught, the way the Director taught him. Even if Jake didn't want that, wasn't like that *now*, then it would be Tobias's fault that he changed, that he started to like hurting freaks, because Tobias was so damn stupid, too damn stupid to know what was happening, too damn, fucking, cursed stupid to . . .

Jake was still staring at Tobias like Jake had been punched in the gut. "Tobias, what—"

He broke off when the waiter brought them two big plates of food. Jake straightened, turned away from Tobias, and nodded to him before he walked away.

Jake stared down at the plates for a second, then swallowed. "Tobias, I don't . . . I don't want to hurt her either. It's okay." That last bit seemed directed more at himself than Tobias. "No one's going to hurt anyone. I'm . . . I'm sorry I said anything." He reached for his fork, then looked at Tobias. He put his hand back down. "Tobias, you should—"

But Tobias knew he couldn't. He knew that if he looked up,

if he so much as loosened his grip on his arms, he was going to fall apart, and it would be so much worse than it had been at the grocery store. It would be so bad that Jake wouldn't have a choice but to take him back to FREACS because a hunter couldn't keep a monster that wasn't under control, and Tobias wasn't under control right now. There wasn't any fucking control in his life, and he couldn't control himself because he was just a freak and he didn't understand what Jake wanted or intended. Every fucking time that Tobias tried to do something, it was the wrong thing, wrong wrong *wrong* in that perverted way only freaks were capable of.

Tobias didn't know what Jake meant about the woman. He had no fucking idea. Crusher would have thought that Tobias would want to hurt her. The Director would have forced Tobias to say—over and over again—what a monster would do to another monster.

Jake had never indicated anything like that. He had never hurt someone in Tobias's presence, never implied that he wanted to. And he hadn't done anything but be good to Tobias, done nice things for him, bought him clothes, given him a room and it was too much, too much for a worthless, stupid, useless ...

Some of his despair and the knowledge of how much he had fucked up must have been visible because Jake turned toward him with so much concern in his eyes that Tobias knew that was his fault too. If he could only be a little less stupid, a little less worthless, Jake wouldn't have to look at Tobias like Jake's world was falling apart too.

"Not hungry?" Jake attempted one of his grins, but it hurt Tobias to see it because Jake was clearly trying so hard, and Tobias couldn't do anything because he didn't understand what Jake wanted or how to help.

∽

JAKE DIDN'T KNOW what the fuck was going on. He didn't know what he'd said or done, but Tobias was clearly on the edge of a breakdown that would make the disaster at the grocery store look like a wiener dog compared to a werewolf.

Jake smiled at Tobias, and Tobias *flinched*, physically flinched like Jake had fucking hit him.

They had to get home. They had to get home *right now*, because Jake didn't know what would happen when whatever was holding back Tobias's panic broke.

He waved for the check and asked for doggy bags, though neither of them had taken a single bite. Jake downed his beer, wishing it was something stronger, and tried hard not to look at Tobias, not to see the trembling in his limbs or his death grip on his own arms.

Jake tried to keep his movements smooth and nonthreatening, but he was fairly sure he was telegraphing his rage at himself. And he knew, sickeningly, that Tobias would think it was directed at him.

Jake didn't know what he had fucking done, but he knew he was responsible for reducing Tobias to *this* when they had been doing so well.

When the takeaway bags came and Jake climbed out of the booth, he briefly thought about handing Tobias the bag—Tobias seemed more relaxed when Jake had him doing things, whether that was carrying a duffel or bringing the glasses from the table to the kitchen—but one look at Tobias's posture convinced Jake that maybe this time he could do it himself, even when he ended up having to balance the food awkwardly to get the car keys out of his pocket.

It felt weird knowing that Tobias was following him to the car as Jake tried not to look at him or do anything else *fucking stupid* to set him off before they could get inside, to the apartment, somewhere safe where no one would try to report Jake for child abuse when they saw Tobias collapse.

But maybe they should. Maybe you shouldn't be in charge of anyone else's life when you're barely able to hold your own together.

Jake told *that* little voice to shut the fuck up and hit the gas a little harder than he needed to get out of the parking lot.

When Jake got the key into their front door, he let out a breath. Being inside his own space gave him the illusion of safety, that whatever had gone wrong could be fixed. Even if he didn't know what had set Tobias off or what the hell he could do about it.

He put the leftovers in the fridge and then went back to Tobias, who hadn't followed him to the kitchen.

Seeing him standing stiff and trembling in the living room made the bottom drop out of Jake's stomach. For a moment he wholeheartedly wanted to retreat, go to his bedroom, and pretend that whatever had happened tonight would go away if he ignored it long enough.

Two things stopped him. One was that Jake Hawthorne might be a bundle of fuck-ups, but he wasn't a coward. Leon Hawthorne had raised a crazy bastard who shouldn't be in charge of anyone's life because he would probably just screw *them* up even more than *he* was screwed up, but he hadn't raised a chicken-livered weakling.

The other thing was that if Jake walked away now, he would be leaving Tobias alone to deal with whatever fucked-up thing this was, to suffer through something that—while *maybe* not completely Jake's fault—he'd certainly made worse at the restaurant. And Jake would not do that.

Though he seriously reconsidered his position when he stepped farther into the living room and Tobias flinched hard away from him.

No, this was just like when he had visited Tobias at Freak Camp. For the first moments of every visit, Tobias had looked like Jake was going to hit him.

Come to think of it, that was how Tobias had looked every day since Jake had gotten him out.

"Tobias," Jake said, unsure where to even begin.

"J-J-Jake?" Tobias kept his eyes locked on the floor between them, twisting his hands like he was trying to rub off his own skin.

Jake took a deep breath to focus himself, making an effort to balance out everything that had happened today and be the strong one, because Tobias . . . Tobias was messed up and Jake was *less* messed up, and so it was clearly his responsibility—

That was when, looking anywhere but at his face because *that* clearly freaked Tobias out as much as anything else Jake might do right now, he focused on Tobias's hands and saw the long, angry red lines.

"Fuck, Tobias." Jake moved too fast. He knew he'd moved too fast, but Tobias was *bleeding*. He grabbed Tobias's hands and felt a little sick that Tobias flinched again, no more and no less than he had from all Jake's small motions that day and the days before. *What the fuck did they do to you, Tobias?*

Though maybe the better question here was, *What the hell are you doing to yourself?*

Jake pulled Tobias's hands forward to see them, then cursed himself silently and steadily for a good minute at the damage he saw.

Some of the damage on Tobias's hands was old, thick welts that looked deliberate and even. It was bad enough getting a good look at how fragile Tobias's hands were—how could he not have noticed when he held Tobias's hand all those times that they were downright *skeletal*, to the point where Jake could easily see the tendons moving over his bones under the skin?

But marked over the old injuries were deep, angry scratches extending from the wrist across the back of Tobias's too-thin hands, lines all red and raw, with some seeping blood through the torn skin. When Jake angled Tobias's arms up so his baggy sleeves slid toward his elbows, he saw more scratches down his forearms. Few were as deep as those on the backs of his hands, but some were red where Tobias's nails had bitten and scraped into the skin.

So help him, Jake's first thought was that he had checked the apartment for ghosts, for cursed objects and mysterious histories, and that there shouldn't be a witch in the country who could snoop around and leave a hex bag without him knowing.

Then he saw the blood on Tobias's nails and fingertips, and he knew he couldn't blame this on anything supernatural.

"What the hell, Tobias?" Jake breathed, stifling his panic as hard as he could. He would not panic. He would not. Someone had to not panic, and it looked like it would have to be him, though he sure as hell didn't want to be the only option right now.

"S-s-sorry," Tobias gasped. "S-s-s-sorry. J-Jake, I didn't m-mean . . ."

Not thinking about this. Jake was going to focus on the basics right now because if he thought about it, he would snap.

"Sit down." Jake half led, half *pushed* Tobias onto the couch. Tobias went easily, shaking, keeping his head turned away from Jake, eyes fixed intently on nothing, the fear in him cramping Jake's gut. But he wasn't thinking about that right now. "Sit there and, *fuck*, don't scratch."

Tobias nodded, but Jake was already moving. He kept the first aid kit in his room because he'd figured that in the case of an attack, that was the best place to retreat.

When he returned, Tobias was sitting exactly where he had told him to, in the exact same position that Jake had left him, his arms half extended as though he didn't quite know what to do with them. As though, because Jake had told him not to scratch, the arms didn't belong to him anymore and he didn't dare lower them, move them, touch them, because that might be violating the rules.

Not thinking about any of this. Jake crouched in front of Tobias and took his right arm, careful not to touch any of the ugly scratches. From long practice, he opened the hydrogen peroxide against his hip one-handed and dipped it against the cotton ball.

Tobias sucked in a breath through his teeth when Jake started cleaning the scratches, but he didn't move away, barely twitched, even though it had to hurt like a bitch. Jake tried to be gentle while working as fast as he could. It unnerved him how Tobias watched Jake's hands moving with fascination. Like he'd never had a wound cleaned before.

The silence between them stretched out, and it hurt. The wounds weren't deep, but Jake wanted to be sure they were clean. He had to feel like he was *doing* something, that even when he couldn't stop this from happening, he had some way to pick up the pieces. Though he had the strong suspicion that that was complete and utter bullshit.

When Jake thought he could keep his voice even—about the time he was done disinfecting every inch of Tobias's raw skin—he reached down for a roll of light gauze and cleared his throat before beginning the process of mummy-wrapping Tobias's arms.

"You aren't allowed to hurt yourself, Tobias," he said. He didn't look up from his work. It probably wasn't necessary to wrap Tobias up. Maybe a couple of bandages on the worst scratches, where Tobias's nails must have found purchase and dug deeper.

But he wanted the gauze. He wanted to know that Tobias couldn't hurt himself this way again. Jake wanted a visible reminder that he had to fucking do better, had to be as vigilant here as he was on a hunt. Tobias wasn't a one-night stand, wasn't a fuck buddy or an acquaintance. He was *everything*, and if that everything didn't include anything but Jake taking care of Tobias until he had no need for Jake anymore, well, that was fine.

But Jake had to get him to that point first. He had to *watch*, because the more Tobias surprised and scared the shit out of him, the more Jake was convinced that he could lose what he thought had been the most meaningful achievement of his life. That one day he would look up and Tobias would be gone, somehow, some way, maybe on his own two feet, maybe because he'd done something like *this*. Jake had to be more fucking careful. It wasn't just his life he was taking care of now, but Tobias's, and wasn't that a fucking joke? He, Jake Hawthorne, taking *care* of someone, when probably the most reliable relationship in his life was with a fucking car.

"You can't hurt yourself," Jake repeated. "I don't want to hurt you, and I don't want you to hurt yourself, and if anyone else hurts you, I'll fucking kill 'em."

That snapped Tobias's gaze up, only for a second, but it was enough for Jake to see the utter bewilderment in them. Tobias had no fucking idea what he was talking about, and whatever had happened at the bar was still messing with his head, because he should not have looked fucking *surprised* when Jake said he didn't want to hurt him.

Jake had given himself permission to not think about a lot of things. But whatever the fuck had happened at the bar couldn't be one of them.

He levered himself up and sat on the coffee table in front of Tobias, carefully pulling his hands away from Tobias's. If Tobias didn't want contact, Jake didn't want to be touching him. This was going to be fucking hard enough when Jake had no idea what he'd done.

～

"Tobias, I need . . ." Jake stopped and took a deep breath while Tobias's nerves tightened. "I know I did something . . . said something that totally fre—messed with your head, but I don't know what, and I . . . I'm really new to this, man. You have to—I need you to be patient with me. Can you . . . Tobias, just tell me what I did, and I'll do better, I promise."

It sounded like Jake was pleading with him, and that didn't make any kind of sense.

Tobias didn't know what to say. Quite apart from the fact that he had no right to make demands of Jake, of *anyone*—it was already too much that Tobias had inconvenienced him in the restaurant and Jake still hadn't had his dinner—Tobias simply didn't know what was wrong with himself other than that he was a weak, twitchy, stupid freak, and *that* he couldn't change.

But Jake had asked him a question, and he could no more ignore that than he could stop himself from making Jake ashamed of him every time they left the apartment.

"I don't w-want to h-hurt her," Tobias repeated, because that, at least, he knew was true.

Jake looked *more* worried and distraught. His hand twitched like he wanted to touch Tobias, but he pulled back.

"I don't want to hurt her either." Jake ran a hand through his hair, leaving it sticking straight up and spiky. Tobias wanted to smooth it down again, wanted more than anything to be able to touch Jake without dirtying him. "Look, I talk shit some-times. I know that, it's a bad habit that I should—well, some-times I *want* to piss people off, but that wasn't what I was doing here. I'm gonna do my best to change anything you need, and you got to believe that I didn't want to hurt her either. I wouldn't, Tobias."

It seemed like the woman hadn't been a monster after all. Tobias had just misunderstood because he was so stupid. But he had to be sure, even though it sickened him to ask. Part of him didn't *want* to be sure, because then his worst fears would be confirmed—fears he hadn't even known existed until Jake had said those things and Tobias had suddenly remembered similar words in Crusher's voice, in Victor's, in all the guards at Freak Camp who had told him what he and every other monster should expect.

"B-but if she was a, a monster ..."

Jake gestured in an oddly hopeless motion, his hands open and imploring. "But she wasn't, Tobias. With monsters, it's different."

Tobias shuddered, the dread that had been haunting him for so long coalescing at last in a sick, dead weight inside him. He had been told that his entire life, but it had never meant what it did when he heard it from Jake.

Jake went on. "I can't say ... fuck, I *want* to say that I don't want to hurt anyone, and I don't normally, but monsters ... A monster is a monster, yeah, not because they're supernatural, but because they *hurt* people. And sometimes when you've finally dusted a djinn or tracked a shifter that's been slaughtering entire families wearing the face of a grandmother ... yeah, it feels good to stab a fucker like that in the heart." Jake folded his hands over Tobias's, careful of the bandages. "I'm sorry, Tobias. I fucking wish I were better for you."

Tobias felt something break loose in his chest. Sure, his heart was still beating like a rain of bullets on a barracks roof, but the horror that had consumed him since the bar—the thought that the life he'd have with Jake would become just like the pain, anguish, and constant dread of Freak Camp—was gone. Not snuffed out, but broken, shattered, snapped into pieces so tiny that yes, they hurt, but they weren't like knives in his chest anymore, hurting every time he took the shallowest of breaths. This was like dust in his eyes, a shard of something under his skin, and it would work its own way out of him. He would heal from the damage it had done.

It still hurt; his terrible fears had hurt and still left him twitching, but he knew they were temporary. In a day, in an hour, they would be gone like the dust and not even the memory would linger.

Tobias stared down at Jake's hands wrapped over his. There it was: everything good about Jake contained in the image of his hands resting over Tobias's bandaged ones, so gently that Tobias could hardly feel them.

When Tobias hurt himself like the stupid freak he was, Jake put him back together. When Tobias had clearly caused Jake pain in some way that he did not understand, Jake still touched Tobias so carefully that even open wounds weren't hurt. Jake took care of him. Jake cared for him. In spite of the freak Tobias was, Jake was there, patient, and he wouldn't get rid of him for these stupid weaknesses—at least, not yet.

That was euphoria. That was joy.

But better yet was the reassurance that Jake was nothing like the guards. Not that Tobias should have ever, ever doubted that. He had almost felt a laugh bubbling up in his chest when Jake talked about what gave him satisfaction in a hunt. Beheading a shifter with silver? Shoving a bloodied knife into a djinn's chest?

Tobias had done those. Both of those, under the Director's orders. The Director and Crusher had called it *too fucking good an end for a filthy freak*. Tobias had always thought of it as a mercy.

Jake's idea of cruelty, of harshness, of harm, was Tobias's definition of kindness. And Tobias's definition of kindness had always been far more than he could ever hope for in Freak Camp.

Tobias bent over their closed hands. He wished he had permission to kiss Jake's fingers, to thank him for everything he had done, to thank him for being so good that it hurt. He was so good that it threatened to break Tobias in half from the joy and unnatural, intense release from fear; it was a freedom he had never felt before.

He managed to force out words, even with his throat closed up from the relief, the heady, blessed, euphoric relief. "You're so good, Jake," he said. "I'm sorry, I'm sorry, thank you so much."

"Hey, Tobias." Jake moved over to the couch, sitting close next to him. "Toby."

"Thank you, thank you, thank you," was all Tobias could say, but at least for now, as Jake shushed him and cradled his head against his shoulder, that seemed to be enough.

5

J ake couldn't sleep that night. He lay in bed, staring at the blank white ceiling, listening to his heart beating too hard in his chest, sometimes turning over to punch his pillow with a viciousness that had no target in life. He couldn't punch something and make the problems with Tobias go away. He couldn't even toss and turn too much because part of him was convinced that Tobias would hear and think that Jake's rage was directed toward him.

It wasn't just the anger, the desire to light something on fire, that kept him awake. There was the inescapable image, emblazoned in his head like the picture he saw once of his mother's pyre, of Tobias leaning against him, arms scratched and bleeding, and his soft, pitifully grateful words.

Sometime between the blank rage and the broken feeling that felt suspiciously like tears, Jake came to a realization.

He, Jake Hawthorne, was in so far over his fucking head that it was a wonder he and Tobias were still breathing. He should have realized that after the horror that had been the grocery store—no, fuck, even before that, he should have known from that nightmarish first night he got Tobias out of camp. But he had ignored Tobias's twitches. He had kept moving, kept talking, hoping that the power of momentum would make anything wrong with Tobias just go away.

But tonight, he had to face the whole, long, brutal, bloody, appalling string of disasters because he couldn't fix this by lighting it on fire. Every setback pointed to one truth lit up with neon lights:

You don't have a clue what you're doing. You can't tell the difference between helping and hurting Tobias. Every time that thought crept into his head, he had told it to go fuck itself because he wanted this—a life with Tobias—and there weren't any other options.

Yeah, that was selfish. Wanting to keep Tobias to himself, to protect him, to make him smile. But that didn't change the fact that Tobias didn't have a lot of choices out there. He had Jake, and maybe Roger or Alejandra, but Jake couldn't go to anyone else with something like this, not when he couldn't even begin to explain what had gone wrong or what the problem was. He just knew that something had fucked Tobias sideways, and Jake had no control over how that was affecting him.

Of course, finding someone to help would also require finding someone that Jake trusted to *let* help. Even Roger—yeah, maybe Roger could come in, but what could he do? Especially when Jake knew enough now to feel more than a little uneasy about pushing Tobias into close contact with other people.

Jake flipped over, twisting his sheets, punched his pillow and then froze, listening, hoping that he wouldn't hear Tobias's whimper, that the kitchen and the living room between them would keep Tobias from hearing Jake and thinking something else completely fucked up. When he didn't hear Tobias, didn't hear anything but the distant sounds of the city, he relaxed into the pillow and breathed through the fabric.

So it was just him against the world, trying to help Tobias, and Jake knew there weren't many people who would give a damn if he died, and not a single soul that really gave a fuck whether or not he ever managed to make Tobias marginally less afraid, let alone *happy* for a minute at a time.

And after tonight, he couldn't deny that he was *afraid* down to his core—something he hadn't felt in years—about the other ways he might fuck this up. About how anything might happen to Tobias, even when he was right next to Jake, just because Jake didn't realize how what he was doing or saying affected Tobias, or he just didn't *notice*.

Jake twisted again, remembering just in time *not* to punch the headboard (two indents in it already, nothing that would even draw the eye, but Jake's knuckles remembered the particle wood). Instead, he stumbled out of bed, swearing at the carpet that snagged his feet, and staggered to the bathroom.

His eyes hurt when he flicked on the lights, but he stared at the mirror anyway.

He looked like shit—which wasn't surprising, as he hadn't been sleeping—with bloodshot eyes and crazy hair sticking in all directions. He looked like a guy who could fail spectacularly at the most important job of his life, not a problem.

Shit, no, he would not fucking accept that. He would not quit less than a week into this. Yeah, he had no right to take care of Tobias—no matter what that little piece of paper said. Yeah, it seemed sometimes like the only competent thing Jake had done was get Tobias out of FREACS—and wasn't it cold fucking comfort to use that for a standard? But he *had* gotten Tobias out, and even if this entire catastrophe now was at least partly his fault for taking too fucking long about it, Jake wouldn't stop trying to make Tobias smile, to give him some kind of security and life.

Jake must have stared at himself for a good ten minutes, letting the yellow light bleach him, his eyes soaking in the exhausted bastard in front of him, until he finally flicked it off and went back to his cold, lonely bed. He would do better for Tobias. Maybe then he could actually sleep.

He was learning every day, he *was*, though each lesson hurt like blessed salt in an open wound. He knew better—now, sometimes—what was going on in Tobias's head. Like after tonight, he was pretty sure that Tobias hadn't even been conscious of hurting himself. Maybe that should have made Jake feel better, but it didn't. Not when he had an inkling that Tobias would never have taken the initiative to deliberately hurt himself, not when he was always looking at Jake for clues for when to pick up a fork or sit down on the sofa. Tobias wouldn't take that much control with his own body (shit, did he think that he was Jake's *property* or something? That was another sick thought Jake didn't have the faintest idea how to go about correcting). And for all that he hated Tobias's unhesitating obedience, Jake had to hope that maybe Tobias had listened to him tonight, maybe he understood that Jake didn't want him hurting himself. Even if it had happened on some fucked-up level of Tobias's subconscious, maybe he would catch himself and wouldn't do it again.

If nothing else, if Jake couldn't prevent Tobias from sliding into the bad spaces, he could at least learn to recognize them and catch Tobias before they hit the bottom.

~

JAKE HAD no plans for the next day, and he intended to keep it that way. Maybe they'd avoid disaster if they stayed inside the salt lines.

One step at a time.

Tobias read on the couch. Jake hadn't put much thought into finding a couch sized for two lanky guys, but when he'd seen this murky orange-brown one at the local thrift store, he'd jumped on it. It was a steal for fifty bucks, especially since it didn't have any weird smells and the armrests had extra padding.

He was grateful he had, and not just because the living room would have looked really empty without the couch and the coffee table. Tobias looked so comfortable, head propped on one saggy armrest, feet not even touching the opposite edge, that Jake wouldn't have changed anything.

Of course, Tobias hadn't started out sprawling. Getting him to actually relax had been a gradual, step-by-step process. At first, Tobias had sat stiffly on the edge of the couch, book held in front of him like he was preparing a lecture on American History. Jake wasn't even sure why he had that textbook; he'd found it buried in the car when he was digging through the trunk for bungee cords to hook the couch to the roof.

Jake couldn't deal with seeing Tobias perched there like he didn't belong, like he expected a pop quiz at any moment. Jake had decided then and there that getting him to damn well *relax* in their apartment was a great first subgoal. After all, this was his place just as much as Jake's.

He dropped down onto the couch next to Tobias, who started up like Jake had sat on the other end of a seesaw. Jake nudged him back against the cushions as he sprawled out like a starfish or a douchebag on a subway. "You know, this couch was actually the first piece of furniture I bought? Like, in my life. It felt big, you know, and I wanted to get a really good one, but the guys at Wise Buys told me, 'You sleep on it, you buy it.' So I had to head out before I gave it a really good test. I know plenty of bad couches from the places we holed up in when I was a kid, and you can't just sit on one for five minutes and think you know what's up. You have *not* known a bad couch until you spend the night with that one piece of rebar digging into your back. So we gotta test this one out, right? Whaddaya think so far?"

Tobias blinked at him. "It's, um—good. Nice."

"Awesome. But just to be clear, I dragged this home on top of the Eldorado, not, like, from a European imports emporium, and I don't give a damn if you put your feet up on it. Or on the coffee table." He kicked his feet up onto the basic pine coffee table that had cost five bucks because one of the legs wiggled, and he rested one heel solidly on the worst coffee stain, sinking deeper into the cushions. "Try it out."

Tobias studied him like he was trying to figure out the joke, but when Jake just smiled, he slowly stretched his legs out, resting his heels on one of the lighter water rings.

Jake beamed at him. "So, where are you at in history? Did ol' George Washington swim the Delaware yet?"

Tobias's mouth curved up in a smile too, which was damn nice to see. "It's the War of 1812."

Jake squinted. "Is that eighteen-twelve military time?"

Tobias's smile widened. "No, in the year 1812. Against the British."

"Oh yeah, round two. We kicked their asses then too, didn't we?"

Tobias made a face. "Sort of. They did burn down the White House first."

"No way!" Jake feigned shock, clutching the back of his head. "How'd that happen in the great US of A? Dude, can you even imagine torching that place?"

Tobias looked a little alarmed, sitting up straighter and eyeing Jake uncertainly.

Jake held his hand palm out, conciliatory. "That was just a joke, don't stress. I've got no plans to burn down any government buildings, even if it might be a little fun. Anyway, what happened in 1812?"

Tobias told him about the Battles of Bladensburg and New Orleans, all the warships that sank in the Great Lakes (and the ghost ships that still hadn't all been put to rest, which of course Tobias knew about from the Freak Camp library even though

Jake's twenty-year-old textbook didn't), and what an absolute dick Andrew Jackson turned out to be (that last part was maybe more Jake's words than Tobias's).

Tobias had seemed initially startled by Jake's invasion of the sofa, but as he talked, animation replaced his nervousness, and Jake recognized that whip-smart, nerdy kid he'd known for what felt like all his life. Jake paid attention to what he was saying, but mostly he just soaked in the sight of Tobias at ease, maybe even *happy*, with a slight flush in his face and a brightness in his eyes.

Jake finally got up to inventory the kitchen to figure out their next few meals, as well as to try to ram the pizza pan into a cupboard that was *too damn small*. He let himself glance over the breakfast bar to see that Tobias had actually slid down onto his side, the book propped in the crook of one elbow and his legs folded up on the couch.

Jake counted it a solid victory. When he brought over a glass of orange juice, he let himself sit on the edge of the couch next to him—though he had to put his hand on Tobias's shoulder at once to keep him from sitting up. He sat there quietly for a minute, rubbing Tobias's shoulder and watching his face, which was very still but had none of the warning signs that said this was *bad*. Jake thought he had learned to recognize those, though it still felt like an awful risk to trust himself that far. But when Tobias's eyes fluttered shut, Jake was willing to bet that was a good thing.

At last, he made himself get up and grab another book off the shelf to read on the other end of the couch. He had had about enough of wandering around the apartment, trying to think of something else to do, and anything Tobias loved so much was good enough for him.

But the book he'd grabbed—an English literature anthology by a dude named Norton—was thick and boring, and it was hard to concentrate when Tobias's feet were right next to him, almost touching his thigh. He dropped the book onto the table and pulled over the Boulder newspaper instead, flipping idly through the sheets to get a feel for what counted as exciting in this town, before reading the articles much closer than he normally did. He didn't expect to find anything super-naturally unusual, but it never hurt to be sure.

Once assured there was nothing out of the ordinary even in Boulder's personal ads, he got up and started tidying. Not that anything really needed to be cleaned, but a lifetime of being anal about weapons and personal care—you never knew when one lazily washed wound could pick up a supernatural disease or contaminant—had made him willing to putter productively. Out of habit, he checked his weapons (weird to not have used a gun or knife in the past week, there wasn't much to clean, sharpen or polish), wiped down the kitchen, and started a load of laundry. He still couldn't believe he lived somewhere with an in-unit washer and dryer that wasn't just a couple of glorified rust buckets.

Eventually, he got desperate enough to tackle the random stuff he'd thrown into the corner of his bedroom. He'd always planned on sorting it out some day—in the Hawthorne world, weapons and first aid took priority and everything else could go to hell—so why not today?

He focused on his room first, grateful to have a place he could retreat to where he didn't have to worry how Tobias would interpret his expression—he straightened the picture of his mom on the nightstand, examined the hinges on the closet door, thought about ways to reinforce the bathroom with steel plating. Then he decided that he'd been away from Tobias long enough, so he grabbed one of the random bags in his closet (how *had* he accumulated so much crap so fast?) and headed back to the living room to dump it out over the coffee table.

The bag was full of crap. Receipts for the stuff he'd bought —normal people saved those, right?—old newspapers, skin mags, a tiny silver knife that looked destined for slaughtering weresardines or something. Most of it was pointless, random, or completely out of place, but some of it was unexpectedly useful. A couple of Boulder delivery menus, a few condoms with wrappers still intact, a *TV Guide*, and a crumpled brochure that turned out to be a visitor's guide to Boulder. It seemed so long ago when he had started thinking about getting a permanent place here for him and Tobias, a time fraught with paperwork, panic, and nerves, but that was done now. Tobias was out, with him, and that was all that really mattered at the end of the day.

Jake unfolded the brochure to find a detailed map marked with shops, restaurants, parks, museums, and random little smiley faces that seemed to be other attractions. His first instinct was to pin the map to a wall, see if anything on it turned out to be a supernatural hotspot. But then he realized it could also just be exactly what it was: a map.

"Hey Tobias!" He held it up. "Check this out!"

Of course, he could have kicked himself when Tobias nearly dropped the book and snapped to attention, almost bolting up from the couch. He only stopped when Jake jumped forward and crouched down in front of him with the map, ass on the coffee table, trying to preserve Tobias's brief relaxation. Tobias froze until the map was resting on his knees, Jake's hands holding it out.

Jake didn't really need to look at the map again—he'd scouted pretty much everywhere in the town, and while he wouldn't have been able to find the Boulder Museum of History, he certainly knew where the best bars were. Priorities, man. He handed the map to Tobias, who took it with the caution of someone just handed a live but nonpoisonous snake.

"I don't know how much experience you have with maps . . ."

Tobias glanced up. "I—I've studied them," he said softly.

"Cool. Well, this is Boulder, our town. I dunno if you wanted to take a look, get a feel for what's here. See, that block, that's where we live, right there. We've got downtown not too far away, and the big college—but yeah, you can see what's marked out. If anything looks interesting, we can check it out. Whenever you want."

Tobias didn't respond, but he focused on it intently, so Jake decided the map was a decent success. He smiled and let go, getting up to finish clearing off the debris on the table.

About this time in the day, not having anything to do, Jake would step out to roam for girls or guys or go to a movie, a bar, somewhere out of his base camp. He would have been scouting the supernatural scene, reading up on local legends, interviewing people involved in possible hauntings. He would be keeping busy. But he'd *done* all that already—in the six months waiting for Tobias, if not that morning—and he wasn't sure what the next step was. Was this when normal people picked up a hobby or something?

As a last-ditch activity, he went back to his bedroom and brought back out the laptop. He didn't really like computers. He could never find anything on the web when he looked for it—except porn—and it was such a hassle. He'd met hunters who insisted the internet was the wave of the future, but Jake couldn't see it. Sure, it was a great way to share info, but if the information wasn't reliable and couldn't be verified, what good was it?

Still, he had one—thank you, ASC Resources and Supply Program—and he could make it work. If not well.

He plugged in this cord and that cord, turned it on, fiddled, hit a couple keys—out of frustration when the thing took *forever* to turn on, or load, or wake up, or whatever it was that computers did—switched on the modem-thingy, and then signed onto the World Wide Web.

When the browser opened up automatically on the ASC

website, Jake was grateful that he was facing Tobias and there was no chance he could see Jake's computer screen.

The page contained the usual advisories for hunters: lists of monsters caught and where in the United States, ghost and demon hotspots, current bounties offered. But right at the top were the articles and notices for non-ASC personnel, normal humans who wanted to know more about the organization that protected them from the supernatural threat. He couldn't avoid reading the headline, at least, and the letters were big enough that Tobias would have easily been able to see them.

MONSTERS AMONG US: WHAT CAN YOU DO?

Jake felt a weird sense of déjà vu, or maybe just nausea. That question was important. People had to know that sometimes disappearances, weird things moving, and light flickers were just random problems, fate kicking you in the balls, but sometimes it *was* freaky shit that had to be dealt with by professionals. Even though Jake wasn't even legal to drink (though that had never stopped him, of course), he considered himself a professional. He had known about hunting as long as he could remember and had *been* hunting for most of his life.

But according to the head honchos who called the shots, Tobias, lying there on his couch, was a monster, one of the freaks about whom the article warned: *can masquerade in the human form to manipulate and harm you or your loved ones.* That idea was so wrong, couldn't possibly apply to Tobias. But it was what Jake believed about every other monster.

He stopped reading. He got out of that page as quickly as he could. Tobias couldn't see it, thank God, but Jake didn't want to look at it anymore, afraid what Tobias would see on his face. As the sky dimmed to dusk through the living room window, Jake stood up and stretched, popping a few joints. His muscles felt stiff. Hell, he hadn't been for a run or done any of his usual workouts since the day he'd picked Tobias up. No wonder everything felt out of whack, like the walls were closing in. This would all be a lot easier to handle if he could work out some of his stress.

Wandering into the kitchen, he debated how to bring that up. It wasn't like he needed Tobias's permission (or that Tobias would know how to grant it) to leave the apartment without him, but every glimpse of the bandages around Tobias's hands reminded him, as they should, that *nothing* was as simple as it seemed. He didn't actually have a clue what might happen to Tobias if he left him alone.

Jake was vastly relieved to see the white Styrofoam boxes inside the fridge. That made dinner plans easy. "Hey, I'm going to heat up our leftovers, okay?"

Tobias answered affirmatively after a short hesitation, but Jake only half heard. He was on a hunt for the tinfoil he could have sworn he'd bought. His first instinct had been to nuke the whole box in the microwave, but Tobias deserved better. If Jake wasn't going to cook, he could at least take the time to heat things in the oven.

Though that definitely took longer, especially since Jake forgot to preheat before he slid the enchiladas—on top of the pizza tray, at least he got to use *that* again—into the oven. He turned on a timer, then wandered into the living room to sit next to Tobias. He noticed Tobias had switched to the start of another book, though Jake was positive he'd seen him close to the end of it earlier.

Jake pointed his chin toward it. "How do you like ol' Huck Finn?"

"Oh—it's good. Really good." He paused, considering. "Not nearly as informative or fact-based as the history book, I think. But that's because it's a story." His voice rose tentatively at the end, like it was a question.

"Uh, yeah?" Even Jake knew *The Adventures of Huckleberry Finn* wasn't an autobiography.

Tobias still watched him. "Is it okay—that I read f-fiction, too? Even if it's not as useful? I mean, sometimes it can be. The research library in the camp had a whole section on so-called fairy tales that I cross-referenced with historical accounts. But I don't know if this—"

"Toby, dude, it's totally okay. All these books are for you, and if they're all *useful* then I'm doing something wrong." Then Jake's eyes fell on the *TV Guide* he'd tossed onto the coffee table. "Hey, let's see if there's anything good on tonight." He picked it up to flick through it, wondering what Tobias would like. *Wheel of Fortune*? *Jeopardy*? *The Young and the Restless*?

Definitely not one of the ASC's tacky "reality" TV shows featuring shiny, Botoxed hunters taking down monsters with a Hollywood camera crew at their backs. Every hunter worth even half their salt hated those sellouts, though the ASC approved them for the sake of "educating the public."

When the timer beeped, Tobias followed him into the kitchen and helped Jake carry the plates and cans of soda, but Jake stopped him before he set everything on the table.

"Let's eat dinner on the couch. I think I found something you'll like."

Tobias changed course easily enough, and Jake felt absurdly pleased when Tobias folded his legs onto the couch beside him. He flicked through the channels until he found the one kicking off a Christmas in July special, with the first *Home Alone* movie about to begin. He figured it was better to start off with something light and safe, and what could be better than a slapstick Christmas comedy, even if it was hot outside.

Jake tried not to watch Tobias obsessively as the movie got underway. It was part of his effort not to drive himself insane with every little thing so that he wouldn't get himself killed before recognizing an actual threat. It was hard, though, as the McCallister family embarked on their absurd antics, not to be hyperaware of Tobias's reactions—or lack thereof. Sure, it was a cheesy film, but Jake had a soft spot for it. He and Dad had spent a few Christmases watching motel cable, drinking hot chocolate and whiskey through multiple repeats of classics like *The Santa Clause* and *A Christmas Story*. Jake thought *Home Alone* was pretty funny.

But Tobias didn't laugh. Not once.

Jake tried not to notice. He tried not to track Tobias's reactions to every scene, because he wanted so damn much to believe this would be okay. That they could watch a classic Christmas movie without falling apart. He should have known better—the bandages on Tobias's hands, the memory of the *grocery store* should have reminded him that nothing was easy or safe, nothing could be taken for granted. And he should never have ignored the first time Tobias flinched when Kevin slapped aftershave onto his cheeks and let out the scream to raise the dead. But he let it go until they reached the night when the Wet Bandits walked straight into Kevin's booby traps.

The moment Kevin took aim with his BB gun at Harry's crotch, it clicked for Jake. Tobias had never made a sound, but every time someone got hurt, made a threat, or a sneering remark, he had flinched, flattened himself into the couch, or balled his hands in his lap. Then it hit Jake without warning what all that body language had been pointing at. Way too fucking late. Jake fumbled for the remote and shut off the TV before Kevin could pull the trigger.

Jake leaned forward, his elbows on his knees and head in his hands, and took a moment to breathe and think what he'd almost done to Tobias. Of what could have happened if he'd let that play out. He remembered now, vividly, what had been coming up: Harry grabbing a red-hot doorknob; Marv's bare foot stepping on a nail; Harry's head torched; the bandits threatening to bite off Kevin's fingers. *Fuck.*

It was a minute before he could bring himself to lift his head and look to see how much damage he'd inflicted. But Tobias, to his amazement, looked okay—no, not okay, Jake knew fucking better than that now, and he was beginning to fear he'd ever see Tobias *okay*—he looked nervous and a little upset, but not in pieces, nothing like he had been . . . those other times. He was looking at Jake, for one.

Tobias bit his lip, hands twisting in his lap. "You don't . . . you don't have to turn it off. I didn't—"

"No, Tobias, it's cool. Stupid movie anyway." Jake leaned back and stared at the smooth plaster ceiling. He almost wished for a few cracks, a spiderweb or two, maybe a creepy water stain. At least then he could pretend he could divine some answers. Instead, he received what he always got from the universe: a blank white nothing for him to fuck up. He kept talking, hoping maybe if he just kept the words coming at some point they would make sense, and what he had almost done to Tobias would go away, and he wouldn't have to think about how dangerous every—little—thing—was, and how inevitably he was going to be blindsided again. And again. "I mean, we could play cards, we could . . . read. Or . . . sleep. I like sleeping, it's . . . restful."

Any normal person would tell Jake that he was a fucking mumbling idiot and there was no way they wanted to hang out with him. He half expected Tobias to start begging or say something about how they could do whatever, he didn't care, he didn't care about anything.

But Tobias said, a little nervously, "Cards . . . cards sound good. If you're not . . ."

Jake never thought that hearing someone else's opinion about what to do for an evening would feel so good. But this was Tobias.

Yeah, it didn't make him feel like the best human being in the world, but it gave him enough strength to look away from the ceiling to where Tobias was looking at him with something close to hope in his eyes.

"Well, hell," Jake said. "Yeah, that sounds good."

They moved to the kitchen table because the coffee table really wasn't tall enough to play cards on. Jake got them a couple more sodas—he didn't think he should be drinking anymore, not right now, when bad things could happen any second that he wasn't paying attention—while Tobias absently, easily, shuffled the old deck Jake had gotten out of his room.

Tobias set the deck on the table between them when Jake sat down across from him. "War?" he asked. When Tobias nodded, Jake gestured toward the deck. "Split it for us?"

Tobias took the cards, tapped the deck twice between his hands to even out the cards—a nervous tic, but one that Tobias had had since they were kids—and split the deck in half with one smooth motion and handed Jake his half.

Jake counted automatically, vaguely dreading finding too many cards in his deck, or even needing to hand Tobias one, but he had a perfect twenty-six.

Jake grinned at him when he was done. Tobias hadn't even bothered to count, just watched him with mild worry. "You're too damn good at this," Jake said.

Tobias shook his head with a small smile and rolled his eyes, and just like that they were kids again, when Jake had finally poked and joked and acted goofy with him long enough to get Tobias to give him an honest-to-goodness exasperated response. Even when Tobias reluctantly took the first three plays—all the fucking twos were in Jake's hand, and apparently on top—Jake couldn't keep the silly grin off his face.

War took forever, but that was okay, because every second the cards passed over the table, Tobias looked a little more relaxed.

Jake swept all the cards up after War and shuffled with practiced ease. He preferred pool hustling to card sharking—part of him admitted he liked the possibility of violence, the fact that any second the con could go wrong and then he'd be up against some pissed-off dudes holding long sticks—but he could still play cards like a Vegas dealer. He grinned at Tobias. "Crazy Eights?"

When Tobias grinned back, real enjoyment in his eyes, Jake thought his heart might stop. "I won last time," he pointed out.

Jake tried to contain the swell of hope and happiness that hit him, all because Tobias was *teasing* him. "Think you remember the rules?"

He didn't expect Tobias's face to pale, his hands to tense on the table. But at least Tobias didn't fall back into his shell, he didn't retreat, and he didn't drop his eyes for more than a couple seconds before looking back up at Jake. "Unless you've changed them," Tobias said softly, "I remember."

Fuck, it had maybe been a year since they had played anything. The whole fucking six months, and then before that because Jake hadn't always brought a deck of cards even when he had been able to get to Freak Camp, and in all that time . . .

Yeah, a guy could forget the rules. But Jake didn't care about that, he just wanted Tobias to stay relaxed, easy, calm again like he had just a second ago while they were playing stupid old War.

Jake dealt out six cards each—their personal variation— and felt his stomach pitch when Tobias didn't pick them up, just watched him.

Jake couldn't meet his eyes. He picked up his cards and turned the top one over. "If you want to play something else, that's . . . I mean, we could stick with War."

Tobias took a deep breath and picked up the cards. "J-Jake."

"Yeah, Tobias?"

"If I . . . If I f-f-forget, will you . . . would you . . ." He fingered one of his cards, as though he wanted to pull it out to play but couldn't quite get up the courage.

"What, Tobias?" Jake resisted the urge to hold his breath. *Please be something I can do.*

"If I f-forget the rules, you'll tell me, right? You won't let me..."

Jake felt relieved, though also unsettled because Tobias's worry had seemed greater than a handful of stupid card rules —though admittedly, their personal version of Crazy Eights had gotten pretty dizzying. "It ain't Dungeons and Dragons, Tobias, you might be the one letting *me* know how things are supposed to go. After all, you've got the kickass memory." He crossed a hand dramatically over his chest. "I promise I'll let you know if I think you're changing the rules on me. And I promise not to try to change them if I think you're kicking my ass."

Tobias smiled, looking somewhat relieved, and they began.

After Crazy Eights—Jake won and was so smug that Tobias rolled his eyes at him again, with more feeling this time—they played a fast and dirty round of Zsíros and Tobias completely cleaned his clock, and by that time it was about one in the morning and Jake could barely keep his eyes open.

"Shit," he said, yawning so far he thought his jaw would crack. "I'm beat, Tobias. You tired?"

And there it was, that beautiful smile that Jake might just one day gamble the Eldorado for. "You're just wimping out because you l-lost."

Fuck, he was trying so hard. Jake could see that he was struggling, but he was actually succeeding at not falling apart. Jake still didn't know what the hell was going on in Tobias's head, but he was fighting it, and clearly had fun tonight. Again, Jake felt a surge of hope. He tried not to let this one sweep him away; his hopes about Tobias had gotten crushed more than once just that evening. But for the first time since he'd gotten Tobias out, their relationship felt exactly as it had when they were kids.

This was the Tobias that Jake had been afraid he would never see again.

6

S aturday morning, Jake grew a pair and pulled out the frying pan to cook up scrambled eggs and bacon. He told Tobias to drop a couple slices of bread in the toaster and pour the orange juice, tasks Tobias handled as precisely as ever. Jake let him carry them out without glancing over once, determined not to make him nervous. It was worth it to see the vast relief on Tobias's face when he set the second glass of orange juice on Jake's side of the table.

Jake beamed at him. "Thanks, Toby. Could you get me a plate and some of those paper towels?"

This was progress, he reflected. They still hadn't been together a full week, so of course things were rough sometimes with hard lessons. But step by step he was figuring things out, and this worked. Tobias liked helping—even if he probably wouldn't admit it if Jake asked—and that was all right, Jake could tell, so it would do for now.

But when they sat down for breakfast, just catching sight of the TV's dead screen sent a foreboding chill through him, and Jake clenched his jaw to stay focused on the here and now. He glanced toward the window instead, at the bright sunlight and birds they could hear in the nearby trees, along with the traffic on the street.

"So," he said, and waited as Tobias stopped immediately, lowering his toast to the plate and looking up. "How'd you feel about taking a walk through town? Just you and me, you know." The reassurance felt dumb. Of course he couldn't promise the streets would be empty, but he hoped Tobias understood what he meant: Jake would be at his side the whole way.

Tobias looked away, his forehead knit faintly, but he said, "Yes—we could, if that's—yes, Jake. I'd—l-like to go out." It didn't really sound sincere, let alone enthusiastic, but Jake took the effort and determination behind the words at face value and reached across to squeeze Tobias's hand. Carefully, though they'd taken the bandages off last night and nearly all traces of the scratches were gone.

Tobias looked back, startled enough to meet his eyes, and Jake smiled at him.

"Good. I think you'll like this town, it's a pretty rockin' place. Had to go over it a few times to make sure no one was making backyard sacrifices to a pagan god on the sly, but—" He could've bitten his tongue as soon as the words slipped out. Hadn't he learned not to talk about the supernatural to Tobias, that yeah, it was a pretty sensitive subject? But Tobias didn't look particularly bothered, just nodded a little uncertainly.

Jake let go of Tobias's hand, clapped his own together, and cleared his throat. "So, yeah, anyway—cool. As soon as we're finished, we'll grab that map in the brochure and head out."

"I studied it," Tobias said to his plate.

"Yeah?" Jake paused, not sure how he was supposed to respond. The way Tobias said that was a little off, but after a second or two of trying to parse out a deeper meaning, Jake gave it up. That wasn't the same as ignoring it. He was sure about that. "Well, that's cool. Between the two of us, no way we'll get lost."

JAKE COULDN'T HAVE ASKED for a nicer day for Tobias's first Saturday out of Freak Camp. Though mid-July, Boulder's elevation in the mountains kept a light breeze moving that took the edge off the warmth. The sun didn't bake or broil them as it would in Roger's patch of New Mexico desert, but the rays still bounced off the sidewalk, bright enough to make them squint. Jake made a note to duck into a store and get Tobias a pair of sunglasses at the first opportunity.

The residential street was quiet, aside from the occasional passing car. No one was out—either sleeping in or already busy with weekend activities someplace else, Jake figured. As they neared the end of the block, he pulled the map out of his pocket and shook it open. It was already worn and falling apart at the creases.

"So," he said, bracing himself to ask even though he didn't have a hope Tobias would answer, "when you were checking this out, did you find anything in Boulder you wanted to see?"

Tobias glanced over, head tilted down—from the glare, Jake told himself—and shrugged, an awkward twitch of his shoulders.

"Well," Jake said, drawing his finger down from their block, "downtown's here, but—let's check that out some other time. There's a few parks, and it's a sweet day for a walk . . . I think this is the main one, Central Park. It's a ways, though—you up to walking that far?"

Tobias nodded.

"You sure?"

Tobias nodded once more, and Jake wondered—but what were they going to do, turn back and stay inside all day? He had to take Tobias at his word or they'd never get anywhere. The best he could do was keep an eye on Tobias for any sign of exhaustion. Add that to the list.

They walked in silence for another block. Out of the corner of his eye, Jake watched Tobias focus on the pavement, placing his feet in an unwavering line, and despite Jake's best intentions to *back off* and not breathe down his neck every minute, he couldn't keep himself from pointing up, ready to grab any opportunity to get Tobias to look less damn stressed.

"Hey, check it out. Some idiot tossed their shoes up into that tree."

Tobias's eyes followed Jake's finger to a pair of battered shoes, linked by their laces, looped over a tree branch. Then he stopped walking, and Jake stopped too.

Tobias's lips parted, and his head tilted all the way back as he stared straight up. The reaction made Jake hold his breath for a moment, but Tobias didn't look upset. On the contrary, this was open wonder, amazement on his face, and Jake didn't think it was about a pair of stupid shoes.

He looked up again, trying to see what Tobias saw. There was just the tree—really tall, yeah, the lowest branch thick as his thigh and higher than he could reach, the whole thing vibrantly green and crawling in ivy, leaves rustling and swaying in the gentle breeze like the tree was talking to itself.

"It's . . ." Tobias breathed, and Jake was amazed to see a real smile growing on his face, an honest-to-God smile. "It's—" He still didn't finish, like he didn't have any words that fit. And for Jake—who had learned in the last few days how damn slow he could be—it finally clicked.

Freak Camp didn't have any trees.

Blinking in a daze, like he'd just been clobbered over the head by an oak branch, Jake caught Tobias's hand. Tobias squeezed back hard as he looked at Jake, turning that breathtaking, fragile smile on him.

"Well," Jake said, keeping his voice normal with a valiant effort, though his cheeks felt awfully hot (July, of course), "sounds like the park was a pretty good idea, huh?"

After that, Tobias didn't watch the sidewalk. He stared up at the trees, birds, and squirrels, breathless and awed in a *good* way, hanging tight to Jake's hand. Jake couldn't get enough of it; he felt light with relief. Finally, he'd done something right. There had been more than a few mishaps along the way—the traces of Tobias's mostly healed scratches were plenty of a reminder for how delicate everything still was and how fast it could slide to hell. But right now, this was good. This was everything.

They paused at the next major intersection (no stoplights, just those funny roundabout things) for Jake to let go of Tobias's hand and pull out the map, but before he could figure out how far they'd come, Tobias said, "Straight, five more blocks to Broadway." Pausing, he added, "Unless you want to take 9th south, then there's seven." He flushed and looked down at his shoes.

Jake stared at the map, counting the blocks. "Holy shit, Tobias. When'd you . . . that's a badass memory you've got."

Tobias turned even more pink, not raising his face. Jake jostled his shoulder gently, and Tobias looked up at him. "I mean it," he said, looking him in the eye. "That's badass."

Now looking like he had a serious sunburn, Tobias ducked his head, but close to Jake, brushing his forehead to Jake's shoulder. That was more than okay, Jake decided. He stuffed the map in his back pocket, still smiling. "Looks like we won't need this."

The streets got busier, lined with shops instead of residential houses, as they got closer to downtown. People were out and about with Saturday shopping, and Tobias stayed closer to Jake's side, but they were still okay. Jake decided on 9th Street as a better bet so they wouldn't go through the heart of downtown.

It was a long walk, and by the time they got close to the park, Jake was fantasizing about refreshment stands with the intensity he usually reserved for a bath at the end of a long, gory hunt. Those slushy lemonade ones in particular came close to certain orgasms on a hot day. Fuck, he wanted one of those, or a *snow cone*, more than he wanted an ice-cold beer or a new handgun for Christmas. And he bet Tobias would like them too. At the least, they would be a cool, sugary treat after a hot walk, and who *wouldn't* want that?

Jake had a vague memory of the park—he hadn't, like, taken a stroll through it, more of a drive-by when he was cruising the area—but he remembered it being big and grassy, and he'd met more than one native Boulderian (or whatever they were called) who adored it. He figured if Tobias could be awestruck by one tree, he'd enjoy a whole bunch of them.

That was, of course, before he had learned to look at things the way Tobias saw them.

When the park came into sight, Jake's first impression was not of the thick, sprawling trees, nor the open space of the lawn beyond, sloping down toward a man-made pond. His reaction was solely, *Fuck, where did all these people come from?* and then *It's a fucking Saturday, Jake Hawthorne, try remembering the days of the week sometime.*

People were everywhere—biking and running along the trails, children racing with dogs over the lawns, couples stretched out on blankets under the trees. It was practically as crowded as a Friday night karaoke bar at happy hour.

They both stopped at the sight of the crowds, and for a moment Jake couldn't look at Tobias, dreading what he would see, at how colossal of a mistake he'd made. He braced himself, prepared to say they'd had enough of a walk and could turn back. But when he glanced at Tobias's slightly paler face, his eyes were focused ahead intently, not on the ground. His left hand was clenched around his right, but he hadn't frozen yet and didn't look panicked.

Jake slid his hand in between Tobias's, loosening them.

Tobias's eyes went to him, wide and startled, and Jake offered a tight smile. "You ready to head back? There were plenty of trees the way we came, and it was, y'know, less crowded."

Tobias's brow furrowed, and his eyes dropped to the pavement, but he just looked like he was thinking about it, not retreating inside himself. "This . . . this is the park?"

"Yep. Trees, grass . . . and people. Just civvies, families, out to catch some rays and play fetch with Fido or whatever. You know, whatever basic stuff normal people do." Jake sighed. "We can always come back later, like Monday. It should be a lot emptier then."

Tobias was watching him again with that furrow of worry. He glanced at the park ahead of them, gripped Jake's hand tighter, and said, "W-we could . . . walk through it. If th-that's what you wanted to do, here. If you think—" Tobias swallowed. "That w-would be okay, with—me."

Jake unconsciously held his breath while Tobias spoke, trying to not just *hear* what he was saying but really *listen* and not miss anything. "Only if you feel up to it, Tobias. I mean— it's not like anyone's going to bother you here." *Just let them try, they'll never know what hit 'em.*

"I'm okay," Tobias said, and surely that determination was enough courage to see them through. Even with—Jake took a moment to appreciate the irony—a walk in the park.

It wasn't so bad once they stepped onto the dirt path under the trees. Tobias wasn't looking around as freely as he had before they were confronted by the Boulderites, but he seemed to be holding it together pretty well. Biting back the urge to start rambling, Jake swept his gaze over the walking options ahead of them and chose a clearing a little farther down as their first marker.

Joggers passed them, but Tobias only twitched closer to Jake's side when a man wearing short shorts and headphones ran toward them with two decent-sized Dobermans in tow. Jake moved to the far side of the path, putting plenty of space between them, and the dogs passed with barely a sniff in their direction.

Tobias was mesmerized by the people, the trees, the occasional bird singing or mouse-squirrel-thing scampering around, but Jake was on the lookout for more diversions, a backup plan of keep-Tobias-smiling. Jake didn't like his odds with the Frisbee throwers, the spandex-clad exercisers, or the stoned-looking smokers hanging out around one bench, but just as he was getting a little nervous, he saw a couple of kids. A small girl in muddy overalls licked at a chocolate ice cream cone dripping with chocolate syrup and rainbow sprinkles as she crouched near one corner of the bench, staring intensely at a line of ants. An older boy sat on the bench and swung his feet while spooning up strawberry ice cream from a small cup. He seemed to be enjoying it, but Jake guessed he was her brother by the way he always kept an eye on the little girl, even when carefully scraping drops of ice cream away from the edge. Some kind of family, at the very least.

But more important than the kids, there was ice cream, which would satisfy Jake's desire for something cold *and* give Tobias the thrill of his life (so far).

"Hey there," Jake said to the kids, as he and Tobias drifted closer. He noticed Tobias twitching when he spoke, pulling a little bit away from the children, making sure that Jake was firmly between them. Jake let him—he had no problem being Tobias's shield—and smiled at the kids, nodding his chin at the ice cream. "Where'd you get those?"

The boy's eyes narrowed suspiciously on Jake, abandoning even the allure of ice cream, but the girl gave him a look that made it clear he was a complete idiot. She gave the cone another lick, and then pointed with one syrupy hand at a food stall labeled Two Spoons about a hundred feet away. "Right over there."

Jake wasn't sure how a kid no more than six could make him feel mentally deficient. "Yeah? It's the real deal?"

The boy set his ice cream bowl carefully on the bench and slid forward, ready to engage. "Who wants to know?"

The girl ignored him and shrugged with exaggerated nonchalance. "It's okay."

"Yeah, thanks." Jake decided that discretion was the better part of valor—and ice cream was more important than getting into a fistfight with an overprotective eight-year-old—and gently steered Tobias toward the ice cream stand.

They were fifty feet away when Two Spoons got swarmed out of nowhere by what looked like half the student body of the University of Boulder. Loud, exuberant college kids. Jake realized, abruptly, that this was a prime example of a situation he should not drag Tobias into.

He stopped, hand on Tobias's elbow as he assessed the situation. They had just reached a neat clearing with a shallow amphitheater set into the ground. Some women sat chatting on the steps opposite as a couple small children played in the middle. The Frisbee kids were on the other side of the clearing, closer to the tree line, and there were trees. Lots of benign, gently rustling trees. Everyone was minding their own business.

Jake turned to Tobias, keeping his hands lightly on his arm. "Hey, I'm going to go get us some ice cream, but just stay here, okay? I don't want you to have to mess with those kids. I'll be right over there and then back in two seconds. You'll be able to see me the whole time. And then, man, are you in for the treat of your lifetime because waffles are the *best* but ice cream is the second best. Does that sound okay? Because if it's not, we can get it together or . . . skip it, for today at least."

He could see the hint of panic creeping into Tobias's face, but he swallowed and nodded once, and Jake was so damn proud of him. He squeezed Tobias's arm once before walking away quickly. The quicker he went, the sooner he'd be back.

~

As Tobias watched Jake go, he tried to suppress the feeling that the park was expanding in every direction to swallow him, dozens of other reals suddenly closer to him than Jake was. But Jake was counting on him to handle this, and Tobias had to show he could. Jake didn't have to hold his hand every time they stepped out of the apartment. Tobias just had to do as Jake said and . . . stay where he was.

But he already knew that standing in one spot and staring at his feet was conspicuous behavior in the real world and something Jake wanted him to stop. So he took a deep breath, pushed his hands carefully into his jeans pockets, and looked around.

No one was staring yet. The three reals about Jake's age continued throwing their disc back and forth, the women on the steps chatted on. Beyond the clearing, children shrieked in happiness as they called for pets or parents. Tobias had been immensely relieved when those dogs earlier hadn't gone after him. Victor had once told him that all dogs knew how to run down monsters, but maybe some reals' dogs hadn't been trained or encountered enough freaks.

"Amy, I want a turn! Give it to me!"

Tobias turned to see two kids near the edge of the lawn— one girl maybe a couple of years younger than him, and a smaller girl beside her. The older girl was running backward, away from her, holding her hands up and watching the sky. Following his gaze, Tobias couldn't stop his mouth from dropping open. A large birdlike creature fluttered—no, not alive, he saw a moment later, though it shivered, dipped, and swayed like a living thing—against the flawlessly blue sky, its skin a patchwork design of the brightest colors he had ever seen, the whole thing somehow hovering above the tree line, controlled from below. Tobias took a few cautious steps closer while the thing wavered and twisted under the bickering children's haphazard control, never letting him get a good look at it.

"Hey, watch out!"

Tobias turned just in time to see an object hurtling toward his head, and he threw himself out of the way. Instinct, honed by years of surviving monster brawls and guard abuse, had him rolling when he hit the ground, twisting to get back to his feet as quickly as possible to face, assess, and deal with (or submit to) the threat before it took his head off with a second projectile.

But instinct had never had to deal with variable terrain, and when he tried to regain his balance, his foot slipped off the edge of the top step.

He fell down the stairs. For a second, he fought with the conflicting need to get away from the threat and panic at the idea of getting farther away from Jake, before the knowledge that he wasn't going to stop until he reached the bottom made him focus on simply surviving the moment.

Hitting the stone ground hurt, but he'd had worse. Tobias focused on pushing himself to his hands and knees and breathing, cataloging damage, seeing what handicaps he'd have in whatever happened next. He kept his eyes closed—easier not to be identified as a threat if he didn't look at reals, same as guards —and tried to catch his breath.

Distantly, he heard laughter, followed by someone yelling, "Don't be a jackass, Andy!" but no one seemed to be chasing him down right away. Projectiles were good, sometimes—if you could survive the first one—because they provided time to recover before the enemy arrived.

Scraped hands, bruised back, one elbow throbbing from bashing it into a stair, and a pain flared in his left ankle every time he tried to move. Fuck. So much for being able to take care of himself for two minutes. When Jake realized he had moved, found out how useless Tobias was, he was going to—

When he heard footsteps approaching, he pulled his legs in to protect his stomach and tried to shift to put his back against the stairs he'd fallen down. He kept his eyes closed and his arms on the ground, hoping that the person would just keep walking and wasn't coming to kick him. Not that that wasn't their right—and he couldn't so much as touch them without maybe losing a hand—but he could hope.

When a worried, female voice right above him said, "Honey, are you hurt?" his eyes snapped open.

The woman from the other side of the stairs was bending down to touch him, her shoulder-length brown hair close enough to swing into his face.

He couldn't stop himself from shoving backward, away from the threat, even though that just scraped his back—and his new shirt from Jake, damn damn damn—along the concrete of the stairs. He had to stop himself. He couldn't run away from reals, not when he didn't know if they were from the ASC, not when he didn't know where Jake was, but he couldn't stop himself.

It only got worse when three reals appeared on the top of the steps. They were *behind* him, he was cornered, and when Jake found him . . . Tobias forced himself to stop, digging his fingers into the thin creases in the blocks of the stairs and willing himself to stay still. It wouldn't be worse if he stayed still than if he tried to run and didn't actually have an escape. His best—only—hope right now was that Jake would come soon. Jake had to come soon.

"Hey, you okay?" the young woman at the top of the steps called. "Sorry about that, we weren't trying to hit you."

Tobias closed his eyes and tucked his chin close to his chest. His best option now was to stay silent, to avoid any questions the reals might ask. Maybe that way they wouldn't know, wouldn't call the ASC, and he wouldn't have gotten Jake into trouble (*and end up back in Freak Camp*). That plan had a modicum of hope. He didn't automatically look like a freak, didn't have vampire fangs or the full-body, genetic tattoos of a djinn. And the shirts Jake had bought for him had high necks so no one could see his scarring unless the collar was jerked down.

But beneath the surface of his calculations, he knew that none of that mattered because he was a freak. They would be able to see right through him. They were reals and they would know and jerk away in horror, and their outrage that he had ever tried to pass himself off as one of them would sweep out of them, and the ASC would be close, maybe one of those very same people who watched him now, and they would drag him back to Freak Camp because *Jake wasn't there.*

Please, please go away.

It didn't work. The woman knelt beside him, right by him, and her voice went even softer. "Where does it hurt? Did you break something?" She reached for the arm he held against his chest, and Tobias couldn't hold back a sharp noise of protest as he pushed himself back again.

"What's wrong with him?" someone above muttered.

"Shhhh. I think he's, like, special needs."

They were figuring it out. Tobias curled over on himself, forehead almost touching his knees, but through his hair he could see the woman staying where she was, raising her hands, palms out. "Okay," she said, voice level. "Sweetie, I'm not going to hurt you. Can you tell me if there's someone I can call? Do you have a card?"

Tobias had no idea how to respond, but he didn't have to. Right then, he heard pounding steps over the grass and a shout of "Tobias!"

He sagged in relief, though he didn't raise his head even when Jake leaped down to the stones beside him. Jake might be angry at him for being so clumsy and stupid and drawing so much attention, but at least he'd make the reals go away.

"Tobias—" Jake took hold of his shoulders, tight but without squeezing to hurt, and Tobias let out another shaky exhale. "Tobias, I'm so sorry. I saw you fall from the stand and —shit, are you hurt?"

Tobias shook his head.

"His elbow's bleeding," the woman said, gesturing slightly, as though hoping Tobias wouldn't notice the motion.

Jake released his shoulder to look at his arm and swore again.

"Hey, dude," one of the reals from above called. "I don't think you should leave your friend alone, especially if he's, like, slow."

"He is not—" Now, Jake sounded furious. "Don't you have some weed to smoke, asswipe? Get lost."

Muttering, they moved off. Jake twisted around to look at the woman next, though he kept a firm grip on Tobias's other shoulder, anchoring him.

"Looks like your friend needs some help," she said, tone unfathomable. "Is he yours?"

"Yes," Jake snapped without hesitation, hand tightening. Though Tobias had no idea what the consequences of this fiasco would be, he still felt a wave of giddy relief as Jake claimed him.

"Well, my sister Janet manages the bagel store on the corner, and I know they have a fully stocked first aid kit. We could go over there to get him fixed up. It won't be a problem."

"I—" Jake began, then stopped. Tobias remained motionless, forehead to his knee, barely daring to breathe. "Yeah," Jake said finally. "That would be great, thanks. Tobias, can you get up?"

Tobias nodded, but Jake still reached under his arms to

help him stand. Tobias sucked in his breath, tested his weight on his ankle, and wobbled.

"Shit," Jake said again. "Did you twist your ankle?"

Tobias hesitated, unwilling to lie directly, not sure anyway if it was true.

"Can he walk?" the real woman asked.

Tobias nodded. He had managed under much worse. To his shock, though, Jake didn't move away, but stepped beside him and slid an arm under his shoulders.

"C'mon, Toby, lean on me. It's not far, is it?"

"Not at all." She turned to lead the way back up the stairs. She scooped up one of the toddlers on her way and said something to her friend before waiting for Tobias and Jake at the top.

Tobias could have been up the stairs—especially if he had been permitted to drop to his hands—in a couple seconds, but it took longer with Jake supporting him. Hurt less too. Tobias swallowed, forced himself to move past the astounding sensation of Jake so close, *supporting* him, to take advantage of the reals being out of earshot. "I'm sorry."

"For what?" Jake snapped. "Falling? Not your fault. I shouldn't have left, I'm the one who fucked up. Goddammit. Don't listen to those douchewads, Tobias, they're just assholes who don't know anything."

It took him a few seconds to realize what Jake was talking about. "Better than the t-truth," he said quietly, and Jake stiffened, stopping them both for a moment, while the woman waited patiently, bouncing her toddler on her hip.

"Well, we'll have a talk about that when we get home," he said at last, and Tobias's skin went clammy and cold, everything swimming before he regained his balance. He wouldn't panic yet about that. Their first destination was a *bagel shop*.

"I'm Maryann, by the way," the woman ahead of them called. "And this little soldier is Thomas."

"Jake. And this is Tobias."

"Are you boys new to Boulder? Students?"

"No—well, yeah, we just moved here, but we're not students. Just . . . looking for a fresh start."

Maryann's cheerful tone didn't waver. "Well, you've come to the right place. Boulder's a good town, not as crazy and crowded as Denver or a lot of other college towns. We do have the occasional fun surprises from the frat boys, but they try to balance it out with volunteer work. And in summer, they're not too bad on the eyes." She grinned. "Now, don't you tell my husband I said that or get any ideas yourself. I'm taken. Whereabouts in town do you live?"

Jake named the cross streets nearest them, and Maryann chatted on about her favorite places around the city—mainly the hiking trails, Boulder Creek, and the Underwater Fish Observatory—as they crossed the street to Moe's Broadway Bagels. Tobias kept his eyes on the pavement the whole way, but he had to glance up as they reached the door, which opened with a cheery bell chime.

The shop was packed with small round tables, reals crammed around, most of them drinking from paper cups, eating strangely shaped round bread, and talking animatedly. Some glanced their way, but no one so much as hesitated in their conversation.

Maryann headed to the back while they hovered awkwardly by the door. Jake shifted, adjusting his grip under Tobias's arm, and exhaled as though about to speak, but he didn't say anything. Tobias bit back the urge to apologize again for ruining their day. Jake didn't seem to like it when he said sorry, no matter how he'd messed up.

Maryann reappeared a moment later, beckoning them through a swinging door in the back, where a large woman—maybe a couple of inches shorter than Jake, and about twice his width—had already opened up a large first aid kit on the counter.

"Boys, this is my sister, Janet. Janet, Tobias and Jake. Tobias had a tumble down those steps in the park."

"Those stairs are a death trap." Janet sighed, popping open a bag of cotton balls. "I just know one day I'm going to see a kid fall and break his head open and then folks are going to come crying to me and I'll have to bite my tongue on all the I-told-you-sos just so they keep buying the bagels. Go ahead, take a seat."

Tobias froze at the idea of leaving Jake's side, not sure if he should obey orders from other reals, but Jake nudged him toward the chair. Tobias dropped into it, feeling his stomach clench and his head start up a steady stream of mostly incoherent panic. But Jake had as good as *told* him to. He took a bracing breath and held onto the edges of his seat like staying in place now would make up for how much he had fucked up the day.

"Where'd you get hurt, Tobias?" Janet asked.

Tobias darted a look toward Jake, who was watching him with a familiar frown, though there was something else about it that Tobias couldn't read. That look squeezed his chest hard, like Victor pressing his boot down to hold him in place.

"I think his elbow got pretty beat up," Maryann said from the doorway, bouncing Thomas gently on her hip. She was watching Tobias too. Jake and two reals focusing on *him*.

Janet reached for him, taking hold of his wrist with one hand as she began pulling up his shirtsleeve with the other, and he couldn't help himself. He didn't try to pull away—he knew what happened when someone resisted—but he made a pathetic, half-choked whimper as he turned his head and body away. *No, not in front of Jake, please don't . . .*

"Hey, hey," Jake said, moving forward quickly. "Let me do that."

His fingers replaced Janet's, much gentler and more familiar, and Tobias steadied himself, breathing a little easier. He felt mortified, distantly aware this was not the way he should be behaving and that there would be horrible *consequences* that he deserved. But for now, at least, he had Jake's hands back on him, and that alone was reassuring. He would never balk from whatever Jake wanted to do with him.

Janet stepped closer to her sister, and the two women whispered together while Jake turned Tobias's arm gently to bring his elbow to light. Tobias couldn't hear what they were saying, but after a moment, Maryann turned back to them. "We'll give you boys some space to clean up," she said, still cheerful, and they and the little boy moved out, letting the door swing shut behind them.

Tobias let out his first full exhale, dropping his head to his chest. Jake's hand was immediately on his cheek, tilting his face back up. "Hey, Tobias. Tobias. No one here's going to hurt you."

Tobias swallowed hard, forcing his eyes to stay on Jake's. "I'm sorry," he said, unable to help it. "I'm so sorry—"

"Stop that." Jake's fingers tightened on his face in emphasis, and Tobias flinched and dropped his gaze. "No, look—you've got to stop thinking everything is your fault. You fell. It was an accident. I'm not *mad* because you got hurt or because you're still spooked around other people. I just want you to believe that these civilians don't want to hurt you. They're trying to help, that's all. You've got to trust them."

Drawing a shaky breath, Tobias nodded, even though he knew he was falling apart. He couldn't do what Jake asked. He only barely believed Jake was telling him this because he trusted Jake to tell him the truth.

"Hey." Jake's voice got even softer. "You believe me, don't you?"

He could tell that Tobias didn't, and Tobias was losing control fast now. Fuck, this day had started so *well*. He sniffed hard, drawing his hand up to press his thumb and fingers into his eyes. "J-just—if any of them knew the t-truth, Jake—"

"Aw, Toby." Jake moved closer, his arms folding around Tobias's back, bringing his head against Tobias's shoulder. It was that *holding* thing again, the last thing Tobias deserved at this point, and it was so bizarre, erasing the last particles of sense in Tobias's world, that it broke him the rest of the way. Tobias collapsed, shoulders shaking as he cried into Jake's shirt, and Jake didn't let him go. He kept repeating *he* was sorry, and he wouldn't leave Tobias alone again.

Tobias got a hold of himself before long. A few deep breaths, clenching his hand in the front of Jake's shirt, and then he pulled himself up, wiping his eyes.

Jake still touched him, drawing his thumb down his cheek, close to the corner of his mouth. "It's gonna get better." He sounded like he was telling himself as much as Tobias. "It'll get better, I promise."

Jake rolled up Tobias's sleeve, pressing a wet tissue to the bloody patch of skin, and opened a bottle of rubbing alcohol to dip a cotton ball in. "This'll burn a bit," he said quietly, meeting Tobias's gaze. "Sorry, I just want to get it clean. It'll be worse otherwise."

Tobias nodded and prepared himself but, like yesterday with the scratches, hardly felt it when Jake touched the cotton to his skin. Jake watched him, brow knit, but said nothing until he finished pressing a large bandage into place.

"There." He sat back on his heels, though he didn't look satisfied. His eyes landed on Tobias's extended leg. "Oh, yeah, your ankle." He grabbed a cold pack from the kit, cracked it sharply over his thigh, then moved to feel Tobias's ankle, between his sock and pants cuff. Tobias's leg twitched involuntarily. "That hurt?"

"No," Tobias said automatically, then forced himself to focus. "It's just—a little throb by the ankle. Doesn't hurt right now."

"Yeah, but it will when you stand up." Jake set the pack in

place—the cold immediately seeping through Tobias's sock—and wrapped a length of gauze around it to keep it in place. "Okay?" He looked up at him.

Tobias nodded, and Jake got to his feet, reaching to brush the back of his hand along the curve of Tobias's cheek. "It's gonna be okay," he repeated. "We'll be all right." He dropped his hand. "I'm gonna go tell them we're done, okay? And then we'll catch a bus or something back to our side of town. I'll be just on the other side of the door the whole time, I promise."

Tobias nodded again, eyes down.

Jake hesitated a moment before stepping away. When the door swung shut behind him, Tobias had to fight the panic crawling up his throat. This time he wouldn't move. He wouldn't so much as flinch, no matter what happened (it was unlikely something else would come flying at his head, but not impossible), because he had to be here when Jake came back. Tobias curled his arm on the edge of the counter, leaning his head against it, and listened to Jake talk.

"Hey, thanks for everything, we're all finished. Let me give you something for the supplies we took—"

"No, no, absolutely not. This is the least I can do for two kids new to Boulder."

"No, really—"

"Put it away, hon. You ain't giving me a penny. Look, you really want to pay me back, come around sometime and have some bagels and coffee. When your friend's feeling better."

"So—" That was Maryann's voice, quiet, worried, but with a layer of steel under the surface. "What's the story?"

Despite himself, Tobias tensed. He knew Jake wouldn't tell these reals the truth and put either of them in that situation, but he didn't know what Jake could say to explain how messed up, how *freakish* Tobias clearly was.

This is all your fault because you can't act normal for a minute, just making trouble, he'll be sick of you so soon.

But Jake was already answering, hardly a pause. "Tobias had a really rough time growing up. His mom disappeared when he was just a toddler, and he went through a whole string of foster homes. None of them should have ever been given a goldfish, much less a kid. Down in Louisiana, you know, the whole system's screwed up there. My dad works in social services, so I met Tobias a bunch of times when he was getting reprocessed after the latest batch of shitheads—well, I know he doesn't look it, small for his age, but he just turned eighteen. I promised him he could stay with me while he got on his feet."

"Damn them and bless his heart," Janet muttered. "I knew it couldn't be anything good, the way he was jumping, but something like that . . . Poor kid."

"Bless *your* heart for taking him in," Maryann said. "Few boys your age would take on a responsibility like that."

"Yeah, well—" Now, Jake sounded embarrassed, unlike the smooth, convincing flow of his cover story. "It's just, Tobias. I mean. We kinda—"

"That's all right." Maryann's tone had a slight current of amusement. "You don't have to explain to us. Just keep on taking good care of him."

"Of course." Jake sounded sure again. "Hey, just one more thing. We walked down from our place, and I thought we'd just walk back, but now . . . Do you know what bus will take us by 20th and Pine?"

"Oh, don't worry about it, hon," Janet said. "I can give you a ride home myself."

"No, seriously, you don't have to—"

"Please, let me. These layabouts can handle the store without me for, what, half an hour, tops? And it'll be easier on your boy too. He's already been through a lot today. An afternoon bus can scare the bejeezus out of anyone, and if you're still learning the system . . . I insist."

"Not to pressure you into anything," Maryann interjected.

"Do whatever seems best for you both. The Number 14 bus can also get you to that area, and there's a stop for it right around the corner."

"Well—" Jake sounded torn. "I wouldn't normally, but—since you offered—it'd probably be better to take on public transport some other day."

"Not a problem. I'll tell Dan I'm heading out, then I'll pull my car around."

Jake came back into the office, and Tobias tilted his head up, relief making him dizzy. "You heard that, Toby?"

He nodded, and Jake crouched down to meet his eyes. "That okay with you? Tell me if it isn't, and we'll work something else out."

Tobias tried to smile, though he wasn't sure it came out right. "'S fine, Jake."

"Okay." Jake rested his hand on Tobias's knee, sending good shivers through his body that he hoped didn't show. "We'll be home soon."

BY THE TIME they got into the backseat of Janet's Honda, Tobias seemed pretty zoned out. He sat with his hands between his knees and head limp against the head rest behind him, eyes partly shut, staring out the window, apparently without registering anything passing by. Despite himself, Jake kept glancing at him every few seconds.

Janet kept up an easy monologue that required little or no participation, pointing out Boulder sights, alternately bashing and praising the neighbors and local government. When they stopped on their block, Jake leaned forward and pulled out his wallet. "At least let me tip you for being an ace tour guide."

Janet chuckled. "Excellent. That'll let me break even on these bagels." She grabbed a five from Jake's hand and handed him a heavy brown bag with a Moe's Broadway logo. Jake almost dropped it from the weight.

"This is way too much." No way he was holding just five dollars' worth of bagels.

"Nope. That's the plan, kid. Do a good deed, get the new kids addicted to the bagels. Net gain of karma *and* new customers. Come by the shop again when you're feeling better, yeah?" She winked. "And if you need a fix before then, give us a call. We deliver for the cute ones."

Despite himself, Jake chuckled. "Will do. C'mon, Tobias." He reached back toward him, hesitating before he made contact, not sure how Tobias would react.

But the second he heard his name, Tobias jumped from utter stillness to scrambling for the door handle. He paused outside the Honda as Jake got out, and Jake lifted a hand toward Janet before he helped Tobias up their stairs and back over the salt lines.

"You look wiped," Jake said, putting the bag of bagels on the table and resisting the urge to brush Tobias's hair away from his eyes. He didn't need to see Tobias flinch again today. "You wanna, uh, lay down for a while, rest up?"

Tobias blinked slowly, eyes not moving from a spot above Jake's right shoulder. Jake wondered if he had hit his head in the fall and the effects were only now kicking in.

"Sure you're not hurt anywhere else?"

"No—I mean, yes, I . . ." Tobias touched his forehead, looking confused, lost. Finally, he said, even more softly, "I'll go lie down."

"Okay, Tobias," Jake said, a little too heartily, and winced at himself. "You do that."

Once Tobias disappeared into his room, Jake went to the kitchen for a beer. He knew by now Tobias would be out for the next few hours at least. Hell, he didn't expect anything less after the day they'd had (Jake's fault *again*), and he might easily pass out himself if he lay down, but that wasn't an option. He had to try to unwind a little, or he didn't know how he'd be able to handle . . . whatever would happen when Tobias got up.

He set the beer on the counter, reached to twist the top off, and paused, looking at it. Then he put the bottle away and got out his single trusty shot glass and the bottle of Jack in the back of the cabinet. He poured himself a generous fingerful, tossed it back, followed quickly by a second. He started for a third pour, then stopped, looked at the label, and set the bottle down. He screwed the cap back on and shoved the bottle into the cabinet before deliberately stepping out of the kitchen.

There weren't a lot of options to keep himself occupied in the apartment, but the last thing Jake could do now was step out without telling Tobias—or hell, even suggest that to him. He turned the TV on low, more for the background noise than to watch anything, and spread everything from his weapons duffel over the living room floor.

He was barely on his backup machete—damn thing didn't need to be cleaned *or* sharpened, but Jake desperately needed something to do with his hands—when he heard a low thump. He froze, his senses straining to identify the source of the sound (could be a garbage truck that didn't run in the afternoon, or neighbors above on a floor that didn't exist), his mind running through all possible defenses. Plenty of ready weapons spread over the coffee table and the floor, salt stored in the lower shelf with the holy water.

By the second low thump, he knew it was coming from Tobias's room.

Jake didn't register getting up. He didn't notice dropping the cleaning cloth or switching the machete to his right hand. He barely stopped himself from barreling through Tobias's door at full speed and taking out whatever evil son of a bitch supernatural fucker was threatening him. The only thing that stopped him was the knowledge that ghosts were *not* the only thing that went bump in the night, and that Jake entering a room with a knife in his hand would likely be even more terrifying.

"Tobias?" he called at the cracked-open door, trying to make his voice normal, even though his throat was clenching and he wanted to growl, wanted to say something in Latin, or beg Tobias to answer him.

He got nothing. Silence. He couldn't hear anything but his own breathing and the beating of his heart.

Cautiously, more terrified than he had been in years—since he thought his dad could beat all the monsters without breaking a sweat—he pushed on the door. "Tobias?"

It squeaked open, and Jake poked his head through. Stupid fucking move, opening his head for an attack like that from anyone standing on the other side. But he couldn't just walk in waving a weapon. Not unless he knew for sure this was a threat and not his own late-breaking psychosis.

Tobias was on the bed, on top of the covers, the line of his back and the planes of his face unmistakable. He was curled up on his side, staring at Jake, his eyes wide.

It seemed to take a second before Tobias realized he was staring. When he did—Jake could practically see the realization on his face—he dropped his eyes, turning his head to bury his face in the covers.

"Tobias?" Jake took a cautious—and possibly fatal, he kept expecting an attack—step into the room.

He barely heard the reply. "I'm sorry," Tobias whispered. "I'm so sorry."

"Tobias, what—" Jake glanced around. The corners were empty, the shadows looked normal, everything seemed to be in place. Then, still moving cautiously, he came to the edge of the bed, set his weapon on the floor—ignoring the little voice that sounded an awful lot like his father telling him he was a fucking idiot for letting go of his weapon—and sat next to Tobias. He took a deep breath. "Toby, are you okay?"

Tobias got out a couple more low *I'm sorrys* before the question seemed to sink in. "I'm f-fine," he said, mostly into the covers.

If Da—Roger had tried to give him shit like that, Jake would have snarled that he wasn't a fucking idiot, but . . . fuck.

"Were you hurt somewhere I couldn't see?" A fall down stone stairs could leave bruises, sprains, internal injuries Jake couldn't have seen from the quick check he gave Tobias at the bagel shop. Tobias could have been bleeding for two hours and Jake wouldn't have known. He couldn't stop his hand from sliding over Tobias's wrist, not holding but just touching the new gauze covering it. "Tobias, if you were hurt, you need—"

"I s-s-swear to you, Jake, I w-wouldn't l-l-lie to you."

Tobias was curling tighter into a ball as Jake sat next to him, the wrist beneath his hand perhaps the only thing that hadn't moved, hadn't tightened protectively. Jake wanted to hug him, wanted to tell him it was okay, but he didn't even know what this was, and the hunter in him had to ask the questions that he maybe didn't want an answer to. "I came in because there was a thumping sound. Did you hear that, or did I . . ."

Tobias flinched and turned his face completely into the pillow. His shoulders were shaking.

Jake didn't need to hear what Tobias was saying to know. When he gently turned him over, the *I'm sorry* hit him like a blow. Even though it might not have been a good idea, even though Tobias hadn't exactly reacted great the last time few times Jake had held him, doing nothing felt far worse.

Jake pulled him up, into his arms, and held him while Tobias shook. "Shhhh, it's okay."

"I'm sorry I'm such a *freak*." Tobias jerked in his arms from the force of the word, rocking the bed against the bedside table with a thud. "I'm sorry I c-c-can't stop. I'm sorry."

Thumping noise. Okay, good, not a monster coming

through the window and the salt lines to kill them. Just Tobias. Fuck.

"It's okay, Tobias," Jake repeated, and let himself touch Tobias's head, stroking his hair. He was pretty sure that any second now he was going to throw up or start bawling himself, but for right now he was going to hold onto the shallow, meaningless words and pray to something that maybe Tobias would hear him. "It's fine."

"I c-can't stop, I t-t-try and they can s-s-see and I c-c-can't stop and I c-c-can't even be al-l-lone five m-minutes and I'm fucking it up and please, Jake, j-just make it g-go away, d-don't—"

"Tobias!" Jake felt horrible for shaking him, even just a little against his shoulder, but he was terrified that if he didn't get through to Tobias *now*, he never would. There would be no way to get past this thing that he didn't understand, didn't have a handle on, and was spinning out of control. "Tobias, what are you talking about?"

"In the p-park when I—you s-said, when they kn-knew, that w-we—" Tobias turned his face into Jake's shoulder and kept shuddering, breathing so irregularly Jake wondered if he was about to hyperventilate. "You h-have to—p-p-p-please, Jake, I'm s-so sorry, I d-d-don't want to, I j-just c-can't—p-p-please, Jake, p-please."

Jake felt a muscle in his jaw jump. Another thing he had done to break Tobias without even being aware of it. Great. Wonderful. Perfect. If he left now to throw up, Tobias would fall over, and it seemed like he had managed to get a grip on Jake's shirt that Jake doubted he would be able to shake. Those were the only two things keeping him still against the new wave of panic and sick disgust at himself. "It's okay, Tobias," he repeated hollowly.

"Please s-stop me, Jake. Please f-f-*fix* me. I j-just can't stop— stop being a freak."

Jake's stomach clenched. "Tobias, you're not . . . It's okay." He kept his hand moving in Tobias's hair slow and even. He wished that he could be somewhere else, that someone else could deal with this. But there wasn't. And, honestly, when Tobias was collapsing, would he really let anyone else hold him like this or say anything that could mess him up even more? "You're one of the least freaky people I know."

Tobias shook his head violently against Jake's shoulder. "B-but they s-s-still knew. They still *knew*. I'm s-s-s—"

Startled, Jake straightened and rested his hand on Tobias's cheek, turning his face to Jake's. "Tobias, no one knew."

"They d-did."

Jake closed his eyes and leaned his forehead against Tobias's. In that moment he wanted to hunt down the Frisbee bastards—an accident, just a fucking accident—and feed them their own feet. He wanted to have actually read the books he was assigned in school or to have watched more chick flicks, because maybe then he would have the words to tell Tobias that it wasn't true when, according to some bastards with shit for brains, it was. So that he could tell Tobias he wasn't a freak and put the conviction of his own heart into it, without thinking about what other people would say. Because Tobias wasn't a freak to him, Tobias was *Tobias*, Tobias was *everything*, but he knew that wouldn't matter to too many people in the world, and he doubted that his own word was enough.

"They didn't know anything," he said at last, heavily. "They saw a . . . a kid, lost, maybe a little . . . scared, but they did *not* see a freak, because you're not one."

Tobias shook his head again. "Jake, you c-can't believe that, you can't l-let your guard d-d—"

"Tobias, shut up." Jake hadn't meant to say that, but dammit. He brushed his fingertips over Tobias's cheek, rested one hand on the back of his neck as he held him. "Shit, I didn't mean that. But you're not a freak to me, ever."

"Then w-w-what..."

"You're Tobias. My Tobias." He sounded like a fucking possessive psycho, but he meant it. And the second he said it, Tobias sagged into his arms a little more, not so much relaxing as collapsing against him. "It's okay. I'm here, I'll always be here, I promise." And to himself, Jake made another promise that the second Tobias didn't want him there, he would be gone. Tobias just had to say the word, and Jake would leave, no questions asked.

No. Fuck that. There would be questions. Like, how much money Tobias needed and where he was going to stay and if he needed a way to get there and if he would really be okay. But that wasn't Jake letting this crazy obsession control him. That was just taking care of Tobias, who owned far more of Jake's twisted little heart than made any sense.

"You'll tell me," Tobias whispered. "You'll t-tell me the s-second I'm t-t-too much. I c-can't change, Jake, but if you t-teach me..."

"You're not too much, you're *never* too much." Jake hoped that Tobias believed it. He could never be the problem. It wasn't that he was too much, but that Jake wasn't enough for him. Not enough for anybody.

"I h-hate... I'm n-not always useless. I s-swear, I can be u-useful, I j-just... I j-just c-can't control... anything. I could d-*do* anything, n-not j-just—"

Jake's grip around Tobias tightened. He hoped he wasn't hurting him, because he wasn't sure that he would be able to loosen his grip. "No, you are *not* a burden, and not useless, get that out of your head. You've gotta quit beating yourself up for this. This isn't a fucking cakewalk. This is major shit that you're —that we're dealing with, getting you out of that hellhole. It's going to be rough, but I'm here for you, and I'm not angry or any shit like that. I mean, fuck, it's only been a couple days, and you're already doing so much better. It's okay."

"N-n-not better. St-still just a st-stupid f-*freak*—"

"Tobias!" Jake wanted to kick himself when Tobias froze in his arms, when his voice cut off, but he had to fucking stop Tobias from saying something like that when it wasn't true and ripping him apart inside. "Hey, we were outside for three hours today, surrounded by a bunch of average Joes. You walked to a park, and you were there with me, man. You were even okay with me walking away from you when I went over to that stall." Fuck, Tobias still hadn't gotten any ice cream. "You were doing *great* up to the second you almost got hit in the head by a flying object and fell down a flight of stairs. It's *okay*."

Tobias's reply was almost too low to hear. "I sh-should be b-better for you. More r-reliable."

Jake wanted to laugh. Or cry. Or shoot something. But what he did was stay where he was, his arms around Tobias, holding him like that could fix everything. "Dude, most people who fall down hard-ass stairs are not as chill as you. And since this was your first time dealing with . . . fuck, anything that you did today, you did great. I'm proud of you, Toby. And it's okay. You'll get better, and the next time we go out I'm going to keep us far away from Frisbees, and baseball diamonds, and squash matches. And, dammit, you've been doing this stuff for less than a week. Any way you react is okay, got that, Tobias? It just means you're you. Not a freak."

Tobias, still not looking at him, doing little more than breathing, jerked his head. But this time it was a nod, a yes, and in that moment, it was everything they both needed.

～

Tobias knew he should probably be thinking about how lucky he was that he had Jake. How little he deserved him, how much pain he would be in if he had screwed up this much performing for the Director or a guard. He should be filled with nothing but gratitude for Jake for being so kind and forgiving that it made Tobias shake to think of all the things that Jake could do, had every *right* to do, and yet didn't, for some inexplicable reason.

Of course, he *was* thinking about all that because his brain hadn't stopped going a mile a minute since they'd gotten back to the apartment. Then Jake had entered holding the machete —not for Tobias, thank God, though he had wondered for a few seconds if his punishment was going to start at last—and just held him.

But what he really couldn't get out of his head, as his body almost involuntarily sagged against Jake, was how the warmth of Jake's arms sank into his bones, loosening parts that maybe hadn't ever relaxed in his life. It made him want to cry and beg and just lie quietly, contentedly, all at the same time.

Jake wasn't angry at him. Jake was . . . *proud* of him for working hard—and Tobias fucking *was* trying hard, keeping himself upright by force of will alone every time Jake suggested stepping outside. It was the only thing Jake had really asked of him so far, and yet he was *still* fucking failing over and over. Jake hadn't given him any limits, hadn't told him he had a set number of times before the pain would start. He'd just said, *You'll get better, Tobias.* When he said it like that, Tobias had to believe him.

Sure, Jake had completely ignored him when Tobias had tried *again* to say that he could be useful, but he couldn't tell if Jake didn't want or need the help of a freak or if he really hadn't heard. He wanted to make it clear that he could do anything— research, blowjobs, clean, whatever Jake needed. He wished desperately that Jake would start using him so Tobias would know what he was supposed to do. But for today, it was okay if Jake didn't want to acknowledge that, because Jake was giving him the grace period Tobias had been terrified he wouldn't get. There was a learning curve, he had said as much, and Tobias didn't know when Jake would be forced to start punishing him, but at least for now, that wasn't happening. Maybe not as long as Jake could see Tobias fighting to be what Jake deserved.

Yeah, Tobias was afraid, not knowing when he would lose Jake's patience, but if there was one thing he had learned in his sixteen years, it was that he could learn. And if Jake said he had time, that a week wasn't long enough to deserve correction, then Tobias still had a chance.

That was good. That was the best, and that was what stilled his shaking and allowed him to let go of the overwhelming terror that had gripped him the second Jake had come into his room, fearing that the talk he had promised would end in pain —or worse, FREACS. But even past that deep reassurance, that *hope*, what Tobias couldn't get out of his head was the feel of Jake's warm, strong arms around him, protecting him, holding him up and not letting him go even when Tobias began to cry on his shirt and there was nothing else to say.

7

They slept in the next morning. Jake wasn't surprised that Tobias had exhausted himself into another deep sleep, but he was a little startled that he himself was still capable of sleeping nine hours straight. Without having overdone it at a bar the night before, anyway.

It wasn't like he'd had any major epiphanies—and maybe that was it, maybe since he was done stewing over everything that went down, his body was just reacting, letting him absorb each new punch and then keep going. Hell, it was as good a theory as any, and Jake was done trying to analyze and predict shit. The last six days had shown him he might as well be a civilian walking into a Chupacabra lair. He couldn't keep Tobias safe in a world that had Frisbees and Christmas movies and, shit, *people*. But that didn't mean they, he, could give up.

But what they had settled last night—and what Tobias wouldn't forget, he hoped—was that they were gonna keep rolling together. No matter how Jake fucked up, no matter what new everyday menace panicked Tobias, Jake would be there to pick up the pieces and do all he could for him. As long as they were both breathing at the end of the day, as long as Jake armed himself with one new thing he'd learned to make Tobias's life easier, he would call that a success. As hunters said, every day you survived was a day you'd earned a drink, right? Damned if that wasn't true.

As they sat down for breakfast and Jake opened Janet's bag of bagels, he tried to think not of what to avoid, but what Tobias liked, what would be *safe* for him.

Trees were good. The Eldorado was good. Security against jackasses invading Tobias's bubble was a definite plus.

Like a flash, between the act of spreading cream cheese over a cinnamon raisin bagel and raising it to his lips, the perfect solution hit: they'd go for a drive.

Fuck yeah, these bagels were delicious. Jake had never been much of a bagel man, but these were miles better than any he'd tried whenever he'd stayed somewhere with a continental breakfast. Like waffles compared to a day-old slice of bread. Maybe part of his appreciation came straight from the energy of Jake's new plan, this idea that seemed *absolutely safe*. But Tobias seemed to like the bagels too, so it couldn't just be in his head.

"Hey, wanna go for a drive?"

Jake was overwhelmingly proud of Tobias when he looked no more nervous than yesterday at the suggestion. He nodded. Jake pressed Tobias's hand, smearing his fingers with cream cheese, and tried to smile out all his happiness. Best of all, Tobias smiled back, something like relief on his face. Yeah, well, Jake was relieved too.

After throwing the dishes into the washer and getting ready to conquer the day, they went down to the car that was, after all, Jake's first home. He settled back against the leather seats and let himself relax, and he saw Tobias out of the corner of his eye doing the same thing. It still felt so good just to be with Tobias and not suspect that he was fucking all this up.

They toured Boulder, starting with the middle of the city,

weaving through downtown so Tobias could take in the colorful shops and outdoor cafes, the walking paths set through cobblestone medians lined with flowers. Then they circled around both halves of the university campus, Jake elaborating everything he knew by rumor or hearsay about college life. After that, they branched out to other parts of the city, suburbs, strip malls, and neighborhood parks. Jake was pretty sure that some of the shop owners whose establishments they passed two or three times thought he was creeping around for nefarious ends, because Jake would circle the block any time Tobias showed any interest, or even if he just noticed the soft light in Tobias's eyes that meant he had found something so foreign it was fascinating.

After getting lunch at a Burger King drive-thru, they passed an hour exploring the suburbs, with some houses set before neatly manicured lawns and others half-shrouded in turbulent greenery. The houses seemed to amaze Tobias almost as much as trees.

"There's really only one family in each house?"

"Yeah, if that. Sometimes it's just a couple and a dog or something."

"It's just like the books," Tobias whispered.

The only rough spot hit when Jake asked him how he was liking the day.

"I love it," Tobias said. "I love being . . . here. With y-you. It's s-so safe."

Jake patted the Eldorado's dash. "I love her too." *And I love being with you, Tobias.* "Gas mileage sucks, but I wouldn't trade her in for anything in the world. Dad—you know, it's been in the family for a while. And it's fucking awesome to know you can go anywhere and do anything whenever you want. You should've seen me before when I had to take the fucking bus home from hunts when D—Leon wasn't around. It sucked. They give you such weird looks if you have any kind of blood spatter or monster goo on a bus. I had to make up a lot of shit about wild dogs and falling out of trees." Then another idea struck, and Jake grinned at him. "Hey, you're sixteen! That's when kids get their licenses. I'll teach you how to drive her."

The offer didn't get the reaction he'd hoped for. Tobias snapped his head around, eyes large and luminous with horror. His voice shook as badly as it had the night before when he said, "You—you don't m-mean—*your car*—"

Jake made a sharp turn into an empty driveway, stopping crooked a few inches before the gray garage door, and had the engine shut off before Tobias could get out another choked word.

"Tobias." Jake reached for Tobias's hand, appalled that he had done something else to set him off. But this had to just be a misunderstanding. "Hey, it's okay, there's no rush, we're not gonna tackle that today. I'm just saying—I'll take you through the paces when you're up for it. There's not many I'd let behind the wheel, but I trust you."

If anything, Tobias looked twice as upset, lifting his free hand up in a fist to his forehead and shaking his head rapidly. "Jake, no, no, I *can't*—"

If Jake had thought Tobias was close to hyperventilating the night before, that was nothing compared to now, when Tobias was clearly, all too familiarly, on the edge of another panic attack. Quickly, Jake slid closer, taking a gentle hold of Tobias's free hand and rubbing his back with his other hand.

"Tobias," he said, repeating it a few more times, steady and soft, to make sure he was getting through. "Hey, it's okay, I'm not going to make you do anything. You don't have to drive until you want to. It's fine, it's fine, we're okay." A distant part of him was chilled at how routine this already was, how it was no longer surprising to have to pull Tobias back from a panic attack out of the blue.

Tobias calmed down gradually, taking deep breaths and

resting—not grinding—his forehead in his palm, elbow braced on the door. His eyelashes were damp with tears. "You can't," he still whispered, and he sounded so broken that Jake swore he could feel his own heart crack. "You *can't* t-trust m-me, please d-don't do that."

Jake didn't say anything. He leaned in instead and tugged Toby to his side.

They sat for a while longer, Jake rubbing Tobias's all-too-frail shoulders with the occasional "It's okay" and "I'm here, you're safe" and any other light, reassuring phrase that occurred to him. He waited until Tobias's breathing had returned to normal before letting go of his hand and leaning back into his own seat.

"No driving," Jake promised at last. He kept the *not yet* silent, and he reminded himself that the day had been going well until then, and Tobias seemed calm again, few traces of his panic left. So there was no reason to turn them back around to the apartment like he had been planning a second ago. In fact, Tobias looked more composed, maybe reassured by Jake's hand on his back or his nonsensical but steady reassurances.

Jake had a sense that a storm had passed, leaving him unscathed. Or better put, he'd managed to fight his way to the eye and the calm. There was still chaos and misery and pain all around them, but here, in this quiet space, Tobias was watching him through his lashes and breathing easier, and Jake felt better for it. Only Tobias's tight fist around the leg of his pants showed that he had even been stressed a second ago.

And shit, Tobias had done things like that even when Jake *hadn't* known that he was falling apart, so being aware of the issue was better, right? Jake hoped so, though he wasn't sure that he believed it completely.

He turned the key in the ignition again and the engine purred under his hands. But for a minute longer he stayed in the driveway of a house that wasn't his, searching for a distraction for them both. Even a topic change would be nice, though he refused to switch to the weather. Though maybe the weather *could* give him some kind of out. It was fucking hot, so he turned the AC on full blast (Tobias jumped, but in the surprised-then-interested way that Jake wrote off as "that startled me but it's fine now" and not "I'm scared out of my fucking mind"). Then Jake knew a surefire bet.

"What do you say we get some ice cream?" he asked, pulling out of the driveway. "We can cool down, get a little sugar in our veins. It's even healthy for you, all that dairy."

Tobias nodded. "A-anything you want, Jake."

Jake glanced at him, ignoring the chill the words gave him. "You've never had ice cream before either, have you?"

"No."

"Yup, didn't think so. I was going to get you some in the park but . . . yeah. Well, delayed gratification is better than just leaving you hanging, right? And, seriously, dude, ice cream is the best."

"Second best," Tobias said. "After waffles."

Jake turned his head sharply, about to gape, and then remembered he was *driving*, so he snapped back in time to swerve around some idiot practically driving in the middle of the road. But he'd needed to see how Tobias meant that. Then he had to get his heart under control, the beats coming far too irregularly because of that shy smile on Tobias's face. Dammit if he wasn't being *teased*.

"Exactly," he said. "Damn, you're smart."

Tobias practically glowed.

Following that promising turn-around, they powered through a Dairy Queen drive-thru and finally got Tobias ice cream. They ate it in the car in a mall parking lot where they could watch people and, most importantly, Tobias wouldn't have to deal with *anything*. If they couldn't be safe within this steel frame and reinforced glass, Jake didn't know that there was any place on earth that they could.

Tobias ate his sundae with infinite care, like something strange and far too wonderful would happen if he rushed through it. Watching him out of the corner of his eye, Jake felt a little bad that he had warned him about brain freeze, because it really wasn't *that* much of an issue. But another part of him loved watching Tobias scoop up small bites of vanilla and fudge, savoring and swallowing with a look of complete bliss on his face.

It was great, yeah, and such a relief to have finally pulled something off right, to give Tobias something good without crashing and wiping out the rest of the day. Jake almost couldn't believe it was possible to end on a good note. He found himself holding his breath at times as they headed west to explore the reservoirs and ranches west of Boulder city limits, bracing for the other shoe to fall . . . but it stayed okay. Better than okay. Tobias was smiling at him, shyly, but miles more relaxed than he'd been even that morning. When they got back to the apartment, Jake whipped together a quick meal of mac 'n' cheese with hot dogs, and they played cards for the next couple of hours, until bedtime.

Monday, Jake decided to take on a different challenge. He didn't ask Tobias to leave the house. They had a leisurely breakfast, Jake nudged Tobias toward the bookcase, and a minute later Tobias was curled up on the end of the sofa with the Norton anthology propped on his legs.

Jake took it easy for a little while longer. He settled on the floor with his back to the sofa to flip through the *TV Guide*, just to see if *anything* looked like it might be safe for them, before tossing it back onto the coffee table and twisting around to look at Tobias.

"Hey, Tobias . . . do you think you'd be okay here if I went for a run around the block?"

Jake exhaled in relief when Tobias didn't immediately panic, break down, cry, or have some kind of spontaneous heart attack. The only sign of his rising anxiety was the tension in his arms and the way he turned his head, looking but *not* looking into Jake's face. "A ru—whatever you want, Jake."

"Hey." Jake rested a hand on Tobias's sock-covered ankle and squeezed gently. "Yeah, a run. You can ask questions, it's okay."

Tobias took a slow shaky breath and carefully put the book on the coffee table. "You'd l-leave?"

"Yeah. Not for long, though. Quick run, maybe around the block a couple times to get out some energy."

"You'd c-c-come back?"

Jake leaned in and rested his chin on his arm. "Always, Tobias. Always. Will you be okay or should I give it a few more days?"

Tobias nodded, though he still wasn't looking at him. "You'll come back. I'll be f-fine. Th-th-thank you for asking me."

"No problem, Tobias. I want you to be okay."

Jake ran harder and faster than usual, and the whole time around the block he felt a tightness constricting his chest that had nothing to do with getting back into exercise. But when he came back, out of breath and covered in a fine sheen of sweat, Tobias was still in the same place. The look of happiness on his face when he saw Jake—quickly eclipsing the panic Jake glimpsed the moment he stepped in—made the idea of leaving all the easier.

Jake drank a glass of water, chatting with Tobias and relishing the feeling of having someone to come home to (and not just someone but *Toby*), and then left for another run.

He went for six laps in all, and by the last one, when he walked through the door and Tobias's face showed nothing but happiness, expectation, and relief. Between that and the endorphins, Jake felt pretty damn good too.

~

IN THE FLOOD OF PAPERWORK, the last time he saw Dad, then drinking like a fish that Roger had to yank out of the water, and the nerve-wracking days after getting Tobias out and realizing just how over his head he was—it had slipped Jake's mind how much Tobias loved books and how fast he could read them. On Tuesday, when he looked over to the couch where Tobias was opening up another book, he realized that Tobias had definitely read that book before.

He'd seen Tobias reading the textbook earlier that week too, as it was one of the eight books on Jake's cheap bookshelf. Tobias had slowly worked his way through each one, his hands on the pages careful, hesitant, and eager in a way that he knew Tobias didn't want him to notice. But it still filled Jake with a cautious hope each time he saw Tobias relaxed with a book in his lap.

He sat down next to Tobias, trying to keep his eyes off the book, but it must not have worked, because Tobias's face shut down a little and he slid the book off his lap and to the coffee table.

"So, what's the verdict?" Jake asked. When Tobias just looked blank, he rephrased. "Just as good as your first time through?"

Tobias nodded. "It's pretty comprehensive, if a little simplistic. There's a lot of stuff they didn't . . . I hadn't known about before."

"Yeah, like what?"

"Just . . . a lot of the overview about the Civil War and . . . everything. There were some zombie issues after Gettysburg, I read about it in a journal, but I had no idea. There's a lot that's new, but I can fit other things into it, you know? I've never read just a textbook about history before."

Jake snorted. "Yeah, well, you get way too much of it in school. But you've read that one before, right?"

Tobias nodded again. "Yeah. I'm skimming this time."

"You think there's some things you missed?" Jake thought books were okay, but he'd rather watch any car-chase, shoot-'em-up movie on TV. He could try, though. They'd been able to talk about a book for hours when they were kids, but that was when he had wanted to talk to Tobias so badly that he would have done anything to give them something to share. Now, like with so many things, he felt lost.

Tobias shook his head firmly. "I have a pretty good grasp of the information." He hesitated, glanced up, and then down again. His hands were limp, palms up in his lap. "I don't know how useful the information is for hunting. I mean, it could be useful if there are ghosts left over from the old battles, or if some of the older massacres were caused by a vampire nest or something like that, but it's hard to pull modern-day connections without other, more hunting-oriented resources." He looked up, catching Jake's confusion, and his shoulders hunched tighter. "I mean, I know you know better, I can do a-anything you need to, I just—"

Jake put his hand over Tobias's. "Hey, I didn't ask you how it was for research. I asked to see if you . . . liked it. I mean, not for research, but just . . . damn, how many times have you read this one?"

Tobias's hand tightened in his and then loosened almost immediately. Jake thought it had been an automatic reaction, but his fingers squeezed Tobias's in response anyway. He liked touching Tobias. And he still hated those little fearful flinches.

"Just twice," Tobias whispered.

"Twice!" Jake started back, and Tobias cringed. Jake swore

silently at himself and tried to point at the shelf more casually, at *X-Men: Days of Future Past.* "What about that one?"

"Three times."

Jake pointed at *Huckleberry Finn.* "And that one?"

"Five times."

"*What?*" Jake knew he was overreacting, but how could he get Tobias what he wanted, everything he needed, if Tobias wouldn't tell him what that was?

He felt so much worse when Tobias pulled away from him into the couch and tucked his legs up tighter. "I l-l-liked it," he forced out. "I'm s-s-s—"

Jake put up a hand. "No, don't apologize. You didn't do anything wrong. Come on." He stood and held out his hand.

Tobias still cringed at any sudden movement or raised voice, or if Jake sat down too suddenly at a goddamned table. But when Jake offered his hand, Tobias took it as quickly and easily as another person would help himself to a second portion of mashed potatoes. Jake didn't know if that was yet another thing broken inside Tobias, or if it meant what he wished it meant: that Tobias trusted him, and this over-whelming fear (overwhelming for Jake; Tobias seemed to accept his own terror as the appropriate response) would fade away.

"We're going to go for a walk," Jake told him. "There's a library nearby. We're going to get you a library card."

TOBIAS FOLLOWED Jake down the street, his heart beating a little too hard. If this had been camp, it would have been a trick, some guard promising something that sounded nice and then taking it away when it would hurt the most. This would have been the Director tying him down and asking exactly what he liked so that he would never see it again. But ... he didn't think that was what was going to happen.

Of course he didn't really think that he could just walk into a building and take out books without any questions. He remembered a little of Becca telling him how real libraries worked and the awe he'd felt, and then Jake had confirmed it as true. Books were ... wonderful, they opened up the world, and he was ... Well, even if the reals around him didn't automatically recognize what he was, he doubted he would ever be able to just walk out a door with a book cradled in his arms. He'd only been allowed to research so much with books in camp because everyone thought that it was a key part of what Jake and Leon Hawthorne wanted him to know.

A lot of guards had made jokes about the *Kama Sutra* being the only useful thing for a freak to read. But Tobias felt confident enough that Jake didn't mean that. He honestly seemed not to care what Tobias read, and he never took a book away from him. He didn't need it to be about hunting or about teaching Tobias what he should do to deserve to stay, though Tobias would've been grateful for that kind of book. He had a little hope now that Jake wasn't going to take him back to FREACS anytime soon, but the old calculations that had given him any kind of grounding, however painful, never made sense anymore.

But for now, Tobias pushed his worries down. The sun was bright in the sky, beautiful and shockingly green trees rustled in the breeze, and his long-sleeved shirt was just the perfect weight to keep him not too hot and not too cold. Being in the right temperature was a pleasure in and of itself, something that had rarely happened at camp. And he was walking with Jake, who didn't look angry, didn't look depressed, just determined. He paced himself so that Tobias stayed at his side, like they'd walked before, though he would've liked to be a step behind. That was where he belonged (unless, of course, Jake wanted him to take a risk first or to be beneath him), but also because when Jake was distracted, when there weren't that many people around, Tobias felt safer just looking. Without Jake's eyes on him, without the threat of a guard or a real who would know that he was a monster, Tobias could let himself watch Jake's neck, the way his shoulders moved as he walked.

He knew that someday Jake would catch him, and Tobias wasn't sure how he would react. Anyone else would hit him, even if they enjoyed the attention, even if they liked knowing that Tobias couldn't stop watching them. Crusher had been like that, though no one had watched Crusher for the reasons Tobias watched Jake. Crusher had been a nasty presence that monsters could neither ignore nor watch too closely. Either choice ended in blood.

Tobias couldn't have said why he watched Jake. Why he was so fascinated by the easy movement of his muscles, the soft-looking skin on the back of his neck, the angle of his jaw revealed when he turned his head. He wished he could stroke Jake's hair or his arm, though he wouldn't dare, of course. He never thought he'd have something so wonderful and sweet in his life. Jake was a gift that he could never have earned (though, God, he would try, if only Jake would tell him how, Tobias would work harder than he had at anything) or maybe a reward for some price he hadn't paid yet. He didn't know what he could give in return for having Jake in his life. Tobias knew his own life wasn't worth nearly that much.

His thoughts were broken when Jake stopped and said, "So, this is the library. Boulder's finest hoard of books and all you can eat—uh, read."

It was a tall building, but far different from the Workhouse or Administration: part brick, part glass rising in a circular slanted prism. There were no bars, peepholes, or checkpoints in sight.

Jake pushed through the big glass door first and held it

open on the other side for Tobias. He used to hold doors open and have Tobias pass through them first. Tobias still didn't know why, but Jake had stopped after a couple of times.

As he passed through the door, Tobias brushed Jake's shoulder. He allowed himself these small pleasures because Jake didn't seem to notice them, and if Jake didn't notice he couldn't mind them or tell Tobias to stop. Tobias didn't want to risk losing something so wonderful, but sometimes he couldn't help himself.

Distracted by the feel of Jake's jacket, smiling involuntarily, Tobias kept his eyes on his feet. When he did look up, he stopped stock-still and stared. He felt Jake's hands touch his shoulders—he'd almost run into him because the stop had been so abrupt, and Tobias felt a flash of guilt for that—but even that pleasant contact and residual worry were swamped by the sight of *books*.

There were hundreds of them. No, thousands. Maybe more. Countless shelves extending out of sight, each one packed with books of different sizes. There were even tables right in front of him with books propped up in a display like anyone, even a freak, could reach out and pick one up without asking permission. He had to suck in his breath and close his eyes to get a sudden wave of dizziness under control.

When he opened his eyes, Jake was grinning at him, mischief and delight sparkling in his eyes. Tobias couldn't stop himself from smiling back. He didn't even try. He hadn't seen that look in Jake's eyes for a long time, and it was somehow even better than all the books before him.

Tobias had read everything in the apartment at least twice, and he'd loved doing so because they were Jake's books and Jake had told him that he could read them. But it had never occurred to him they could get *other* books. The camp's library was a fraction of what he could see now, and most of the texts had been old, thick copies of grimoires and bestiaries from every century for a thousand years. Tobias didn't know what all the books before him were about, but he dared to imagine they weren't just about the supernatural.

And Jake wanted him to read *these* whenever he wanted. Well, maybe not whenever he wanted, but Jake would not have brought him to this place, would not look as happy as he had the first time Tobias ate a waffle, if he was just going to turn them around and cut Tobias off from this beautiful reservoir of knowledge.

"Like it?" Jake was still grinning.

Tobias nodded quickly. He couldn't find the words to say how much he loved it. Even if he tried, he would stutter and freeze up because this was *such a wonderful place*. And he loved Jake even more for bringing him here, though he'd thought he couldn't feel more grateful, more indebted, more dazzled by Jake.

"I thought you would." Jake still looked as smug as he had when telling Tobias how he and his father had taken down their latest wendigo. "C'mon, let's find the librarian and get you a card."

The line was short. Apparently, Tuesday afternoon wasn't a crowded time in the library. Tobias made a note of that. If Jake ever let him come to this paradise by himself, he wanted to come when no one else was there, when he could disappear amid the tall aisles of books and not be in anyone's way, not be found. Though he doubted that he would ever come here without Jake, and he didn't think that Jake would want to escort him all the time, just to make Tobias happy. Jake had better things to do, and nothing a freak wanted was that important.

But he brought you here today, didn't he? a small voice whispered. *He saw that you wanted more books, and he didn't take them away. He brought you to a library and says he's going to get you a card so you can have more. He might come back with you. He might actually want you to have this.*

Hard to believe. Stupid to put his hopes on that. But the closer they got to the desk, with Jake's hand resting gently on his shoulder, the more he dared to believe it.

When they got to the counter, Jake didn't move past him. With a spike of panic, Tobias thought Jake might leave and make him talk to a real without being there to claim him when he fucked it up and everyone found out he was a monster. But Jake didn't leave, didn't even step away. He just stayed beside him with his hand on Tobias's shoulder a steady comfort, not at all in restraint.

The librarian smiled reassuringly. Tobias took a deep breath and forced himself to look at her, though not at her eyes —he couldn't do that, so dangerous, there might be something in his face that she would see that proved he was a monster— and waited for a clue of what to do next.

"What can I do for you?" she asked.

Tobias was pretty sure she knew there was something wrong with him, but there was no hatred, loathing, or threat in her eyes, so he didn't think she had figured out he was a monster. He could deal with this. Jake expected him to deal with this.

"Ummm," he started, and then glanced back.

Jake was glowing at him. Tobias was relieved that he had tried looking and talking to the real woman before Jake told him to. Every time Jake smiled, Tobias felt a strange level of buoyancy filling him up like light.

"Tobias wants a library card," Jake told her. "We live down Bluff Road. Right, Tobias?"

Tobias nodded and turned back to the librarian. "Yes. I . . . I am here for a library card. Please."

She hadn't stopped smiling. So far, so good. "That's no problem, library cards are what we're here for. Here, fill out this form and bring it back when you're done, and I'll get you your card right away."

Tobias took the piece of paper gratefully and turned away. He almost handed it to Jake but then, glancing down at it, realized he could do it himself. He knew the address and Jake's phone number since Jake had shown it to him the day after they'd arrived in Boulder. The form didn't ask much else.

He took a pen from an alcove with two computers labeled CATALOG SEARCH, and slowly, in his best handwriting, filled the form in. Jake was still smiling, hands in his pockets and leaning against the computer table, looking up at the second floor like he had no doubt Tobias had this handled.

Tobias hesitated over the name line, and then carefully wrote *Tobias*. That was the name that Jake always used, and it would be a dead giveaway to put down 89UI6703.

Once finished, he brought it up to the counter. He was careful not to let the librarian touch him when she took the form. He didn't want her to touch a monster, even unknowingly.

"Tobias," she said, and he managed not to flinch. "Do you have a last name, hon?"

Tobias froze. He opened his mouth and then closed it again, fear hitting him like a fist to the diaphragm. He had hoped, he had really thought that this was going to work, that he was going to have a *card* that said he could check out books, that he would just be able to hand in the piece of paper with a few lines of information on it, and everything would make sense because that was the way it worked in the real world.

That was how it would work if he hadn't been born a monster. He should have known that he wouldn't be able to get away with it.

"I thought . . . N-n-no . . . s-sorry." He tried to reach over to take the form back. Maybe if she didn't have evidence of him, she would forget this and wouldn't remember the stupid monster that thought he could act like a real for a day.

Then Jake put his hand back on Tobias's shoulder. "It's

Tobias Hawthorne," he told the librarian. "Hawthorne with an E at the end."

The woman's smile returned full force. "All right," she said, made a note on the sheet, and began typing on the computer.

Tobias felt the world sliding sideways. Jake had said . . . Jake couldn't possibly mean that. He had to blink rapidly because his eyes were full of little bits of sparkles, and he felt light-headed. He must have misheard. Jake wouldn't have . . .

But Jake was still speaking, this time in a low voice to him.

"I hope you don't mind, you didn't have a last name in your file," he said, and if Tobias hadn't known better, he would have thought that Jake was nervous.

Tobias just stared at him, full in the face. "You mean that's really my name? L-Legally?" He couldn't hide how much this meant to him, and he didn't know how it showed on his face.

"We can change it if you want to." Jake did look worried now. "I mean, it would take more paperwork, it was hard enough convincing them—" He glanced at the librarian. "Well, it was a hassle, but your last name can be whatever you want it to be. I mean, I know that Hawthorne can be . . ."

Tobias couldn't stop the smile, but he could duck his head. Then he remembered that Jake liked to see him smile. That he looked the happiest when Tobias could bring himself to look him in the eye. "No, that's—that's good. Hawthorne is . . . perfect." *Because it's your name.* He would be able to keep Jake's name forever. Even if they took it away from him someday on paper, he would know that for a time he had been Tobias *Hawthorne.*

❧

FOR JAKE, bringing Tobias to the library had turned into a treat all by itself. Much as he hated Tobias's double-twitch every time he saw something he loved (twitching once to hide whatever reaction he'd had, twitching twice because he hoped that Jake hadn't noticed the first one), he loved to watch Tobias awed and wide-eyed. It let Jake see the world in a new light. Especially the parts he never really thought about, like libraries.

The only stomach-dropping stop was the second after he told the librarian Tobias's last name, because . . . well, he hadn't exactly shared that with Tobias yet.

But the radiant smile he got in return went a long way to convince him that giving Tobias the Hawthorne surname was, at least, not one of his fuck-ups.

"Hawthorne is . . . perfect," Tobias said, and for one minute, Jake was blissed out with unaccustomed success.

They checked out a few good-sized books, including a biography of Mark Twain, and walked back home. Jake couldn't stop smiling, and every time he looked at Tobias clutching the books close to his chest or saw him reach into his pocket to feel the brand-new library card, he thought he was going to crack from the rush of relief and happiness.

When the librarian handed over the card with another bright smile, there had been a space on the back for the cardholder's signature. For the first time, Tobias had written his name, Jake's last name, in careful letters that wobbled just a bit.

He couldn't imagine anything better than this.

As they reached the apartment, Jake's cell phone rang, and he jumped in a totally professional hunter-reflex way. Tobias jumped too, of course, and Jake tried to wave at him reassuringly as he yanked the phone out of his pocket. He didn't even know why he had it on him when it only rang once in a blue moon and nearly gave him a heart attack when it did.

Then he saw Roger's name on the screen, and the unease in his chest broke apart into something light. "Hey, Rog." He unlocked the door with his other hand and waved Tobias in with another gesture that hopefully communicated he'd be back in a minute. Tobias actually beamed at him, his arms full of books, before turning into the apartment. Jake shut and locked the door before heading back down the stairs to amble along the sidewalk.

"Hey, kid. Any word on the paperwork?"

For a moment, Jake was lost. How did Roger know about the library form? And why didn't he also know it had already gone super smooth? "Paperwork?"

Roger's voice turned incredulous. "Yeah, the ASC paperwork. The thing you've been waiting on for months and pining over like a Victorian lady?"

"Oh!" Jake stopped walking as the realization hit him. It had been, what, a little over a week since he'd picked Tobias up? It had felt like years but also like no time at all. "Yeah, I got him!"

"You *what?*"

Jake winced, pulling the phone away from his ear. "Yeah, I picked him up on the sixteenth." He didn't think he'd ever forget the date. Even though his cousin Leah Dixon had sounded grim on the phone, he'd done several fist bumps as she told him, *You may retrieve your monster from FREACS on July 16th. Remember your ID and make sure you read the intake paperwork we've sent to your address on file.*

"You—" Jake had never heard Roger speechless before. "You troll-headed *moron*, you didn't think to pick up the phone and let me know?"

Jake just managed to keep from laughing. "Sorry, Rog, it moved kinda fast."

Another moment of silence made Jake glad he was several hundred miles away from New Mexico and not in head-slapping range. "Well? What's he like?"

Jake rolled his eyes. "Tobias is great. Wouldn't hurt a fly. I told you that."

"And I told you, even if he's fully human, that place would fuck anyone's head up," Roger snapped.

"Dude, I know!" Scowling, Jake glanced around to check for privacy. "Look, he's shaky. This is all really new to him, so we're just taking baby steps. Even the grocery store was pretty intense."

"You brought him to—" Jake heard Roger take a deep breath. "Jake. You ain't dumb, no matter how much you like to act like it. I know you believe in the kid, but tell me you're using that head of yours."

Jake scowled. "Of course I am."

"Yeah? Nothing's happened yet that made you think you're maybe out of your depth?"

Jake winced again. Roger could read him too well even long-distance. "We got it handled, okay? I told you, baby steps."

A pause on the other end of the line. "All the same, I'd feel better if—why don't you take a few days to come by and see me? Both of you, I mean. Alejandra's been talking about swinging by. You know she'd like to finally meet him."

Jake felt another surge of unease he didn't want to examine. Roger's place had always been the closest thing he had to home, but he wasn't sure Tobias would feel the same. Plus, as much as he owed Alejandra Rodriguez for helping to vouch for Jake's character to the ASC so he could get Tobias out, Jake didn't know her nearly well enough yet to pull Tobias in for a meet-and-greet.

"What, already? We're still getting our feet under us in Boulder. Give us some time before we take on the open road."

"Jake. Don't make me come to you."

"Hey, no!" A bolt of alarm went through Jake at the idea of Roger descending upon them here in Colorado. Nothing good happened when Roger had to stir outside his self-marked territory around the little town of Truth or Consequences. "All right, we'll come see you. Just give us a little more time. I swear we've

got it under control. Look, I've gotta go back now and just—
keep him company. He's fine, really. He just does better when
I'm around. You don't gotta worry, he's too scared to *talk* to
anyone."

"Jake—"

"I'll call you later." Jake stabbed the off button and braced
himself for the phone to start yowling again, but Roger didn't
immediately call back.

Dropping the phone into his pocket, Jake turned back to the
apartment. He and Tobias had just had an awesome day. The
library was a definite winner, and they could build on that.
Roger worried too much.

BACK AT THE LIBRARY, Jake had filled out a card for himself and
browsed the movie section while Tobias pored over the books,
and he finally picked out a couple of things he felt reasonably
confident would not shatter Tobias.

He ordered pizza delivery from a local pie shop, and it
turned out to be a hell of a lot better than the frozen ones he'd
gotten at the grocery store. Tobias even reached for his own
slices (okay, maybe only after Jake took one of his own) and
didn't even try to hide his smile.

After dinner, Jake pushed in the VHS tape of a nature documentary, and they settled down in comfy clothes onto the
couch.

The documentary was ass-boring, which was exactly what
Jake had hoped for. He didn't have a thing to complain about,
because Tobias was currently slouched against his chest, so
relaxed he had dozed off. As hesitant as Tobias was to initiate
contact, if Jake stretched his arm across the back of the sofa,
Tobias would immediately sit right beside him. Once there, he
practically melted into Jake's arms.

Nature documentaries really were underrated, Jake thought. Hell, he should've had a pile of them ready to go from the very first night. Before Tobias's eyes had fallen shut, he'd clearly been enraptured, and in a good way. This one was about a couple of birds going after each other, and the biggest action scenes were just a couple of brown birds swooping and diving. Nothing noisier than the soothing murmur of the narrator's voice offering them bird fact after bird fact.

Jake might just send this Marty Stouffer some kind of gift basket. Chocolates, whiskey, a taxidermy possum, whatever the man liked.

Tobias's slow, even breaths and his light, relaxed weight against Jake's side felt better than anything he could remember. Fuck yeah, Jake had kept his promise. Tobias was safe, alive, warm, and comfortable enough to sleep right next to him. If Jake just focused on this and today and nothing else, he could believe that everything he'd hoped for had come true. There wasn't another damn thing he needed. He'd told Roger the truth: they were doing just fine.

He realized he was bone-tired, sunk into the couch like he had one of Roger's trolls sitting on top of him. Even if he was willing to wake Tobias—and he'd rather have bitten his fingers off, unless the apartment was on fire—the steps between here and his bedroom seemed stupid and unnecessary. Not when he'd clearly found the best thrift couch in the world. Plus that whole thing about Tobias being *here* and finally at peace. Jake wasn't going to give this up a second before he had to.

Tobias, of course, could go to bed whenever he woke up from his nap. Jake wouldn't be keeping him here if he shut his own eyes for a minute or two.

Shifting slowly, he turned to stretch out along the couch. Tobias never woke up, never pulled away from Jake's body, but nestled back against him with a soft murmur once they were horizontal. Jake tugged a pillow under his own head. Tobias was using Jake's bicep as a headrest, which was just fine with him.

Their legs were notched together, but Jake wasn't sure where to put his free hand. After a moment, he gingerly laid his arm across Tobias's ribs, letting his fingers curl onto the edge of the couch.

It felt good. Better than good. Better than anything he had words for. He buried his nose in the back of Tobias's curls, inhaled him, and closed his eyes.

JAKE WAS PULLED out of sleep by a distant choking cough that grew louder the closer he came to full awareness. But he didn't have the foggiest clue what was happening until he opened his eyes and saw Tobias hunched over, knees pulled up, clutching his throat, struggling to breathe.

That was the end of Jake's early morning daze.

He shot up in panic, scrabbling at Tobias's hand to try to figure out what the fuck was hurting him. For a few red-raging seconds, he thought some kind of spirit had gotten through the wards and he was going to kill that motherfucking son of a bitch a second fucking time and make it *hurt*. But Tobias shook his head, eyes closed, working to inhale, even as he choked, each breath an awful rasp.

Jake wasn't sure if he was glad that it wasn't something he could kill. Because yeah, maybe it was reassuring that Tobias knew what this was, seemed to have a handle on it, but that also meant there was not a damn fucking thing Jake could do while Tobias was choking on something Jake couldn't see or understand. Maybe this was the way civilians felt, able to do nothing in the face of the unknown but hold on to their loved one's knee and plead incoherently for it to be all right. "Breathe, Tobias, please, just breathe. Don't do this to me. I need you to breathe, c'mon, you can, it'll be okay."

After what seemed like hours—entirely too damn long, *fuck* —Tobias gradually relaxed, managing short but even breaths, and then deeper ones, sagging against the cushions in exhaustion.

"God," Jake breathed, and pulled Tobias forward, folding him against his chest and not caring for once about how he'd react. "Holy shit. Way to scare a guy shitless in the morning. Christ."

"So—" Tobias gasped against his chest, voice raw. "Sor—"

"Shhhh." Jake closed his eyes, unconsciously rocking Tobias back and forth. He couldn't hear another *sorry*, not now. He focused instead on how Tobias relaxed against him, no tension or anxiety in his muscles. Tobias wasn't confused about what had happened, didn't seem to be fucking scared out of his mind like Jake. Which meant that this wasn't the unknown for him. Fuck, fuck, *fuck*. After a minute, he forced out the important question. "Does that happen often?"

Tobias shook his head, nose brushing Jake's chest. "Only a c-couple times since I came here."

Jake swallowed, not wanting to think about Tobias choking alone in his room. Fuck, what if he'd passed out or something? "What about . . . back there?"

"No. It never happened . . . before."

"Hm." Jake readjusted his grip, shifting his legs so they could sit more comfortably, and tilted Tobias's head back to look him in the face. "Any idea what sets it off? Is there anything that—helps?"

Tobias shook his head, gaze sliding down as he rested his head against Jake's shoulder.

"Well, we'll see if we can figure something out." Jake ran his hands over Tobias's head and back again, feeling panic's echo in his pulse. He couldn't get over how little he fucking knew about taking care of Tobias. How Tobias could be so close—lying right beside him in a salt-lined room—and those bastards hundreds of miles away could still do their best to choke the life out of him. *So close, so close.* Tobias had one hand lightly clutching Jake's T-shirt, forearm bare, and the light lines of scratches—mostly healed, but still visible—clenched Jake's chest unexpectedly.

With an effort, he let him go. "Good. Okay. We should totally get dressed and shower and shit, and I'll meet you out here in fifteen. We're going somewhere awesome for breakfast."

TOBIAS FOCUSED DOGGEDLY on the task at hand, on Jake's directions as he showered, dressed, and then ended up waiting in the living room. He could hear Jake's shower running. Tobias hesitated, then took a seat on the end of the sofa, folding his legs under him.

So much had happened in the last twelve hours; his heart still beat a little too fast, a little less than smooth. He had never allowed himself to think for a second that Jake would want to sleep beside him. And not to do anything except hold and sleep and listen to each other breathe. The idea that he could ever have something as wonderful and perfect as that—it still made his hands shake when he thought about it, but he pressed them tight between his knees. He didn't want Jake to see and think there was anything wrong when there wasn't, there couldn't be.

Jake hadn't even been disgusted when Tobias woke him with his hacking—Tobias couldn't control it, couldn't help that edge-of-waking sensation that he was hanging by the collar he no longer wore, choking, dangling, scrabbling to support himself on toes that didn't quite touch the floor until he couldn't breathe, couldn't scream, couldn't think. But instead of being frightened or angry, Jake had been—there was no other way to describe it—*worried* about Tobias.

Tobias didn't completely understand, and that should have worried him more—terrible things happened when you didn't understand all the rules—but it was hard to panic this morning. Hard to worry when Jake had settled against him for the whole night, when he had felt Jake's touch for far, far longer than he could have ever expected.

When Jake emerged from the hall, his damp hair dark, Tobias tried not to jump or straighten or do anything but smile and look Jake in the face. He had learned that much, at least, because Jake's whole face broke into an answering smile, bright and easy like Tobias hadn't seen since the first day Jake took him away from camp.

Jake came over and held out his hand to pull him up. "C'mon, Toby."

They didn't drive far, just to a donut shop a few blocks away that Jake had pointed out on Sunday. He'd acknowledged that bagels were pretty good ("Especially with that chick's cream cheese. I don't know what they put in it, maybe cocaine, but it's fucking worth it"), but they couldn't come close to sugar-glazed donuts.

It was getting easier to trust Jake when they went out, Tobias thought as he stepped out of the car. Jake wouldn't bring him somewhere people might recognize him for what he was, and he wouldn't force Tobias into something he couldn't manage yet. Of course Jake knew what he was doing.

Tobias still stuck close to his side as they went through the door, and Jake rested his hands on Tobias's shoulders as they stood in the back of the shop. Focusing on breathing slow and even, Tobias made himself look around instead of staring at the floor. Some reals stood in line before the counter, behind which were shelves of what Tobias supposed were donuts. They looked like delicate bagels with different colored toppings and textures. Other reals sat at small tables, eating the donuts with their fingers and drinking from white paper cups.

When they reached the counter, the young woman behind it flashed a smile, eyes flickering past Tobias to Jake. "What can I get for you?"

"We'll take a dozen mixed," Jake said. As she rang it up, a man next to her turned to start filling a box, and Jake dropped his mouth to Tobias's ear. "Do you want coffee or milk?"

Tobias shivered, feeling Jake's breath over his ear and neck, aware of how close Jake was behind him, hands still on his shoulders. "Milk's fine," he whispered, and Jake squeezed his shoulders.

Jake got a coffee for himself, and they took their drinks and the donuts to an empty corner table with a window. Tobias tried not to think about all the eyes that might see him, instead focusing on the box Jake had just opened. Jake pulled one out of the middle that was a light yellow with a crumbly glaze of white sugar that stuck to his fingers. He tore it in half and offered Tobias the bigger section. It was warm and softer than a bagel.

When Tobias bit into it, he expected something bagel-like, but the flavors hit him from the tip of his tongue to the back of his throat: the rush of sugar, the sweet burst of a flavor that he could never have imagined. His senses couldn't quite believe that anything so good, so real, could be happening to *him*. He had to close his eyes while the sugary softness swept from his mouth to his stomach and somehow through the whole rest of his body. When he came back to himself and looked up, blinking dazedly, he saw Jake grinning even wider, like he was barely containing laughter—but not *at* Tobias.

"Pretty good, huh?" Jake asked, licking his fingers clean of the white sugar flakes.

Tobias waved the last piece of donut. He wished he had words that could remotely describe the sensations from just that bite, or the bright dazzling feeling of lightness inside him, like a kind of happiness that might have him floating away, if not for the surety of Jake's grounded presence. Jake, who carried him through the worst of the real trials, then gave him the best parts of the real world as a reward for Tobias's bravery.

8

They spent the rest of the day at home, but it felt better than the last few days. Maybe it was because, for the first time since Jake had realized just how badly those bastards had messed up Tobias, he felt confident about some things. He could tease Tobias (carefully) and knew that he would get a small smile if he was obvious enough about it. He could leave the house for a run—damn, it felt good to be moving again—and Tobias wouldn't spontaneously combust in the time it took him to circle the block three or four times at an easy jog. And Tobias liked donuts and learning things about the real world, including stuff it had never occurred to Jake to explain before.

"So, he puts on a bat costume . . . to fight crime in the night?"

Jake grinned at him, flipping the grilled cheese and ham sandwich in the frying pan. "Yup. And he's incredibly badass. Of all the superheroes, Batman's the best."

Tobias absorbed that, leaning against the counter next to him. He looked perplexed but thoughtful. "Would you ever dress up as a bat to go hunting?"

Jake sighed. "Nah, don't have the tech for it. I always thought that a grappling gun would be super cool. But without that and, like, the mask, I might as well stick with the denim and plaid uniform. Easier to blend in anywhere, you know? And besides, I don't know that the bat schtick would work anywhere but Gotham—that's a made-up city, but it's based on New York."

Jake had belatedly realized he ought to brush up Tobias's comic book knowledge, since Tobias had already read the X-Men volume a bunch of times and seemed to enjoy it. They'd covered Superman, Wonder Woman, and Spiderman before getting to Batman. Tobias was fascinated by the colorful world of mutants, aliens, and billionaires that fought baddies long before the world knew the supernatural type of monster was real. When Jake had tried to casually check that Tobias knew none of it was real, he'd gotten a look somewhere between pity and concern, which for some reason made him grin like a lunatic.

After dinner, Tobias asked hesitantly, "Will you be l-looking for a hunt? Anytime soon, I mean? I'll be okay—I mean, you don't have to stay home for me."

Jake paused, mind whirring. In the months he'd spent finding a place in Boulder and waiting for that damn call, he'd assumed he'd take a break from hunting after he got Tobias. He hadn't put much thought into when he'd get *back* to hunting. "Boulder's pretty clean, I'm keeping an eye on things."

Tobias was quiet for a moment. "I don't know m-much about . . . never mind."

Jake tilted his head back, catching Tobias's gaze. "Hey, you got questions, I want you to ask them."

Tobias fidgeted with the napkin, brow knit, and then tried again. "It all seems—the donuts and meals and everything you keep g-giving me—I, I don't know how much money it is, but I don't want y-you to, if it's costing you too much—"

Then it clicked. "No way. First off, dude, I'd rob Fort Knox for you. Second, I'm not about to run out of money, don't sweat. The ASC sends me a chunk of change every month."

Tobias's eyes widened, and Jake hurried on. "It's not 'cause of you, it's—they do it for everybody who signs up for this life, all the active hunters. It's not hard to register after you get your license. Then if you report your monster kills—missions, I mean—a few times a year and stay in the network, they keep you on salary, and it ain't bad. The Dixons are good for one thing, at least. And the ASC money is better in our pocket than theirs." That was something Leon had always said, though Jake was suddenly unsure how it would sound to Tobias.

But Tobias just nodded, seemingly unbothered. Maybe even a little reassured.

~

"Laughing Goat Coffeehouse," Jake repeated. "No shit. That's what it's actually called."

Tobias blinked at him over the top of his new book: *Oxford History of Medieval Europe.* "Why?"

"That is a good question." Jake sat back, dropping the well-worn brochure map of Boulder. It felt like he had been going through the thing with a fine-toothed comb for hours, trying to figure out where their next exploratory adventure would lead them. They should probably go back to the grocery store—the orange juice had disappeared so fast, Jake wondered if maybe he had been pouring more down Tobias's throat than he should have, but vitamin C was good for you, wasn't it?—but Jake didn't think either of them were up to that at the moment. Another restaurant sounded like the best bet. "What do you say we go find out?"

Tobias hesitated, lowering the brightly colored book slowly to his lap. Jake knew he still wasn't completely sold on leaving the apartment. Sometimes Jake just wanted to agree that they didn't have to go anywhere, but he knew the best thing for them both was to go out again and again, getting a little better at it each time, until Tobias really truly believed that the normal people out and about on their day were not going to hurt him, hate him, or even butt in front of him in line at a stupid coffee shop. So that was the mission: find places with stuff that Tobias had never seen before (hell, Jake had never been to a coffee-house that featured goats, laughing or otherwise) so that Jake would have something to delight and distract him from whatever made him nervous.

"Sure," Tobias said at last, the would-be casual tone still forced, but it still made Jake glow with pride. He reached over to rest his hand on Tobias's ankle, and a smile bloomed over Tobias's face.

"I think you'll like it. It's downtown, we passed it when we were circling around last Sunday, remember? It had that purple-and-green canopy and the little round tables outside."

Tobias nodded. "I remember. On Pearl Street. It looked . . . nice."

"Well, that settles it." Jake clapped his hand lightly over Tobias's calf, then hoisted himself to his feet. "They're supposed to have some pretty sweet drinks, and an 'intimate, organic elegance,' whatever that means. No happy hour, but I think that's probably a good thing." Jake shuddered dramatically. "If there's chuckling goats there, anyway, I'd hate to see the place when they get a little alcohol in them. And you can't tell me that people don't slip the goats a little extra."

"Are there . . . actual goats?" Tobias looked unsure whether Jake was teasing him. Jake wasn't completely certain himself. Maybe he was a little nervous because this was a place he usually wouldn't set foot in (unless it was for a case, but he had done some pretty weird shit for cases).

"Tobias, I couldn't tell you. I guess we'll find out."

YEP, Jake decided the moment they stepped through the door. This was definitely one of *those* coffee shops. The kind he'd never be caught dead in—that is, before he had Tobias with him. It was full of the usual cushy armchairs, preppy-looking people, and the sweet smell of java exposed to so many sugars, syrups, and esoteric processes that it couldn't rightly be called coffee anymore. The only thing different was the goats. Everywhere. With every sweep Jake made of the room, more goats— pictures, models, pottery, signs, thankfully no actual stuffed goat heads—popped out at him. Creepy. How had this place not pinged his hunter radar the first time he scouted out the town?

But Tobias seemed chill with general goatiness, even the porcelain head that looked more like a pissed-off, blue-veined cow, so Jake shook off his personal nerves and turned his attention to the menu scrawled across a huge chalkboard above the counter. The lower corner, enclosed in a big pink heart, advertised a special on free-trade soybeans from Tasmania.

There really were no limits on what he would do for Tobias.

Jake aimed a smile at Tobias's shoulder as they moved toward the counter, a smile that widened and broke open when Tobias reached back, one hand tangling with his.

The girl behind the counter blushed when she saw them, but she was grinning too. "What can I get for you guys?"

Jake threw his arm over Tobias's shoulders, pulling him close while scanning the menu for the drink loaded with the most sugar and syrup. "Let's get, uh—a hazelnut mocha with whipped cream. And chocolate sprinkles."

Jotting the order down on a cup, the barista tipped her head toward the counter next to them. "All the toppings are over there."

"Awesome. I'll take a cup of plain black Joe—if you *have*

coffee in its natural state." He glared at the menu with suspicion. "I dunno if it already comes to you soaked in vanilla sugar extract or something."

"Nope, I gotcha covered." She punched a couple more things into the cash register. "That'll be six seventy-two."

Jake paid and then tugged Tobias over to wait for their order. He couldn't help scanning the room, waiting for a threat that he knew, rationally, would probably not appear. He hadn't expected it to be this crowded on an early Friday afternoon, and the seating was pretty limited. When a table opened up in the back corner, Jake took Tobias over to grab the seats, and then returned to pick up their drinks. The table was crowded next to a cluster of way-too-hyper high-school girls, but they would have a comprehensive view of the room and their backs against the two walls. Even better, they were close to an emergency exit, aka the bathrooms and kitchen.

Tobias took his chair gingerly, as though it might break under his weight, and Jake did his best to unobtrusively scoot his own closer so he could nudge Tobias's shoulder with his.

"Watch out," Jake told him, as Tobias wrapped his fingers around the cupholder. "They make it hot enough to scald your tongue."

Tobias flinched, just slightly, and let go to rub his hand nervously on his knee until Jake caught it. Closing his fingers around Tobias's hand was like coming home. "If you take the lid off, I'm sure it'll be fine in a minute."

Tobias gazed at Jake's hand around his, then looked up with a hopeful smile that felt even better.

❧

TOBIAS HADN'T KNOWN what to expect when Jake described the coffee shop. Not that he'd known what to expect when they went anywhere, though he was getting better, he *knew* he was.

But now that they were here and settled down with their coffee, he . . . liked it. The shop had bright paintings and people who seemed nice. The coffee was sweet despite a bitter aftertaste, the music overhead was soothing, and Jake was making jokes and still holding his hand.

It was a good spot too, where they had their backs to a wall and Tobias had a good view of all the reals in the place. Nothing would be able to sneak up on him. He knew that Jake would protect him, but it was always better to see all possible avenues of attack.

The only thing jarring was the group of young women right next to them. They were louder than anyone else in the room and excited about something, jumping forward in their seats at times. Tobias couldn't help tensing, because that was a surefire way to pull a guard over, and nothing good would follow.

But there were no guards here. No one paid attention to the girls. Jake grinned at him, occasionally nudging their shoulders together, and the coffee was rich and filling. Tobias was pretty sure he could've had just one of these mocha things for an entire meal. He was in a public place and breathing okay, not embarrassing Jake or doing anything to draw attention.

Jake downed the last of his coffee. "Hey, will you be okay here for, like, two minutes while I take a piss?"

Tobias nodded. That wouldn't be so bad, knowing the whole time where Jake was, knowing he was coming back. And the reals in the coffeehouse weren't going to try to attack him the second Jake stepped away. They *wouldn't*. He was almost positive.

"Sure. I'll be right here." Tobias did his best to smile and got a brighter one back as a reward. *Good choice, maybe you're finally figuring out what makes him happy.*

He couldn't keep his eyes from following Jake around the corner, out of sight. Then Tobias dropped his gaze to the table, working to keep his posture casual, no different from any of the reals around him, though he no longer had the confidence to look up and check. He tried to slow his heartbeat. *It's going to be fine. Just like when Jake goes on a run. He'll be back to check on you in a few minutes.* But this time he wasn't locked safely in the apartment. A dozen reals sat mere feet away, and if Tobias made any wrong moves, they would be able to tell.

He turned the coffee cup slowly in his hands, focusing on the creamy liquid and how good it tasted, how wonderful Jake was to bring him here and buy it for him. That was the trade-off, wasn't it? Jake brought Tobias places, gave him good things, and in exchange Tobias had to cope with the people around him. He could do that. He could learn and do better each time. He still didn't understand why Jake wanted him to interact with reals or just be around them, but Tobias didn't have to under-stand a task to perform it well. This was no different from a task from the Director or an order from the guards, except that it was so much more important. But he couldn't think about how very important this was, either, because that didn't change anything, only made his chest clench more, made it harder to breathe. He wouldn't disappoint Jake. Period.

After a minute of staring at his coffee—he had automati-cally started counting his breaths the second Jake disappeared —Tobias summoned the courage to lift his eyes and look around the room. This was possibly his favorite place so far, except for the library and their apartment. The pictures hung on the brick walls showed lush meadows, a bright blue sky, and animals—most frequently goats—in warm browns and oranges. The reals around the room were smiling and more relaxed than even in the donut shop. Yes, this was a good place.

He also liked the music playing from somewhere overhead. It wasn't at all like Jake's, but it was soft, and—he didn't have words to begin to describe it, but it was just *nice*.

The song faded to a close. Tobias had a second to savor the ending before one of the nearby girls slapped her hand on the table and let out a shriek that cut through the background murmur of conversation. Tobias flinched and dropped his eyes.

"No way—no *way!* You're totally bullshitting me. *Tell me* that's bullshit."

Keeping calm was hard when the real girls talked so much louder and angrier, drowning out every attempt Tobias made to block them out and focus on something else.

"I swear to God, Tina, I saw them myself."

One of the girls, numerous bangles dangling around her wrist, gestured dismissively—Tobias couldn't stop himself from glancing up at the sound, instinct telling him that it could be some kind of attack. She sniffed. "Well, excuse me, but next time I see that ugly whore I'm gonna punch her face in!"

"Jeez, Tina," another girl said, rolling her eyes. "Way to be harsh."

"Whatever, I don't care. She *is* a whore, and just thinking about her plastering those fat lips all over his face makes me sick. I'm gonna vomit, not even kidding. I mean, what the fuck makes her think she deserves . . . *anything* from a guy like Brad? Oh my God, someone needs to warn him before he gets a *disease.*"

The coffee shop lost focus, and Tobias couldn't draw air or fight the sudden dizzy nausea in the pit of his stomach. He dropped his forehead into his hands, squeezed his eyes shut, and struggled to breathe. He couldn't draw attention to himself, that was the last thing . . . the very last thing . . . and when Jake came back . . .

Tobias couldn't finish the thought. Everything that had made him happy a second ago—the idea of looking into Jake's face, the sweet taste of coffee—soured in his mouth, because he had *remembered.*

There was some dirty freak whore out there that these reals had discovered and despised as much as the Director had despised Tobias. He never should have forgotten.

It didn't matter that none of the reals recognized him yet. It didn't even matter that Jake didn't seem to care that Tobias was nothing but a freak (how could Jake know and care and still hold him, touch him, even sleep next to him?). Jake had always known that Tobias was a monster—unidentified, yes, but that didn't really make a difference—and had still treated him like a real, like he cared what happened to him. Tobias could almost believe that Jake's kindness was permissible. Not deserved, but if Jake wanted to be kind to him, it wasn't completely wrong, completely an abomination.

Jake had always known what Tobias was. But he couldn't possibly know what Tobias had *done*.

If he did, he'd be . . . disgusted would be the best of it. Angry. Furious. Violent, and rightly so. Tobias had basically been *lying* every time he let Jake touch him, every second Tobias had tricked Jake into treating him like he was something clean.

The Director had said more than once that monsters corrupted as easily as they breathed, because it was what they did naturally. That he had to gag Tobias sometimes just to stop him from instinctively trying to deceive, manipulate, and warp the reals around him.

But what shredded Tobias now from the inside, what made him almost want a hunter to walk in and tell Jake everything, was because he knew now, again, what he was.

Not only did he not have the right to touch Jake, but he had to watch himself. If he didn't have the strength or permission to relieve Jake of the danger of contact with him, he could at least —he had the *obligation* to—watch himself so that Jake wasn't contaminated by a freak. So that he wasn't being manipulated, corrupted, forced into that denigration.

∾

JAKE FELT PRETTY good as he came out of the bathroom—discovering a new thing Tobias liked always made it an awesome day—right up to the second he caught sight of Tobias. Then he sprinted the eight feet from the bathroom to the table, dodging chairs, adrenaline making him wish it were a hundred yards so maybe he could work out more of the panic before he had to try to be sensible for Tobias.

He was right where Jake had left him, his half-full coffee resting about the same place, but he was a different Tobias entirely from the cautiously happy, smiling, slightly nervous one Jake had left no more than five fucking minutes ago. This was the Tobias of last week: hunched in his chair, head in his hands, shoulders tight as he tried to make himself as small as possible.

Even before Jake had properly landed in his chair, he grabbed Tobias's arm. "Tobias, are you hurt?"

Tobias dropped his hands, jerking back as though Jake's fingers burned his skin. He would have fallen from the chair if he wasn't wedged against the wall and if Jake was ready to let go of him that quickly. There could still be blood or an injury *somewhere*.

Jake swallowed painfully and forced himself to release Tobias's arm. Sick, too-familiar panic was crawling in him, growing and twisting with every second.

Tobias didn't move when Jake cautiously shifted away, didn't make eye contact when Jake said his name. "Tobias. C'mon, man, look at me. Please." *Shit*, what had happened? "Please look at me, Tobias. Tell me what happened."

Tobias didn't look up. He just shook his head quickly, breathing shaky and uneven. Another panic attack, then, or close enough. Jake felt lost, drowning. Every other time he'd had an idea of what set Tobias off. He had to know, he *had* to so he could stop it, so he could take out anyone or anything that so much as made Tobias cringe. "Did someone say something to you? Did someone—touch you? Tobias?"

Tobias shook his head again, frantically, and Jake knew he had lost him. There was nowhere good to go from here, and they had to retreat to familiar ground, *now*, before whatever the hell this was got worse.

Jake stood. "C'mon, let's get out of here." He moved back, making room for Tobias to pass between the wall and the cluster of gossiping girls.

Tobias rose stiffly, holding his cup of coffee between both hands, head bowed to his chest. When Jake followed, he laid a hand on Tobias's back. That same move that had calmed him every single other time Tobias had been upset, but now he *shuddered*, so hard the coffee spilled over his fingers. He didn't pull away, but the taut muscles jumped under Jake's touch.

Jake jerked his hand back.

He couldn't look at him in the car. Tobias didn't look out the window, didn't look at Jake, didn't drink from the coffee cup cradled in his hands. Once they reached the apartment, Jake took his time putting away his keys and wallet and hanging his jacket before turning back in time to see Tobias carefully set the cup down on the breakfast bar and clamp his arms over his chest. His posture was too much like the night Jake had caught him scratching his arms. It looked too fucking much like Tobias was in pain and Jake could do nothing.

Moving forward, he grabbed Tobias's hands—more forcefully than usual, but he had to break through this shell. He was determined to reach the Tobias he had had barely half an hour ago, who had met his eyes and *wanted* to move closer to him. But Tobias's hands—after Jake unpinned them from Tobias's chest—were limp in his, unresponsive.

"Tobias. If you don't talk to me, I can't—I want to *help*. If could just understand whatever the fuck—dammit, Tobias, *look at me*."

Tobias pulled his head up, but his eyes were blank and fixed on some point beyond Jake, nowhere near his eyes. Then he spoke painfully. "You shouldn't. You shouldn't touch me, I should've never—"

With a sharp inhale, Jake let go and stepped back.

"Sorry, Tobias. I shouldn't've ... won't ... yeah."

He flexed his hands to see if they really were working—everything felt numb, and he wondered seriously if he'd short-circuited something in his head—and then grabbed the remote from the coffee table. He needed noise right now. He needed something to think about that wasn't Tobias *pleading* for Jake not to touch him, to keep his pushy hands to himself. Jake didn't look at Tobias to see if he was watching Jake with loathing or fear. He couldn't take either.

He put the volume on high, walked to his bedroom, and closed the door.

Tobias didn't want to watch the television. The flickering lights reminded him of the strobes occasionally used in interrogations, or the spotlights that cut through the yard during the demon attack years ago. The lights didn't bother him when Jake was next to him, or when he could sink into a book. But now, Jake was in the other room, and even thinking about reading made Tobias sick. With short, halting steps, he moved to the couch and sat down.

It felt like forever. It felt like no time at all. Tobias was so sunk into his own despair (*he was just a whore; he'd managed to make Jake even more upset; he wished he could turn off the light and noise and be alone with his misery, but Jake had turned it on and he didn't have the right*) that he didn't hear Jake leave his room, didn't know he was coming until he was just *there*, staring at him from beside the television.

Looking into Jake's blank, drawn face, Tobias tightened his hands over his own arms and bowed his head to his knees. Here it was. Jake couldn't just ignore it anymore. Tobias had absolutely, definitely done something wrong, and there was only one logical result.

"Tobias." Jake's voice sounded rough, like he'd been screaming. "Can I sit down?"

Tobias's hands tightened involuntarily until he felt his nails digging into the flesh of his arm, and he abruptly let go. Jake had been very clear about that rule, that he could not hurt himself—*wouldn't do a good enough job, anyway*—and he couldn't. He would not break any rules. He was obedient. Not good or clean or worthwhile, but obedient.

He couldn't answer, though. It had been a question, but there was no possible answer that Tobias could give. The couch was Jake's, and Tobias was Jake's, and he could do what he liked on and with his property.

"Yeah, I'll sit down then." Jake lowered himself—had he been hurt? Why was he moving that way, like something was broken?—onto the couch more than a foot away from Tobias. He picked up the remote and turned off the television. The sudden absence of light and noise hurt almost as much as its presence had grated. Like cold water on a fresh burn.

"Tobias."

He flinched. He had always loved that Jake used his name. Without Jake, he would have lost that years ago and been nothing but *Pretty Freak* and *Whore*. But now it hurt because in reality, the other two names were all he was. Maybe it would hurt less if Jake acknowledged that.

Jake continued, not really waiting for any kind of response. Not that Tobias expected him to. "I know you've been . . . they hurt you. Those bastards at camp. I've seen the black eyes and the . . ." He gestured at Tobias's forearm.

Tobias's mouth went dry, and his right hand tightened

around his left wrist. He could feel the bones grinding together and couldn't stop himself.

"But I think . . . if I hadn't been such a coward, I would've asked you right after the first night, when . . ." Jake closed his eyes and took a deep, pained breath. Had he broken a rib? *How?* "Tobias, did they . . . fuck, I don't even know how to ask."

Tobias didn't know what Jake was asking. He didn't want to know. Even though Jake couldn't possibly have learned in such a short period of time, it seemed like he was asking about *that*.

"*Fuck*." The word was quiet and heartfelt. "Tobias, I know they hurt you, but did you . . . look, I need to know . . . did they . . ."

Then Tobias knew exactly what Jake wanted to know, and he couldn't hold back the panic with the blinding realization that Jake wanted to know if he had been fucked.

He hadn't. Jake had to believe that, or this was all over. It would be over tonight.

"No!" The word was too violent, too much like a lie, so he tried to drag it back, but Jake *had* to believe him. "No, no, no, Jake, they didn't, I d-didn't l-let them, I p-promise. No, please please please, they n-never did, I *swear*."

He was almost clawing at his leg with his left hand while crushing his wrist with the right. He could feel his throat closing up, and *fuck*, how could he be close to crying at a time like this, when it mattered so much that Jake believed him? Tears, begging—those never persuaded or staved off pain.

When Jake caught his wrists, gently pulling his hands apart, Tobias sobbed once and forced his body to be still, tried to be obedient, whatever that meant at this moment, whatever Jake wanted, whatever would relieve the pain Tobias could see in Jake's body. But Jake just planted Tobias's hands together on the couch next to his own thigh.

"Okay, okay, it's okay, Tobias. I believe you. It's okay. Don't do that, don't hurt yourself. I believe you, it's okay."

Jake didn't sound like he completely believed him. He sounded like Tobias had to do more to prove himself. He had heard that tone many times in his life, and he was still here, alive and sitting on Jake's couch because he had obeyed, because he had proven his sincerity in any way that was necessary, and he would again.

"They didn't, Jake. I swear they didn't." When Jake reached for him, Tobias curled up in spite of himself, even though everything he was belonged to Jake.

"Tobias." Jake's hand brushed over his hair, then nudged his chin until he'd raised his head to see Jake. The touch was still so gentle, soft, and Tobias didn't understand why there wasn't any pain. Where was the fucking pain? "I believe you, Toby." Jake sounded like he was trying to prove it to Tobias. Tobias didn't understand. "It's okay. I'm glad those bastards didn't . . . It's okay."

Something was wrong with Jake. Even though Tobias didn't know what it was, he couldn't stop shaking, couldn't keep his hands still on the couch, couldn't even keep his eyes on Jake without trembling.

"Yeah, I'm glad they didn't." Letting go of Tobias's face and wrists, Jake leaned away. He rested his head against the back of the couch and stared at the ceiling. "'Cause that's just not okay, Tobias. No one should do that. You get that?"

"Y-yes, Jake. I und-d-derstand. They d-didn't." There was something sad in Jake's eyes, like he really didn't believe Tobias at all, like he regretted what he would have to do to Tobias because he was lying. But Tobias *wasn't* lying, he hadn't, he wouldn't, and if Jake didn't believe that, Tobias would be lucky to end up dead by morning.

The other option, if he couldn't prove now that he had done everything he could to stay whole for Jake, was that the Director would hand him straight to Crusher when he was returned to FREACS, because he wouldn't even be worth training anymore. "They d-didn't, I s-swear."

"Not okay for anyone." Jake sounded now like he was talking to himself. Tobias couldn't think, couldn't think of anything he could do to prove to Jake that he was still undefiled for the taking.

Tobias had almost decided to go to his knees to try to show Jake something he was good for when Jake got to his feet. He still looked hollowed out, in pain, and he didn't so much as glance at Tobias.

"All right, Tobias. Go to bed or something. Read, watch TV, I don't . . ." He shook his head. "I'm going out. I'll be back in a few hours." He glanced back once, and then away. "You'll be safe here, I promise."

Jake picked up his jacket, wallet, and keys. Tobias had no idea what was going on. He would be *safe*? But where was Jake going? What? Why?

There had been orders, but Tobias couldn't process them because Jake was pulling on his jacket and opening the door.

Tobias watched. He *stared*, even though that should have earned him a beating all by itself. This had to be a test, a joke, maybe even a punishment. Any of those things he would understand. But not Jake *leaving*.

Then Jake glanced back, but this time his eyes didn't even make it to Tobias's face.

"You'll be safe," he repeated, his voice harsher, not like Jake's at all. Then, almost inaudibly: "Safe from *everybody*."

The door slammed shut after him.

9

Tobias had only been sick two or three times in all the time he had been in Freak Camp, but he still recognized it when it came. First a cough that he couldn't quite get out of his throat, no matter how hard he tried to control it—though he had managed never to cough when Jake was in the same room—then shivers down his arms and his back, nausea and tremors that he couldn't stop. In the last few days, since he had remembered why Jake should despise him and never touch him, it had been harder and harder to hold down the rich, greasy foods that Jake shared with him.

He hated throwing up any food that Jake had bought for him—*ungrateful, useless whore*—and he didn't think that he would survive if Jake caught him doing it. He wouldn't have to wait for Freak Camp if he turned away from vomiting up the latest burger or bowl of chili and saw Jake's horrified face looking down at him. So he managed to eat, to smile, even to look Jake in the eye while his stomach clenched and writhed, and then quietly excused himself to the bathroom where he emptied everything out again.

His stomach he could handle, but the cough was getting

worse every day. Holding it in felt like he was choking himself. He was dimly, bitterly grateful that Jake had stopped touching him. How horrible would it be for Jake to touch not only a monster and a whore, but a diseased, pestilent one?

Friday night was when he first felt the chills and the world slid in and out of focus, sick dread filling him. Why the hell was he getting sick *now* of all times? He had been healthy for years and years in Freak Camp in infinitely worse conditions, and only now did it really matter.

By Sunday, he was done feeling sorry for himself and cursing the universe and the immune system that was stabbing him in the back. It hadn't mattered that Jake didn't hit, burn, or beat him, and he'd given Tobias the best food and conditions he could imagine. Tobias was a monster, and this was just what had to happen. Even if he hadn't fucked up everything with his behavior (though he must be doing something wrong, or maybe Jake *knew*, why else would he hardly look at him anymore?), his body had done it for him.

Tobias sat on the soft bed in his generous room and let himself shake because he couldn't help it. He didn't have the strength to stop the tremors anymore. He felt so damn cold, but he knew that getting beneath the covers wouldn't help. If he tried to take a hot shower—even assuming he could get as far as the bathroom without Jake *seeing*—it might help the horrible feeling that he was freezing to death in a warm room, but he didn't think he'd be able to stay upright for long under the pounding water. Much safer to stay in his room where Jake wouldn't see him, and let the shaking take him, let the sickness churn through him while he hoped it would leave him, that Jake would somehow forgive him.

He couldn't believe a shred of the hope.

Few monsters got sick at Freak Camp. Most were immune to what could get passed around. If one did, no one would touch them or even look at them. No one wanted to risk catching one of the few diseases that could spread through all monster species. The guards wouldn't touch a freak if they could tell that he had something. The only option was to lie on the hard, cold bunk and shake. Either you got up again in three days, or you went to Special Research, where no monster was ever seen again.

Tobias had no idea how it would work for him in Jake's apartment. He knew that reals had hospitals and doctors, but he neither expected nor wanted to go somewhere with sick reals, who needed the least amount of natural and supernatural contamination. He was sure that whatever disease he had, it would be devastating for a real. Monsters were supposed to be stronger, harder to kill, and now he could barely draw breath.

He didn't know what Jake would do when he found out. He hoped that Jake would just let him lie in sticky sweat and try to burn the illness out. He would get up or he would die. That would be nice, but he didn't have much confidence it would be that simple. Why would Jake want him dying in this beautiful room, this comfortable bed? Monsters didn't deserve this, least of all when they finally expired.

He had to clench his eyes shut and fist his hands to hold back the nausea when he realized the walls were thin enough that he would hear the phone call Jake made to the ASC for freak pick-up. Tobias couldn't contaminate the Eldorado on the drive back to Nevada. Dirty black vans with chains on the walls waited for things like Tobias.

He thought he had time. This was the first day he hadn't left the room. When he had stepped out yesterday—sat with Jake for three meals at the kitchen table, held his breath when he'd gone through Jake's bedroom to shower in his bathroom, stared at a book while Jake flipped through channels on the TV, his movements jerky and unhappy—Jake hadn't seemed to notice anything wrong. At least he hadn't called him out on the unsatisfactory behavior, hadn't given him an ultimatum. This was his first day down, and Tobias thought that he could get himself back up in a couple more, at least enough to maintain the illusion that he was reliable enough to keep around.

He thought he had fucking time.

But then he heard Jake at his door, his footsteps coming to a halt. "Hey, what do you want for dinner tonight? I'm thinking Chinese or pizza. Your call."

Jake expected an answer. He would stay there until Tobias responded. Tobias opened his mouth to say "pizza" or "I'm not hungry" or *something*, but all that came out was a choked, croaking noise that he didn't think reached the door.

Panic didn't help him clear his throat. Worse, he couldn't clear his throat without coughing, which would give away how sick and useless he was. He swallowed convulsively, his shoulders shaking as he tried to clear the phlegm and bile without making a sound that would give him away.

Jake knocked on the closed door again, harder. "Hey, Tobias, you've got to answer me, man. I haven't seen you all day, the least you can do is tell me what you want to eat."

JAKE FUCKING HATED THIS: standing in front of Tobias's shut door, asking him what he wanted for dinner when he really wanted to ask him where the fuck Jake had gone so wrong as to make Tobias hide from him like this, like he was even *more* afraid. Ever since that stupid fucking goat coffee shop, Tobias had become miles more withdrawn, less willing to speak or even stay in the same room with Jake.

It hurt. It hurt more than Jake had expected, even compared to when he'd thought about how it would feel if Tobias didn't need him anymore, if he had the strength to tell Jake he wanted to leave and never see him again. Tobias had hardly spoken on

Saturday. He'd come out for meals, to pretend to read—Jake wasn't fucking blind, even if Tobias remembered to turn the pages every once in a while—before disappearing into his room again. He looked pale and withdrawn, like he was being haunted.

But he wasn't, because Jake had checked the wards four times over yesterday, even laying an extra line of salt out over the carpet, and nothing did the trick.

Then Tobias made his excuses to go to bed early, leaving Jake with a deck of cards in his hand and the stupid hope that they could put something together again. Jake had put the cards away and grabbed his coat to hit the second-closest bar. He'd gotten wasted at the closest on Friday, and he didn't like to repeat himself too often.

But by the time he had got back to the apartment—drunk, but not shit-faced—he'd decided that it was fine if Tobias didn't want to talk for a while. If he wanted to spend the least amount of time in Jake's company as possible. He needed his space. Jake shouldn't have pushed about that whole abuse thing. He should have just left Tobias the hell alone, especially when he already looked so shattered and unsteady (*damn* fucking goat shop). But Jake had pushed him, so the best thing he could do now was just back the fuck off and let Tobias recover. Because Tobias *would* recover. And if it took him not talking to Jake or being able to stand his company for a little while, that was a-okay. Jake could deal.

That plan was fine—okay, not at all, horrible and miserable and fucked-up, but the best one he could come up with.

Then Jake woke up hungover past noon on Sunday, stumbled to the kitchen, swallowed his aspirin with some orange juice, and put out the dishes for a late breakfast. He figured he'd wait for Tobias to appear—Tobias seemed to generally wait until Jake was up before leaving his room—before making anything. If meals were the only thing they would have together, the only time Tobias could bear to be near him, then that was what he would take, but he wouldn't cheat himself of that. So he waited, drinking the orange juice against the nagging pain in his skull, trying to ignore the call of the whiskey in his cabinet.

At two-fifteen, Jake finished the last of the orange juice, got up, and put everything away. He hadn't a clue what he wanted to do, but he opened the laptop in the living room, looking for hunts he probably wouldn't take. He cleaned his knives. He checked the salt lines. And the door to Tobias's room remained noiselessly, completely shut until the sun went down and it was dinnertime again. So Jake went over for one more try, another stupid attempt, because Tobias *had* to eat, and it was the time to eat, so it followed that Jake would see him again.

He asked at the door, trying to lock down his stress and gnawing desperation, and got nothing.

He had been ready not to see Tobias much. To give him some space, maybe just talk with him at meals, or maybe not even then. But not seeing him at all for *an entire day* was too fucking much. And now he wasn't saying *anything*, and all Jake wanted to do was charge in there and grab him, maybe shake him until he fucking realized that Jake didn't want to hurt him. Which Jake knew made no sense and was about the stupidest thing he could do, but it was hard to think of a better plan when his muscles itched to move and his nerves crawled at the silence, the dead accusations behind that door.

He settled for knocking on the wood again, harder. "Come on, Tobias, don't leave me hanging here. Just tell me what you want and I'll get the fuck out of your hair." He knew he sounded angry, and he didn't care. Not too much. Didn't a guy fucking deserve to be angry once in a while?

But when the silence lasted longer than some kind of shunning or guilt trip usually would, a little voice wondered if Tobias was even in there.

Jake couldn't imagine Tobias on his own in the world. He couldn't see Tobias willing to go out and interact with people, but now he couldn't shake the gut-deep fear that maybe Tobias hadn't been able to take it anymore—whatever the fuck had happened between them—and had left.

Every day, every hour that Tobias refused to talk to him or even stay in the same room as him, the little voice inside Jake got louder. That the struggle to get Tobias out of Freak Camp, the half-nightmare, half-dream of the last three weeks, was nothing but an elaborate illusion, fantasizing the happiness and the pain together because he was that lonely and messed up.

It was a stupid idea that didn't make sense for a second, but Jake couldn't stop his hand from turning the doorknob, even as he reminded himself that he was just being a fucking stalker again, invading Tobias's privacy when he clearly wanted nothing to do with Jake. Jake braced himself for the flinch, the accusing eyes, the silence. He'd open the door and take the consequences, another knife in the gut because he couldn't accept the obvious meaning of Tobias's silence and leave him the fuck alone.

But Jake forgot all of that when he saw Tobias hunched on the edge of the bed, supporting himself with his thin, stiff arms and shaking like a leaf.

For a second, Jake thought that he was the reason that Tobias shook. Then he saw the sweat glistening on his skin and the way his teeth clenched every time a tremor took his body— as though he was trying to fight them off.

Jake moved in without conscious thought. Tobias tried to move away from him—*Of course he doesn't want you near him, why would he?*—and would have slid off the bed, but Jake was there, catching him, pulling him back up, and sitting down next to him.

This close, Tobias's way-too-thin body in his arms, Jake

could feel the shakes moving through his body and hear the rough rasp in his throat. He put a hand to Tobias's forehead, ignoring the way Tobias flinched—of course Tobias still expected to be hit—and almost jerked away from the heat radiating from him.

"Fuck, Tobias, you're burning up."

Tobias dropped his head, briefly touching Jake's shoulder before swaying away. He might have fallen over if Jake didn't have his arm around him. He tried to speak—Jake could feel his lungs expanding, could see his throat working—but all that came out was a fit of desperate coughing. Tobias turned his mouth into his own shoulder, shuddering.

"I'm s-s-sorry," he rasped when the coughing had subsided. "I tried not—"

"Shhhh." Jake pulled Tobias closer. Tobias continued shaking against him, the vibrations moving from his shoulder into Jake's chest. No damn way was he going to move away when Tobias might collapse without him, when Tobias was hot enough, if not to fry an egg, then to reheat pizza. "You hungry at all?"

Tobias shook his head, still hiding his face. He was limp in Jake's arms, but not like he trusted Jake. It was more like whatever was going to happen, whatever Jake wanted to do to him, Tobias couldn't work up the energy to resist. He was just a willing, empty vessel of skin and bone in Jake's arms. Shit, had he gained any fucking weight since Jake had gotten him out of the camp?

"Come on, Tobias," Jake said, shifting him carefully, suddenly sure he was holding something precious and breakable. "You're soaked. You need to get into dry clothes and under the covers."

Tobias nodded again. His hands moved to his chest, fumbling at the buttons on his shirt, until Jake braced him against his shoulder and reached for the top button. Opening a shirt was strange from that angle, both like and unlike when he worked on buttons on himself or opened a partner's shirt from the front, but he managed it.

Undressing Tobias felt wrong and made him uncomfortable in a way he didn't want to examine closely. Tobias didn't need to be afraid of him, not ever, and certainly not now.

Then he saw the first scar, and it got a lot fucking easier to focus. It wasn't much by itself: a white starburst about the size of a dime, visible on the already pale strip of skin exposed when Jake pushed back the shirt. But that scar had a partner an inch away. Beneath that was a thick, ragged furrow that trailed down the side of Tobias's ribs. Jake followed that white trailing scar, pushing the shirt farther back on Tobias's shoulders, baring most of his chest and his upper arms, and he realized that those ugly raised marks were only the beginning. It was as though he had followed one worm down to a nest and found hundreds.

Straight white scars forming grids, crooked scars, fat welts, thin scores, palm-sized pink plains of scarred skin and burns, layered over and over each other like the weave of an old rug: horrifying and almost beautiful if one could ignore that it had been carved into human flesh. Jake couldn't. What he saw in Tobias's skin was *pain*, so much pain, years and years of it woven into Tobias's skin where neither of them could escape or forget it.

Jake pulled the shirt off harder than he should have and pulled Tobias around so that his face pressed against Jake's chest and Jake could look over his shoulder, run his hands down the textured sea of old wounds.

Tobias's back was worse than his chest. Worse than anything Jake had seen before on a human body, and all this had happened because he had not rescued Tobias sooner.

Fine, dammit, what had happened at Freak Camp was not

Jake's fault. He hadn't held the knife, brand, whip, or whatever the hell had left those ugly little starbursts. Probably most of this damage had happened long before Jake had his ASC license. But he could have done *something* if he had gotten his head out of his ass long enough to actually *see* what was going on around him. He should have paid more attention. Fuck, he had known since the day he saw that damn smiley face scar on Tobias's forearm that he was being hurt. He had probably been hurt *every fucking day*, but had Jake done anything to stop that? Had he done one damn thing to stop those bastards other than branding one of their sadistic, sneering faces? And even that had been motivated by rage more than any thought of helping Tobias.

He had failed Tobias again and again. And the worst part was that Tobias didn't expect—had never expected—anything better of Jake than he had of the bastards who carved their marks into his skin.

TOBIAS HELD AS STILL as he could in Jake's arms, shivery face pressed against Jake's shirt, and wished he knew what the fuck was going on.

Jake wasn't angry, not that he could be wholly sure with the way the world was going in and out of focus. He was *holding* Tobias like he hadn't in days and telling him he had to go to bed, and Tobias didn't understand any of it. He had always known that Jake was better, kinder than the guards, that he would never hurt him unless Tobias deserved it—*What if he did hurt you? Wouldn't it be a relief to know what would finally push him over the edge? Wouldn't it be a relief to be treated a fraction like you deserve?*—but he couldn't begin to understand Jake *holding* him while Tobias coughed into his shirt and sickness burned from him.

Then Jake started taking his shirt off, and all Tobias could think was *Oh God, finally?*

But why now? Why when Tobias was so feverish that he couldn't concentrate on anything, could barely bring Jake's eyes into focus, but he could feel Jake's hands on his chest, unbuttoning his shirt? He closed his eyes and tried to breathe as deeply and evenly as possible, fighting down another cough that threatened to close his throat and rattle him in Jake's arms.

He couldn't think straight, couldn't make sense of his environment, but he tried to brace himself nonetheless. It was impossible to wrap his head around why Jake would get off on him being sick and nearly unable to draw a breath. But if it were true, he wished he had known earlier. *I could have faked this*, he thought. *I could have done this for you if I had just fucking known.*

Then Jake found a scar and followed it with his fingers. Tobias felt him tense, felt his interest change. The hands sliding the shirt off his back and turning Tobias's body never became violent, but Tobias knew Jake wasn't happy anymore. One quick glance at his face confirmed all of Tobias's worst fears again. Rage, disgust, horror.

Oh shit, Tobias thought, *he doesn't like scars*. He had to fight down a bubble of hysteria, something that rose up from his gut and threatened to choke him more thoroughly than the coughs. *Well, I'm fucking screwed then.*

But even while he fought that burst of delirium, a part of himself that he had tried to break a long time ago—the part that *wanted* things—whimpered and whined in the back of his mind, a place he could force himself to ignore except when Jake wrapped him in his arms. *I can't change that anymore. I tried not to get caught, I tried not to get beaten, but I couldn't . . . I couldn't stop them. What did you expect me to do?*

Something, clearly. Jake hated the scars. Would shove him away at any second.

There had to be something worse than Jake pushing him away. Being sick and alone had been Tobias's best option earlier, but now it seemed the worst. Worse than death, worse than Freak Camp.

The rational part of his mind knew that wasn't true. There was nothing worse than Freak Camp and nothing safer than death. But Jake leaving him now . . . what would be the point of getting healthy if Jake hated the scars, would never look at him without disgust because of them?

I've done so much worse, Jake, Tobias thought. *So many better reasons for you to hate me.*

Eventually, Jake's hands running gently up and down his back came to a stop, and he rested his head on Tobias's shoulder.

This is it, Tobias thought. *Go ahead, Jake, just leave me.*

"You need to rest," Jake said at last. There was something wrong with his voice, something tight and choked, and Tobias shivered for a reason other than fever. Jake couldn't be getting sick, not this fast, but he sounded like he felt as queasy and weak as Tobias. But his arms around Tobias's shoulders never loosened, and Tobias couldn't hear anything wrong in Jake's lungs. He would be able to with his ear pressed so close to Jake's chest. "Lie back."

Jake started to push him away and down, and Tobias rallied the remainder of his resources to grab at his arm and hold his shirt. "Jake," he rasped. But that was as far as he got before his chest clenched, and anything he tried to say dissolved in coughing.

Distantly, he felt Jake pushing him down on the bed, reaching for his pants. Tobias tensed and tried to turn himself, tried to help Jake as much as he could, even though the room was spinning and he couldn't separate the feel of Jake's hands from the pressure of his back on the bed and his clenched fists.

One second he was lying there, wondering if he was hallucinating, fantasizing about being claimed, finally taken by the only person in the world he had ever wanted. The next second, Jake was pulling a pair of sweatpants into place over his hips and working a shirt over his head.

Tobias gasped, bucked a little, struggling for breath, and Jake put a hand on his chest. "Shhhh." He tugged the shirt the rest of the way down. From the side table he picked up a steaming mug (where had that come from?), fit his other arm under Tobias's back to lift him into a sitting position halfway up, and gently brought the mug to his lips. "Come on, Toby, drink."

Tobias did as he was told, even as his stomach twisted on itself and he couldn't quite swallow properly. Jake had him take a small sip and then waited patiently while he forced it down. Oh God, what if he threw up on Jake?

Tobias would not let himself think about that. He couldn't. Instead, he concentrated on the astonishing feel of Jake's arm supporting him, the rim of the cup against his lips, the warm liquid moving down his throat. About three swallows down, he realized that he was hungry, and thirsty, and that he was still shaking but didn't feel quite so damn cold. He looked down and saw a couple of water-filled soda bottles packed around his legs. Those were the sources of warmth. He had thought that it was just a normal reaction to having Jake still be there.

He had no idea how much time he had lost. He didn't know what had happened. But he didn't think it had been what he had expected. He didn't think Jake had taken him. And yet, inexplicably, Jake was still there, feeding him soup and wrapping him with warmth and gentleness. It was so wrong. If a monster was sick, he didn't deserve to be put in a warm bed in clean clothes, bundled with hot water bottles and . . . *touched*. He deserved nothing. Healthy he was damn near useless, but *sick* he was a burden, nothing but a dead weight. Tobias could hear every word of what the Director would say.

It was wrong to have Jake still beside him. So wrong and so wonderful. He couldn't imagine anything better. There was nothing better.

When Jake took the mug away, Tobias couldn't keep from smiling, couldn't hold back the happiness, even though that might make Jake angry or make him think that Tobias didn't know what a *fucking useless burden* he was. But Jake only looked a little relieved when he saw Tobias's smile. He even smiled crookedly back at him, and that made Tobias feel loopier than he had at any point in the last two days.

"Hey, Toby." Jake's voice still sounded wrong, but Tobias reassured himself that Jake didn't look sick. He just looked *sad*. He pulled the covers up to Tobias's chest, picking up the towel he had set under Tobias's chin. "You're really sick. You need to sleep, okay?"

Tobias nodded. He took a breath and managed to exhale without coughing. Settling into the covers, he closed his eyes but snapped them open again when he felt Jake get up from the bed.

"Don't go." Now, why had he said that? Jake was helping him, he hadn't thrown him to the curb yet, and here Tobias was fucking it up by being a needy, useless monster, so much more trouble than he was worth. He'd even involuntarily reached for Jake, fucking *reached* for him when he was sick and sad and wanted more than anything for Jake to stay.

It was a stupid, impudent thing to say, but the look on Jake's face—surprise, hope, unnamable things, and a slow touch of wonder—said it hadn't been stupid at all. Maybe it had been exactly right.

He came back.

Tobias still closed his eyes when Jake eased down on the bed and reached for his face. Jake didn't like it when he flinched, and if Tobias saw the touch coming, he wouldn't be able to stop himself. Not when hands in the past had ground against his eyes, his nose, forced hard gags into his mouth and applied knives and hot rods close to his face, though not so high that it would leave marks where the guards had to look at him every day.

But all Jake's hand did was rest on his hair. Then slowly, softly, he began stroking downward from his forehead to his neck, over and over again. Tobias's eyes flickered open briefly and then closed. He was afraid to look, afraid to do anything that would make Jake stop.

"I'm here," Jake said. "I'm here, and I'm not going anywhere. Get some sleep. Just relax, Tobias, I won't let them hurt you ever again."

Tobias tried to keep awake, tried to savor the contact. Who knew when something this good would happen to him again or how long Jake would stay?

But he couldn't fight sleep when his body was exhausted and shaking for rest and healing. He drifted in spite of himself, drawn by the steady, soft brush of Jake's fingers over his feverish skin, into his first deep, dreamless sleep in days.

The next morning, Tobias managed to drink some of the broth Jake gave him, but that night when Jake brought him mushroom soup (*Sorry, this is all we got left. I'll hit the store later, get you some chicken broth*), he couldn't hold it down.

He made it as far as the bathroom—tile, he could scrub tile, he wasn't sure he could get the stains out of carpet—before he was on his knees, vomiting into the wastebasket. He flinched when Jake touched him—*Please don't hit me now, I don't want to throw up on you*—but Jake just tugged him gently over to the toilet. Tobias felt a dull moment of dread when Jake opened the seat and pushed his head toward the bowl, but he stopped well before Tobias's face was anywhere near the water. Then Jake let go of his head, crouched next to him, and rubbed Tobias's back while he shook.

"Hey, it's okay. You're gonna be okay, Toby."

But Jake didn't sound okay. He sounded like he had a nail in his hand and it hurt every time Tobias shook.

"You shouldn't—" Tobias blurted out, then had to stop while another wave of nausea rose from his gut. The after-shocks made him close his eyes, left him close to sobbing. "You s-shouldn't t-touch me," he gasped.

Jake's hand on his shoulder froze. "Tobias, I'm sorry. Did I . . . ?"

"I'm f-filthy, contagious. I'm disgusting. I'm sorry sorry sorry, so sorry. P-please don't get sick. Don't l-let me make you s-sick."

~

"Tobias! Don't—" Jake broke off because what the fuck could he even try to say? He tried to tug Tobias back toward him. For a second, Tobias clung to the toilet bowl as though he were drowning and the white porcelain was his only lifesaver. Jake could see the act of will it took for him to release his hold and let Jake pull him away.

Jake maneuvered Tobias until he was cradled against Jake's chest, his fingers again moving through his sweaty hair. Tobias turned his head away, and in the part of Jake that wasn't just trying to *deal*, that hurt. "It's okay, it's okay." He didn't know if Tobias heard—or believed—a word he said.

When the shaking eased up and he thought Tobias could sit unsupported, Jake got him a glass of water and a damp washcloth to wipe the bile and sweat from his face. Tobias looked horrible—pale, shaky, devastated—but the expression of near-adoration on his face while Jake wiped the tearstains from his cheeks made Jake downright uncomfortable. It wasn't like he was doing much. Cleaning Tobias and bringing him some water after he'd damn near poisoned him with that soup was the least he could do. It shouldn't have been that special next to all of Jake's other screw-ups.

Tobias was calmer after the water and the washcloth. After several more minutes, when he seemed less likely to lose the little liquid he had left in his stomach, Jake helped him up to splash his face one more time. They stumbled back to Tobias's bedroom like a couple of drunks heading home at two a.m.

Jake put a wastebasket next to the bed for Tobias. Tobias's sprint for the bathroom had been one of the most terrifying things Jake had seen recently, at least before Tobias's scars, his panic attacks, and when he fell down a flight of stairs. He tried to make him more comfortable. The shaking had worsened again after just that short walk.

So Jake sat on the side of the bed, adjusted the blankets, rubbed away a speck of soup that had been flung onto the headboard, and generally tried to feel useful in the face of Tobias sick and feverish, teeth chattering. He couldn't keep from touching Tobias's forehead again and again, smoothing his warm and damp hair uselessly.

"Shit, Tobias. You're . . . really sick." He could say that with certainty, and that was when Tobias was still and too quiet. When he coughed, it sounded like he was going to lose a lung. "I think . . . fuck, I hate hospitals, but I should probably take you to a clinic or something, get a doctor to check—"

"No!" Tobias fought to sit up, back braced against the headboard, eyes as wide with horror as Jake had ever seen them. "No, Jake, no, please. It's only been a d-day, please g-g-give me at least one more, please please, I'll get b-better—"

"Tobias." Jake grabbed his shoulders and tried to ease him down again without shoving. "Look, it'll be okay—I'd *never* let them hurt you, I swear, I'll be there the whole time. They're just gonna see how sick you are and get you a prescription or something."

Jake thought he was being reasonable. He thought that he wasn't panicking or suggesting something crazy. He just really didn't want Tobias to die. But Tobias seized Jake's sleeve, and his eyes and cheeks were bright with fear as well as fever. "D-don't, Jake. Please, *please*, I swear I'm n-not that sick, I d-don't need to go, please don't take me . . ." He couldn't finish, curling over his knees with another fit of coughing that racked his body.

Jake could see the outline of Tobias's bones through his rumpled nightshirt: vertebrae, rib, and clavicle with hardly anything in between, bound together by taut skin. Jake swallowed hard against the terrible conviction that Tobias couldn't sustain this wrecking illness, that he had no reserves or resources. *He survived eleven years of Freak Camp, I won't lose him now to the flu.* If it even *was* the flu. Shit, all his medical knowledge lay in stitches and blood loss and concussions. He couldn't fucking gamble with Tobias's life, not an inch.

"They're not going to hurt you. You gotta trust me. I won't let anyone hurt you, swear to God, Toby." Jake would take him. He *had* to get help. This wasn't some fucked-up thing between him and Tobias but fever, sweat, and vomit. He could ask for help for this, and maybe get it, without feeling like a failure.

He was just about to carry Tobias straight to the Eldorado and find the nearest emergency room, when Tobias looked up at him, lips trembling, eyes wide and desperately lost. "P-please," he whispered. "Th-they'll *know*."

That hit Jake straight in the solar plexus. It was his turn to lean forward, trying to breathe through the anguish in Tobias's voice and the lack of any kind of hope. Maybe it was past time that Tobias lost faith in him. Only years of fighting things that filled other people's nightmares kept his voice steady as he looked Tobias in the eye again. "They can't take you away from me, Toby. They *can't*. I'll never let them."

Tobias stared at him wordlessly, then clenched his eyes shut. He turned over, or tried to, as his limbs seemed too heavy for his waning strength to move.

Jake should have taken him to the hospital, gotten a doctor

to fix him, called *someone* who would know what kind of drugs would bring the fever down or if any restaurant in the area would deliver broth to their door. But somehow the hopelessness he had seen in Tobias's eyes drained him of all that energy. He doubted his own conviction that any doctor could make this better.

Instead of carrying Tobias out to the Eldorado, Jake tucked the blankets tight around his shivering body and wished he could do more. He was ready to climb into bed with Tobias if that would stop the shivering, but that was off-limits for fucking sure. So he did the only thing he could think to do when hospitals, holding, and hope were off the table.

"You need broth and stuff." Jake stood. Tobias turned to him, his gaze blurry. "I'm going to run to the store. Don't . . . don't die on me, Tobias."

Tobias's eyes widened. Jake could see the spike of panic. "You're—" He had to break off for a coughing fit. Not one of the worst ones, but not good either. Jake waited. "You're coming b-back?"

"Half an hour. Tops. I promise. We just need some stuff. *You need some stuff that I can't get, but I'll buy other stuff for you anyway.*

Tobias nodded. "I'm s-sorry," he said in a small voice. "So sorry."

Jake couldn't respond to that. Didn't trust his voice not to break. He might have felt better if he were in some kind of physical pain instead of whatever the hell kind of pain *this* was. He turned and left.

As the front door closed on his heels and he locked it automatically, it occurred to him that he'd been doing a lot of leaving lately. Despite how he knew that Tobias had no one else, and he was near-hopeless without Jake right now, he couldn't shake the thought that maybe that was for the best.

The local all-night supermarket wasn't that far away, and

Jake cut minutes off the usual time. Yeah, he was speeding. Yeah, it was eleven p.m. on a Monday and no one was around.

He parked the Eldorado messily close to the front and jogged in. The staff glanced at him and then away, unconcerned.

Not until he was standing in the middle of the soup aisle with his arms full of things—white bread, NyQuil, Kleenex—did it hit home that he didn't have the first fucking idea what he should be doing. He couldn't even think back to when he'd been sick, because Hawthornes didn't get sick.

Okay, not quite true. But he hadn't gotten sick much as a kid, and when he had, Leon had just...

Fuck it, sometimes Leon had just *been* there, and times like that he hadn't been *Leon*, he was *Dad*, and Dad had been perfect. Like he'd always known how to figure out the focus-object for a ghost or how to sneak up on a swamp monster, he just *knew* how to make Jake feel better. He had been there, with nasty cough syrup and hamburgers and the conviction that because Jake had always followed his orders, he would obey now when Leon told him *Get your strength up.* When Leon had said, "You'll be fine, Jake," it wasn't a reassurance or a platitude. It was an order and the *truth,* and Jake knew it would be true just because his dad was saying it.

Other times Leon hadn't been there, and Jake had just curled up on whatever bed, cot, mattress, or couch there was in their latest motel, apartment, hovel, or cabin, and slept until he could breathe again.

But now Jake was all that Tobias had, and he couldn't waste time having some kind of mopey existential crisis in the middle of the fucking grocery store when Tobias *needed* him.

Jake bought six things of the wateriest chicken noodle soup he could find, plus some more cough drops. He had to shove the last can in his pocket, and the late-night cashier glared at him at checkout, probably convinced he was shoplifting whole turkeys in some pocket yet untapped. She asked him whether he wanted paper or plastic, and it didn't sound like an offer, so he bagged his purchases himself and hurried out.

Carrying the stupid plastic bag was easier than holding everything in his arms. Jake couldn't count the disasters that could have befallen Tobias while he was gone (falling out of bed, fever spiking, choking on vomit, just *dead*), and he tried not to think of them as he sped all the way home. It was probably dangerous the way the road blurred in front of him, swamped in images of Tobias shivering, Tobias coughing, Tobias unconscious or worse, but he didn't fucking care. He had to *get* there and stop it, everything that was rapidly becoming his worst fear.

It was a kind of panic clogging his veins, his heart beating far too fast for the short trip from the grocery store to the apartment, and Jake thought that it would only get worse until he could see Tobias safe again.

He brought the Eldorado to a stop in the parking lot, and he realized that now, in order to make sure that Tobias was safe, he had to go inside. Suddenly, it was hard to put his hand on the door and push himself out of the car.

Jake leaned his forehead on the steering wheel and sucked in one deep breath after another, trying to get a grip on himself. He had to leave the safe shell of the Eldorado. He had to walk up those stairs with his stupid little cans of soup and help feed Tobias because he didn't know how Tobias would get through this without him. Granted, he didn't know how Tobias would get through it even *with* him, but Jake was the best option he had. Even though Jake didn't know if he could hold it together long enough to do any good. Not when every time Tobias flinched away from him, it drove home the reminder that Tobias had no reason to trust him, and Jake was fucking this whole thing up, and how could he fix that? How could he survive *not* fixing that?

A huge part of Jake could not bear to go back inside to face Tobias's fear with the knowledge that at least part of that terror was completely justified. But, eventually, the rest of him—the part convinced Tobias could die at any second, and the part who refused to ever walk away—got him out of the Eldorado, up those stairs, and through the door to where Tobias, and all he meant, waited for him.

~

THE FOLLOWING AFTERNOON, Jake sat on the side of Tobias's bed and pushed a few damp hairs off his forehead.

Tobias had slept most of the day after drinking another mug of broth that morning. Jake figured that was good, even though Tobias's temperature was still pretty high. He worried, but at least Tobias hadn't been coughing as badly (though maybe that was normal, seeing as he'd been sleeping almost constantly), and he hadn't vomited in nearly twenty-four hours.

Jake had tried to research Tobias's symptoms online (the method worked for mutant spider bites after all, so it *had* to have some answers about whatever the hell Tobias had), but he'd ended up cracking and calling the local doctor's clinic, just to see if he could get some general advice and a sense if this was serious or not. The nurse he spoke to was pretty nice—she didn't ask any invasive questions that pinged his hunter radar, though she urged him to bring Tobias in. But she'd said it sounded like a run-of-the-mill viral infection that should disappear after a few days, and Jake should only worry if the fever spiked or continued for more than forty-eight hours. Jake thanked her, hung up, and tried to feel relieved. He'd gotten a professional opinion, after all. He tried not to think about how the nurse had no idea Tobias had been a FREACS inmate for most of his life. If this was something he had caught there, it might not be a run-of-the mill virus. And if he'd contracted the cough after they left, there was no guarantee that his skin-on-bones frame could fight it off.

So Jake had gone back to his vigil at Tobias's bedside, watching him toss and turn with labored, gasping breaths. He wasn't sleeping easily, but Jake hoped the little rest he got would help.

He wiped Tobias's forehead again with a cool washcloth, then sighed and picked up the thermometer on Tobias's bedside table, alongside the wide array of medicine he'd set out, Tobias's two full water glasses, and a couple of dishes of broth that Tobias hadn't eaten. He'd been judging Tobias's fever roughly by the heat radiating from his forehead, but that wasn't really accurate if Jake had to watch for spikes and couldn't rely on his own nerves to judge what was *too hot*.

"Hey, Toby." He brushed his thumb over the corner of Tobias's mouth. "I need you to open up for me. Just for a sec."

Tobias moaned, twisting onto his other side with his eyes screwed shut, but Jake persisted. Eventually, his coaxing opened Tobias's mouth enough to slip the thermometer between his lips.

He didn't like how still Tobias went the second the metal instrument touched his tongue, as though the thermometer held him immobile. Resting his hand on Tobias's neck, Jake could feel the rapid pulse beneath his fingertips, but he couldn't remember if it had been any slower just before.

When the thermometer beeped and Jake withdrew it— 100.8 degrees, okay, that was a start of a decline—Tobias's lips parted, and he panted hard before rolling onto his face with a heartbreaking, agonized whimper, so wretched that Jake felt it physically go through him like a wendigo's claws.

"Hey, hey, Toby," he said, leaning close and rubbing his back. "You okay? Something hurt? Talk to me, man."

Tobias didn't answer. His hands were scrabbling uselessly at the sheets, and his breath was even more labored. It sounded almost like he was on the edge of another collapse.

Repeating Tobias's name, a litany as desperate and earnest as an exorcism (and not helping, *fuck*, Tobias wasn't responding at all), Jake maneuvered Tobias onto his side so he wasn't mashing his face into the pillow, giving him room to breathe, room to move. Maybe just so he could be doing *something* while Tobias—still mostly delirious—panicked right in front of him for reasons he didn't understand.

Tobias sobbed, a broken and hopeless sound, and shrank away from Jake's touch, drawing his arms and knees to his chest in a ball. "No, no, please, Jake—please don't—I'm sorry, I'll be better, just please don't—"

It took a second for the words to sink in, and then Jake bolted from the room so fast he nearly flung the door off its hinges. He made it to the wall outside the bathroom, the one Tobias had used when he had the strength to hobble out. He wasn't sure if he was going to vomit. His stomach was roiling, his hands shook, and he could still faintly hear Tobias's sickening pleas drifting from the bedroom.

He sounded afraid and despairing. Utterly without hope that Jake would listen. That Jake would be any different from the bastards who had cut into his skin and broken something inside him.

Jake had tried to believe that Tobias knew he wasn't like those sadistic sons of bitches. He had tried to convince himself that Tobias wasn't afraid of him in addition to his general fear of reals and asking for things and looking him in the eye. Though Tobias would never have said otherwise because he was so desperate to please that he wouldn't have said a single thing to upset Jake.

But that nightmare—fuck, Jake hoped that it was a nightmare; he couldn't contemplate that horror in Tobias's voice being part of his regular dreams—showed that Tobias wasn't just afraid of Jake. He was *terrified*.

If Jake could have, he would have walked out right then. He would've left because Tobias was so clearly wrecked by his mere presence, and every time Jake looked at Tobias with that knowledge, it hurt like a wicked bitch. He would *go*, willingly, if it would make life just a little bit easier for Tobias.

But he couldn't. Because Tobias was feverish, half-starved, and sick, and Jake was the only one there. That scared him shit-less more than anything else that had happened in these three fucking roller-coaster weeks. He couldn't leave because Tobias needed him, even if he would never ever trust him.

Jake swallowed painfully until he was sure he wouldn't need to barf out his stomach when he stepped back in that room and had to hear Tobias's whimpering with perfect, painful clarity.

Then he turned and went back in. Because it had to be done, and he was the only one who would.

TOBIAS'S FEVER broke that evening, and Jake knew he should feel relieved. But what he really felt was numb.

The next morning, Tobias felt well enough that he asked to sit in the living room (a weirdly precise request, among the thousands of things Tobias wouldn't ask for—like more water when his glass was empty—but it seemed important to him to get out of his bedroom). Jake helped move him, opened the windows, threw Tobias's sheets into the wash, and cleaned to the best of his ability, trying to get the smell of sweat and sick-ness out of the walls, though they were probably more in his head than anywhere else.

He tried to stay out of Tobias's sight as much as possible. It was better that way for both of them. If Tobias wasn't confronted with Jake at every moment, he wouldn't be terrified all the time, right? And Jake wouldn't have to see the fear in Tobias's face, just below the surface.

He had scared people before, but those had been civilians, and he was a hunter. He'd been doing his job, and it hadn't mattered what they thought of him when he blew out of town.

Tobias mattered. No matter all the hunts Jake had been on, he'd wanted to save Tobias's life more than anyone else's. He couldn't think about how much he was failing because he *still* had a job to do, and studying his fuck-ups could only distract him from feeding Tobias, getting him healthy, and maybe giving him enough confidence to survive on his own. Because Jake sure didn't see any way they were going to make it work together.

The plan had been working (do the job, get out, don't get attached) until Jake was cleaning up from a meal that he'd made for Tobias (more broth, beef this time) and hadn't bothered to eat himself.

Tobias pushed himself up on the couch—Jake was watching, even though he was in the kitchen, even though it was probably creeping Tobias out *more*—and he looked so hopeful, like he *wanted* to ask something, that Jake had to step out of the kitchen, wiping his hands on a towel. Maybe this time Tobias would tell him what he needed. Even a hint would be nice.

"Yeah, Tobias?"

"Jake?" Tobias looked down, then up again. "Are you . . . are you okay?"

"I'm fine. You need anything?"

Tobias started to shake his head, and then the motion twisted on itself until it was like a shrug-nod, or maybe just a shudder. "I feel good, Jake, really good, but you're . . . did I . . ."

"Did you what, Tobias?"

Tobias took a deep breath, closing and opening his eyes,

keeping them fixed on the carpet. "Did I d-do something wrong, please tell me, Jake, I can be b-better—"

The words made the bile rise in Jake's throat, and he almost wanted to turn and walk away before Tobias could plead with him, before that broken tone reemerged. But something stopped him. Something perilously like hope. Maybe he could take this chance. Maybe he could just ask and learn what Tobias needed, and then he wouldn't shake and cringe and beg, and he would be *okay*.

That was all Jake wanted. Everything Jake wanted. So he crossed the living room and sat on the coffee table. Tobias looked up, and Jake could see him swallow from the effort that took him.

"You're afraid of me, Tobias," he said, looking him in the eye, even as Tobias cringed again. "Every day, you're afraid of me, of what I'll do. No, don't shake your head, I'm not *stupid*, and the way you flinch away from me is . . . yeah, well, it's pretty clear. But if you meant it, if you really want to help *us*, you need to . . . I want you to . . . tell me. Tell me how to make this better for you, tell me how to"—*stop making you afraid of me with every breath*—"help you. What will make this easier for you, Toby?" Jake forced a small smile. It hurt a little but was worth it when he saw Tobias relax fractionally.

He didn't expect Tobias to answer—yeah, he hoped, but he had learned better than to believe—but after a moment, Tobias inhaled shakily.

"You . . . you could . . ." He stopped, shoulders tense, eyes on his knees. His hands clenched once, twice, and then flexed out until Jake could almost hear the knuckles cracking.

Jake held his breath. He hadn't dared to expect a real answer, but maybe the direct approach was finally going to fucking work. "What?" he whispered. "Just tell me, Tobias, anything."

PART OF TOBIAS knew he should be glad that Jake had finally realized he shouldn't be near or touch a freak. Jake was safer that way, and Tobias should be glad. But he couldn't help the growing, selfish, monstrous worry that he had done something wrong and driven Jake away at a time when he couldn't control himself. He worried more each hour that Jake would get tired of this burden and this weakness. He worried about Freak Camp. He worried about what he could do to make Jake touch him again.

And now Jake was asking what he could do to make this easier, telling him in so many words that he didn't want Tobias to be afraid, didn't want him cringing, and Tobias could try. There was one thing, one precious promise that Jake could give him that would maybe scrub away his deepest fear, the one he'd had nightmares about all through his sickness. Maybe, with that fear gone, he could do better at conquering all the little terrors.

Tobias drew in another deep breath and tried to convince himself it wasn't much to ask. Just one bullet. It was the same as Jake would grant any monster.

"You could—you could p-promise me," he tried again, and found the courage, somewhere, to put his greatest need into words. The greatest need, at least, that he thought he could actually receive. "That you'll n-never . . . that you'll put me down yourself . . . rather than r-return me to F-Freak Camp."

Tobias knew he should let Jake think through the request—Jake was a hunter and a real and so much smarter than him—but when he didn't answer, Tobias couldn't stop his mouth. He almost wished for the closed throat from the cough because now that he had started, all his bottled fears were forcing their way out of him in a dangerous rush. He didn't look up, too terrified to see Jake's face. "I kn-know you t-told me you w-wouldn't, you p-promised, I kn-know, but you d-d-don't know . . ." *what a fucked-up piece of shit I am.* "You haven't"—*fucked me, used me, found any use for me*—"you c-could change your m-mind, and y-you don't know how . . ." *I always fuck up eventually, because that's what monsters do.* "It would h-help, Jake, just to hear you s-say it again, to know you'd give m-me a bullet before . . ." *they have a chance to take away everything I ever wanted only for you.*

JAKE FELT something in his chest snap—maybe that was his heart, it certainly seemed to be beating louder than usual—but it wasn't a new pain. Not one that would kill him.

He hated that Tobias had asked that. He had told Tobias he would never bring him back to Freak Camp, and he had meant it. He would crash his car, kiss Dixon boots, and light the state on fire before he ever let Tobias walk back through those doors. He wished like hell that he had the words to clear away the fear he could see in Tobias's eyes, even when they remained fixed on his hands. Or rather, he wished he had different words. Because in that moment, he finally realized that Tobias meant it. Tobias thought that Jake could throw him back to those sons of bitches. He thought Jake had the capacity to shoot him. And yet he still believed that Jake's promises were good, so Jake could say something, right here and now, that could possibly pull that fear out of Tobias, or at least tuck it so far inside that he wouldn't flinch every time Jake reached for something near him, and he wouldn't cringe like he expected to be hit when asking for something he needed.

Just like that, Jake knew that he was going to say it, because it might, just might, give Tobias hope. It should have been an easy promise—after all, he would never let Tobias go back to Freak Camp, even if it wasn't the way he expected—but it felt like defeat. In that moment he had to admit to himself that he didn't know any way out of this downward spiral ripping Tobias apart. He was caught there in its depths, pulled along without a way to break free. Jake had already made his decision, maybe when he was fourteen, maybe when he looked in his father's face and knew he was walking away, but he had made it, and there was nowhere else for him to go. They would rise and fall together, but Jake didn't like the odds for buoyancy.

He reached over and touched Tobias's face, ignoring both Tobias's automatic flinch and his own self-loathing at seeing it. After that initial reaction, Tobias looked up a little, and his entire body turned toward Jake like a flower turning toward the sun or a child feeling the hand of a parent promising it would be all right.

"I promise, Toby," Jake said, half fervent, half heartbroken. "I would put three rounds through your heart and burn your bones before I let those bastards take you back to Freak Camp. I *promise*."

The relief on Tobias's face almost broke him again—the joy, the way he practically threw himself into Jake's arms. Jake pulled him close and tucked his cheek against Tobias's and felt the relaxation in him, as though a layer of tension had been stripped away, duct tape yanked off an old wall, ripping away paint and baring the plaster.

Jake touched Tobias softly over his back and held the rest of the promise to himself. Not just the fact that he would kill anyone and anything before he put a bullet in Tobias. No, there was another part he barely wanted to admit to himself because he didn't know how Tobias would take it. He wasn't sure that when he was better—*if* he got better, if he ever even got *okay*—Tobias wouldn't need him anymore, and he would just . . . step away, step out, leave like so many people Jake had cared about had left.

Jake wouldn't blame him. He was an overbearing asshole sometimes, not as smart as Tobias, not as kind. He was trouble and couldn't make the right decisions. Mostly he tried to believe it wasn't his fault that Mom had left, and mostly he managed, but he knew beyond a shadow of a doubt that he was the reason that Dad left. He could still remember the words.

He could probably survive Tobias leaving him. He expected it sometimes, even bitterly hoped for it when he was drinking or in the darkest hours of the night when he couldn't escape how much damage he was inflicting. But even knowing Tobias didn't want to stay with him would be balanced by the triumph in the knowledge that Tobias could survive without him. If Tobias left Jake, it would be because he had the strength to stand on his own.

If Jake had to pull the trigger—*I never will, don't even think of it, Hawthorne*—he was pretty sure he would next turn the gun on himself.

10

Tobias was relieved by how quickly his condition improved after the fever broke. For days he couldn't see straight, couldn't always tell the difference between the mattress underneath and the plain white ceiling above. Only Jake had been his constant presence through the hellish nights, propping him up with pillows to feed him soup and crackers, lowering him again and brushing his hands through Tobias's hair through the long, unfocused days. He never once mentioned how he shouldn't be touching, caring for, or dealing with a filthy monster, or what Tobias would have to pay for this kindness, or if there was any kind of punishment to be found at the end.

Tobias was starting to cautiously believe there might not be. And if there was, that didn't matter, because Jake had promised Tobias he would *never* go back to Freak Camp, and that was the best thing. Tobias was in the safest place in the world every time Jake touched him. Every time he opened his eyes and felt the blankets over his shoulders, he knew he was in the best place he could ever be.

It kept getting better. One night drenched in sweat, sure he was going to die any second, coughing out every rebelling freak organ in his body, to a couple of days later, being able to wash the dishes and walk to the bathroom without steadying himself once on the walls. Thursday morning he had even woken up before hearing Jake's quiet steps in the living room.

Tobias had put away the half-empty bottle of whiskey on the kitchen table and washed Jake's glass before deciding that he didn't want to go back to his room. The sheets were clean and the window was cracked to let in fresh air, but Tobias could still feel the days of being sick. Not so much in the scent, sight, or feel—he hadn't ever vomited onto the carpet, thank God, and Jake had never so much as slapped him, so there wasn't any blood—but in the memories of words and murky nightmares.

So he stayed in the living room, propping himself up on the couch, and opened one of his books from the library. Jake had seemed happy when Tobias had read before, and now that he was better, it wouldn't strain his recovering body.

In Freak Camp, he had never worried about straining himself. He had done what he had to do. But now he knew that taking care of himself was important to making Jake happy— Jake had clearly been worried and upset through the entire run of the fever, though Tobias wasn't sure why—so he would do his best. He drank a little water from the tap in the kitchen before settling down on the couch, feeling a slight tremor in his muscles: easy to ignore, but a clear sign that he should continue resting. Jake had said that he should drink a lot of water, but Tobias wasn't sure if that counted as a rule, a suggestion, or a fact.

When Jake shuffled out of his bedroom a couple of hours later, he made it to the invisible line that divided the living room from the hallway before he saw Tobias. He froze and blinked a couple of times. Tobias thought he saw him swallow, and there might have been something like relief in his face before it faded back to wariness.

"Hey, Tobias."

"Hey, Jake." Tobias's hands were shaking slightly now. Maybe he'd been holding the book up too long. He lowered it and tucked his hands beneath his knees.

Strange how the weakness of his body used to be a threat, something that had to be compensated for so that no other monster could take advantage. Now it was still a sign of weakness, but he didn't have to push through at the long-term expense of his endurance. He didn't need to damage himself more so that he wouldn't get jumped in the showers. It was like the one time he had been in the infirmary for weeks and hadn't had to watch his back, he'd only had to get better so that he could keep surviving sessions with the Director. Except when he had been in the infirmary that time, he hadn't been thinking about anything but surviving out of habit and the recitation of an old promise.

But it was all different now. Rather than being hollowed out, he had Jake and his fulfilled and new promises. And those gave him . . . something very like hope. And maybe happiness.

"You're doing better."

Tobias wasn't sure if it was a question or a statement. "Yes, Jake. Much better. Thank you." He knew he was smiling and couldn't quite control it, but he was pretty sure now he didn't have to.

Jake almost smiled in return, and then tension slid back into his shoulders. "That's good. That's really good." He turned and went into the kitchen. Tobias leaned his head against the back of the couch and listened. Cupboard, refrigerator, pause, close refrigerator.

"Tobias?"

It could all go to hell so quickly, really. Tobias felt his entire body clench. Jake didn't sound angry, didn't sound like he was going to hit him or even yell at him, but he still didn't sound happy. Tobias braced a hand on the couch and tried to get up, to figure out what he had done wrong and fix it, but when his arm shook, he sank back into the cushions. Better not to risk it. Tobias desperately wanted to do whatever Jake wanted, but he was afraid that stumbling into the kitchen would not be the way.

He hoped he didn't sound afraid, answering. Jake didn't like it when he was afraid. "Yes, Jake?"

"Where did you put my bottle?"

"The w-whiskey?"

Jake didn't answer for a second. "Yeah."

"In the second shelf from the refrigerator, where you u-usually store it."

The sound of the cupboard opening again and a couple cans of peaches being moved. "Ah. Thanks."

Tobias waited for the sound of liquid pouring, maybe the freezer opening so Jake could get some ice, but nothing happened for a long second. Then the peach cans were shifted around again, a glass was returned, and Jake left the kitchen.

Tobias smiled, expecting him to come into the living room, to sit and turn on the TV, or open his laptop. But all he did was walk close, put his hand against Tobias's forehead for a couple seconds, sigh in relief, and then turn away again. At the threshold of the living room, Jake stopped to say over his shoulder, "If you want breakfast, there's cereal or . . . you know, whatever, help yourself," before he disappeared down the hall, and his bedroom door clunked shut.

Tobias didn't realize he was staring after Jake until he had to blink his eyes several times because they felt painful and dry. He rubbed at his face, and then tried to focus on the book in his lap again, but it wasn't as easy as it had been.

THERE WAS ONLY SO much time that Jake could spend in his room before admitting to his own cowardice. As he lay on his bed and stared at the ceiling, he wondered exactly how long that was.

He thought that the situation would get better when Tobias did, when he could move around on his own and Jake could give him his space again, but somehow it was worse when he could walk into a room and Tobias was there, *looking* at him, expecting things from him that he was becoming more and more convinced were impossible for Jake Hawthorne to provide.

Certain thoughts gnawed at him. Chief among them was worrying whether Tobias really was getting better, whether the current improvement in his health was just a temporary thing. But right up there, where it maybe should have been from that first fucking night, was sex.

Jake was honest with himself: he thought about sex a lot. He was twenty, hot, and liked pretty much anyone with a willing smile and a set of hips.

Thinking about sex had never before made him feel physically ill.

Jake wasn't an idiot, even if he often acted like it. He could see the signs. He knew that they meant Tobias was pretty fucking messed up (had *been* messed up, and one day someone was going to pay for that).

What he didn't know, and what circled in his head like an abandoned dog, was how much of this was his fault and only getting worse because of what Jake had done.

When Jake had him close, Tobias had seemed as happy as he ever was, as happy as Jake was. But how much of that was an illusion, Tobias interpreting what *Jake* wanted and trying to give it to him? How could Jake trust himself ever again when he couldn't read Tobias's reactions and know they were genuine?

He couldn't. He couldn't trust himself with Tobias, because

everything he did was a long line of mistakes, stupidities, and probably borderline molestations.

But staying in his room for the rest of his life, counting the bumps in the plaster of the ceiling, wouldn't undo any of that or make him a better person. He would suck it up, go out there, and do better.

Any minute now.

IT WAS, at least, still Thursday when Jake finally got up again and dragged himself out of his room. He wandered into the kitchen first—thought about a drink, decided against it—and felt his heart sink. There was no evidence that Tobias had made himself breakfast or anything since he'd seen him that morning. Granted, there might not have been. Cereal only took a bowl and a spoon. Tobias could easily have eaten and put everything away again so perfectly Jake couldn't notice. But, then again, he could also have *not* eaten. Jake was starting to suspect that if he didn't watch Tobias, if he didn't see him eat and drink, it might not have happened at all.

Tobias was still in the living room, reading. He was pale and his wrists were far too thin, but he looked a thousand times better than he had that weekend. Jake took a cup out of the cupboard, and Tobias's head twitched in his direction before he stopped himself and huddled closer to the book.

"Hey, Toby." Jake walked into the living room and leaned on the armrest of the couch. Tobias jumped when he spoke, but his face brightened as he looked up at Jake, like he might have smiled if he got any kind of encouragement. "How are you feeling?"

"Much better, Jake."

"You eat anything?" *While I was wallowing in my room?*

Tobias looked away. "Y-yes. C-cereal."

Jake felt something in him relax. Tobias should have probably been eating every couple of hours, given how much energy his body had to be expending to recover, but at least he had eaten. That was progress.

"Probably about dinnertime now, though. What do you think of spaghetti?"

Tobias closed the book quickly and straightened. Jake moved off the arm of the couch when it looked like Tobias would get close enough to touch him. Tobias didn't need any of that shit.

Briefly, Tobias looked lost, staring at Jake's face like he had forgotten why he put down his book. Then his eyes dropped to his hands, wrapped around each other. "C-can I help?"

Hanging out with Tobias in the kitchen, close enough to touch, bump into, feel his breath on his skin, sounded wonderful and was one of the last things that Jake wanted. But looking at the hesitant, fragile look in his face, Jake couldn't tell Tobias no. He didn't have a good reason to say it, either. After all, Jake's issues weren't Tobias's fault.

"Yeah," he said, trying to sound enthusiastic and failing grandly, "that sounds great."

Making the pasta with Tobias was as good and horrible as Jake had suspected. It was an easy meal—boil spaghetti, heat a jar of pasta sauce, zap vegetables in the microwave—but every time he turned around, Tobias was there, looking up at him, smiling, his body and hands too close. His expression was still this side of afraid, inches away from the panic Jake had seen again and again. Panic Jake had caused because he couldn't make good choices or keep his hands to himself.

Jake filled the pot and cracked the spaghetti in half, got a bag of peas out of the freezer, and couldn't think of anything to say, even when Tobias's eyes followed him and he wanted to smile, wanted to talk about some random tangent. But what was the point? Anything he talked about could turn into something that would rip Tobias apart. So he kept silent and ignored the way Tobias opened his mouth sometimes, as though he wanted to talk but couldn't. Or maybe he just saw the same problem, had nothing to say to Jake, didn't know how to fix it.

Jake was pretty sure that was his fault too. A tightness grew in his chest with the conviction that he was only making all this worse, along with a deep, slow self-revulsion every time he caught himself watching Tobias's hand while he stirred the spaghetti ever so carefully, or when he reached over to help Tobias open the jar. Tobias's hands shook a little, but whether from sickness or fear, Jake couldn't tell. When their hands brushed together, Jake couldn't help feeling how Tobias's fingers twitched under his, the soft heat of his body.

That was enough. Too much. Jake jerked away from him, emptied the jar into a saucepan and set the burner on low. The pasta was done, but he couldn't stay until everything else was ready. He couldn't sit down to a meal with Tobias right now with this shit in his head.

Jake dumped the pasta and boiling water in the strainer and tried to bolt out of the kitchen, but Tobias was there, Tobias was right there, and Jake couldn't be in the same room any longer.

"I'm gonna shower," Jake said in a rush. "Back in ten. Can you watch the sauce and maybe zap the peas?"

If anything, Tobias's face got paler, but Jake didn't know if it was from the suggestion that he microwave something by himself or because he'd been standing for too long. "Yes, Jake."

"Yeah. Good, I'll . . . I'll be back." Jake almost touched Tobias's face before he left. His hand rose halfway. But he caught himself and rushed out of the kitchen.

He showered. Technically. He turned the water as hot as he could stand, bracing himself against the tile wall. He *had* to start giving Tobias more space. Maybe he should get a fucking civilian job.

Jake stepped out of the shower feeling almost worse than when he had gotten in, scrubbed at his face hard with the towel, and dressed. They needed to eat, though even the thought of food was like lead shot in his stomach. He couldn't let his own weakness, inadequacy, and lack of self-control hurt Tobias. At least, no more than it already had.

Jake was holding it together. He wasn't happy—about as far from it as a man could get short of being splayed out on the floor bleeding—but he was still moving.

Then he walked into the kitchen, water droplets still trickling down his neck, and found Tobias on his hands and knees, carefully picking frozen peas off the tiles. He had a bowl cradled in his arms—like a woman might hold a baby who could start crying any second—and, one by one, dropped the peas in the bowl.

Jake's first reaction was a kind of sick amusement and relief that it hadn't been the bubbling sauce or the steaming pasta. He didn't really like peas, but he had a vague idea that they were good for something health-wise and therefore Tobias could probably use as many as he could get. But if they didn't make it to the dinner table, no harm no foul. At least Jake could still get some carbs into him.

Then Tobias glanced up and turned as pale as the white porcelain bowl. He dropped his eyes and carefully set the bowl down on the floor. From the doorway, Jake could see his hands shaking enough that the peas jumped around in the bowl, threatening to leap over the rim.

Amusement and apathy instantly transformed into a furious fire in his stomach. Jake didn't know what this was, what the fuck this was *again*, but he couldn't deal with it. He didn't want to face this fucking thing again. The cowardly, honest, angry, *hurt* part of him—the voice that hissed that Tobias had never actually liked him or thought he was any kind of friend, that Jake had just been the best option in the sea of sadistic bastards

—wanted to turn back around and slam the door on his bedroom. Who gave a damn if Tobias crumpled in on himself, blank-faced, hopeless, purposeless? Who gave a fuck if Tobias had issues that Jake hadn't even dreamed existed, and he might do anything—including hurt himself—if Jake wasn't there?

Jake didn't want to care. He didn't want to be the only one dealing with all this shit that had been his only hope for a real purpose, something that was worth losing his father. Tobias had no one but him, and he had fucking no one else either. *Even now, Dad, I fucking wish you would come home someday, like you used to. You always found me eventually.*

Jake didn't move past the kitchen doorway. Maybe this was why Tobias wouldn't look at him or anybody. Maybe this hopelessness, the understanding that nothing would change and nothing could get better, was what he lived with every day.

"What are you doing?" Jake asked, even though he didn't fucking want to know. He stared at the refrigerator and waited for it. *Go ahead*, he thought, angry and ashamed of himself for being angry at *Tobias*, for Christ's sake. *Go ahead, kick me in the teeth.*

"I'm sorry," Tobias whispered. "I was p-putting the peas in the bowl, for the m-microwave, like you told me, exactly like you told me, but m-my hand—I'm so clumsy, I'm stupid, but I can do better, I promise I can do better, Jake, I j-j-just . . . They fell, but I'm p-picking them up. I'm n-n-not wasting—"

Jake's head snapped down. "You think I wanted you to cook food after it fell on the floor?"

He added himself to the long list of things that he hated when Tobias flinched away from the question like he'd been hit.

Tobias looked back up in horror, shaking his head. "Not you, I would n-never give you . . . I'm s-sorry, no, I would never. I just thought that maybe I . . . maybe you would let me . . ." His hands fluttered over the bowl, unsure where they could land, and Tobias looked anywhere but at Jake, distress pouring off him.

He wouldn't ever give Jake food that had been on the floor, food that was less than perfect, but he hadn't expected anything better. He never fucking expected Jake to give him anything decent.

Jake walked slowly into the kitchen, and Tobias slid onto his hands and knees, head down, tension in his back palpable. Jake hadn't seen that posture in days, maybe a week, but it still made nausea rise in his throat and his hand clench.

Other days, Jake would have crouched beside Tobias, like vague memories of how his mother had reached for him. He would have told him it was all right, would have explained *again* how Tobias could eat any fucking thing he wanted, how Jake would never do that to him. How Jake wasn't fucking much but he was better than the sorry excuses for human beings that had fucked up Tobias's life so much.

Right now, Jake couldn't do it. Couldn't scrape up the energy or push past the hatred and self-loathing to try to make Tobias feel better, because it wouldn't fucking work. It never fucking worked.

Goddamn, some days Jake wondered what the fuck Tobias would do if he really did slug him, if he just gave him one solid hit across the jaw that carried all Jake's anger, sadness, and horror. What the fuck would Tobias do if Jake started doing every goddamned thing that Tobias expected of him? If Jake made him live off his leftovers or hit him when life wasn't going his way, when he was tired, or just because he wanted to? *What the fuck would you do then, Tobias?* Jake wondered, staring down at him.

He didn't say it out loud. He had the sick suspicion that if he started doing all those things—became a fucking monster like the guards and hunters Tobias had known all his life—Tobias would trust him just as much. Maybe love him more.

He could imagine Tobias, pale and calm, eating nothing while Jake ate. He could see Tobias relaxing into the blows, no matter how violent, letting the force of Jake's fists paint new bruises across his back and abdomen. No matter what Jake did to him, Tobias wouldn't make a sound because he thought that was what Jake wanted.

In Tobias's world, what a hunter wanted, a hunter got, and that was all Jake was: a fucking hunter, another fist, another voice, another dick. Jake could imagine himself doing all that to Tobias—nausea an old friend, holding back the rage—but what he couldn't imagine was Tobias saying no.

Tobias would never say no, no matter how bad it was. And Jake would never know what had gone wrong.

"Do you even fucking want to be here, Tobias?" he asked. He wanted to know. He seriously wanted to know. And he didn't think that Tobias would ever tell him, unless Jake started to hit him, to beat the truth out of him.

Tobias glanced up, panicked, and then away. The line of his back was a tight, graceful curve of bone and sinew. "I'm sorry, I'm sorry, I'm so sorry, the peas just . . . I won't . . . I promise . . . A-anything for you, Jake, I didn't mean . . . I'm sorry, s-sorry. *Please*, don't—"

Jake made a sharp gesture with his hand and Tobias cut himself off mid-phrase like Jake had hit him to shut him up. Maybe he should, just once, to see if being the monster Tobias expected would make him love him. How could he cringe away every day, how could he keep looking at Jake like he expected to be beaten over fucking *spilled peas* and not hate him, hate him so much for what Jake had been raised to be?

"This isn't about the peas, Tobias, this is about"—*how you hate me*—"you flinching every fucking time I come into a room. About you expecting me to be some kind of . . ." *monster, like you're supposed to be*, "sadistic fuck with a hard-on for blood. Why the fuck would you stay, Tobias? Why the fuck would you *want* to stick around? What the fuck do I have to offer . . ." *Nothing*, that's what the fuck he had to offer, and some day Tobias would figure it out, like everyone else in Jake's life had figured out.

And it wasn't fucking fair. Jake had burned bridges, had lost the most important things in his life, but he would lose Tobias now, because he had never really had him. The Tobias he had thought he knew was an illusion he constructed during all those brief visits in camp, a fantasy Jake had created for himself so he could believe he was some kind of good person.

But he wasn't. Tobias made that perfectly clear every time he flinched.

Jake reached down and grabbed Tobias by the arm, pulling him to his feet. The rational part of his brain started ringing alarms and screaming about his stupidity the second he started pulling Tobias toward the door, but the rest of him was so consumed by the festering, formless rage that nothing sane could be heard.

"Do you want to leave, Tobias? So fucking convinced that I want to hurt you all the fucking time, why would you stay with a son of a bitch like me?" Jake couldn't control anything, not the words coming out of his mouth or the pressure he was exerting on Tobias's arm.

"J-J-Jake . . ." Tobias tried, but Jake shook him a little, and he shut up.

Part of Jake liked that Tobias wasn't talking, apologizing, begging for things that he damn well deserved to have without even asking. The rest of him knew he'd just broken any trust they might have built with that shake. He had hurt Tobias to make him do what Jake wanted.

Jake yanked the security chain out as he flung the door open, barely feeling the metal whip past his face even as he jerked Tobias back. The danger from that little chain was nothing worse than an inconvenience, but he would step between Tobias and a hell of a lot worse without hesitation. He just wished he could protect Tobias from Jake himself.

"See," Jake said. "There's a fucking door to this apartment, and the lock sucks. I'm not holding you here. You can go any fucking place you want. I didn't spring you from FREACS so you could be my *slave* or . . . or whatever the fuck. If you'd be happy somewhere else, then go. Save yourself, get away from me before I become every fucking thing that you're afraid of, what you—" Jake bit himself off. He'd already said way too much, fucked them both up so badly, and Tobias . . .

Tobias stared at him, horror making his eyes huge, his throat working. One hand wrapped around Jake's hold on his arm, the other fisted itself in Jake's shirt. Jake knew it couldn't be a conscious move. Tobias wouldn't voluntarily touch him, never let himself make contact unless Jake touched him first.

"You want me . . ." Tobias panted. "You want me to l-leave?" The words fought their way out of his throat, caught and choked by panic. "You're throwing me . . ."

And just like that, it all crashed. All of Jake's rage, the undiscriminating conflagration of hate and shame burned away, and he was left with the pain that was all his own. Smiling bitterly to himself, Jake pulled Tobias closer to him. He loved the way Tobias fit in his arms, like he had been specially ordered for Jake to wrap his arms over the warm curve of his back and tuck him close. He hated the way Tobias just yielded in his arms when Jake knew he would have been just as compliant with a blow. Hell, he could still be anticipating violence even as he relaxed against Jake's chest.

"No, I'm not," he said heavily, letting his hands move over Tobias's back, because he was already a fucking bastard. One of the worst people in the world, but still better than everyone else in Tobias's life. "I'm not fucking kicking you out. I just . . . I can't stand it. I can't fucking stand the way you look when you think I'm going to hit you. I'd give you anything, Tobias, anything you want. But what I need you to have the most is a place where you feel safe. How can you want me, how can you possibly want anything to do with me when"—*you see me as a monster*—"when you're always fucking afraid? Do you . . . do you even want to be here?"

"I don't w-w-want to go b-back—" Tobias began painfully.

Jake loosened one hand to touch Tobias's chin, and Tobias looked up. "I promised, and I never break my promises. Freak Camp isn't even on the table. You're never going back there. I didn't even consider it. This isn't a question of me or Freak Camp." Jake hoped he would fucking win that contest. Hoped. "This is whether you want to be with me or with someone else. Somewhere else where you won't have to be afraid all the time, where you won't cringe all the time and you can eat whatever the hell you want without me watching you."

Jake didn't have the foggiest fucking clue where he could find Tobias a place like that. Didn't know who he would ask or where he would look. But if Tobias chose that, right now, he would find it, build it, create it. If he had to build him a cabin in the Everglades, or hide Tobias in a castle and spend the rest of his days driving off monsters, Jake would. And he would start right now if Tobias could only tell him that was what he wanted.

Tobias looked away, looked anywhere but at Jake. When his hands slid up over his face, Jake let him go and stepped back.

Tobias took a deep, shaky breath, and then another. And then, so quietly that Jake could barely hear him over the beating of his own heart, Tobias whispered, "I w-want to be with you."

He hesitated over the word *want* like he always did. When he turned away and dropped his hands from his eyes, Jake saw wet spots on his hands, on his cheeks, eyes that wouldn't look at

him. He was closed off, shut down, as though he expected nothing, expected a blow, didn't believe that Jake would give him
what he asked for, might even throw him out now *because* he
had dared to ask.

Jake reached out, desperate to give Tobias whatever comfort
he could. Then he let his hand fall. He wouldn't be able to
touch Tobias right now and live with himself afterward.

"Then stay," he said roughly. "I need a drink, I'm going out.
Watch TV. Eat pasta. Do whatever the fuck you want."

Tobias nodded tightly. His face showed nothing, just a great
emptiness. He looked brittle enough to shatter if he hit a sharp
corner. "You're leaving?" He said it like a man who just wanted
to be sure of an important, irrefutable detail: the date of his
execution, the amount of poison he had just ingested.

"Be here when I get back," Jake said. "I'll be back. If you
want me . . . just fucking be here."

He walked back into the bedroom to grab his wallet and his
keys—decided to leave the gun, no reason to court stupidity—
and then left. Tobias watched him all the way out, like he was
watching the sun go down and didn't know that it would ever
rise again.

A COUPLE OF HOURS LATER, Jake had nowhere near enough
alcohol in him to let him forget the look on Tobias's face—
accepting, peaceful, relaxed—when he thought Jake had been
almost about to slug him one, but enough alcohol to make his
hands fumble for his phone without much conscious thought.

Roger was number two on the speed dial. Four rings in, Jake
decided no answer was probably for the best. No one should
get in his way tonight, as one drunk would-be tough guy and
his own blood alcohol level proved. He was fucking everything
up and couldn't even remember it going by.

Then Roger picked up. "Jake Hawthorne, that had better be you."

Thank God. Hearing that gruff, uncompromising voice broke down every defensive instinct he had. "Rog."

"Are you on your way yet? Don't tell me you're a mile outside town 'cause you figured I never get company. Or did you get lost?"

"Lost. Yeah. I wish. Fucking lost. No, we're still in Boulder. I just . . . I can't, I can't fucking do this, Roger." That confession broke down every wall Jake had, everything he'd been holding inside for the last few days. Words tumbled out, slurring and twisted and hardly comprehensible even to himself. He barely had enough to time to wonder if they could do as much damage to another person as they did to him. "I don't know what the fuck I'm doing, and I don't know how to stop. And it fucking hurts to *watch* him . . ."

"Jake, what happened?" He wasn't so drunk that he didn't hear Roger's sharp tone. "Did he hurt you? Fuck, Jake, are you—"

Easy to reclaim the rage when it felt so much better than gnawing despair. "Fuck yourself, Harper," he snarled into the phone, getting a couple worried glances from the bartender and his closest bar mate. He pushed himself off his stool, stumbling only a little as he moved toward the door. "Tobias, Tobias's no . . . *he's* not the one. I'm not hurt, he's . . . you should see him, Roger. He's terrified. Of me. Fucking petrified. Calcified. *Dinosaurified.* I'm hurting *him.*"

"Jake, pull your shit together." Roger's voice had enough command in it that for a moment, Jake almost thought it was his father on the other end. "Freak Camp is a shithole. Nobody's got the full picture, and what he's been through . . . It's not just gonna go away in a couple of weeks." Jake thought he could hear secrets in Roger's voice, but he didn't have the energy to hunt for them. Not when he would follow any voice and take any advice that would dampen the fear and rage tangled up in his chest.

"Fuck that place," he said. "And fuck the government. I can't do this, Roger. Yeah, not goin' away in a week, shit like that, but this is *Tobias*, and every fucking time I try, he just . . . fuck. Fuck."

Jake could practically hear Roger processing that through the airwaves, maybe trying to parse what Jake couldn't say. He wondered if he was making any fucking sense through the booze and the pain. Probably not. What the fuck else was new?

"So, what's the plan?" Roger's voice was neutral. Absently, Jake wondered why he cared. Yeah, Roger had helped him through a lot of the shit he'd done in his life, and he'd co-signed the paperwork to get Tobias out, but this was the first time Jake had heard that wariness in his voice. "Take him back?"

"Fuck no," Jake snapped. "Never. I just—I can't even tell if he should be around me. I . . . fuck, if there was *anywhere* else . . . if I could do anything better, but everything I do just fucks it up more. There's got to be someplace else, someone—"

"Shut up, get a grip, and listen," Roger snapped. "There ain't. There's nowhere else. You're all he's got, and he trusts you."

"No, he *doesn't!*" Jake's voice cracked like he was fucking thirteen again. "He doesn't trust me—he's fucking terrified every day that I'm gonna start beating him or kick him to the curb and I don't know *why!* I'm—I'm fucking losing it here, Rog!"

The silence stretched for a long time. Uncomfortably long. Jake was trying to remember through the alcohol haze what he'd said, maybe muddle backward until he figured out where he'd put his foot in it, what he'd said to fuck up *this* relationship, when Roger spoke.

"What's the worst part? What gets under your skin the most?"

Jake thought. It wasn't like it was a hard question. He knew. But it took a second to get it out. "He looks at me like I'm gonna hit him," he said dully. "Not just sometimes, but . . . fuck, Roger, every day. Sometimes . . . sometimes that's the only thing I can see on his face."

Another silence. "Jake. It's . . . it's not personal. He's not afraid of *you*, he's afraid . . . hell, he's just afraid. You . . . you care about that fr—that kid more than anything but maybe that damn car of yours, and that means you're the best chance he's got. Where's he now?"

"Back at the apartment," Jake mumbled, cradling the phone against his chin, sure he'd done something wrong but not sure what or how bad it was.

"Then the first step is to get your ass back so he knows you ain't gone. You can't do a damn thing for him from some seedy bar, moron."

Jake nodded, even though Roger couldn't see. "Yeah. Yeah, you're right. Like fucking always. Thanks, Rog. I'm goin' back."

"Drive safe," Roger said, and then Jake cut the call and pulled himself to his feet, one hand fumbling for his car keys.

AFTER JAKE LEFT, Tobias stared at the door. Somewhere in the course of five minutes, his world had shattered to pieces. He had no idea how it had gone so wrong so fast, nor did he know where to begin picking up the broken shards, or if there was any point to it.

He wasn't sure how long he stood there. He hadn't thought to check a clock when Jake had come into the kitchen, and after that he . . . hadn't been able to think of much of anything. But finally, he got himself moving, fixing on the last orders Jake had given. He could no more stop himself from following them than he could have disobeyed Jake and slit his wrists.

Watch TV. Eat pasta. Do whatever the fuck you want ... until I come back.

Tobias turned on the television with shaking hands—he kept the volume down, he didn't care what the plasticized, smiling people with the shiny machines were saying—and went to the kitchen. Eating was almost impossible, even though the pasta was soft and bugless, the sauce without taint or rot. Both were almost unpalatable with the ragged hole Jake had left behind him, the front door's slam still echoing in his ears. But he choked it down because Jake had told him to. His body needed the food, and it tasted good, but the only way he could keep chewing and swallowing was by remembering Jake's voice, his promise to return. He had to meet Jake's expectations to make that happen.

Cleaning the meal up after that was almost easy. He stored the extra pasta and sauce in Jake's plastic containers, washed the pots, and carefully swept up every last soggy, half-frozen pea. He was numb enough by that point that dumping the peas into the garbage can almost didn't hurt.

Then he collapsed. Not literally, he wouldn't do that to Jake, but he made it as far as the couch before the energy that had driven him, the resolution to *obey*, gave way to confusion and despair.

Jake had been so angry, and definitely at Tobias this time. Tobias knew he should've been more careful with the peas, fucking freak hands shaking too much at the wrong time. But he wasn't convinced that Jake had actually been angry about the logical thing. He had shouted, and threatened to throw Tobias out, and had shaken him—though less than Kayla had done most Thursday mornings. Tobias didn't know if this was just another strange real thing that Jake was doing, another thing that he was too stupid to understand, or if this was the breaking of the floodgates. Would Jake beat him when he came back? Would he continue avoiding him like he had for the last few days?

Of the two options, Tobias knew which he preferred.

When Jake finally came back (Tobias refused to look at the clock, he didn't want to know, he was just blindingly relieved that Jake *was* back), Tobias was half asleep, stretched out on the couch, staring at the light and color the television threw over the walls. He couldn't have said what was on, and it became even less important the second Jake walked back through the door.

Tobias closed his eyes and fought down the dizzying relief. He tried to keep himself as still as possible. Jake would know that he was awake, but it wasn't Tobias's place to resist what was coming.

Jake slammed and bolted the door, his movements sloppy, his eyes unfocused and half closed when he glanced at Tobias on the couch.

Tobias braced himself when Jake moved away from the door, but he just stumbled to the bathroom and turned on the light. Tobias heard him unzip, pee, and fumble at the sink before reappearing.

Jake walked unsteadily to the TV and hit the off button. Tobias shifted uncertainly in the sudden darkness. It was a shock, like when the light had been doused in an interrogation room before a blow. In the thin, soft light from the bathroom, Tobias saw Jake move slowly toward the couch.

Here it comes, Tobias thought, and all he felt was readiness and relief. Jake had come back. It would all be okay. "Jake," he whispered, when the silence stretched long enough for fear to sneak in under his skin.

Jake held up a hand. He was swaying even as he stood still, and his words were slurred. "Don't say anything, Toby. Don't . . . just please don't. Just . . . scoot over."

Tobias moved, heart beating too hard. He wanted to ask if he should turn over or crawl down to the floor so Jake could stretch out, but Jake had told him to be silent. Jake sat next to his legs and clumsily knocked his boots off.

Tobias couldn't choke off a little noise—maybe a whimper, just out of surprise—when Jake fell over, half beside, half on top of Tobias.

Jake patted him absently. "'Sokay," he said, sweet alcohol on his breath and eyes already closed. "It'll all be okay."

With the next sigh, the rest of Jake's weight slumped against him, like he'd fallen asleep. Tobias couldn't quite believe it, but he didn't know why Jake would try to trick him. Cautiously, he lifted his one free hand and stroked the back of Jake's hand, hanging off the edge of the couch, with his forefinger. And then again.

Sometime later, after Jake's even breathing didn't change, Tobias, too, exhaled and closed his eyes.

JAKE DIDN'T SLEEP WELL. He woke at daybreak, groggy and confused about why he was half smothering Tobias on the sofa, and then the memories of last night slammed into him with the hangover. With a supreme force of will, he did not vomit on Tobias. Instead, he peeled himself off and staggered for his bedroom. By the time he showered, washed his mouth out— which did nothing to ease the nausea or help him feel clean— and changed clothes, his head was pounding like a goddamned drum corps. He dry swallowed aspirin and ignored the pain, aware he had fully merited every throb.

When he returned to the living room, Tobias was sitting up on the sofa, staring down at his hands, left twisting his right. Jake had to swallow back bile a couple of times, remembering what he'd done yesterday, the things he'd said. And Tobias was the one looking like a guilty child.

In this light, he was too young, too fragile to have survived half of what he had.

When Jake finally managed to speak, it came out as a hoarse croak. "Hungry?"

Tobias's head snapped up before dropping again. He squeezed his hands tighter, shoulders a mass of tension, and Jake tried not to think about what Tobias thought would happen to him if he didn't find the right answer.

Finally, Tobias spoke in no more than a whisper. "I . . . I could eat."

Jake groped along the breakfast bar for his sunglasses. "Get your shoes, then. We're going out."

The cafe was close, one of the first places recommended to Jake when he'd arrived in Boulder. The owner was a sixth-generation Boulderite, and the service was so famously friendly that the place was packed to the gills most mornings and bursting on weekends. Jake told the apologetic hostess that yes, the patio was fine, and kept his sunglasses on against the god-awful glare.

The waitress was a slim young college girl Jake would have flirted with any other day, but this morning he could barely look at her. Tobias was even more subdued than the last time they'd gone out, staring down his menu as though it contained endless, alien mysteries. Jake ordered coffee for himself, juice and milk for Tobias, and two breakfast specials: pancakes, bacon, eggs, hash browns. Tobias didn't react, even when the girl gently pulled the menu out of his hand.

The meal passed in silence. The food was good; they both ate, and Jake felt better, physically.

He thought about saying something like: *If I ever treat you like that again . . .* but had no way to finish the sentence. Tobias couldn't stop Jake, retaliate, threaten to leave. Nothing. He was trapped, so it was up to Jake to be a decent human being. That was all. Shouldn't be so hard.

He swallowed the hard knot in his throat and spoke. "I'm sorry. What I did last night. It was fucking wrong, okay? No one should ever put their hands on you like that. Especially me. *Don't* say it's okay, because it's not."

Tobias didn't say anything, of course. And Jake was out of words, so after swallowing again, he pushed the syrup over to Tobias. Slowly, so he wouldn't jump. Tobias froze, but after a moment, he took the sticky little bottle. After another hesitation, he poured it over the rest of his pancakes like Jake had and set it back down.

The waitress came back to refill Jake's coffee and ask if they were satisfied with the meal. When their plates were clean of every last bite, she laughed and said it must have been good enough. Tobias nodded without looking up, and Jake thought, *Well there's that, at least.* He hadn't been able to ask Tobias himself, not while he knew Tobias felt obligated to tell him whatever he thought Jake wanted to hear. He didn't think Tobias felt the same need to lie to strangers.

They sat there for several more minutes after the bill was paid. No one rushed them. The place was starting to empty out, breakfast rush over and lunch crowd still too early. The street was quiet with only the occasional passing car. They watched birds peck at a crust of French toast wedged under a nearby table, until an enormous pigeon came in and snatched it away, ending the tussle.

Jake exhaled, massaging his eyes under his sunglasses. Then he looked Tobias full in the face for the first time since he had woken up that morning. "Do you want to go to the library?"

Tobias started, looked up—though only for a second before dropping his gaze to the ground—and began twisting his hands. "Ah. There's still . . . a c-couple books I haven't r-read yet, in the ap-apartment . . ."

Jake lifted one shoulder. "You can take back the ones you've finished and get some more."

After a moment, Tobias nodded, blinking. "Okay. Unless . . . there's a-anything else y-you wanted to do, because I can always—"

"There's nothing I want to do, Tobias," Jake said. "Nothing in the world."

He hadn't meant it to sound like—anything, really, not angry or sarcastic, or as tired as he felt, but at the words, Tobias pulled his legs up to his chest and hugged them, tucking his chin between his sharp, bony knees. He looked wretched, and it hurt Jake more than the unforgiving sun, so he pulled the glasses off when he stood up. "Let's go."

Without hesitation, Tobias stood and followed him.

11

To be honest, Tobias had no idea what the fuck was going on.

Jake went from hot to cold, from caring for Tobias during his sickness to staying—*hiding*, part of him whispered—in his room, from being so angry that Tobias knew he was about to be beaten, to just . . . not.

Jake shouted at him but told him to eat. Jake left him but came back and slept beside him. Jake took him to a restaurant and seemed thoroughly miserable, then took him to a library. Surrounded by the thousands of books, the smell of paper and the safety of quiet, Tobias had forgotten to watch Jake. When he realized what he had done and glanced back, Jake had been smiling faintly, as though Tobias's happiness was contagious. As though he were happy *for* him.

Tobias was almost painfully confused, but as the day passed and nothing bad happened, he was willing to cautiously classify this as *better*. He and Jake ate together, spent time together after dinner, and Jake seemed more . . . open. Accepting.

More than once he found himself thinking about Jake sprawled on top of him on the couch, being able to feel Jake's heartbeat. Though he knew he shouldn't, Tobias hoped it would happen again, especially when they sat together on the couch, especially when Jake came close enough to touch. But it didn't. Jake stopped at the edge of the living room to tell him goodnight, and for a moment he hesitated, as Tobias sat with his eyes on the carpet, hoping—but then Jake disappeared down the hall.

Tobias feared the resignation he caught in Jake's face sometimes. He could remember that look in Becca's eyes, and he suspected it had meant horrible things he couldn't have imagined then. But at least he still had Jake close by, and he had to count that as better.

He just hoped that it wouldn't get worse as fast as the last time had.

~

WHEN JAKE WOKE up the next morning, he had a plan.

Part of him chafed at it, sure that it was the kind of concession that only weak bastards and cowards would make. He hated even considering playing by the rules of Freak Camp and the sons of bitches who had fucked Tobias up in the first place. The very last thing he wanted to do was surrender to what they had done, tacitly saying, "Yeah, you fucked Tobias up, and I'm okay with that."

He hated it. But he knew he was balancing on a thin edge and any misstep would slice into him (or worse, into Tobias) like the sharpest knife. Even he could tell that when a guy threatened to throw a defenseless trauma victim out of the house, got hammered, and then collapsed on that same survivor, he wasn't exactly in the sanest headspace.

This was no game, but maybe he and Tobias needed some ground rules.

If *anything* would make it easier, he had to do it. He wasn't sure he could stay sane if this whole fucked-up situation with Tobias kept spiraling.

They had more delicious Eggos for breakfast and chilled on the couch like usual. Tobias read, Jake pretended to watch TV, and then a little before noon, he got up. "Hey, I want to talk with you about something."

Tobias closed his book carefully. "Yes, Jake?"

"Let's . . . go to the table. I'll make hot chocolate."

Right before lunch was the perfect time. Jake had a vague conviction that food fixed things, so if this went badly, he would make grilled cheese. But a little drinkable chocolate beforehand couldn't hurt either.

It took longer to get the chocolate together than he'd expected. He was probably stalling. He didn't want to do this. But he also really needed it to work.

When Tobias was seated at the table with a cup of hot cocoa piled high with marshmallows—warm, but not actually hot, Jake had made that mistake only once, when Tobias just *drank* it—Jake sat across from him. Tobias's eyes were locked somewhere in the middle of the table.

"I've been having a really tough time with this whole thing, in case you haven't noticed," Jake began, ignoring the way Tobias's arms tensed and the marshmallows shook on top of his cocoa. "And I think we've got to shake some things up."

Tobias let go of the mug fast, sloshing liquid over the top. "I'm s-sorry," he said, looking anywhere but at Jake. "L-let me go wipe it up, I'm sorry—"

When Tobias would have bolted for the kitchen, Jake caught his arm and tugged him back to the table. It was a loose hold, a toddler could have broken it easily, but Tobias dropped like he'd reached the end of a chain. Jake once again had to fight the slow, smoldering desire to hit something until everything that had ever hurt Tobias was dust and bones.

"So I'm going to lay down some rules," Jake said, keeping

his voice even, nonthreatening. "And I want you to do the best you can to follow them, okay?"

Tobias nodded, almost frantically, and then took a deep breath and became almost unnaturally still. Jake could see him bracing himself. And that was exactly why they needed rules: Tobias could search for all the inner peace he wanted, but he should not believe that he needed it to survive what was coming. Jake would protect him no matter what. And Tobias had to know that that meant Jake would stop himself too.

TOBIAS WISHED he could stop being afraid. He really did, because the more he acted according to how he'd been trained, the more Jake retreated from him. And the more he saw the blind rage in Jake's eyes—or worse, the dull hopelessness—the more it ripped away any shred of comfort he'd gained.

But rules—he could do rules. He could do anything Jake needed him to do, anything he wanted, if Jake would just *tell him* what it was.

If Jake told him to drop to his knees, make him dinner, cut himself open on one of the small knives, Tobias could do that. He was ready every moment of every day for anything Jake wanted. And now, *now*, if he was finally laying out his expectations, Tobias was more than ready to listen, remember, repeat back, and obey.

At least that was what he told himself as he folded his hands over the table to hide their shaking.

"Rule one you already know," Jake said. "Don't hurt yourself."

Tobias forced his eyes to Jake's and nodded.

"Rule two: you can only apologize once a day. Do *not* say you are sorry for everything, Tobias, because it's not your fault, and I don't blame you."

Jake watched him steadily. Tobias didn't have the foggiest idea what his reaction was supposed to be, but he had to smother the desire to apologize and the equally crazy instinct to laugh hysterically. He wished Jake would stop. These rules didn't make sense, and though he was *so good* at following commands to the letter, he already had the awful premonition that these would be impossible.

But Jake continued. "Rule three: if someone is hurting you —and I mean in any way, Tobias—you hit them back. Even if it's me. Or yell at them, or just get out any way you can. If I'm there, I swear they'll pay."

"Jake! That's not—" Tobias bit it off. Freaks could not fight rules. Freaks got hurt if they fought the rules. But these rules were all wrong, and even though he knew that Jake meant them, Tobias could not imagine hitting any real, especially Jake. He couldn't even try to think of it without wanting to curl up into a ball.

"But the most important rule," Jake said, speaking so softly Tobias had to control his breathing just to hear him through the pounding in his ears. "The most important rule is that you have to tell me what you want. And when something's happening that you don't like, you have to say *no*, you have to say *stop*. If I'm doing it, I'll stop. If someone else is, I'll stop *them*. But you have to tell me what you want and what you don't want, because if I hurt you because you didn't tell me what was going wrong, I'll never forgive myself. Tobias, look at me. Do you believe me?"

Tobias stared at Jake, and in his face he saw nothing but sincerity and earnest hope.

Jake didn't want him hurt in any way. Tobias could hurt Jake just by letting the pain slide by like he always had before. This was so different—*So wrong*, a small voice said, *why should he care about a monster?*—but it might not be bad. It could be . . . it could be something that Tobias couldn't have imagined, something so much better, with four simple rules.

He nodded.

Jake looked happier, steadier. "Great. That's awesome. But there's one more thing you need to remember. I really want you to follow these rules, but I also want you to know that no matter how many times you break them . . . nothing is going to happen to you. Absolutely nothing. I won't be angry, hurt you, or kick you out. Got it?"

No was on the tip of Tobias's tongue. That didn't make any sense whatsoever because rules included punishment whenever they were broken. But he looked at Jake and considered how the structure of his world had turned upside down since Jake had taken him away. How good life could be when it wasn't falling apart.

Tobias chose to believe him.

"Yes, Jake," he said, and he breathed in the light of Jake's smile. This was going to be damn hard, but he would try.

A COUPLE HOURS after Tobias and Jake split two large pizzas for lunch (meat lovers and veggie, for the vitamins and protein), Roger called.

When the cell phone wailed in his pocket, Jake almost went for the gun he wasn't wearing—startling Tobias, tucked on the other side of the couch with his feet almost touching Jake. Jake rested a reassuring hand on Tobias's calf while he dug for the stupid thing.

He held his breath until he saw Roger's name on the screen, then stood up and flicked it open, walking around the coffee table. "Hey, Rog, what's up?"

"Kid. Just making sure you're holding it together."

Jake cleared his throat, not sure that he wanted to hang out awkwardly in the middle of the living room for this conversation. Would stepping out onto the landing give Tobias the wrong idea? "No, everything's better. Loads. We're doing . . . okay." *I'm not drunk and shouting at Tobias, anyway.*

"Good. Glad to hear it." Roger sounded as matter of fact as he would checking on the aftermath of any hunt. But he hadn't actually gotten any new information about how it had wrapped up, and that made Jake nervous about what was coming next. "Hey, I wanted to give you a heads-up: you're going to be getting a package from me in the mail soon. Don't do something stupid like light it on fire or some other fool thing."

Jake huffed. "C'mon, Rog, you know I'm totally professional about lighting shit on fire. What is it?"

"It's a book," Roger said, meaningfully. "Which is why I'm telling you not to use it for tinder. I want you to *read* it, Jake, and when you're done, read it again."

"Huh." Jake glanced over at Tobias, still holding the book in his lap but watching him from under his bangs. "Do I get any hints?"

Roger harrumphed evasively. "It could help. Maybe. I dunno. It's not like there's a damn instruction manual for taking care of a kid that's been raised in that hellhole, but I did my best. So you're going to *read* it and think about what you've read and if you start falling to pieces again, you damn well call me. And not at three a.m. Got it?"

For a moment, Jake held the phone to his ear in silence. Tobias was still watching, and Jake had to turn away, not sure how anyone would interpret the relief on his face. "Thanks, Roger. I appreciate it."

"Yeah, well, don't nominate me for sainthood yet. Damn book might be no more useful than the paper it's printed on. And it's that thin modern plasticized stuff that don't burn for shit too, so that might not be much."

Jake leaned against the kitchen doorway. "Thanks anyway, Roger. For thinking about us."

"Yeah, kid. I still want to see you with my own two eyeballs before long, but just keep it together for now."

Jake heard the click, and Roger was gone.

AFTER WEEKS of struggling with what felt like a smothering hood over his head, losing his sense of up, down, and survival, Tobias could finally take full breaths. Jake had, at last, told Tobias explicitly what he had to do to please him, and regardless of whether or not that would be easy, how long it might take him to learn or what might happen in the meantime, Tobias felt stable for the first time in the real world.

He recited Jake's rules constantly in his head, running over the exact phrasing until he could repeat each rule backward and forward at a moment's notice. Jake had yet to test if he'd been listening, if he remembered, but that was unimportant. Tobias had rules now, and he had to be prepared.

Tobias had decided almost immediately that Rule Two would be the easiest. Despite the urge to tell Jake how very, very sorry he was every time he fucked up—he could do better if Jake would be patient and give him another chance—Tobias had forced himself to be silent under far more strenuous circumstances, so he should be able to control himself now, especially since Jake had promised he would not, no matter what, put Tobias back in FREACS.

Rule One wouldn't be much harder. He hadn't consciously chosen to hurt himself, but he could break the urge. He had done more difficult things before and with less forgiveness.

Rules Three and Four were much harder to parse. Tobias understood the individual words, but he couldn't visualize situations in which these rules would come into play.

For example, if he was being hurt—in *any* way, Jake had said—Tobias was supposed to *hit them back*. Barring any alternate real-definitions of that phrase, Tobias had to take that to mean he should initiate a literal, physical attack. So there were certain times—obvious to Jake because he knew his way around the real world—when Tobias was supposed to respond with violence.

If Jake had been referring to situations with monsters, the rule was perfectly applicable, but almost unnecessary. Jake had told Tobias that he didn't want him hurting himself, and as far as Tobias was concerned, letting another freak get the better of him would be about the same as clawing up his own arms.

But Jake couldn't have meant him to use force on reals, and absolutely not against hunters, because the repercussions— Tobias shuddered hard, involuntarily, even considering them. Even more baffling, Jake had said *you hit them hard . . . even me*, which was absolutely nonsensical. Not only because Jake had *never* hurt Tobias, but because he was *Jake*.

At least he had offered him an alternative. *Or yell at them or just get out any way you can*. That should be easier than physically retaliating, but Tobias didn't know if he could do either of those things, at least not until he was tested. He might not do it well the first time. He wished he could be tested just to get the failure out of the way and figure out what he had to do to make his body obey.

But he had to trust Jake too that he had meant the last caveat. That was as impossible to imagine: how could *nothing* happen after he disobeyed a rule?

Rule Four was just as difficult, though it didn't scare Tobias quite as much, because it didn't demand any aggressive acts. It demanded *words*, yes, words that would not be easy to voice, but he didn't see how Jake would know for certain every time if Tobias was breaking it. Yes, sometimes he gave himself away with noises he couldn't prevent and defensive motions he should have broken himself of years ago, but Jake had never liked those anyway.

For the first time since leaving Freak Camp, he found himself again balanced on the knifepoint of behavioral requirements and expectations. But for now, at least, he only had to focus on the first two rules (*don't hurt yourself* and *don't apologize*) and keep the other two in mind.

And every hour that Jake didn't reprimand him for his failings, didn't tell him to kneel while Jake took out his knives, it got easier. First, because this was obedience, and Tobias could overcome a great deal of instinct with that excuse. But secondly, every time he choked off another apology or explicitly named what he wanted, Jake smiled a little wider, relaxed a little more.

He was doing what Jake wanted and making him happier. For now, that was enough. He didn't have to worry about the harder rules yet.

JAKE LIKED how dinner had gone. There had been a tense moment when Tobias dropped a fork while he was setting the table—he'd frozen like a rabbit about to bolt, before letting out a shaky breath, picking it up, and returning to the kitchen to replace it with a new fork—but otherwise, it had been good.

Jake had made chicken cordon bleu—sliding it from a box in the freezer into the oven, but sue him, his skills weren't in the kitchen—and the conversation had moved along steadily from Jake laboriously piecing together Tobias's favorite parts of his latest book using the most innocuous questions he could think of to Jake recounting his last major pool hustle. It had involved three idiots, their blond bombshell (and much smarter) sister, a ferret and two pigs, and by the end of the story, Tobias was smiling over his glass.

When Jake polished off the last piece of oozing cheese,

Tobias got up, that same half-smile lingering on his lips. "Can I do the dishes?"

"Go for it," Jake said. "Though if you need help, just say. It's not like I really cooked or anything."

Jake felt lazy letting him do all the work, but Tobias looked happier, steadier when he was doing something. Jake had to remember that while he needed things (rules they both lived by, assurances that Tobias was twitching just because he was twitching and not because Jake was hurting him), Tobias had needs too. And if he wanted to set tables and clean and cater, well, Jake could live with that. Granted, it was easier, too, to sit there with a couple beers and a decent dinner in him.

Outside, a car door slammed, followed by a couple of muted adult voices along with the high piping of a little girl. Jake guessed it was the family that lived under them. He'd seen the parents several times since he'd moved in, though he hadn't done much more than nod and flash a smile on his way out. They were a young couple with a yappy dog and a pink-cheeked toddler with curly blonde hair, and they looked about as apple-pie civilian as you could get. Maybe sometime when Tobias was more comfortable (and that would be *when*, not if), he and Jake could introduce themselves. It would help Tobias to meet people who treated him decent, for him to see that they saw him as nothing more threatening than a shy kid.

The family must have just reached their front door when the mutt started barking, and the girl greeted him with an earsplitting shriek of joy.

A second later, Jake heard the unmistakable smash of glass in the kitchen. Jumping up, he hurtled around the corner.

The glass had shattered around Tobias's feet. No blood, and Tobias was wearing shoes. He'd be able to walk off the tile without cutting his feet so Jake could sweep up the glass.

It was okay. Everything was fine—an adrenaline kick, but manageable—until Jake looked up and saw the pallor of

Tobias's face. His eyes were wide, horrified, staring blankly at the shards. When he noticed Jake, he flinched away with a gasp.

"I'm s—" he started, and then bit off the word. Jake saw a shudder race through him, and Tobias shook his head. "I'm sssss—" He gasped, fighting for breath. He made a low noise, part hiss, part moan, and practically caved in on himself.

I'm sorry. Tobias was trying to follow the rule. Jake, sick and horrified himself, lunged forward to catch him before Tobias's knees hit the floor.

"It's okay, Toby, you're fine, I'm fine. It's just a glass, you'll be fine. Step over it, we're going to the living room. Big steps, no glass shards, okay?"

Tobias was warm and shaking in his arms. Jake knew it was unreasonable, but he wished they'd somehow gotten past these breakdowns. Every time Tobias collapsed in his arms, it cracked his heart open again.

They didn't make it to the couch. Jake got Tobias into a chair and pulled the other one close to him. "Toby, *breathe*. It's okay. You're okay, I swear."

Hands covering his face, Tobias was still making that low keening sound, cutting off the apology fighting to get out.

Jake knew that he shouldn't get too handsy, but he wrapped his arm around Tobias's shoulders, rubbing his back. Anything to stop that horrible, pain-filled noise.

"It's okay, Tobias, you can say it, it's okay." Jake pulled him into a hug, drew his head in close. Fuck it, he had to, afraid otherwise that Tobias would shake himself apart. "Say it!"

"I'm s-s-sorry," Tobias gasped, and buried his face in Jake's neck. "I'm . . . rules . . . *Jake.*" He took a desperate, shaky breath, and Jake could hear the apology and desperation in his name. And because he had been at that same point only a few days ago, he could hear the despair here too. "Jake."

"No, it's okay." Daringly, Jake stroked his hair. How long had it been since he had touched Tobias this easily? Just a few days? And he had missed this more than the time he'd locked himself out of the Eldorado for more than a day, until he could scrounge up the cash to pay a locksmith. "I asked you to. You don't have to apologize, there is absolutely nothing you have to apologize for, but it's okay that you did. These rules aren't supposed to hurt."

Tobias made a little choking noise that seemed almost like a laugh. "Rules," he whispered, but slowly—far too fucking slowly for Jake's peace of mind—his shudders subsided.

When Tobias was calm and still in his arms, Jake pulled away slightly to study him. Tobias looked okay. Maybe a little shell-shocked. Probably trying to put himself back together, and Jake could understand that taking some time. "You okay?"

Tobias jerked his head toward the kitchen. "Glass?"

Jake waved his hand dismissively. "Cheap. We've got five more. I'll clean it up." Tobias flinched, and Jake rested his hand on his arm again. "*We* can clean it up, Tobias. If you want."

Tobias nodded, and then visibly gathered strength. His voice, when he spoke, was even quieter and more hesitant. "Girl?"

"Um." Jake blinked. "Girl?"

Tobias twitched all over and ducked his head. "The scream . . . th-the girl. Never . . . never mind."

Realization dawned slowly. "I don't . . . I don't think that was anything. I can check if you want." Jake half stood before Tobias shook his head, and he lowered himself into the chair again.

They sat together for a long time, and then Jake got the broom and swept up the glass. Tobias held the garbage bag open for the shards and wiped down the counter afterward.

They were doing okay, Jake thought. They were learning to rebound.

~

THE NEXT MORNING dawned gray and drizzly, but Jake felt cheery. Yeah, it had gotten rough yesterday, but they were up, eating Lucky Charms, and the day looked manageable.

They spent the morning watching TV, reading, and playing dominoes. By lunch, between Tobias's quiet and the rain, Jake had way more energy than options. He dampened some of it by making grilled cheese with bacon and, while they ate, bombarding Tobias with things they could do around Boulder when he was ready.

But after half an hour of talking about hiking, opera, rock climbing, butterfly pavilions, and baseball (spending ten of those minutes comparing the advantages of the history museum over a local meadery; "I mean, one place you learn history, the other one you get to drink it, Beowulf-style!"), he noticed a trend.

He would suggest a place, and Tobias would say, "That sounds good." He'd mention another, and Tobias would agree that too was wonderful. He'd try to wheedle an opinion out of him and get a mild preference—boating briefly gained a narrow margin—before it reversed completely a couple minutes later. Sometimes Jake could tell that Tobias really would rather go hiking than shopping in the closest mega mall, but if he had just been going by his *Yes, Jake* and *that sounds wonderful*, they would be signed up for skydiving and ballroom dancing by the end of the week.

At last, Jake sighed. "Tobias." He leaned forward, narrowly avoiding the remains of lunch with his elbow. The frozen french fries had turned out a little soggy, but Tobias still seemed to like them. "I'm gonna add another rule."

Tobias froze, the last quarter of his grilled cheese sandwich raised to his lips. He put it down and hastily wiped his fingers on his napkin. "Yes, Jake?"

Jake met his eyes and felt heartened when Tobias didn't drop his. They didn't even waver as much as they had yesterday. "Every day, I want you to say 'no' to me at least once."

Tobias paled and ducked his head, tucking his hands beneath the table.

"Hey. You know I wouldn't ask this if I didn't think you could do it." Jake waited, but Tobias continued breathing shakily with his eyes down. Jake took a jagged breath himself and kept his hand gripped around the edge of the table. Maybe Tobias wouldn't notice. Ha. "You never say no, Tobias. And it's really important to me that you tell me what makes you unhappy, uncomfortable or, hell, even if you would rather do one thing instead of another. I'm not asking you to tell me where to shove it—though go for it if you want to, it'd make my day. I just want one little word, once a day. I promise I'll make it real easy. Look." Jake picked up the saltshaker and held it over Tobias's plate. "Should I dump this entire thing of salt over your sandwich?"

Tobias stared at him, visibly shaking now. Jake could see things he didn't want to see fighting it out in Tobias's head. "If you . . . n-no. No." He shook his head violently and shrank on himself.

Jake's throat tightened. One day he was going to get a list of exactly which of those sadistic bastards in Freak Camp had done this, and he would extract everything they owed. Jake had *asked* Tobias to say no, had given him a perfect opportunity, his intention couldn't be more obvious, and Tobias was still shaking like he had run a mile all-out.

Jake put down the shaker and reached over, palm up, hoping to draw Tobias's hand from beneath the table. "That's good, Toby. I won't. Thank you."

Tobias's hand clenched his, shaking as much as Jake had expected, but after a few seconds of Jake offering whatever soft reassurances he could think of, Tobias relaxed, and Jake felt something untwist in his gut.

He squeezed Tobias's fingers before letting go. "See? You can do it. One day at a time."

Tobias made a muffled noise that was almost a laugh but much closer to a sob.

After dishes were put away and Tobias was back on the couch with a book, Jake went for a run. He didn't mind a little rain.

THE PACKAGE WAS WAITING when he came back from his run. He carried it to his bedroom to open with his knife, just in case. Roger's description had been vague to the point of ominous, and he had decided that anything that made him nervous he shouldn't do in front of Tobias.

But when he pulled off the plain brown wrapping, it was just as Roger had warned him: a book. A good-sized book with thin pages and medium-size print. *Recovering the Survivors: A Practical Guide to Handling Post-Traumatic Stress and Trauma-Related Behaviors* by Lakshmi Chandramohan. Skimming the table of contents, Jake unexpectedly felt a coil of anxiety in him relax. He didn't know where Roger had found it, but holding proof that someone else had dealt with these problems, had put in enough work that she'd literally written a book on it, made him feel less alone for the first time since he'd taken Tobias away.

He considered covering the book the way he had been required to wrap his textbooks, but immediately rejected it as dumb. Tobias wasn't going to pry, and if he did, so what? This was supposed to help him too. They didn't need secrets.

The first time through took him a day and a half. He read

nonstop for hours, focusing like it was research for a case with a string of bodies, barely aware of how Tobias kept peeking at him over his own book. He seemed concerned at Jake's radical behavior change and watched him during meals like he thought Jake might shake him and stomp out again. When it finally clicked for Jake just how much Tobias's anxiety was ramping up again—when through dinner, Tobias could barely force out more than a couple words through the stutter that had been hardly noticeable the day before—he made a special effort to smile, to squeeze his hand, and took a break to play cards again, dragging his mind out of the book and back to the here and now.

Tobias didn't look completely reassured, but he ate better and seemed less nervous. Jake, gaining insight with every page, counted that as a win.

The second reading took three days, and he had to stop often, dropping the book in his bedroom and taking grueling runs around the block, once running all the way to the park just so he could go up and down the killer stairs Tobias had fallen down. He needed the adrenaline, the extra pump of his heart to give his brain space to work. He couldn't stop reliving every hour of the last four weeks and seeing how they slotted into place. He had to know down to the last detail what he had done wrong and how to avoid repeating those mistakes.

Of course, not everything lined up perfectly. The book itself said that each case was different. A lot of Tobias's behaviors were just a little different from the textbook cases, and other parts were completely missing.

Rage, for example. It was supposed to be a primary response, outbursts and irritation a normal outlet for the survivor's past and current helplessness, but Tobias didn't display that. Not even a flicker.

Other things were so word-for-word exact that it sent chills down Jake's spine. Hell, the book even mentioned breakdowns in grocery stores. More than once he ended up swearing at himself, pacing his bedroom and raging—if Tobias didn't have anger, Jake certainly did, and sometimes he wondered if he should be more concerned about that—at all the catastrophes they could've avoided if Jake had done a little research on this shit during those six months he'd kicked his heels waiting for the word he could snatch Tobias out of the ASC's special torture factory.

But he hadn't known this. He couldn't have predicted it. Not even Roger had suggested it to him then, and Jake suspected he knew more than he was letting on. But there was no use looking back. What he had to do now was take what he learned, apply it, and hope like hell he hadn't messed Tobias up too bad already.

No, he wasn't going to think that way. From here on out, it was going to be positive thoughts all the time, because Jake had scraped the last of his pride away when he'd hit rock bottom. He was ready to take every bit of professional advice he could get. Tobias *was* going to get better, Jake *was* going to get his shit together, and they would be okay. One day at a time.

Two whole chapters dealt with physical contact and how both crucial and dangerous it was for trauma survivors. There were plenty of warnings about how it could set them off, trigger bad reactions, and send victims spiraling to the worst places in their head, especially when the contact was unexpected or undesired.

But conversely, there was a lot about the effects of touch deprivation, especially for kids. The book said that sometimes touch, the good kind, could be vital. "Good touch" had to be from someone the victim trusted and could only happen in a safe, consensual environment. No pushing and no strangers.

Jake had broken that rule often enough he could throw up thinking about it, but beating himself up didn't help either of them. They were on a better track now, and he could tell Tobias was feeling better with rules to obey, even when they some-times backfired.

He didn't want to automatically consider himself someone Tobias trusted—not when the image of Tobias pulling away from him was seared into his brain. But he couldn't forget all the other times Tobias's perpetual tension and fear eased when Jake took his hand or pulled him close either. The time Tobias had said, "Don't go," and *reached* for him. Jake couldn't forget those moments, because they were all that had kept him going last week.

Roger had told him too. *He trusts you. You're the only one.* Maybe so, and if he was—well, too late to undo all the damage, but he had to at least try to make amends where he could.

When he sat down on the couch next to Tobias that night, he didn't crowd him, but he didn't put a foot and a half of space between them as he had the week before. Tobias looked up, eyes wide, and Jake could almost believe he was more startled than afraid.

"Hey, Toby, there's something I should talk to you about."

Tobias drew in a breath, almost inaudibly. "About the —rules?"

"No—well, yeah, sorta. About part of one."

The intensity of Tobias's gaze was unsettling, reminding him how seriously Tobias took his words, how careful Jake had to be. He had always thought himself a pretty smooth talker, but he was nowhere near smart enough for this, when Tobias's life and well-being were at stake.

JAKE LOOKED TROUBLED. Not as closed-off and unhappy as he had recently, but more weighed down than before the package had arrived. Tobias assumed it was the book Jake had been reading the last few days. It wasn't any of his business, of course, and he would never so much as spy on the cover without Jake's permission, but it made him nervous. He tried very hard not to think of all the possible objects and instructions Hunter Harper could have sent Jake. But Jake had said Roger was a good old friend and an excellent hunter. Tobias had glimpsed him a couple of times in the camp, though never lingering, and only once in an interrogation room. Even then, Tobias had never seen him hurting a freak, even his worthless self.

Tobias still worried.

Jake took a breath, placing his fingertips carefully together. "Y'know the rule about not letting anyone hurt you—"

"Rule Three," Tobias said.

"Right, and the one about telling me what you like—"

"Rule Four."

"Yeah, exactly. Well, I'm going to add something."

Tobias held his breath instinctively, waiting to take in every word Jake said, even as his mind (stupid, unreliable freak mind) raced ahead with different possibilities. *Punishments don't apply. I'm the exception to both rules, you keep your mouth shut no matter what. Haha, just ignore Rule Three, that was a joke to see if a stupid freak like you would believe it.*

Somehow, he heard everything Jake might say in Victor's voice.

Jake exhaled slowly, closing his eyes, and, in a flash of panic, Tobias remembered the night he thought Jake had broken a couple of ribs, he was moving in so much pain. "You probably know . . . I like touching you, Tobias. I've done more of that than I should, I know that now, and I'm . . . sorry, I really am, for whenever I pushed you too much, crossed lines I shouldn't. The last thing—the very last fucking thing I want to do"—Jake was so emphatic here, leaning forward with each word, his gray eyes boring into him, that Tobias was gripped with the deadly, terrifying awareness that this was vitally important, he *had* to understand, even though he really didn't yet—"is put you in any situation where you don't like what's going on. Do you get that?"

Tobias swallowed hard. He didn't know what Jake meant by times he "pushed" Tobias too much. Unless he meant the one night he shook him, and Tobias had barely felt that. He'd definitely deserved it anyway, for spilling the peas and being so stupid that he upset Jake. He wished he could say he understood, but he couldn't lie to Jake.

Jake must have seen his confusion. "Because that counts. Anytime I . . . I put my hands on you, even if it's a single finger, in any way you don't like, that counts as hurting you, and you should tell me to stop."

"But Jake, you haven't . . ." Anguished, Tobias pressed his hands over his eyes, then remembered that Jake liked it when he looked at him. "You don't do that, Jake. You never have."

Jake seemed unconvinced. Tobias felt despondency taking hold of him—not the leaden, numb hopelessness he'd always felt before, but an acute pain as he lost something precious (how had he dared let it become precious to him?). This was even worse because it was so backward: Jake wasn't threatening to take his touch away because he'd found out how much Tobias liked it, but because . . .

Tobias shuddered in a breath, rocking back and forth as he struggled to force the words out. "When . . . when you t-touch me—like you did the other day, after I broke—I . . . I feel better, like it's—easier to breathe, and I don't have to worry about a-anyone, or . . . It helps, Jake. It helps so much."

"Okay." Jake caught Tobias's hands, and Tobias stopped rocking. He exhaled shakily. "Okay. Like this?"

Tobias nodded, unable to speak, too shaken by his own vulnerability.

"Okay." Jake squeezed Tobias's hands. "But even if you like this now, there may be other times when you *don't*, and that's okay. It doesn't mean I'll never touch you again. It just means you want hands off right then, and I *want* to know, I really do. Rule . . . Four, right? You just have to say one word, or make a noise, or even pull away a little, and I'll get it and give you some room. Promise you'll let me know, Tobias. Do you promise?"

Tobias swallowed. He couldn't fathom the scenario, much less how he would comply, but with Jake looking that desperate, he didn't have a choice. "Yes, Jake. I promise."

"Good." Jake sighed in relief. He didn't let go of Tobias's hands. "Thank you."

TOBIAS WOULDN'T HAVE BELIEVED a week ago that things could improve so much. He hadn't known where they were headed the night Jake shouted at him after the peas were on the floor, but he wouldn't have dared dream they'd come back to a place where Jake would pull him close on the couch and *let* Tobias stay there against Jake's side.

A place where Jake would finally give him *rules* to follow, even if they were strange and daunting in a way he wasn't used to.

A place where Jake looked *happy* again, and not like Tobias caused him pain just by being near him.

Jake still left the apartment every day, though now it was for runs and not drinking at night. Tobias had started waking up early too, listening for Jake, then leaving his room to say good morning. He'd get a bowl of cereal because Jake liked to see him eating even though he waited until after his run and shower for his own breakfast. While he was in the shower, Tobias would start the coffee just like Jake had shown him, and he'd toast a pile of Eggo waffles for both of them.

The morning after they talked about Rule Three, Tobias came out as Jake was tying his tennis shoes.

Jake grinned up at him. "Hey, I was thinking. How about we paint the whole apartment green, right now?"

Tobias considered this carefully. "No, Jake."

Jake beamed and came over to pull Tobias to him in a half-hug. Then he released him and headed for the door, calling, "Forty-five minutes, tops."

Every morning, Tobias recited the rules in his head. Adding what Jake had told him last night was harder than expected. Not the words—he could summon Jake's exact phrasing, but he had trouble distilling the conversation they'd had to a core rule. Was it *Anytime I put my hands on you, even if it's a single finger, in any way you don't like, that counts as hurting you, and you should tell me to stop*? He'd told Tobias specifically what that meant: *You just have to say one word, or make a noise, or even pull away a little, and I'll get it and give you some room.* And he'd made *Tobias* promise. It worried him that Jake would accept his promise—the word of a freak didn't mean anything—but Tobias couldn't fix that, so he focused on the rules.

He understood the words, but he couldn't understand why Jake thought the new parts were so important. Especially since Jake had never touched Tobias in a way he didn't like, and Tobias didn't think he could recognize the situation if it happened. How would Jake know? Rules Three and Four were difficult and uncertain anyway.

Then an idea struck him like Kayla's elbow jabbing into his ribs. Maybe he could . . . ask Jake. Talk to him. Find out exactly what he meant Tobias should do, who he wanted Tobias to hit if someone tried to hurt him.

It took the rest of Jake's run and the eight minutes of his shower for Tobias to convince himself this was feasible, that nothing bad would happen because he admitted he hadn't fully understood the first time, that he needed Jake's help. It was difficult to overcome the old fear and training, despite all of Jake's kindness in the last few weeks.

Tobias waited until after they'd finished the waffles and coffee plus the scrambled eggs Jake had thrown together (more than enough food for just one meal, but Tobias had learned it was best to stop remembering *before*, to stop comparing). He waited for Jake to bring out his book and join him on the sofa, and then he took a deep breath.

~

"JAKE . . . I HAVE A QUESTION." Tobias faced him on the couch, one leg drawn up under him, hands folded tightly over the shut book on his lap. But he met Jake's eyes, despite all the hesitancy and apprehension written on his face. This wasn't easy for either of them.

Jake turned to him, giving Tobias his full focus and determination. "Lay it on me."

Tobias took a deep, rallying breath. "R-Rule Three."

Jake rubbed behind his ear, trying and failing to recall. "Uh, right. Which one was that?"

"If someone is hurting me and I mean in any way I hit them back," Tobias recited at top speed. "E-Even if it's y-you." He faltered for a moment, then continued, "Or yell at them or just get out any way I can."

Shit. Jake had been afraid that Tobias would probably take the rules way too seriously. But at least he was coming to him now instead of something worse happening, especially when Jake wasn't watching. The rules had to help, even if they took some adjustment. He couldn't think about what kind of dead end they were at if they *didn't* work.

"Yeah," he said at last. "What about that one?"

Tobias took in another slow breath and shut his eyes for a few seconds, reopening them to speak. "I-I don't understand. I mean . . . I understand the *words*, but . . . I don't know what you m-mean. Wh-who am I supposed to hit? If they hurt me?"

Jake took his time before answering. "I mean anyone, Tobias. When we go out, and if I'm not watching—and I'm going to do my damn best to watch out for any assholes and keep them away from you, but if I—if one of them ever slips through, you defend yourself. I don't care if it's some guy who lives down the street, or works in a store, or passing in the park."

Tobias's face went a shade whiter, though his eyes never left Jake's. "You mean r-reals."

"People. Yeah. Anyone. No one has the right to hurt you, Tobias."

Tobias flinched back, his control breaking. He squeezed his eyes shut, shook his head rapidly, then covered his face with his hands. Jake reached for him but stopped himself. He swallowed hard at how raggedly Tobias was breathing.

"I mean it," Jake said, more forcefully. "*No one*. That means civilians, monsters, or hunters." He thought about the bastards he'd met hunting, the guards laughing at jokes he'd barely understood as a child but made his blood burn now. "*Especially* hunters."

At that, Tobias keened, a sound of abject shock, horror, and despair, and Jake moved in close to touch his back. "Hey, hey, I know. They—they hurt you. I'm not gonna let them anywhere near you, but if they ever touch you again—"

"*Jake*," he begged, and there was a sob just underneath. "They'll call—they'll call the A- ASC . . ."

Fuck, Jake was pushing him too hard. "Okay, don't worry about hunters yet. I'm not letting them near you, I swear to God. But you got to know you have my permission to fight back if those sons of bitches try to hurt you. I won't be mad at you if you can't, but if you do, you won't get in trouble. And like I said, if you can't, just try to get away, call for help, something."

"Can't, can't, they'll h-hurt you if I . . . I'm sorry, so sorry."

Jake smiled sadly. Tobias hadn't apologized at all yesterday, cutting the words off every single time. But he'd decided to use them now, when Jake was telling him he should protect himself. Fuck, this hurt. "They can try," he said. "But they won't be able to. And we're not going to run into hunters if I can help it. I'm keeping an eye on things, and Boulder is clean. No one needs to come visiting, but we'll be ready if they do. Tell you what, we'll take this in baby steps."

Tobias choked or maybe laughed. It was hard to tell. "B-baby steps?"

"We'll leave the house, you and me. Maybe go to the park or something."

Tobias shuddered in his arms. "C-can't hit a real."

"Hey, I'm not asking you to!" Jake nudged his shoulder against Tobias's. "But if a Frisbee tries attacking you again, you're going to beat that flying sucker into the ground, right?"

Jake knew he was talking nonsense and he didn't know why he thought it would help. But Tobias's stare cracked into a smile —an actual *smile*. The he ducked his head against Jake's chest. "I can do that," he said into Jake's shirt.

Sometimes his nonsense turned out okay. Jake brushed his fingers through Tobias's hair. "Awesome. That's what I'm talking about."

He hadn't been going to push for the park that same day, but Tobias brought it up after the breakfast dishes were done.

"Would t-today be a good day . . ." He glanced out the window to the sunlit street and took a shaky breath. "It's nice," he offered.

Jake might have been an idiot, but he wasn't that dense. Not when he could still see the tear tracks from their talk. He squashed the impulse to keep Tobias safe inside. That wasn't going to help either of them. "Well, I guess. It's a Tuesday, should be less crowded. You *want* to?"

Tobias searched his face, a careful scrutiny he performed every time Jake asked him something now, looking to see if *this* was the time he was supposed to say no. Jake bore it out because this stage wasn't going to be easy for either of them. Baby steps.

"Yes," he said at last.

Jake felt his face break into a smile, and he nudged some of Tobias's newest library books with his knee. "Maybe you could bring a couple books, read on the grass, catch some rays." He'd skimmed one of Tobias's health books, which had reminded him of the importance of sunlight for vitamin D and serotonin and all that crap. Tobias could use as much as he could get. "We could even drive there, make it real easy."

Tobias looked down at his book and ran his thumb over the page in a gentle, nearly reverent gesture. Then he looked back up and actually smiled. Small, tentative, but there. "Okay, Jake. I'd like that."

"Awesome." Jake squeezed Tobias's hand once, and Tobias actually squeezed his in return. "Let's go. Pick out your books. And hey, let's hit up the bagel shop on the way, see what they've got for lunch."

It was definitely a much better day for visiting the park, Jake decided. Way fewer people, plus he was less of a dumbass than before. And Tobias was handling everything so much better, though Jake steered them away from a group playing Frisbee, just in case.

Moe's Broadway Bagels was only half full, and as they neared the front of the line, Janet appeared from the kitchen to beam at them.

"Well, hey there, strangers! It's great to see you again. Wasn't sure if my bagels had landed you in the hospital with a bona fide food coma, or whether I should be proud or ashamed of that."

Tobias fought the urge to hide behind Jake. He could do this. He'd had much more practice being around reals since he'd last been inside this store, even if it hadn't all been good. Jake believed he could, and therefore Tobias would.

He managed to hold his head up and smile at her as Jake snorted.

"Maybe we did, I dunno. A few days were pretty blurry."

"As long as you're not here just because you got run over by something again." Janet eyed them for injuries.

"Nope, strictly lunch business today."

After they ordered a couple bagels with sausage and cheese to go, Jake and Tobias sat down with their cans of soda to wait at a table near the door, and Janet pulled up a chair across from them.

"How's Boulder been treating you?"

"Oh, it's been awesome," Jake said, and he glanced at Tobias as though for confirmation.

"I—I like the library," Tobias managed. He felt his face heat up, overwhelmed with the certainty he was doing an awful job of pretending to be a real, but Janet looked pleased.

"You're a bookworm, huh? We always need more kids into books. I should introduce you to my niece, she's about your age. Maybe you'd be a good influence on her."

Tobias choked a little on his soda, and Jake leaned forward to jump in. "He's definitely a good influence on me. I got through this whole book in less than a week, and it wasn't even a good story. More of a science text. I'd never have done that before."

Janet's eyes crinkled in amusement, and she nodded as though impressed. "Well, I'm glad to see you back and that the city's treating you right. Ah, looks like your bagels are ready." She stood. "Always good to have repeat customers, especially when there isn't a bodily injury bringing them in. You stay here, I'll grab that for you."

As she went to retrieve their order from the counter, Tobias was still uncertain but cautiously relieved. He didn't think Janet was on her way to call the ASC to report a freak. Jake's dazzling grin toward him confirmed that Tobias had done okay. It made him weak-kneed with relief.

After leaving the bagel shop, they gave the built-in amphitheater a wide berth as they entered the park. Jake took them away from the trails and toward the sprawling trees and ample grass in between. Jake suggested that Tobias pick one, keeping his tone nonchalant—*all the same to me, no preference here*. Tobias hesitated for a minute, then chose a large cottonwood in the middle.

Jake spread out a large towel he'd lifted from a nicer motel. He stretched out on his back, sunglasses on and hands behind his head, while Tobias settled down next to him.

It was a lot nicer than he'd expected. The bagels were damn good, and Tobias had his books in a spare duffel. The weather was just right, and without the shrieking crowds that had been there last time, Jake could have dozed off, knowing he could crack open his eyes and see Tobias sitting next to him, reading contentedly.

It was beautiful and almost perfect, so he really shouldn't have been surprised when it ended.

The first warning was a whistle blast, followed by the laughter and chatter of a crowd approaching. Jake opened his eyes, saw Tobias turning his head, and sat up.

There were a couple dozen people about Jake's own age wearing matching tie-dye T-shirts. Their leader, a short blonde, also wore an oversized Dr. Seuss hat (*Cat in the Hat*, Jake thought), a shiny red cape, and a backpack slung over her shoulder. She was twirling a baton with more enthusiasm than skill and marched ahead of the group like she'd just escaped from a Saturday morning cartoon. She stopped abruptly, waved the baton dramatically, and then dropped into a crouch. Five or six of the group immediately dropped down with her, the rest following suit in a couple of seconds, with a couple more stragglers joining the huddle slowly and with an obvious lack of enthusiasm.

The group spread out in a circle, holding hands—oh, some of the boys didn't like that—then lay down all at once except for the leader, who sat upright in the middle. She blew her whistle and shouted something, and one of the guys jumped to his feet, grabbed a stuffed bear from the leader, and took off running across the lawn. The Dr. Seuss girl blew her whistle again, and this time a girl jumped up and did the same thing, though she ran in the opposite direction.

"What," Tobias said. "What are they doing?"

"Something I definitely didn't know about before I decided to move here."

Tobias shifted, and the book slid off his lap. When Tobias didn't catch it, Jake noticed him twisting his hands together, and he laid his hand on top. Tobias's fingers relaxed.

"B-but what is it?"

"Peer pressure." Jake squinted at the kids. Most of them had run off by this time, and it looked like the leader was homing in on her least-willing participants. He abruptly realized that it was mid-August. About the time the school year started up. And Boulder had a university. Fuck. "It's gotta be part of the college crap. For the fish."

Tobias glanced at him. "Fish? You mean like . . ." He wiggled his hand in a swimming motion.

"Freshmen," Jake amended. "Kids starting their first year of college. They do all these touchy-feely bonding games." And this wouldn't be the end of it. The fraternities would start up with God-knew-what bullshit. He'd been to enough college parties (research, absolutely all research) to know that Tobias and affectionate first-year hazing would go together like eighteenth-century lace and gasoline.

With a sigh, he stood up as Tobias watched the Cat-in-the-

Hat girl with fascination. "C'mon, let's take off before she starts offering us green eggs and ham."

"That would be bad," Tobias agreed, getting up and sliding his book into the duffel. "Especially since we just ate sandwiches without mold."

Maybe Jake should slip some Dr. Seuss books into Tobias's next library stack. "You hungry still?"

Tobias shook his head. "No. The sandwiches were delicious."

Their walk back to the car was uneventful, even as they passed more groups of college kids running around. It looked like each group had a theme, and there were far too many of them. Jake shook his head as he pulled his car keys from his pocket, then looked over the metal frame to where Tobias waited by the passenger door.

"Hey, Tobias."

"Yes, Jake?"

"Let's have nothing but cheese dip for dinner."

Tobias looked confused. "But we don't have any—no. No, Jake."

Jake grinned and swung his door open. "Damn right."

EVERYTHING MOVED SLOWLY. Jake didn't know why he expected otherwise. Whether staking out a suspected witch's house or sitting in an emergency room to find out if Dad was going to live, nothing went fast in his life—except the moments that were immediately terrifying, and he supposed he was grateful they hadn't had many of those.

Jake kept rereading Roger's book, though he found himself skipping some sections that were too painful to think about and lingering over others that offered more hope. He knew he was looking for quick answers (and damn, had Roger chewed his ass that one time he'd discovered Jake looking for a guy with GED tests for sale) and wasn't going to find them in those white pages or in Tobias's wary eyes.

Still, it got easier every day. Comfortable in a danger-could-be-anywhere kind of way. Jake found himself smiling sometimes without knowing why. Once, when Tobias looked up, Jake didn't even notice he was staring at him until Tobias smiled: a slight, honest quirk of the lips that made Jake grateful all over again that he'd called Roger instead of just drinking himself insensible and getting run over by a Volkswagen or something.

It was late on a Thursday evening, just a little bit over one month since they had arrived in Boulder. Jake left the kitchen after doing the dishes, beer in hand—he drank a few at night sometimes, but he'd managed to avoid repeating another truly fucked-up binge—and couldn't keep the smile off his face when he saw Tobias half buried in his latest book propped up on his lap.

It was a coffee table book or something (big enough to *be* a coffee table, if someone attached little legs to it) and had an enormous picture of white-capped mountains on the front cover. Tobias looked so fixated, Jake would have worried the book was a matter of life and death if his expression hadn't turned to wide-eyed wonder every time he turned a page.

Jake watched, enjoying the peace. Then he realized that Tobias hadn't turned the page in at least a minute.

He cleared his throat and took a sip of beer. "Whatcha reading?"

Tobias looked up, blinking in surprise, and then his cheeks went a little pink. Like he was embarrassed, but *just* embarrassed. He didn't look at all afraid, and it was amazing the things Jake counted as a victory these days. The things that made him as giddy as his first kiss. "Not really reading," he said, holding Jake's eyes with such strength that—between that and the blush, goddamn—it knocked Jake's breath away.

He tilted his head, aware he was grinning like a loon. "Not reading? But it's a book. Whatcha doing, then?" He set the beer on the table and came to sit down. Tobias spread the book flat on his knees.

The photo was a full double-page spread showing St. Louis's arch at night, silhouetted against a dark city background with brilliant, flowering fireworks splashed across the sky. Tobias's fingers ghosted over the glossy page, tracing the arch reverently.

Looking down at the photo, Jake realized that Tobias hadn't been there. Tobias hadn't been anywhere except a shithole prison in Nevada, a handful of places in Boulder, and this apartment. Jake had promised him so much more.

"It's beautiful," Tobias whispered. "I like . . . I like just looking sometimes." He glanced at Jake and then down again. "Just looking without reading or . . . anything else."

It wasn't so much a plan as the knowledge that *they could, so why the hell not?* Nothing was holding them there. Nothing could stop them from anything they wanted. The only thing keeping Tobias cooped and confined was Jake's fear.

Jake grabbed Tobias's hand and pulled him up from the couch. "Let's go," he said. "Let's go see it."

Tobias stared. "Go . . . where?"

"Here!" Jake rapped the book with his knuckles and couldn't stop grinning. "I'll show you the Arch, the Great Lakes. I'll show you the Grand fucking Canyon." *You deserve it all, way more than I ever have.*

"I . . ." Tobias looked nervous, staring, and Jake realized maybe this wasn't what Tobias wanted. Roger's book had said sometimes people close to survivors projected their own desires and shit onto them. Maybe that was what he was doing now,

pushing Tobias where he didn't have the resources—yet
—to go.

Jake backpedaled. "I mean, that is, if you . . ." He took a deep
breath and let go of Tobias's hand. Just because they didn't go
today didn't mean they could never leave. There would be
other days, and what Tobias needed now was most important.
Even if suddenly the thought of sticking around Boulder felt
like picking the scab off a wound. "Only if you want to, Tobias."

Tobias swallowed. "Want to . . . what?"

Jake waved a hand at the book. "Go there. Go everywhere."
Just like I promised you.

"Like . . . like in the pictures you used to bring? Is this a 'no'
question?"

"No, I promise this is serious. You can say no if you want to,
but yeah, it's like the pictures I used to bring."

Tobias turned and looked at the book. Jake saw his throat
work and his hands clench. "C-can we? Am I allowed . . ." He
shook his head. "Yes, Jake. I want to. If we can."

Jake almost whooped with joy. He wanted to grab Tobias
and hug him. But he managed to restrain himself to squeezing
Tobias's hand. "Awesome. Let's go. Right now."

Tobias stared when Jake rushed to his room. He found the
spare duffel they'd brought to the park, dumped the towel out
on his bed, and brought the empty bag to Tobias. "Here, you
can pack your stuff in this."

Tobias blinked at the bag. "What should I bring?"

Jake spread his arms wide. He couldn't stop grinning.
"Everything! It's an adventure."

"Like . . . clothes? Toothbrush?"

"Yes and yes, anything you want. Hell, you can probably fit
all your worldly possessions in there. We haven't bought you
nearly enough stuff, even by my standards."

Tobias stared at the bag, and then slowly raised his eyes. To

Jake's delight, he was smiling too. "Yeah. I can fit everything in here."

"Awesome." Jake let the elation and whirlwind of action carry him into pulling Tobias close for a hug before he let him go. "Be back out here in fifteen?"

Tobias's cheeks were pink, and his smile hadn't faltered an inch. "Okay."

They were ready in forty-six minutes, running long only because Jake decided they should throw their food in the car too. They tossed their duffels in the back seat, cereal boxes and fruit on top of them, and a spare blanket, pillow, and Jake's armory in the trunk. They finished off the rest of the milk and orange juice, straight from the bottles and ice-cold, and Jake tucked the last two beers under his seat. He quizzed Tobias on the stuff he'd packed, making sure he had clothes, a tooth-brush, and at least one of the books from Jake's shelf.

They swung by the library on the way out of town to leave Tobias's books in the book-drop. Jake had no idea when they were coming back to Boulder—he didn't want to think that far ahead—and Tobias had refused to keep his books past the due date. Small delay, but it made Tobias smile again, like his world was fucking perfect right then. Jake would have done a hell of a lot more for a smile like that.

By midnight, they were roaring along I-70 east, leaving the lights of Denver behind them. It was a dark, clear road, empty but for a couple semis, and Jake reveled in the purr of the engine, his hands on the wheel, and the vast expanse of empti-ness and freedom before them. Best of all, Tobias was right next to him, so close that Jake could almost hear his breathing under the low croon of the Rolling Stones. He was safe.

Jake drove, and Tobias eventually fell asleep with his head against the window, and the stars burned as bright as the possi-bilities before them.

The series continues with FREEDOM, available for pre-order now!

Thank you for reading FEAR!

It would mean so much to me if you would consider leaving a review. I love to read every one.

Do you want advance access to the next book, extra stories, and other exclusive Freak Camp content? Sign up for the monthly Freak Camp newsletter at **freakcamp.com**

ACKNOWLEDGEMENTS FROM LAURA

When I declared my intention to publish not only my first but my second book in the same calendar year, it was with the same ferocious optimism that often makes Bailey (co-author and best friend extraordinaire) shake her head, but there is a reason it worked out and I'm not simply a delusional madwoman. That reason is my team.

Of course, A Monster By Any Other Name would never have been written in the first place without that co-author in crime, Bailey R. Hansen. Huge thanks also to whereupon who has supported and built this world with us from the beginning and has made me a much better writer.

I am so grateful I also got to work once again with my editor Mackenzie Walton, and the impeccable Adam Mongaya for catching all consistency errors in this universe we created. All remaining errors are my own defiant ones.

Thank you again to Christine Griffin, the brilliant illustrator and designer of this book's gorgeous cover art, who also has supported this story for so many years. Your illustrations and enthusiasm helped make its potential so much more real to me.

Thank you to Kate Rudolph and Melanie Greene, fantastic romance authors, for letting me pester them so often about how to do this whole publishing thing professionally. I don't know where I'd be without you both, Quell and Mel (and my whole slack family. I appreciate you guys and bitches so much.).

Many more thanks go to all my beta readers and proofreaders: Amanda Stenson, CarolAnn Grafe, Just H, Paige, Rebekah JJW, Sumbul Danish, Shea Brannen, and many more.

Thank you to Angela James and her communities Book Boss and From Written to Recommended, which gave me so many of the tools and confidence to really finish this story with a bang and do it justice.

Finally, thanks to my mother who is the best and most cinnamon roll of all mothers, and also to Jud, for joining our family with true Viking spirit during some of the hardest years.

ACKNOWLEDGEMENTS FROM BAILEY

When we first started writing Freak Camp, I could have never imagined how big it would grow or how many lives it would touch. I am humbled and honored, and so profoundly grateful for Laura Rye. While this Monster was a mutual labor of love for a very long time, in recent years she has done literally everything to get A Monster by Any Other Name into your hands. She is the best friend and co-author a girl could want.

Writing a book takes a village (or at least writing and publishing a good book!) and Laura has already done a great job of calling out the many people who made this work better along the way. Once again, I want to thank my personal first readers (love you, Mom and Dad!) and the first readers of Freak Camp who traveled through the darkness of Book One and stuck with us through the hurt and comfort of Book Two and beyond. Laura and I wouldn't have created the book in your hands, or become the writers we are today, without you.

9781088119228